The American Duke

The American Duke

A REGENCY-ERA NOVEL

AUGUST JADE STERLING

Krystal Kat
PRESS

Published by Krystal Kat Press, New York City
https://augustjadesterling.com

Designed by Girl Friday Productions
www.girlfridayproductions.com

Cover design: David Fassett
Image credits: Envato/PixelSquid360, Shutterstock/KathySG, Rawpixel, Shutterstock/Darya Komarova

ISBN (paperback): 979-8-9863933-0-8
ISBN (ebook): 979-8-9863933-1-5
Library of Congress Control Number: 2022921481

This book is dedicated to my parents, Marylou and Quinton, who lovingly taught me you can achieve anything you desire; to my sister Quinnette, who has been with me through each step of this process; to the truth that was hidden and never told or taught; and to the faculty, administrators, staff, workers, students, and alumni of Wilberforce University, Wilberforce, Ohio, U.S.A.

WHO'S WHO

———

THE ROXBURYS

 Sterling Adam Roxbury—British, the sixth Duke of Westmoure, lives in England

 Avery Roxbury—British, lives in America, brother of the sixth Duke of Westmoure, Sterling Avery Roxbury; Anne's husband; father of Sterling Avery Roxbury, Meredith Anne Roxbury, and Elizabeth Beverly Roxbury; co-owner of the Avery Jacob Shipping Company,

 Anne Roxbury—American, wife of Avery Roxbury, mother of Sar, Mer, and Beth

 Sterling Avery Roxbury (Sar)—American, son of Anne and Avery Roxbury

 Meredith Anne Roxbury (Mer)—American, the oldest daughter of Anne and Avery Roxbury

 Elizabeth Beverly Roxbury (Beth)—American, the youngest child of Anne and Avery Roxbury

 Charles Roxbury—British, brother of Avery Roxbury and Sterling Adam Roxbury, the sixth Duke of Westmoure

 Frances—British, mother of Joycellyn

 Joycellyn—British, daughter of Charles and Frances

Alexius Standerson—British, daughter of Caroline and Sebastian

Anthony Daggs, the Marquess of Dearne, Inspector Daggs of Scotland Yard—British, one of the elite operatives who works for Berkley on an as needed basis

Ashby (Ash) Wyndham, Earl of Danford—British, an aristocrat who served in the elite group of noblemen under the command of Berkley during the war

Aurelia Rothingham, Duchess of Edgerton—British, wife of David, good friend of Caroline Standerson

Basil Willingham—the future Duke of Brockton, nephew of the current Duke of Brockton

Brian O'Keefe—British, accomplished actor

Captain Coomes—British, sea captain, works for Westmoure Shipping Company

Caroline Standerson, the Marchioness of Broadhurst—British, wife of Sebastian, daughter Alexius

Charlotte Peach, Countess of Fatson—British, a member of the aristocracy

Chief Red Cloud—American, second in charge of the Avery Jacob Shipping Company

David Rothingham, Duke of Edgerton—British, an aristocrat who served in the elite group of noblemen under the command of Berkley during the war, married to Aurelia

Diana Ryerton, Duchess of Northampton—British, wife of Marcus, good friend of Caroline Standerson

Earl of Landingham—British, a member of the aristocracy

Earl of Severson—British, a wealthy aristocrat

Earl of Thornton—British, a wealthy aristocrat

Easton Willingham, Brockton, The Duke of Brockton—British, an ally of the Crown

Edward and Little Elizabeth—British, street orphans

Ethan Quinn, the Marquess of Perth—British, head of the Foreign Office

Evan Marston, Duke of Carrington—British, an aristocrat who served in the elite group of noblemen under the command of Berkley during the war, married to Georgina

Evelyn Quinton, the Marchioness of Briarcliff—British, wife of Richard Quinton, Julien's mother

George Mason—British, works for Berkley in the Home Office

Georgina Marston, Duchess of Carrington—British, wife of Evan, good friend of Caroline Standerson

Grayson, the Duke of Grayson—British, Caroline's father

Harold David Hearthstone, cousin of Duke of Westmoure—next in line for the title

Hortense Hamilton, the Dowager Duchess of Horton—British, the most revered woman of the ton

Jackson (Jack) Abbott—British, one of the elite operatives under Berkley's command

Jacob Goldsmith—American, co-owner of the Avery Jacob Shipping Company

Jonathan Simmons, the Earl of Carlyle—British, field surgeon and physician, an aristocrat who served in the elite group of noblemen under the command of Berkley during the war

Julien Quinton, the honorable Earl of Sutton—British, son of Richard and Evelyn, one of the elite operatives under Berkley's command

Lady Sarah Jersey—British, head patron at Almack's along with the other patronesses at the time, Lady Emily Cowper, Lady Anne Stewart, Marchioness of Londonderry, the Viscountess of Castlereagh, Lady Sefton, Countess de Lieven, Baroness Willoughby de Eresby, and Countess Esterhazy, arbiters of le bon ton

Madame Burgoff—British, modiste extraordinaire to the ton

Marcus Ryerton, Duke of Northampton—British, an aristocrat who served in the elite group of noblemen under the command of Berkley during the war, married to Diana

Margaret Lambeth, Countess of Milford—British, a member of the aristocracy

Mildred Cook—British, cook and integral part of the Westmoure household

Miriam Wyndham, Countess of Danford—British, wife of Ashby, good friend of Caroline Standerson

Miss Engles—British, deportment, all things British

Morgan—British, the sixth Duke of Westmoure's (Sterling Adam Roxbury) man of affairs

Mrs. Kiggins—British, housekeeper, companion, friend of Lady Hortense

Mrs. Spencer—British, chatelain of the Westmoure's homes

Oliver—British, majordomo of the Westmoure household

Perkins—American, Sar's right-hand man

Richard Quinton, the Marquess of Briarcliff—British, husband of Evelyn Quinton, Julien's father

Royce Thortonshire, the honorable Marquess of Shone—British, one of the elite operatives under Berkley's command

Samuels—British, soldier, attached to the Home Office, works for Berkley

Sebastian Standerson, the Marquess of Broadhurst—British, the senior diplomat in the elite group of operatives under Berkley's command, married to Caroline, daughter Alexius

Seymour—British, majordomo of the Broadhurst

Smytherson—Valet to the Duke of Westmoure

Sylvia Meacham, Viscountess of Truvo—British, a member of the aristocracy

Thomas Berkley, the Duke of Hampton, a royal duke, moniker, the general—British, head of the Home Office, leader of the elite group of operatives, cousin of the king

The Wolfhounds: Duchess, America, Baby, Bella, Oscar, Felix—British, trained at Whitehall

The American Duke

———

Two Hundred and Fifty Miles off the Coast of America,
Captain's Cabin
1791

The captain of the British ship *Standish* pronounced them man and wife. Avery looked into the deep-brown eyes of the honey-haired beauty standing before him, his wife. The kiss was a promise of their future, and Anne felt it to the tip of her soul.

Eleven Years Later
London, England
August 15, 1802

The London Daily

———

Bill to Prohibit Transporting Slaves
Supported by the Duke of Westmoure

The Duke of Westmoure announces he is supporting the movement to end the slave trade, and is introducing a bill in Parliament to prohibit British shipping companies from transporting slaves. Westmoure joins forces with Anand, Thomas Clarkson, William Wilberforce, and Olaudah Equiano who have been leading the vigorous campaign to abolish slave trade for over a decade.

After visiting America and witnessing the massive number of slaves sold there from Africa and Ireland, their unconscionable treatment, and their transportation under inhumane conditions, the duke stated it is morally intolerable and reprehensible.

"We are responsible for this atrocity against mankind, and we are obligated to end it immediately. Satan's highway to hell must be stopped."

The duke owns Westmoure Shipping Company. His company has never transported human cargo. Westmoure Shipping Company, one of the largest in the world, may not depend upon the huge revenues generated from transporting slaves, but many other companies do. It is likely these owners will lobby strongly against this bill and prohibit its passage.

Five Years Later
March 26, 1807

The London Daily

The British Shipping Act Passes:
Slave Trade Prohibited

Both houses of Parliament passed the bill prohibiting English vessels from transporting slaves. The initiative for change started moving forward quickly after the Duke of Westmoure announced he was supporting and working with the various committees and anti-slave transport leaders to abolish transportation of slaves. He campaigned endlessly for support and passage of this bill.

The Abolition of Slavery Act became law yesterday, March 25, and becomes effective May 1. Continued transportation of slaves is an act of piracy and a felony. Slave ships will not be allowed to trade at British ports. The Navy will patrol the seas off the coast of Africa and Ireland. Suspected British ships will be stopped, confiscated, and fined if they are transporting slaves.

The Duke of Westmoure stated, "This is just the beginning of the campaign to end the inhumanity of slave trade and slavery."

He will continue to work for full emancipation of all slaves throughout the world.

The Sixth Duke of Westmoure's Private Study
March 27, 1807

His personal journal, the pages of his life and innermost thoughts were laid out before him—the two-edged sword, the past and the present. His ducal power had ruined his brother's life. Now, the ducal power must shape his brother's future. Somehow, the mistakes of the past had to be rectified and made to mesh seamlessly into the present. The dukedom's future depended upon Avery and his heir. Closing the journal, the duke shook his head, trying to erase the cobwebs of his memories, and started his weekly letter to his brother.

March 27, 1807

Avery,

Yes indeed, it's a wonderful day. The law officially passed. British ships can no longer transport slaves from any country, including Africa and Ireland. I hope this helps your cause. We can do nothing about the slave laws within America except exert diplomatic pressure. I have assurances from the ministers this will be done. We'll continue to work for full emancipation throughout all of Great Britain.

Pausing, he thought of the many letters between the two of them, threads binding them after years of estrangement. The haunting memories of those years dominated his actions. What a fool he'd been—time wasted, shame and remorse. For a while, even after the truth was known, he hadn't allowed himself to think about how much damage had been done or how much he'd missed his brother Avery's quick wit and steady nature. During his trip to America, the two of them reconciled, but the pain lodged deep in his heart told him it wasn't enough. Would anything ever be enough? The duke sighed. Knowing how pleased the passage of the law would make Avery, he slipped the article from the *London Daily* into the envelope along with the letter.

As he continued to reflect, the sadness in his life caused his breath to catch—mistakes, deceit, and more mistakes. He still pictured the smug look on his brother Charles's face when he confronted him with the truth, the hate that burned in the woman he married, and his daughters who cared naught for anything but his tremendous wealth. Not one of them loved him, each other, or the responsibility and honor of the title. But the joys made all of this bearable: Joycellyn, his brother Avery, who found a way to forgive him, and the woman he loved above all others—the secret love of his life. Thinking of the future, he silently prayed he was creating ways to protect them and the dukedom long after he was no longer on this earth.

The first part of his plan was successful: the abolition of slave transportation—a gift for his brother Avery and his beloved wife, Anne—another way to make amends. His next step depended on the court's decision. Petitions were filed, and the court would hear the matter next term. *God, let me live long enough to ensure the future of the title and my family.*

Three Years Later
The Sixth Duke of Westmoure's Private Study
June 14, 1810

Avery,

The court heard the petition. After much debate and many long delays, everything has been recognized as legal and any hint of illegitimacy has been removed. I'm pleased everything will pass to you. I feel as though I know your son, my nephew, from your letters. Your son will make a fine duke one day . . .

Eleven Years Later
The Sixth Duke of Westmoure's Bedchamber

Dismissing his man of affairs, the duke started writing what he knew to be his last letter. It had to be right. The future of the family was at stake. He'd beg forgiveness on his eternal soul with his last breath if necessary, but it wasn't necessary. He'd been forgiven. Struggling with the pen and formation of the words, he hoped to express his love and expectations for the future.

November 10, 1821

Avery,

The pains are coming more frequently, and I tire quickly. The doctor says it is only a matter of time. I'm sorry I was such a fool and didn't listen to you thirty years ago. Our meeting in New York brought me much peace. Thank you for forgiving me.

I leave everything in your trusted care. Teach your son well, for everything will eventually pass to him. He will be a peer, and the title will continue in honorable hands. Teach your daughters everything about Westmoure's. Continue to include them in business matters when you are in England, even if this is not what society thinks proper for young ladies of their station.

Take care of Joycellyn. She has brought light and sunshine into my life. Joycellyn is a glorious child, more like my favorite grandchild. Please watch over the love of my life, the woman I should have married years ago.

I wish I had met your wife Anne; I am pleased yours is a love match. She will find her way as a duchess and probably wreak havoc with the ton. I leave everything in your trusted hands.

With affection,
Sterling

It took a week to complete the letter. He read it again. Satisfied, he watched his man of affairs slip the letter into the envelope. With veined, shaky hands of old age, the duke sealed it and sent it to the carrier bound for America that afternoon. Now, everything was in order. He leaned back and closed his eyes for a long rest.

London
November 21, 1821

The London Daily

The Sixth Duke of Westmoure Dies

The sixth Duke of Westmoure, Lord Sterling Adam Roxbury, has died at the age of seventy. The duke owned Westmoure Shipping Company. He was one of the forces behind the initiative and passage of the British Shipping Act, which prohibits British ships from transporting slaves.

The title passes to his brother, Lord Avery David Roxbury, who lives in America.

Whitehall
November 24, 1821

"Sebastian, Julien, Royce, your assignment by special order of the Crown."

Thomas Berkley assessed the men, three of his top operatives. This time their mission didn't include marching armies, the roar of cannons, or orders to find and destroy. Underscoring the urgency of what needed to be done, he simply stated they were the escort for the new Duke of Westmoure.

Pushing back the fallen lock of black hair threaded with gray, he also tried to push back the harsh reality of the assignment. Instead of war, there would be intrigue, power ploys, and nonacceptance by society. This time duplicity and death would pit Englishmen against each other. Although the instruments of destruction on the playing field had changed, there were no easy assignments, and everything boiled down to the same common denominator: good versus evil, right versus wrong. In that regard, this mission was no different than any other.

Sebastian Standerson, the Marquess of Broadhurst, was older than the other two by seventeen years—the senior operator, the diplomat, the man of steel. "Sir, the Crown wants us to meet the new duke when his ship docks at Southampton, correct?" His guarded movements bespoke of one who spent too many years behind enemy lines.

"No. You're to travel to the former colonies and bring the duke and his family to England."

Julien Quinton, the Honorable Earl of Sutton, sat with long

legs stretched out before him. Only a fool would think he was relaxed and not listening intently to the conversation around him. But for his razor-sharp reflexes, all three would have met their end when French agents came upon them in the forest outside of Lyon just before Waterloo. The hiss escaping from his lips was the only indication he understood the magnitude of the undertaking.

Leaning with one shoulder against the wall and his legs crossed at the ankles, Royce Thortonshire, the future Duke of Aston, studied the room. Royce was the detail man. If asked, he'd recall every aspect of the room in precise order, including the ink pot on the desk. Coupled with sound thinking and clear logic, they made a formidable team.

"I assume we're proceeding with utmost caution."

"Yes."

The last time they'd been together their mission was to find and destroy. To this day, the government still avowed no involvement in the deaths of a British traitor and his French counterparts. Now they were needed again. The sixth Duke of Westmoure, a good friend of the Crown and their personal friend, had died. With his death came the responsibility of protecting the new duke. Berkley hoped they'd return unharmed and alive, but their mission guaranteed violence.

As the meeting progressed, Berkley noted the change in his men from merely curious to protective predator: an operative of the Crown, the mental shift from observer to participant.

"Any questions?" Berkley didn't expect an answer. "After the funeral, a ship will be waiting to take you to America. Jack will be awaiting your return at Southampton with everything you need. Sebastian, you'll ride with me to the service; we can discuss everything in detail. Royce, Julien, prepare for every eventuality. Travel to Ivy Hall together."

"We'll stay at Rushton." Julien nodded.

Berkley, the general, as he was called by everyone under

his command, continued. "This will be convenient for us." Rushton, the ancestral home of Julien's family, lay adjacent to Ivy Hall, the ducal residence of the Westmoures. "Be ready to leave at first light. I apologize for taking you away from your families during the holidays." The clipped orders of the general were to be obeyed without question.

On the other side of the office door a man silently slipped down the dimly lit corridor, making sure no one saw or heard him. At the designated place he left the sign for a meeting.

CHAPTER 1

The New Aristocrats

America
January 1822

Poppa, Poppa, what are we to do now? The silent words stuck around the lump in her throat. Tears slowly trickled down her cheeks. The hole in the ground in front of her held the box where her father lay. Time had stopped when Sar found their father's lifeless form in the garden. The gunshot between the eyes ensured that Poppa would never see again. Tiny specks of dried blood still clung to barren branches of the rose bushes. The cold of the January day had nothing to do with the numbness and pain surrounding her heart.

She was born in this little close-knit community in America near the Canadian border. Here, there were no strangers. Less than ten yards of lake divided the two countries and towns. Citizens of both countries traveled back and forth over the footbridge as though crossing a street. They were friends, family. One helped the other . . . until two days ago.

Detecting the slight tremor of her mother's body ripped Mer's heart in two. The casket nestled in the cavity before her hammered home the reality of the tragedy. She leaned into her brother's arm, and her sister Beth leaned in to clutch his hand.

Sar stared down into the death pit as the winter sunlight bounced off the coffin in a shimmering rainbow of weak color. His chest tightened. Only concerns for his mother and sisters kept him from leaping into the cold depths to pound on the piece of wood and wail, "Wake up, wake up!" Sar shivered from the ice and rage around his heart. Whoever did this would pay.

The faces surrounding him appeared indistinguishable through his grief. All good men, he once thought. There had never been a murder in the community until the day before yesterday—murder, cold-blooded murder. In a blink, everything had changed. His guarded look scanned the crowd. For thirty years his father made this border town home. He'd met his mother within two months of arriving in America. *I saw her and fell in love with her that very moment.*

As the often-told story goes, they married three times— once in Canada to honor his father's British roots, once in America at the family church down the road, and on the high seas in international waters for the romantic adventure of it. Sar's copies of all three certificates sat in the lockbox in the desk drawer.

Mer tried to focus on the moment, but another fleeting look at her mother's trembling figure, and pain like she had never felt before seared her body. It was as though she was looking at everything through a haze; nothing was clear. She recalled Poppa laughing at breakfast. The next time she saw him he was laid out in the ice house. Try as she might, she remembered nothing in between. Her foot tapped softly on the frosty earth. Like a soothing balm, good memories rushed forth.

She was now twenty-two, but Poppa frequently reminded her she was still in diapers when he carried her into the shipping office for the first time—and she'd been there every day since. The family business was as much a part of her as breathing. As children, the ships became castles with princesses and princes, and set the stage for fights with pirates, round-the-world trips, and hidden treasure. Playing aboard the decks usually landed the three of them in hot water with a captain at least once a week, but the crews adored them. Whenever possible, they persuaded them to be pirates.

As Mer grew older, she discovered her uncanny ability to organize everything from shipping schedules to orders, filling the ships going from America and those coming into the ports in New York and Boston. Along the way, she was guided by her parents and her father's business partner, Jacob Goldsmith. One of her father's favorite litanies played in her head: *You must know your business from the ground up, inside and out.*

The puff of wind caught a strand of Mer's honey-colored hair; it hung in the air like a fluttering butterfly. Large, expressive brown eyes glossed from the sheen of tears. Every possible emotion had been wrenched from her soul, and she was empty. How were they going to move forward without Poppa? Her very essence ached.

With one last look at the newly turned grave and a nod to the minister, her brother led the family back to the house. Neighbors, friends, and acquaintances followed, expressing condolences and chatting in the hushed tones that always followed the awkwardness of death. Poppa loved a good party, and Mer wondered what he would think of this. Again, the front door opened, and three men stepped through the entry. Mer's gaze slowly took in the trio, and her eyes shifted back to the one with cinnamon-colored hair. Her heart stopped, and a flutter in her stomach occurred.

Who is he? Unconsciously, she started taking steps in his

direction. "Mer." Mrs. Thornton, their nearest neighbor, gave her a hug.

Julien felt eyes boring into him. When he glanced up, it felt as though he was looking directly into the very essence of himself. Mentally shaking his head, he wondered why it felt like she belonged to him, this woman with honey-colored hair, huge expressive brown eyes, and a sadness that wrenched his soul. From their briefing in Whitehall, he knew this was one of the daughters. He wasn't able to break his connection with those mournful eyes. It was as though an invisible thread was pulling him into her. The armor protecting his heart couldn't withstand the onslaught, and he felt a strange sensation deep within. Too close, his inner self responded, too close. The invisible thread kept reeling him in.

On the other side of the room, Perkins quietly spoke to Sar as he cautiously glanced between Perkins and the men in the foyer. The scowl on Sar's face spoke silent volumes. Mer watched the two of them while somehow trying to appear to be attentive to Mrs. Thornton. When the old lady paused for a breath, Mer thanked her for coming. She trusted that was the correct response, because she had no idea what had been said. Giving the old lady a hug, she escorted her to a seat near her daughter.

Perkins leaned in closer to Sar. "Sar, the men wished to speak . . . ahem"—Perkins cleared his throat—"to your father."

"Didn't you tell them this is a house in mourning?" "Yes, they said they knew."

"Then why did they ask to speak to my father?"

"Before I could say anything, they demanded to see the master of the house, and said they'd wait. This is strange."

"It's probably a business matter. Send them away . . . another day, next week maybe, but not now, Perkins."

"They claim it is most urgent. Something isn't quite right. They're most adamant and demanding."

"Urgent or not, today is not the day. Send them away!"

"I don't think that's possible. They are willing to wait . . . to wait however long is necessary."

"Then they can wait until hell freezes over."

Sar's glimpse at the men made him wonder if he had a choice. The predatory stance and determined look of the three gentlemen with broad shoulders and heights towering over six feet filled the large entryway, overpowering the space. Their elegantly tailored jackets, waistcoats, and highly polished Hessian boots were a beacon proclaiming their presence. Sar noticed one surveying the room looking for the person who would silently announce, *I am lord and master of all here.* Hell probably couldn't move them.

"Damnation, Perkins. Show them to the library; I'll join them shortly."

The gentlemen carried themselves in a manner that let everyone know they were not commoners. Instinctively, everyone moved aside as they were led to the quiet sanctuary. Sar headed to the library with a heavy heart and steps as grave as a man taking his last walk to the guillotine.

"Perkins, we won't be long."

With a nod, Perkins closed the library door.

Could she get to the room next to the library undetected, or should she stay and accept the condolences of the mourners? An unknown force was compelling Mer to go. Something pushed her to the stranger, an inner awareness of something illusive, a sense of some type of danger.

Another hand touched her elbow, and she looked into the water-filled eyes of the minister's wife. Mer inwardly sighed. The library would have to wait.

"My lord." Sar glanced at the man in the finely tailored black jacket. "You have our deepest condolences. We didn't realize the news had already reached you. Hopefully, we'll be able to leave sooner than anticipated. Would it be possible to speak with the master of the house, Lord Avery David Roxbury?"

Just hearing his father's name was like a fist being plowed into his stomach. "What manner of game is this?" he was about to shout, when the gentleman pulled out a miniature at least thirty-five years old. Instead, one word was softly spoken: "Dad." At the same time, the three gentlemen took note of the man standing before them. He was much too young to be Avery David Roxbury. The next in line to inherit was the youngest brother Avery, age fifty-eight. The man standing before them was no more than thirty.

"You're not Avery David Roxbury." The definitive statement rather than a question dangled in the air.

Sar shook his head. "No."

The man compared him to the miniature. Except for wavy hair, everything else was identically the same—the son. Once again, he asked, "Your name?"

Sar's grief and anger resonated beneath his apparent cool façade. *What is this madness?*

Glancing at the miniature of his father clutched in the stranger's hand, and taking a deep breath to gain some self-control, he hurled his own question at the stranger. "Why do you wish to know?"

"We're on the king's business; it's imperative we speak to Lord Avery David Roxbury immediately. He would be expecting us."

"Speak to him . . . immediately . . . expect you?" Sar railed. "Look around you! Does this not speak of a house in mourning?"

"Excuse me, my lord, is this not the house of Lord Avery David Roxbury?"

"Just who do you think you are speaking to?" He reacted to their intrusion and words as though a knife sliced through his heart. "His Majesty's business or not, this is America. The former colonies are free of English rule. I'm not a lord, nor was my father. What do you want?"

Unperturbed, the questioning from the man continued. "Your name?"

Exasperated, the answer came forth with barely an ounce of control. "Sterling Avery Roxbury, the one and only son of Avery David Roxbury, who was laid to rest a mere hour ago and murdered two days ago. Now, if you gentlemen will *please* excuse me." He turned to leave.

"And, your mother?"

With icy-cold eyes he stared at the gentlemen. "Beside herself with grief after thirty years of marriage."

"Do you have proof of that marriage?"

The audacity of these strangers to enter his house and insult his parents and himself by insinuating he bore the shame of being born outside of a legal marriage blinded all rational thought. A bastard was nothing—a non-person—socially ostracized and damned. "How dare you!"

An explosion of rage, frustration, and anger poured from him. With the need to pound the British gentleman within an inch of his life for his insulting implication, Sar lunged at him and gripped the lapels of his jacket. Contempt and grief flowed from him as he tried to lift the man from his seat. He couldn't. Strong vice-like hands on either side of him restrained his arms, forcing him to release the lapels.

The man he had just tried to beat didn't seem overly perturbed. His eyes bore into Sar with steadfast intent. "Again, do you have proof of the marriage?"

Sar struggled with his thoughts and looked his adversary in the eye: definitely steel and determination. "Yes, and what business is it of yours? What do you want?"

Through his fog of anger and grief, his father's warning sprang to life. *One day you might need proof your mother and I are married. The British government may need legal proof.* His father never explained why. During the last six years, his father repeated that warning frequently. Sar assumed it concerned the shipping company. Maybe after his father's death, in order to collect certain claims, his mother needed to provide evidence of proof of a legal marriage. *But they hadn't known of his death,* the voice in his head reminded him. He quickly dismissed the thought of a long-lost relative leaving a fortune and bitterly laughed to himself. This was the only family. His father was alone until he met his mother.

Sar looked intently at the gentlemen, puzzled by what they wanted and confused about this strange coincidence—the British government arriving on this day of all days demanding proof of his parents' marriage.

"Answers to my questions first, then we'll talk."

"For God's sake, man, my father was just buried."

"Proof of the marriage, now." Sebastian pushed for the information. With the murder of Avery Roxbury, everyone was in danger. The sooner they were on their way to England, the sooner he could begin to level the playing field.

Hesitantly, Sar went to the desk drawer that held the lock box and the papers he promised to protect with his life. The old lock wouldn't give. Maybe it was a sign not to open the box; maybe it was Pandora's Box filled with untold mystery, pain, and sorrow. Maybe, maybe, maybe, but he knew the box had to be opened. Finally forcing the lock, he opened the creaky lid and spread the contents on the desk. There for all to see were exact copies of three separate marriage certificates: one from the Canadian church, one signed by the captain of the British ship attesting to the marriage in international water on the high seas, and one from the church down the road.

Everything was exactly as Sebastian was told to expect. Regardless, his man would be dispatched to review the churches' marriage registries in the morning.

"Your Grace."

"Your Grace?" Sar never got further.

"Our condolences again," Sebastian continued. "We thought you knew of the passing of the sixth Duke of Westmoure."

"And?" Sar replied dryly with one eyebrow arched. "The sixth Duke of Westmoure . . . ah, Westmoure Shipping. You'll have to see our agents in New York." His single thought was to get them out of his father's library. The memories and the lingering scent of his pungent cigar smoke still filled the room. This was his father's special haven, and these strangers were an invasion of those memories. He wanted it left exactly as it was—a shrine in honor of his father.

Sar's mind suddenly caught up with the present moment. *Your Grace?* Why were these men using the title of an English aristocrat? Turning towards the gentleman who just spoke, he willed himself to focus.

"You don't know about the sixth Duke of Westmoure? Perhaps your father mentioned him. You carry his name."

"No." The tone of finality of the answer echoed throughout the still room. "Gentlemen, this is not the day to discuss business. Even if Westmoure's is one of the largest shipping companies in the world, we can discuss your matter next week." As he moved to summons Perkins, Sebastian rose to his feet and bowed.

"Your Grace, you are now the eighth Duke of Westmoure. You've inherited the title, lands, and wealth of one of the most honored families in all of Christendom. We apologize for intruding on you this day. The title passed to your father in November, making him the seventh Duke of Westmoure. We were sent by the Crown to escort him and his family to England. There is much to discuss, but we agree, today is not the day. Mayhap tomorrow, if you would be so kind? We'll need your family and attorneys present. Again, you have our condolences."

As Sebastian delivered his velvet-cloaked order, he

assimilated the new facts. His mind quickly reached the obvious: murder due to the succession to the title, and a spy and murderer lurking within Whitehall.

Sar's grief-filled, anguished mind tried to sensibly assimilate what he had learned. And, just like that, with the utterance of a few words, the family's life was turned upside down again. First a gunshot and now words.

Mer extricated herself from the sobs of the reverend's wife and secretly made her way to the room adjacent to the library. She was too late. Leaning against the wall, all she heard was Sar requesting that the gentlemen spend the night. Tomorrow they'd explain their business. Mer quietly tip-toed out of the room.

CHAPTER 2

Life-Changing Truth

Sar jerked upward as the cool liquid trickled down his thigh. Sitting in his father's favorite chair, he watched the amber-colored brandy spread on the rug and the glass roll to the corner of the room. Dawn had stolen the night. It had been another restless night in which peaceful sleep eluded him. His mind was beleaguered with thoughts about his father, the family, and the farfetched tale of the Brits.

Though he wanted time to sort everything out, now there was the matter of the British strangers to sort through first. Surely it was a mistake. Yes, his father was from England, but his family was all he had. Lessons taught by his father swirled in his head. *Family is the most important thing in life, always take care of and provide for them. Respect every woman you meet. Regardless of the difficulty, always do what is right.* The litanies played over and over in his mind as he splashed hot water on his face and continued to dress. Sar wondered what his mother's reaction would be to their English visitors. Well, there was no time like the present to find out. He ambled down the hallway to her bedchamber.

Even though it was early, he doubted she'd slept. As he raised his hand to knock, her worried maid opened the door. "I was just about to go looking for you, Sar." She pointed to his mother. "She dismissed me last night, saying she didn't need any help. The missus is in the same spot where I left her."

His mother was sitting by the fireplace, staring into space and clinging to the birthday gift his father had given her the day before he died. The pain of her grief hit him like a thunderbolt, her shock palpable. Since the age of eighteen when she married his father, their lives had been one. She sat dazed and catatonic.

Mer awoke at dawn. Sleep had been an adventure down memory lane: Poppa teaching her about shipping schedules, Poppa cautioning her about the young men who would woo her for the family's wealth and status and insisting she marry for love, Poppa hugging and laughing with Mother, and Poppa warning her not to worry, everything will work out. She knew she had cried and laughed during the dream. If she hadn't known she was sleeping, she would have sworn her father was in the room talking to her. Gooseflesh rose on her arms. None of this eased her grief. She'd find Sar, find out what the gentlemen he'd talked to in the library wanted, and then spend time with Beth and her mother. After she was introduced to the man with the cinnamon-colored hair, the fluttering of her heart and stomach would end. It was all due to the sadness of the last few days. She was being a silly twit. A man had never affected her like this. She just wasn't her normal self.

Her feet touched the cold floor, and she willed herself to get up and move. There was no answer when she knocked on Sar's bedchamber door. Cook hadn't seen him, and he wasn't at the stables. Using the side entrance, she peeked into the empty library and then went to find Perkins. Where you found

Perkins, you usually found Sar. Perkins couldn't be found. Hearing voices coming from her mother's room, she slowed her pace and silently eased down the hall. Pressing her ear to the door, Mer tried to decipher what her mother was saying. Her soft voice made it impossible.

In the bedchamber, Anne's flailing arm barely missed the statue on the mantle as she turned and pointed to Sar. "We were never going to tell you. You must believe what your father told me. You must! I don't care what the British say. If your father said he didn't do it, he didn't. Above all, he was an honest and honorable man. I know . . . I lived with him for thirty years."

Bile rose in her throat. Taking one step forward, Sar caught her as she slumped to the floor. To tell her son the *other* secret would be even more painful. Maybe he didn't have to know. Maybe they could go on as before, but she knew the *before* of their lives had been swept away with that single shot and the arrival of the British. Anne started to tremble as tears coursed down her cheeks. Avery had warned her that one day the British might arrive. If they came, he had to be prepared and be able to prove their marriage was legal. Until this moment, she had never thought of *how* he was going to be able to prove it. Always lurking in the back of her mind was the truth: their marriage was illegal. By law, it didn't exist. Her children were bastards.

She shivered violently. Her mind raced through the years. It seemed it was only yesterday when Avery asked her to marry him, and she had willingly—three times, once for each country, his and hers, and on the high seas as a romantic adventure. Avery's words danced through her jumbled thoughts. *This is to prove the abiding conviction of my deep love for you, Anne. I will always protect you as my wife.*

She rocked back and forth, bemoaning the loss of innocence, the death of Avery, and the losses yet to come. "Believe what your father told me. You *must* believe what your father told me. You must!" She couldn't look at her son. She didn't want to see his confusion, anger, and the deep sorrow of betrayal. Avery wasn't here to provide the answers and ease the pain. All she had to offer was blind faith in a dead man and the secret that would destroy them all.

Like her, Sar didn't have to believe the story she had just told him, but the secret was irrefutable, a fact no one could deny.

"What is the manner of their business?" she murmured through choked tears. "Did they come to take him back to England to stand trial? Why now?" Anne stared straight at her son but didn't see him.

Perkins tapped Mer on the shoulder. She turned, glared at him, and mouthed "Go away." Whatever was being said on the other side of the door was important. She raised her eyebrows and, with her hands, shooed Perkins. Afraid she'd miss something, she turned back and pressed her ear to the door. Sar's angry voice was more distinguishable.

"No, that would make our life a lie, a mockery. Secrets like the one you just told me and the story the British bring betrays us—us! The father I thought I knew would have told me. May he rot in hell!"

Damn, she couldn't make any sense out of the snippets she heard. Sar's angry voice resonated in her ears. She'd never heard him so incensed or speak in such a matter about Poppa, let alone talk to their mother like that. Her foot moved unconsciously as she strained to hear more. Perkins gently pulled her away from the door. The warning in her dream came back to haunt her. She heard her father's words. *Not to worry, everything will work out.* Frustrated, she went to find Beth, to tell all, and see if they could figure out what was going on. Perkins replaced her with his ear glued to the door.

After the morning meal, the family and Jacob gathered in the library. Her mother looked as though her inner life had been extinguished. The man called Sebastian and the other two gentlemen, Julien and Royce, joined them. It was obvious by their lofty demeanor they were part of the elite of British society. When the family's attorneys, Arnold Morrison and Abe Berg, walked into the room, Mer's raised foot stopped and froze in midair. Something was wrong.

Their attorneys never left their law offices except on matters of grave importance, and they'd left their offices two days in a row.

Julien tried not to stare at her, but his quick glances weren't enough to satisfy his curiosity. What would it be like to touch her silky hair, brush his lips across that full mouth, caress her breasts, and feel the softness of her inner thighs? Was she only interested in the latest gossip, balls, and finding a husband? Why wasn't she married? Julien wondered where these thoughts were coming from. Although the journey had been much faster than anticipated, fifty days without a woman was too long. And he was feeling it to the bottom of his boots if he was hungrily looking at the honey-haired beauty sitting across the room—an innocent, an obvious innocent.

Julien, get a hold of yourself. She is an assignment, yours to protect. But the invisible thread wouldn't let go and pulled him tenderly to her.

Sebastian cleared his throat. "We have much to discuss. Would you like to begin?"

Arnold Morrison peered over his spectacles, and Abe Berg nodded. Whatever was going on, the two acknowledged Sebastian's statement as if they all knew the outcome.

"Again, our sympathy, Sterling." Abe Berg opened the discussion for the attorneys. "Gentlemen, proof of your business."

The man named Sebastian handed a packet with two seals

on it to the attorney. Berg examined the seals, comparing them to the sketches in his folder. "Yes, this seems to be authentic," he said and sliced it open.

After a very slow reading, he passed the packet to Morrison. Abe Berg reached into his file and handed another packet to Sebastian, sealed with an exact duplicate of one of the seals on the packet Berg had just opened. Sebastian sliced open this packet, and a thick gold signet ring rolled to the floor. Quiet filled the room as all eyes focused on the ring spinning round and round.

Mer watched as her mother reached out to Sar and touched his hand as her tears continued to fall. Mer's eyes shifted from one to the other. The bits and pieces she heard earlier left her confused and anxious. Sar had damned their father. Her mother hadn't stopped crying. Besides her grief, something else wasn't right. Mer's foot was moving in a steady beat of its own accord.

Sar could no more control his meandering thoughts and frustration than stop the ebb and flow of the morning tide. What about his father's crime? His mother's story? What about the Brits tale of a dukedom? Confusion etched his deep-furrowed brow. He wanted to know what had been kept from him all of his life and why—and he wanted to know now.

"Sterling." The sound of his name brought him back from his wandering thoughts.

As if reading his mind, Arnold Morrison spoke. "We think we should start with an explanation. Your father was the youngest son of an aristocratic family. Twenty-four years ago, through sources unknown to us, Avery learned of the passing of his brother Charles. There were three boys born to the family: His Grace, Charles, and your father.

"Avery came to us with information regarding his family, which we compiled and documented. Letters from the solicitors in London confirmed the death of his brother Charles, and that your father would inherit the title upon the death of his oldest brother. From the day he asked Anne to marry him, Avery's thoughts and actions were always directed towards protecting his wife and the family to come.

"I doubt if you know, but your father left England under a cloud of suspicion and dishonor. He never thought he'd return to Britain nor need the documents in our file."

What? Had she heard correctly? Her father, leaving England under a cloud of suspicion? Suspicion of what? Blinking, Mer tried to absorb the information . . . Her father, the family, their life as they knew it, all a charade. No, this couldn't be possible. Poppa was the kindest and most honorable of men. And what was this "grace" business. Her foot started shaking, and she looked to her mother for answers. All she got were blank stares and sensed Julien looking intently at her.

Julien caught himself as he was about to rise to go to her. She needed him. What was it about this woman who had him acting totally out of character? *Come on, Julien old man, she's just an assignment.* But he couldn't dismiss the need he felt. And that strange feeling encased his heart, and the thread of connection tightened.

"As Attorney Morrison stated, this letter, the family signet ring given to Lord Avery upon his twenty-first birthday, and the original marriage certificate from the ceremony performed on the high seas are authentic, proof your father was the youngest brother of the sixth Duke of Westmoure. I'll try to fill you in with as much as I know."

Sebastian continued. "When your father left England—excuse me, ladies—it was under the suspicion of having compromised an eleven-year-old servant and molesting her in a horrible manner. From the trauma of the abuse, she stopped talking. Articles of your father's clothing were found in the child's room. Being very firm about honor, the sixth duke exiled your father immediately, severing all family ties. The duke kept the child and her babe under his protection."

Anne sat with her children, silently stunned at this revelation of the man they loved. He'd betrayed them. Mer's mind was trying to comprehend Poppa compromising an eleven-year-old servant and abusing her. *No, no, not Poppa.* He would never. She could hear his laughter, and her mind's eye replayed the gentleness that had guided his children through the years. They never feared him. When he disciplined them, he was never violent. And when he did discipline them, they needed it. *A child of eleven!* Mer closed her eyes as her entire body started shaking.

"Six years after the incident, the girl came face to face with your late Uncle Charles and started screaming and clawing at him. At first, everyone thought she was having a breakdown. When she started to talk, it was babble like that of a child first learning to speak. It took some time before she was finally understood. Charles had taken repeated liberties of the child and threatened to kill her if she told anyone."

Mer's foot tapped uncontrollably. Waves of emotions flooded her senses—rape, accusations, another whole family, connections they never knew about, and murder. *Poppa, oh Poppa, what are we going to do now?*

Julien looked up to see the sheen of unshed tears in her brown eyes, felt his heart clutch, and knew he was being drawn to her by forces beyond his control.

"Debauching innocents wasn't within the family code of honor. Charles's duplicity, and knowing Charles was to inherit the title, placed the duke in an awful dilemma. His Grace banned Charles from the house. From that day forth, he had no contact with him. The duke met with ministers of Parliament, the government, and his solicitors to find a way to legally remove Charles from the line of succession. Short of a royal proclamation, there was no solution."

Sebastian cleared his throat before he continued. "The duke was mortified by the magnitude of his mistake. He'd banished your father for something he didn't do and separated him from the rest of the family forever. Five years later, His Grace came to America and found your father in New York."

Anne's eyes widened. She remembered that particular trip. Avery had returned unsettled and vague. She could never pinpoint the change. Every day since then he told her, "I will always love you, and I will always protect you." Sometimes she had an ominous feeling of doom when he uttered those words. His love was not in doubt, but the words created a silent barrier of untold mystery. A shiver ran down her spine to her toes. She tensed and her stomach revolted. She knew what was yet to come. Her secret would be a secret no more; she'd lose everything. There was no way Avery could protect them now, and Anne looked at the children she would lose with the utterance of six words.

"In the meeting in New York, the duke begged forgiveness and pleaded with your father to return to England immediately and take his rightful place in the family. Your father refused. It's my impression His Grace left New York much relieved, even though your father said no to returning to England until necessary; that would be when the title passed to him. Both men went their separate ways with peace in their hearts.

"There is much more. Morgan, the late duke's man of affairs, knows all. Your Grace, if you'll tell us about your antecedents, we'll be able to finish putting all of the pieces together and clarify why we are here."

Sebastian sat back in his chair and observed. From the rapt, stunned attention of her children, it was obvious they neither knew nor suspected the rest of the story. The next few minutes would tell the character of the family and give him more insight as to how to handle the trip to England.

Anne didn't have a choice. Her words would irrevocably change their lives. Forbidden thoughts crowded her mind; she shuddered. As difficult as it was going to be, the secret had to be bared, laid out for inspection, and their life destroyed. There was no turning back, and the voice in her head reminded her not to cower before this group, regardless of their lofty positions and titles.

Anne squared her shoulders and felt the presence of a protective arm around her and wanted to reach out and touch Avery. She paused, looked at her children, and saw questions, confusion, and concern on each of their faces.

"My children, you are not white. I am the granddaughter of a freed Negro slave." The air in the room stopped. "That makes you, like me, my children, Negroes . . . mixed blood." She looked from one child, to the other, and then to the other. Shock and disbelief were on each face; Mer's tapping foot stilled. Anne pressed on.

"In this country and in Canada, marriages between Negroes and whites are forbidden. These laws make our marriage illegal. If I am correct, this prevents Sar from having any claim to the title."

Sebastian nodded in agreement.

If a mother's love could protect them, she'd wrap them in her arms forever, but the harsh reality of the world and truth instantly made all of them different—pariahs, according to most. She thought her parents had been legally married, but her mother's death-bed confession about being mixed blood had left questions—unanswered questions. Her father was from England, and her mother was the daughter of a freed slave. She'd never met her grandfather, and her father had died when she was five.

"In this country, if the authorities knew of my marriage to your father, we'd be stripped of everything and maybe lynched or sold into slavery through nefarious means." Trying to gather her thoughts, she paused again. "We live in a small community. No one knows or suspects I am of mixed blood. When your father asked me to marry him, he understood the risks. Nothing would deter him from making me his wife and holding ourselves out as married, even if the marriages were not legal. My children, you are mixed, Negro bastards."

So much . . . so much we kept from you in our effort to make your lives easier, she thought. As pain clutched her inner being, she wanted to scream at the injustice of it all. Anne watched emotions wash across the faces of her confused, bewildered children and didn't know how many times a heart could break. Words wouldn't ease the shock, but she tried anyway.

"Your father and I weren't going to tell you. Just as your father wanted to protect the sanctity of our marriage, we wanted to protect you." In a calm clear voice, she continued. "Telling you our secret would have placed you in known danger and questioned the validity of our marriage. In order to live as a family, we couldn't let anyone know of our predicament. People see me as white. Therefore, they acknowledge you as white.

"No, I am not ashamed of who I am. Your father and I did what we thought was best for you. We didn't want you to face the degradation or stigma of being labeled, disrespected, and abused. We wanted you to have the best America offers. We did it because we love you."

She knew she was pleading, pleading for understanding, begging for their love, beseeching for a chance to be their mother. Her entreaties were met with stunned silence.

Angrily, she turned to Sebastian. "Why are you here telling us about a title that my son can't inherit? But for you, no one would have known of our secret. Look at what you've done to my children, our family. We are no more. We are nothing. Do you hear me? Nothing!"

Jabbing her fingers in his chest, words tumbled from her. "Do you have any idea what it is like to be a Negro, a mixed breed, an outcast in this country? Do you understand the consequences that affect every aspect of your life? Will you be there to defend them from the hate? Will you protect them when someone tries to kill them for the life we have been living?"

"Yes." Sebastian's firmly spoken word resonated through the room.

"Go! Leave us alone so we can get on with our lives as best we can." The air shimmered with barely controlled restraint. She collapsed in the chair and buried her head in her hands.

"Anne, I think it is best if I explain from here." Abe Berg admired her courage, saw she was visibly shaken and the children baffled. He hoped she was able to withstand what was yet to come. "Even though Avery prepared well for this eventuality, he assumed he'd be alive to prove the legitimacy of the marriage and to offer comfort to his wife and children when he assumed the title."

Sar walked to the sideboard, filled a glass with brandy, and swallowed it in one gulp. Then he poured another. He tried to place the glass in his mother's hands, but her trembling prevented it. Instead, he put an arm around her shoulder and held on. An openmouthed Mer placed one foot on top of the other to try to stop the tapping. A wide-eyed Beth continued to chew on her lower lip.

"There have never been any laws prohibiting inter-race marriages in England," Abe continued. "Your father prevailed upon the captain of a ship registered in England and flying the English flag to marry them in international waters. Under the time-honored principles of international law, a wedding ceremony performed by a licensed captain on the open seas in international waters is legal and binding if the country under which the ship is registered and flies its flag recognizes the marriage as lawful. The signed original marriage certificate with the official seal of England is proof the marriage is legal and binding.

"In our folder is additional documentation. Copies were sent to the solicitors in London fifteen years ago. Anne, all of the children were born of a legal marriage. The local minister, as the vicar, thought nothing of marrying two people so in love. They never knew. Avery sought to protect you and remove any stigma of illegitimacy."

The words washed over her numb body. She was legally married . . . married. It took a moment for the impact of the reality to sink in. Married, but not in this country. Avery's often-spoken words about protecting her and the family had caused the greatest sacrifice of all: his life. The simple ceremony aboard the ship made the impossible possible. *Avery, I didn't understand then. You loved and protected us as you said. Thank you, my love.*

Mer could hear words bouncing around her. She was viewing her life through a thick fog and was fumbling about through the muck, unsure of a direction, unsure if she would ever find her way out. She *wasn't* who she thought she was. Would she be treated as an outcast by many, a person who was less than human because of mixed blood? She was part Negro.

She shook off her mother's hand and ignored her words. Mer lowered her head between her knees and prayed she wouldn't faint. Spots danced before her closed eyelids. Julien wanted to reach out, hold her, and comfort her. She was his to protect.

"Your Grace, Lord Avery took extreme precautions to ensure you were his lawfully wedded wife and the children born of a legal union," Sebastian continued. "During the interim years before the late duke died, Lord Avery communicated regularly with him and his lawyers.

"The late duke also discussed this matter with his peers and solicitors. After thorough and extensive research, the proper petitions were filed in court for the British government to recognize the marriage on the high seas as legal and binding. Due to the laws of the former colonies, the late duke and Lord Avery wanted to make sure the succession of the title was in order beyond a shadow of a doubt and above a whisper of the law.

"Let me explain. There has never been a legally recognized mixed-blood duke among the peerage. The aristocracy believes their bloodlines are pure, and they instill that notion in every child born. In England, slavery was prohibited in 1609, and unlike America, inter-race marriage is common. Your marriage isn't the first union between a member of the aristocracy and a Negro.

"I cannot lie and say there hasn't been opposition to this by some of the peers. Several years ago, due to the interference and influence of some highly placed members of the aristocracy, the court nullified the marriage between a countess and her Negro footman, because she could still bear a child. Even though the earl had died, the thought of a lady bearing an inter-race baby was repulsive to many members of the aristocracy. Within the aristocracy, some try to cling to the belief of purity of lineage and will do anything to prevent the bloodlines from being mixed."

He didn't need to fill in the unspoken words: *even murder.* Sebastian imagined the wagging tongues of the ton once the news of Avery's death reached London. There was little doubt his murder had everything to do with inheriting the title. One murder or two, it didn't matter. A mixed-blood duke compromising purity of lineage was intolerable to many. Breeding was essential. His instincts warned him Sar was next. A glance at Julien and Royce told him they'd reached the same conclusion.

Those behind Avery's murder would make sure the right gossips knew the pertinent details. Quicker than an instant it would appear in the Society News. As usual, the general had been right. All hell was going to break loose.

"Your Grace, in the matter of your parents," Sebastian continued, "the English court heard the petition presented by the late duke in closed session. After much debate, which centered on the laws of the former colonies, the court recognized the marriage on the high seas as legal and binding. In Britain, in order to inherit a title, you must be born of a legitimate union. By law, you are entitled to inherit."

Thoughts, problems, concerns, anxiety, and fear swirled through Anne's mind. *How do we go on? Were we foolish to marry?* She felt paralyzed by an innate feeling of irreversible loss. *Avery, I need you so much*, her mind shouted. Unfortunately, there was no reply and no answers. The pain in her chest became unbearable; she couldn't inhale. Hoping her leaden legs would support her, she stood and left with the dignity of one born to the aristocracy. The men rose and watched Her Grace leave.

"Enough! This is exhausting to all. My mother is distraught." Acting as though he was used to giving orders and being obeyed, Sar took charge, making it clear what they were going to do and so ordered it. Reaching out for Mer and Beth, he pulled them to him. They formed a closed circle from the rest of the world.

"I suggest we continue this discussion tomorrow morning. We need time to try to understand and begin to come to terms with finding out we are not at all who we thought we were. Being mixed blood in this country and having Negro blood in our veins means we are nothing. We have no rights. It's not every day a man finds out he is nothing and is considered less than human in the country in which he is born, yet is a duke and a peer of the highest realm in another country.

"Gentlemen, you can continue your work here—whatever it is that needs to be done. Dinner is at seven." Clinging to each other they left the room.

Julien watched them leave. *She should be clinging to me,* his inner voice chimed.

Tension fringed the air at dinner. Mer and Beth toyed with their food, looking through red-rimmed eyes for guidance from Sar. Clenching the stem of the wine glass in front of him as though it was his only lifeline, Sar glared at Sebastian. The glass shattered like gunshot.

Everyone jumped. Sar pushed back his chair with enough force to send it crashing to the floor and left the room as though the demons of hell were nipping at his heels. The English gentlemen and lawyers continued to dine as though it was business as usual.

***

Unable to sleep, Sar walked to the lake, thinking about his lives—the old one, the one he never knew about, his new life, and the future. He wasn't surprised to see Jacob. When there were serious matters to discuss, Jacob and his father came here to talk. The cold of the late-night air matched the chill in his heart and the questions he had to ask. Jacob motioned to the seat where Avery usually sat.

"I've been expecting you."

"Do I have any rights in the country?"

"No, Sar. We both know in America Negroes—mixed bloods—are considered inferior and less than human. Most white Americans don't think of them as anything but property to be owned and used by what they believe to be the superior white race."

"Why?"

As a white man, Jacob didn't know if he could answer. "I have no idea how people think, or how they learn to harbor hate because people are different."

"Because of my mother . . . Is she the reason our ships never carried human cargo?"

"Sar, your father and I sat here and talked about the injustice of transporting human cargo and slavery on many occasions. In our opinion, both are wrong, unconscionable. Once, we had the opportunity to board a slave ship confiscated by the British Navy. Humans had been packed in every conceivable area like salted fish and transported on shelves in spaces of less than twenty-three inches per person for the long journey. They were branded, put in manacles, and tied to each other. Heat filled the cramped, airless spaces. There was filth, disease, and little food. Many died from suffocation and starvation.

"The British commanders told us about the horrors they witnessed. Slave traders dumping slaves overboard if they were running low on food or to decrease their fine if the ship was about to be seized by the Navy. Thousands died. Irish women sold into slavery to breed with the African slaves were cheaper to buy. Slavers jumped on this opportunity to increase their profits. Unable to withstand the intolerable conditions on the slave ships, some of these women drove nails into their brains."

Jacob paused. "British ships are prohibited from transporting slaves. Less than honorable British companies are still in the business. Although Britain can pass laws to govern its country, it can't pass laws for the world. Sebastian told me your uncle, the late duke, campaigned endlessly to ensure the bill prohibiting slave trading passed—a gift for your father and mother."

"I didn't even know he existed." Never in Sar's wildest imagination did he ever consider the passage of a bill in

England, American slavery, and a dukedom would irrevocably impact his life.

"Your father and I couldn't carry human cargo. It's wrong. It's murder. Slavery is immoral. A man owning another and treating another human as such is shocking and unacceptable. As a Jew, I know about oppression, but it is nothing like that of being a Negro. All I have to do is change my name, practice a different religion, and I'd instantly be accepted as just another white man.

"I'm not ashamed of my heritage, and you shouldn't be ashamed of yours. Life can be unfair, cruel, and hard due to the ignorance, greed, and unfounded hatred of man."

He'd never heard Jacob speak in such a passionate manner. He now understood his integrity and the depth of the friendship he shared his father. This was an honest man—one you could trust with your life—and Sar felt the shift of the responsibility of his father's principles slip slowly onto his shoulders and his father close at hand.

"Did you know my mother was a Negro, or a *mulatto*, as some people would call her?" He spat out the offensive term.

"No, your father never told me. I feel he didn't want to burden us with the truth or put us in jeopardy."

"Would it have made any difference if you had known?"

"Truthfully, yes. It would have been a surprise at first. Then I'd have been more protective of you and your family. It would've been hell always being on the lookout for someone who could harm you. The way Avery and Anne planned everything, we went about our lives suspecting nothing. And no, I didn't know he was an aristocrat. However, now that I think about it, I should have picked up on our differences when we made our trip across to America."

"Did I really know my father?"

"Without a doubt, Sar, without a doubt."

"What sort of man was the man I called father?"

"Your father was probably the most honorable man I have ever known. He married for love, and he loved his family. Sar, I am a Jew. It made no difference to your father. That is why he married the woman he loved. Above all, carry his name and all you do in his honor and act as he."

Sar sat and witnessed the quiet of the night turn into the wee hours of another day. Everything weighed heavily on his mind. He'd never completely understood the plight of Negroes in this country. How could he? He *was* a white man, an observer. He couldn't truly feel the anguish or experience the depth of humiliation and hatred, because he wasn't a Negro . . . until yesterday. The stark truth of his mother's revelation changed his entire life and perspective in less than two seconds. He laughed to himself at the irony.

Neither man spoke as they returned to the house. The companionable silence of the two was a testament to a new-found understanding of life and their friendship.

***

First light came with the dawn of a new day in so many different ways. His sisters found him with questions and confusion in their wake. Anxiety tumbled from Mer as she unconsciously tapped her foot. Beth stood on the other side of him, biting on her lower lip. From the shadow of the bluish tint underneath their eyes, it was apparent neither had slept.

Always direct and to the point, Mer blurted out question after question. "We are mixed with Negro blood. I don't feel differently. Does being white one day and mixed blood the next change a person's attitude towards you?"

She could almost see her brother's mind spinning and searching for the right words to say. As a family, they had spoken of the dilemma for Negroes. Ingrained in her very being was the fact that slavery and inequality were intolerable.

Julien stood in the shadows with a clear view of Sar and his sisters. Mer's foot was rapidly tapping as questions erupted from her. Her manner reminded him of an inquisition by the general—direct, to the point, thorough. An argument with her would match the sharpest blades, and someone would draw blood. He shuddered at the thought of her future husband trying to tame her. She stared at a point to the left of his shoulder. There was nothing he could do but watch and protect. As though hearing him, Mer slowly turned her head. Chocolate eyes locked with his. He sensed her sigh of relief.

As Mer's questions kept coming, Sar could tell there was more than worry in her voice. Underlying her shock was fear, anxiety, uncertainty, and confusion. She hit upon every major point that would make their life unbearable: the unfairness of the laws, nonacceptance, always guessing if you had a true friend, unfounded hatred. He knew what many people in America believed, that Negroes were untouchables, chattel, of inferior intelligence, and a slovenly race good for working only if a stern overseer was watching. These chilling thoughts occupied his mind.

A cold sweat broke out on his forehead as he thought of the humiliation Negroes endured. In a country where all people were equal, that was true only if you were white—pure white. Drops of blood of another race could not be mixed. America boasted of its freedom and equality for all yet allowed one man to own another because of the color of his skin. And now they were one with them—people of color. Even if they were free, Negroes were still nothing. Had their work with the Underground Railroad led the slaves from one hell to another? And, he wondered about the unspoken: for Negroes, the fear and hatred harbored from the abuse at the hands of white Americans, or the hate and ignorance of white Americans passed down from one generation to the next. Before yesterday, he never entertained thoughts such as these. Their lives had changed course through crossed and twisted lines of fate. Now there was no going back to yesterday. Sar couldn't answer their questions, but he'd try to find a way to make them understand.

"As mother stated, we are Negroes. Life *may* be a little *different*. As for our future, after this morning, I am sure we'll have much to think about." Life could never be the same. There was no option. In England, their lives might be difficult because of the aristocracy, but they'd have rights and freedom.

The meeting in the library was a necessary formality. Sebastian brought forth document after document. Some were for close scrutiny and others for signing. The staggering wealth was beyond comprehension.

"Your closest relatives are the former duke's two daughters, a distant cousin Harold, and the child born out of wedlock. Her name is Joycellyn." Sebastian droned on, "Harold will inherit everything upon your demise if you do not have an heir. As for the late duke's daughters, they know of the title passing to your father and the marriage of your parents. They wish you do not call upon them in London. I'm sorry, Your Grace.

"After being presented to His Majesty, you will take your seat in Parliament. My wife, my marchioness, will be more than pleased to sponsor your mother and sisters to ease their way into society. Alexius, my daughter, is about the same age as your sister Beth. Her Grace must also be presented to the king. Do you have anything to add?" He glanced at the attorneys.

"We will speak to the family in private." As Morrison spoke, he saw pain and confusion on the faces of the family.

CHAPTER 3

Opening Volley

Southampton, England
Two Months Later

Sar stood on the port side of the boat, welcoming the occasional salt spray shower. He felt as unsure of himself as the bobbing waves. Thoughts of the last two months were his only companion—his father's death, mixed blood, a dukedom, the flight from America to be safe and free, and the voyage itself. Ship life was a regimented schedule of lessons. Among the servants transforming them were three maids, a valet, a woman engaged to teach deportment and all matters of society, a seamstress with three assistants, a tailor and his assistant, and a dance instructor.

Looking over the deck, he spied the man in brown threadbare work trousers, a coarse shirt, gloves, and a black coat with a dark brown cap pulled low over his head. There was little contact with other passengers, but the man with the limp was never far from sight. Whenever he saw him, Sar silently spun various tales, making up the man's story. A fire had burned his face; it was grossly disfigured. He was headed to England to try his luck there. *Ha, that's a change . . . going to England to seek his fortune, rather than America. But wasn't that what they were doing?*

Maybe relatives were helping him to return home, because his luck ran out. *Maybe, maybe, maybe . . .* Regardless, he was there heading towards a new life.

Julien tried to ease the harshness of truth as he explained the intricacies of society facing them. "Of course, being mixed blood and a peer changes everything from how people respond to you, to the questions they ask, and the prospect of you and Beth finding suitable husbands. Added to this, you are from America, a most uncivilized place in many imaginations. A titled wealthy lord, especially a duke, can always find a bride."

Looking at Mer, his thoughts went in an entirely different direction—one he couldn't control if he tried. Julien didn't remember when the urge to hold Mer had become so strong. From the beginning, there was a silent communication between the two of them—a knowing, a sense of trust, a connection, a bond, and the need to feel her heat. When he was with her, he felt a sense of contentment, although she challenged him in every way. Arguing with her was just as he'd imagined: an explosion of fireworks. Sparks flew from her eyes, and she unconsciously tapped her foot. Her laughter eased his worry.

Underneath it all was the burning desire that was a building inferno. Like a moth, he flew closer and closer to the flame, and then retreated when his heart sent him a warning of danger—too close, too much, she wants love. Her full, sensuous mouth begged to be plundered, and skin soft as silk cried out to be touched. It was becoming more and more difficult not to grab her, find a secret passage to explore that inviting mouth, and discover if all of her was just as soft. Thoughts of kissing her witless always brought images of long, creamy legs wrapped around his waist, luscious, honey-colored hair of silk brushing naked skin, and moans and screams of unbridled passion as they climaxed together. She hummed along in his veins like blood, and he hadn't even kissed her.

Mer stared intently at Julien as he regaled them with story after story of the intricacies of the lives of the aristocracy and the way of the ton. She didn't know whether anything would apply to the family, except to stay out of *their* way. After all, the new duke and family were different, very different, and the opposite of what was acceptable within the ton. She'd never marry; she'd be the object of ridicule and gossip. What to do, what to do? She wanted love, marriage, and a family. She also wanted someone who understood she was more than just a wife and wouldn't have a heart seizure if she worked in other endeavors besides charity undertakings. Although she was deeply in thought about her life, she could feel the presence of Julien in her very being.

Deep in thought himself, Sebastian worried about keeping the new duke and his family safe as he watched the duke's family and their reactions to Julien's answers.

"It's amazing what instantly happens in most minds when one's skin color isn't white, or you're labeled as different, and lineage dating back to an invasion isn't perfect. You're dismissed by many in society as nothing." Julien's description of the ton competed with the slap of the waves against the ship: hard and unrelenting.

***

Days filled with lessons and fittings, sisters turning into total strangers *oohing* and *aahing* over their new finery, manners foreign to them, and increasing expectations of their new life had brought them closer and closer to the shores of England.

When not learning about English society, Mer was asking Julien pointed questions. Sar laughed to himself. Poor Julien, if he only knew. He was a patient man to try to answer her. Mer's foot always seemed to be unconsciously tapping, which was a sign of her rising temper, irritation, or disagreement with whatever the other person was saying. Unlike Beth, it would be more difficult to find her a suitable husband. Sar's impression of males of the aristocracy was that they didn't like clear-headed, logical, intelligent women who were twenty-three, by most standards too old and already on the shelf. Added to this was their lineage, mixed blood.

The docks of Southampton, with sights, sounds, smells, and all things familiar to Sar, finally greeted them. Everywhere he looked there were stacks of cargo and not an inch of space. He felt at home amidst the crowd, people darting in and out and standing on crates shouting at others, and the hustle, bustle, and scurry of the everyday business of shipping.

Liveried footmen in gold and green met them with a very-fine, well-sprung traveling coach emblazoned with the ducal crest. By the time the baggage was gathered and instructions given as to the remainder of their possessions, the sun was low in the sky, making it impossible to travel far on the eighty-mile trip to London.

Sar leaned forward to give final instructions to a footman, when a muffled *crack* filled the air. Mer watched as her brother pitched forward. Vice-like arms grabbed her from behind and wrapped around her torso. Her feet flayed, trying to connect with shins and knees as she was lifted off the ground, and just as quickly she went still. His scent penetrated her senses.

"I'm putting you in the coach for your own safety."

The smooth timbre of his rich, silky voice brushed across her ear. She relaxed into a wall of muscle. Arms of steel supported her. His closeness sent spiking currents of tingles throughout her body. If only she could turn her head, she'd be able to more deeply breathe in his unique scent of spice with undertones of soap and masculinity. Being in his presence affected her like no other man. In America, there had been suitors, but she never felt the need, the desire, the connection. With Julien, she experienced it all. The warmth suffusing her body almost made her forget about the present.

"Go and help Sar. I'm fine."

His arms skimmed her breasts as he gently placed her in the carriage. Her nipples puckered. Heat pooled in her stomach. She ached for more. With a nod, he turned and left. Mer opened her reticule and checked her traveling pistol.

Sebastian was already barking orders. "I'll see to the duke. Royce, see if you can pick up the blackguard. Jack, get the doctor; he's three coaches behind. Send the other coach up here now! Julien, see to the women and get His Grace's coach out of here. You know where we'll meet."

They moved with a purposefulness, speed, and stealth, silently announcing they had been in similar situations before and were prepared for danger.

Julien jumped inside the duke's moving coach. He had to say something of comfort. "The duke, Your Grace, is with Sebastian. The doctor is but three coaches down."

"How badly is he hurt?" She stared unseeingly into the evening twilight, too numb to shed a tear.

No! her mind was screaming. *No, not my son too.*

"He is very much alive." Julien hoped this was the case and turned and looked directly into the most beautiful pair of tearful brown eyes he'd ever seen under a tangle of luscious honey-colored hair. Heat pooled in his loins, and he uttered one word: "Mer." Even though most inappropriate, he extended his arms to both sisters. They rested wearily against him. It was going to be a long night, a very long night indeed.

Shifting in his seat to ease the discomfort of the growing bulge in his pants, he looked down at the head resting on his shoulder. It felt right. *Where did that thought come from?* This feeling didn't need analysis. He'd been cooped up in close quarters on a ship for two months and hadn't nestled between the thighs of a woman since before he left England last year. He'd been mentally devouring Mer because he needed a woman—any woman except Mer.

Sar was lifted into the other coach. After years of war, Sebastian was on full battle alert. Blood pooled on the floor. "Where the hell is Simmons?" The door flew open, and Simmons was shoved into the coach.

"Save him!" Sebastian snapped.

Jonathan Simmons was used to Sebastian, having worked with him in the field. Too many times he'd put his men back together under conditions much worse than this. "More superficial than anything . . . most likely the pain caused him to lose consciousness. If he'd been standing upright, it would have been a clean shot through the neck, the outcome totally different."

The coach moved at a clipped speed toward the rendezvous point. "Anything else, Simmons?"

"The usual. He'll be back to right in no time. Whoever did the deed is a fine marksman. Never a dull moment with you, my lord." Both men looked at each other. The times reflected in their eyes, and one other thing: respect.

***

In one of the worst areas of the steaming docks, where rats scurried around as though they were the citizens, a man slightly hunched and limping, with a brown hat pulled low on his head, made his way up the stairs to the second floor of the Anchor Inn. The room was in the back, overlooking the stables above the noisiest part of the tavern, the taproom. Positioning himself in the seat behind a roughly hewed table, he waited.

Some time passed before he heard the distinct shuffle of someone climbing the stairs.

The door opened. Another man entered. In the dim light, this man could not see the face of the man at the table, but he knew the man sitting was a nob. "And?" the man behind the table questioned.

"The old duke is dead."

"And the son?"

The man, also dressed in identical brown threadbare trousers and black coat with a brown hat pulled low over his head, limped to the table. "I shot him, but he is not dead. Next time I'll complete the job."

The man behind the table looked him directly in the eyes. "There can be no mistakes, no link, no trace." He aimed a pistol directly between the eyes of the man standing in front of him and fired.

The man behind the table quickly stood, crossed the room, and opened the door. Seeing no one was about, he locked the door and limped down the tavern stairs, making sure the innkeeper saw him before disappearing into the night.

***

Gasping and attempting to wake and open his eyes took too much effort. Needles of sharp pain danced down his shoulder and greeted him. Sar thought he was being pulled through a dark tunnel. *Think, Sar, think,* he repeated to himself, trying to remember where he was, but unconsciousness pulled him back into an unknown zone. Simmons knew the duke would be fully awake soon.

On the lower floor of this very secluded house, three men sat in the library trying to piece together the events of yesterday. In the dim alcove, Mer stood silently and listened. Daring not to breathe, she heard every word. When Sebastian ordered

Julien and Royce back to the docks, she quietly backed out of the room the way she came.

Slipping noiselessly though the hallways, she found her mother and Beth in the dining room. Huddled over the table speaking softly, she repeated what she'd heard. "A man by the name of Berkley is in charge. They call him 'the general.' By order of the Crown, he sent Sebastian, Julien, and Royce to escort us to England. They were under direct order to bring the new duke back alive . . . that was Poppa. Now that Sar has assumed the title, for the first time a mixed blood is a duke, a legally recognized peer. The aristocracy is no longer pure. Some of those who know about us think it's better to kill the new duke and his heir rather than have the sanctity of pure bloodlines sullied."

Mer couldn't help but roll her eyes as her foot did a tap dance under the table. "Berkley predicts all hell will break loose when the entire ton finds out. Sebastian sent him a report informing him Sar is now the duke."

Anne looked at her daughters and marveled at how they had weathered the crises. The present danger drew her thoughts full circle. She knew her daughters cried at night for their father, their change in status, the confusion and shock of being mixed blood, and having to leave America to be safe and free. They may be free in England, but they weren't safe. With someone out to kill Sar, they had to form a wall of protection around him.

Gathering Mer and Beth closer, Anne started laying out their plan. "Now, this is what we are going to do . . ."

***

As difficult as it might be, Sebastian had to speak to the ladies. They were probably frantic with worry—first a husband and father, now a son and brother, both shot. How much heartbreak could they handle? How much danger could they cope with? Somehow he'd find a way to reassure them. Quickly, he walked down the hall to the dining room, where he found them hunched together in whispered conversation as though plotting a conspiracy. Together they turned and silently looked at him. Three sets of eyes bore into him; it wasn't a comfortable feeling. If looks killed, he'd be dead three times over.

"Good morning, Your Grace, Lady Meredith, Lady Beth. I checked with the doctor. His Grace is going to be fine. I thought we'd discuss the events of yesterday after the meal."

"No, we will do it now." That was it. No hesitation from Meredith. "And please do not try to tell us it was a random incident. We were born in America and know the ways of deceit and intrigue. We shoot better than most men."

"And do not," Beth added, "dismiss us as merely silly, frivolous women."

Sebastian quickly changed tactics. American ladies were very different from most English ladies. They were given much more freedom except for two females in London he knew. He smiled to himself. His wife will love them, and his mind reeled at the thought of any of them hurt.

"May I please call you Sebastian?" Without stopping, Her Grace continued, "My children were conductors of the Underground Railroad. Our house was a stop."

Sebastian's breath seized in his lungs. Well, that answered that. Eventually he'd have to tell all, and it would probably be sooner than later, or they'd figure it out for themselves and put everyone in grave danger.

"On more than one occasion, they were inches away from being caught or killed. Avery instilled in them the belief of freedom for everyone. He did that for me. My son's life is in danger. My daughters and I talked; we reached our own conclusion. Simply put, the government, someone within your government, or members of the aristocracy are trying to kill

my son, the eighth Duke of Westmoure, and probably murdered my husband."

What he didn't dare say out loud, Her Grace had. What
he didn't want to accept—traitors within the government and
among the aristocracy—she had announced with the confidence of one who was accustomed to dealing with the lowest
of the low. It was useless to wonder how they reached their
conclusion so quickly.

"Shall we compare notes in the library in an hour? Until
then." Sebastian rose, forgetting his meal.

The day did not start well, but so it went many days. The
meeting in the library would have to wait until later. His Grace
awoke. The rider accompanying Royce and Julien returned
with a message. After reading it, Sebastian penned the reply
in code: *Get note. Clear out of area immediately. Meet at next
place by midnight. Must reach London before dawn.*

He went in search of Simmons, who heard the urgency in
the approaching steps. Action was imminent. "Simmons, we
must leave at once. Prepare the duke."

Simmons's reply of "an hour at most" fell upon empty air.

There was no need to go in search of Perkins; he was waiting for Sebastian. "Perkins, since you have a penchant for
eavesdropping, how soon can we be ready to leave?"

"Within the hour."

"Make sure all is ready—and leave nothing of our presence."

"Of course, my lord."

"Perkins, you know what to—" but Perkins had already
left. Of course he knew what to do. He too had helped runaway
slaves.

Sar slept most of the time thanks to the laudanum. When
awake, his questions were piercing, and his observations and
conclusions surprisingly accurate. This was not an empty-
headed young man with a title, Sebastian mused. But damn it,
why did he involve his mother and sisters?

Around dinner time they approached the second house. An uneasy calm sent a shiver down Sebastian's back. Abruptly, he brought the coaches to a halt. "Jack, come with me."

Leaving the others, they headed for the house. The eerie still reminded him of moments before battle. Everything was wrong. Living here were three men who took care of the property and any operatives who needed use of the house. He couldn't ignore the feel of death.

Jack silently made his way to the back of the house. Sebastian worked his way to the front. With a quick push of the door, he had his answer. All three men were gagged, bound together upright, and tied to a column in the hallway, staring straight ahead with a hole between their eyes—three good men in service to the Crown, dead.

Checking quickly, he noted the bodies were cold and nothing else seemed to be out of place. "Jack, men to clean up everything. They'll know what to look for. I need you to head to London. Find the general, regardless of the time. Have the men ready fresh horses for Julien and Royce. They're to proceed to London with all haste and watch for signs of the route we take. Check the stable, and I'll write the message for the general. I'll only be a few minutes. We must hurry."

When Sebastian returned to the family, he wasted no time. "Your Grace, ladies, if you need to refresh yourselves, you should do so now. We must leave for London immediately."

Horses were changed, and the journey started again with a feel of utmost urgency. Trying to put what he knew in some type of logical order, Sebastian didn't notice the countryside rushing past the speeding carriage.

"Sir, how many were murdered?" That direct question from Mer jolted Sebastian from his thoughts. Something about her piercing gaze warned him not to lie.

"All . . . all three men."

The ladies were staring intently at him with no signs of

swooning or fear. It was then he noticed pistols primed and ready on their laps. The duke chuckled. "Ah, it pays never to underestimate an American woman—especially one with a hair trigger finger." Sebastian needed no other reminder.

They could ill afford to stop, but one last change of horses was necessary. The stillness of the empty posting inn yard attested to the late hour. Two men stood concealed in the shadows of the stable door, watching. Their stance was predatory and dangerous. As the horses ground to a halt, the men leapt from the darkness and rushed the coach.

***

Julien opened the door to make sure she was safe. The game had turned deadlier than ever. Her brown eyes haunted him during his ride. Pictures of her unpinned hair curling around his body, with her naked beneath him, kept dancing through his mind. To feel and taste her was whipping his inner demons into a frenzy. They wanted release. Lust, pure unadulterated lust made him ache for completion whenever she was near or whenever he thought of her, which was most of the time.

On the ship, he'd seen wind plaster Mer's garments to her body, molding her. Long legs and large breasts were parts of the package he itched to unwrap. They'd be a perfect fit. Her frame would meld to his as though she had been especially made for him. With her passionate fire, he pictured himself dominating and pleasuring her in bed and teaching her to do the same. Wishful thoughts of brown eyes, honey-colored hair, a body perfectly made for him to caress, and a wet, tight, hot sheath to sink into were the center of his attention. Forbidden tantalizing thoughts, a sister of a duke. He wished not to be shot.

He shook his head to clear the prohibited thoughts and images. Why now? Why was he attracted to this innocent?

There was no doubt in his mind she was inexperienced. Sar would have killed any man who touched her. Julien's reaction to her was strange, different. There were others, but never the need—no, the craving—to keep her near for himself.

Since the first time he'd lifted the skirts of a willing milk maid when he was fourteen, he'd never dallied with virgins and had avoided the parson's trap for twenty-nine years. He was looking forward to being a rake for a few more years. Eventually he'd marry a lady of the ton, have the usual marriage of his class, an alliance, and beget the requisite heir. Hopefully he'd find an affection with the lady, but not love. Love was a fanciful notion. The thick armor around his heart bespoke of witnessing the marriages of the ton. Having more than one married lover taught him there was very little love and faithfulness among the married elite.

Tempering his thoughts, Julien reached for Mer. The frown on her brow eased, and she smiled softly. "Your Grace, ladies, we are changing horses. You might like a cup of tea. The innkeeper will be most accommodating."

As he helped Mer out of the carriage, he wanted to pull her into his arms and wipe away the fear lurking behind her wary eyes. Instead, he held onto her hand longer than appropriate, feeling her icy calm of fright. It transmuted to something fundamental within him, something he couldn't describe. *His,* said the echo in his head.

"The footman will escort you. Please excuse me."

He abruptly turned and walked toward Sebastian. "Do you know they have pistols? Do you think they know how to use them?"

"Without a doubt, Julien, without a doubt."

They secluded themselves in a corner of the stable to discuss their findings. Sar strode purposefully towards them. "Your Grace."

"Sar."

"Sar it is, then." Sebastian approved of this young duke. The title hadn't changed him. He was Sar and all that came with it, not the other way around.

"Since this is about my family, my title, and me, I shall be a part of this investigation and everything else it entails. Your reports, gentlemen. Then we'll begin to solve these murders."

Sebastian's mouth turned into a half-grin, and a known feeling spread through him. He could trust Sar with his life. He was one of them, a protective predator. Like his mother and sisters, His Grace knew someone was out to kill him.

"Well then, let's get to the heart of it: the reports."

She couldn't see the stable from the window of the inn, but Mer stared into the night. Where he had touched her hand, it felt hot, as though she was being forged into him. For reasons she didn't want to explore, she wanted to kiss his full lips and run her hands across the wall of muscles of his chest. She was in England now. Wishing for things she couldn't have was pointless, and Julien was definitely on her cannot-have list, for many reasons. She started ticking off the reasons in her head, when she thought, *Why not?* She was right—she was in England playing by a set of rules she didn't understand and facing exclusion because she was mixed blood. Why not indeed. Holding on to that thought, she turned to answer her mother's question.

Sebastian knew what started in America was following him home to England, and the next installment of subterfuge was sure to come. London was a mere three hours away. Before dawn, they'd slip into Whitehall, see the general, and give their report. Secrecy was becoming more important by the second. Within Whitehall operated a spy, a traitor. Unless they found the assassins first, nothing would stop the conspiracy to kill the new duke.

Never thinking he would see such carnage with intended purpose of evil within the aristocracy against another aristocrat took Sebastian back to the covert operations on the Continent and images of war. He could smell burning skin and see death and destruction from impressions buried deep within him. At times like this, he needed reassurance of good, life, and love.

Hopefully he'd be home before Caroline awakened. After twenty-one years of marriage, she represented all that was good in this world, and he needed her.

CHAPTER 4

First Impressions

London, England

Before dawn, they arrived at the duke's house. The door opened immediately, and Jack raced down the stairs. "Your Grace, the staff is abed, except for Morgan, your late uncle's man of affairs."

Morgan bowed. "Your Grace."

"Morgan, this is Perkins," Sar said. "Show him around and introduce him to the staff in the morning. Jacob will be going to the shipping office. Make sure everything he needs is made available to him."

"Is there anything else, Your Grace?"

"Yes, no one is to enter this house without Perkins knowing it."

***

Though the corridors at Whitehall were empty, light filtered into the hallway from beneath some of the office doors. Without so much as a knock, Sebastian opened the door at the end of the hall.

"Gentlemen."

Berkley didn't glance up from reading the report on his desk. His moniker, "the general," given to him during the war by the group of elite aristocratic operatives he'd commanded, had carried over to his current position. As director of the Home Office, he was one of the highest officials of the Crown. It was his job to bring to justice those trying to kill the new duke, and he didn't like what he read.

Gauging the measure of the American, Berkley could tell the new duke was used to hard work and taking charge. According to Sebastian's report, His Grace addressed wrongs even if there were laws to the contrary. His involvement in the Underground Railroad was just one of the examples of such behavior in the report. Berkley saw the pain on the duke's face and wondered if it was from grief or a gunshot wound. He was pressing on regardless. His stance spoke of an aggressive predator—and His Grace knew he was being observed.

Without any preamble Berkley spoke. "According to your reports, there have been four additional murders since the duke's father, and someone shot the duke upon his arrival in England. Please stop me if I'm wrong or missing any of the major facts. We'll get to the details in a few moments. The second murder occurred in the Anchor Inn not far from where the ship docked. Murders three, four, and five were committed at the same time. All of those murdered were shot between the eyes, obviously facing the executioner. A note was left on the body of the late duke: 'One down—more to go.' Another note was found in the pocket of the dead man killed at the Anchor Inn.

"Your Grace, I need all of the details regarding your father's murder."

"It's Sar, sir. My father was in the garden determining the best place to have the gardener plant a rosebush in early spring in honor of my mother's birthday."

The memories crowded his mind. The annual ritual of planting a rosebush for his mother's birthday also included planting one for the birthday of each of the children. A riot of lush blooms filled the garden in summer. They had uprooted all of the roses and brought them to England.

"The garden has a separate entrance at the back of the house. It's also the trade entrance. Standing very close to my father, the assassin fired while looking directly into his eyes. There were powder burns around the hole. My father fell forward onto the staked-out area. Dropping the note on his body, the murderer walked away."

"Your impressions?"

"There was no sign of a struggle. He probably befriended my father. The murder was committed quickly. The assassin doesn't mind working in broad daylight and having his victims look directly at him. He is for hire and part of a carefully laid plan. The note attests to that."

After a pause, Sar added, "I'm one of the remaining victims. Who are the others?"

A hard glint encased Berkley's eyes. Yes, the new duke will do. Hopefully one day they might meet under ordinary circumstances. But there was no ordinary in his life; his life was dedicated to the business of the Crown. "Murder number two, Julien, Royce."

In precise order of detail, Royce reported, "The tavern is one-half mile from where the ship docked. When the maid went to clean the room, she knocked, and then pounded on the locked door. There was no response. Not having a key, she went in search of the innkeeper. He found the victim crumbled before a table, shot between the eyes. The room was in perfect order; nothing had been disturbed."

Julien continued. "Whoever he is was shot at close range. Our examination of the body showed power burns around the hole, no sign of resistance, and no other injuries. The room hadn't been let again, so we were able to do a thorough search . . . nothing. Because the magistrate found the note in the victim's pocket, robbery wasn't the motive. The victim looked familiar—brown work trousers and black coat."

Sar could see the man in his mind's eye just as Julien described. But where? When? The laudanum made him less than clear-headed. *No more, the pain be damned.*

"I assume you have the note."

Julien pulled it out and handed it to Berkley.

"Anything else? No weapon? Not even a knife in the boot?" He looked at Royce.

"Nothing else, sir."

"Sebastian, I have your full report. Has anything been omitted?"

"Nothing."

"Let's take a look at the notes. The first one says, 'One down—more to go,' and the second one says, 'Two down—three more to go.'"

They pulled everything apart over and over again. There were pieces of a puzzle with nothing in between connecting them.

"It's apparent the duke is next to be murdered. The men murdered at the second safe house probably weren't the intended victims of note number two; they were just there, their deaths a silent message to us. There's a mole in the Home Office, and a high-ranking official of the government is involved. Only a select few knew about your assignment to the former colonies. This also implicates several members of the aristocracy. My hunch is the other victims are Her Grace and her daughters. Whoever is behind this won't stop until the duke and his family are dead."

No one said a word as the magnitude of Berkley's last statement hung suspended in the air. "We must quickly make the next move, alter their pattern, and force our adversaries to us—and everything must be done in the utmost of secrecy."

Two nights without sleep showed. Reasoning became more difficult, and Berkley knew they were getting nowhere.

"Gentlemen, until tomorrow. May we have the honor of calling on Your Grace at home at three." It wasn't a question but a command.

"Of course." Sar could barely get the words out.

"Sebastian, tell your wife I will attend the ball to introduce the duke and his family to the ton. Shall you start the season with a crush? Let us say in a month, a costume ball? You know I do so detest those gatherings."

So, the first move is being made in the general's usual crafty manner, Sebastian mused.

"Our pleasure, sir. I'll inform her that we'll be giving the opening ball of the season and of your acceptance." Sebastian laughed. "Caroline will love planning the party, and Seymour will take on his favorite role: protector of all he holds near and dear. Will you please send the list of people you wish to invite around immediately? The usual precautions?"

The general simply said, "Yes."

***

In a fashionable house in Mayfair, Seymour, the butler, handed the *London Daily* to his most admired mistress, the Marchioness of Broadhurst. Lady Caroline read as she ate.

Society News

We have it on the best authority that the government sent envoys to America to escort the seventh Duke of Westmoure to England. The new duke was (and I wrote was) the heir to the title upon the death of the sixth Duke of Westmoure, Sterling Adam Roxbury. The title passed to the seventh Duke of Westmoure in November. Readers, please read the following carefully. This will affect the entire ton.

The seventh Duke of Westmoure, Avery David Roxbury, was murdered two days before our ambassadors arrived in America. The seventh duke married the granddaughter of a freed Negro slave. The heir apparent is now officially the eighth Duke of Westmoure. Sterling Avery Roxbury is a mixed blood. His mother is now a duchess.

Twelve years ago, petitions were filed. In closed chambers and amidst great secrecy, the English court recognized the marriage of the late seventh Duke of Roxbury and the free Negro as legal and binding. The marriage occurred on the high seas in international waters on a British ship. England does not prohibit marriage between races. American laws do.

This means, dear reader, that the purity and sanctity of the lines of the aristocracy have been compromised and will continue to be once the new duke marries and begets an heir. To further complicate this matter, the new duke has two sisters of marriageable age. Who would marry them, even if the family is one of the wealthiest in all of Great Britain?

One other note of interest: the new duke was shot upon his arrival at Southampton. Someone doesn't want the new duke to live. To pollute and dilute the blood of the aristocracy is unacceptable to many. After all, the aristocracy is above all others who have been intermarrying for centuries. Yes, the new duke is still alive.

If the new duke dies without an heir apparent, the Ninth Duke of Roxbury will be Harold David Hearthstone, a distant cousin. We know that bloodline is pure.

Caroline couldn't believe the column. Hate . . . pure hate. Her husband had been asked to escort the family back to England. Well, she really couldn't say asked, because the general never asked—he ordered, he demanded, he commanded. Because this bit appeared in the news sheet, Sebastian was in England and would be home shortly. She was glad; after all their years of marriage, she missed him. The surprise trip to the former colonies had made the holidays unbearable. Now it appeared there were other problems. With the death of the seventh duke and attempted murder of the eighth duke came the activity that always surrounded her husband's involvement in government affairs: danger. She rang for Seymour.

"Seymour."

"Yes, my lady."

"You read the Society News before I did. As you know, my husband will be home shortly. Ask cook to prepare his favorite dishes tonight." The Marchioness of Broadhurst handed the news sheet back to Seymour. "We're in the middle of intrigue again, which suits you perfectly. Lately, things have been a little too ordinary and boring for your liking."

Caroline bit back her smile. Seymour had been born into this house and trained by his father. Since the beginning, Seymour's family's primary duty had been to protect the household, with life and limb if necessary.

"Yes, my lady. It appears we are back to normal." Seymour bowed, smiled, and headed to the back of the house to check his pistol.

***

In the bedroom of another house in Mayfair, he handed the news sheet to his lover. "He and his sisters must die; the aristocracy cannot be tainted with mixed blood."

"I know."

"Make sure that branch of the family dies."

"Consider it done."

"Thank you, my love."

***

In a fashionable mansion in Grosvenor Square, two men talked. The news sheet lay open to the Society News.

"He's alive and so—"

"He must never find out."

"I know."

"It's business as usual. No one has figured anything out for the last six years. This duke won't either. We'll continue and keep a watchful eye. Tell our crew to keep their ears open and report everything they hear. Don't forget, no one has the intelligence of those of the aristocracy, let alone a mixed blood. He must die."

The talked turned to finding new mistresses.

CHAPTER 5

A Taste of London

The door to the London mansion of the Duke of Westmoure automatically opened as Sar climbed the stairs. "Oliver at your service, Your Grace."

"Oliver." Sar was attempting the second flight of stairs to the family quarters when Perkins fell into step beside him.

"And."

"All is well."

"Has anyone awakened?"

"Jacob went to the shipping office."

"Wake me at five. I understand the fashionable hour to dine is seven."

"Your Grace, Smytherson will wake you."

"And who is Smytherson?"

"The duke's valet, of course. In service to the late duke for twenty years. The Smythersons have always served the dukes of Westmoure from the first."

"And where is Peterson?"

"He's now Jacob's valet."

"And Jacob approved?"

Perkins looked at Sar with an expression that asked the question "are you insane?" and answered with a slight smile on his face. "Not quite so, Your Grace, not quite so."

Sar knew Jacob had blistered Perkins's ears with his objections. *Well, life in England will certainly be different.* He would have laughed if he hadn't been so tired.

"Perkins, we forgot Mer's birthday. Will you find out from whatever her name is who teaches deportment what the proper gift is for a twenty-three-year-old sister? If we were in America, she'd beg for a pistol to add to her collection. Brother that I am, I would have gotten it for her, but we can't do that here. Ask the teacher where to purchase the gift and buy it."

"I took it upon myself to pick out a little gift for her and the other ladies. Ah, just a little something to welcome them to England, Your Grace."

"What is a little something, Perkins?"

"Cute little dogs that aren't so friendly to those they don't like."

"How little is little did you say, Perkins?"

"Oh, about ten and one-half stone. I thought each of the ladies would like one. Three females are being delivered tomorrow, accompanied by their dog handler. Sebastian thought it was an excellent idea. He arranged for the dogs and the handler. A man at Whitehall trained them."

"I see the way of it, then. Make sure the dogs are with the ladies whenever they are out without me, and have two men follow."

At this Sar chuckled—three killer dogs with three ladies trained to kill without hesitation if they had to. *Nice touch, Sebastian, nice touch.* He was glad someone had thought of it, and he would thank Sebastian when he saw him.

"Tomorrow I have a meeting in my study. After that, I

see no reason why we can't have a small celebration for Mer. Ask Cook to make a cake and whatever else the British do for birthdays."

Before he could turn the knob to his bedchamber, the door opened. "Smytherson, wake me at five. I'll need a bath before dinner."

***

When he woke, it was morning.

Anne heard the laughter as she approached the breakfast room. Before she greeted them, she stood in the doorway observing their bobbing heads and animated hands. Their excitement and high expectations of London was contagious. The meal was laced with laughter. With Miss Engles at their side, they'd move forth without the worry of making too many mistakes, but she knew that wouldn't be enough to win over the ton.

"Your Grace, are you receiving?" Oliver presented a card on the silver salver: the Marchioness of Broadhurst and her daughter.

"We'll receive in the blue room, Oliver. Please have Cook prepare refreshments."

She turned to her daughters, all of them laughing at this early morning encounter with society. Apparently, it didn't take long for the busybodies to ferret out the latest on-dit for the gossip mill. In less than forty-eight hours, they had callers. Ah, the beginning of endless days of . . . of what? The question left Anne unsettled. "Shall we? Our first callers."

Their visitors turned out to be Caroline and Alexius, Sebastian's wife and daughter. Although it wasn't the fashionable time to call, they wanted to be the first to welcome them to London.

During their visit, Anne learned about the ball in their

honor, where to shop, where to be seen, and how to handle the highest sticklers of society. The season began in a month, the day of her presentation to the king and the ball.

"Either no one will come to the ball because you're mixed blood, or everyone will come out of curiosity. It'll be the latter, for the ton must have gossip to fuel itself." Caroline laughed; her eyes danced with the anticipation.

Later that day at the appointed hour, Berkley arrived by the back and made his way to the study. As a frequent visitor in the past, he knew his way about. They were waiting.

"Gentlemen. Sar, have you recalled anything else?"

Interesting, Sar thought, *no wasted words.* "The man killed at the tavern, could he be the one who was on the ship with us? The description matched the man with the limp darting back and forth on the deck."

"That's it! I knew there was something familiar about him. As I recall . . ." Julien hesitated. "The magistrate couldn't give us his name. The only thing found on him was the note."

"Julien, Royce, first light, back to the docks. Talk to the ship's captain; look at the manifest and the passenger list. Take it if you have to. Speak to the innkeeper. Find out everything. Take two men with you. Report directly to this house upon your return. Westmoure will get word to me and the others."

With the general snapping out their strategy, they discussed the possibilities and shifted the clues once again. "Whoever is about this knows Whitehall very well—too well."

"Mer's twenty-third birthday was last week. So much has happened that we didn't celebrate. We're having a little party." Sar extended the invitation, hoping the gathering would ease some of the family's anxiety of the last few days.

For the first time in years, Berkley was attending a birthday party. *Ah-ha, this is the perfect way to meet the duke's family without arousing suspicion. I'll make my assessment, fade into the background, and be on my way within minutes.*

Everyone was leaving, but Julien needed more time with her. "Mer, would you care to go for a ride in Hyde Park?" Julien smiled down at her, making his aristocratic bearing and chiseled face more handsome.

"That would be wonderful. Let me get my wrap."

"Don't forget your maid and your dog. This is London. Have you named her yet?"

"America," she said with a laugh.

Handing her into the carriage sent a shock reverberating through Julien's body to his toes. When she was this close, he could smell her almond scent laced with something seductive and heady . . . maybe jasmine. He longed to explore every inch of her luscious body. Without a doubt, he had to rein himself in and break the effect she had on him. Thoughts of her turned to wistful longings of the heat of a kiss, which turned into visions of legs encased in silk stockings wrapped around his waist and a slick, hot passage. He was uncomfortably aroused again. *One kiss*, he thought, *just one kiss and she'd be out of my system*. His very hard arousal signaled it had better be one kiss very soon.

As they laughed and talked through Hyde Park, Mer was oblivious to his aroused state and the curious stares. The gossipmongers were going to have a field day trying to figure out who she was. He'd sit back and wait for them to approach him.

Being with Julien kept the reality of her troublesome world at bay. Since the day she landed in England, she'd smiled so much she thought her face would crack. It was all for appearance's sake.

The ache over the loss of her father was always close at hand. The circumstance that landed them in England was another concern. On top of that, she didn't know who she was. Yes, she was Mer, but *who* was Mer? One day the world was at her feet, and the next moment she was an outcast. How did it feel to be mixed blood, a Negro? Was she different? Was she less than?

Conflicting thoughts, a bleak future, hatred directed at her because an aristocrat married a Negro, and fleeing to England to be free always underscored her actions and thoughts. She cried herself to sleep every night.

Something had shifted in her thinking when she learned she was mixed blood and an aristocrat. Marriage was never a primary thought. Of course, she assumed one day her one and only would come along and she'd marry. But now, as a part of the English aristocracy, marriage wasn't a possibility. Learning about the aristocracy and listening to Julien describe the ways of society, no gentleman, let alone a lord fitting for her station, would marry an intelligent twenty-three-year-old mixed blood from America and sully the bloodlines of some ancient family.

Maybe Sar should put an announcement in the *London Daily*: "Meredith Roxbury, mixed blood, sister of the eighth Duke of Westmoure, in need of husband. Aristocrats need not apply. Very large dowry."

This was England, and class lines were pronounced and etched in stone. One wasn't expected to move up in life and cross class lines, not like in America . . . if you were white. That sharp reminder made her realize how futile her situation was among the aristocracy. Marriage wasn't an option. She was off the marriage mart before she could even participate. *Just once I want to experience the ultimate pleasures between a man and a woman.* And, as she figured out days ago, she was not going to be denied. *I'll have to take what I want.* Intuitively she knew there was no one better to teach her than Julien. During the voyage, they'd become friends, but for her, there was more. Whenever she saw him, her heart raced. She dreamed of kissing those full lips and being embraced.

Taking a sideways peek at him, she noticed his broad shoulders filling out the bottle-green jacket and tapering down to a lean torso and waist atop well-formed thighs and legs.

Remembering the barrier of muscle she was pinned against when he held her at the dock, she imagined a well-defined wall of marble form like that of the pictures of Michelangelo's *David*. Longish, cinnamon-colored hair begged to be touched. These thoughts didn't make her blush, but she tried to hide the bright red of her cheeks when ideas of what she was planning filled her head.

Their turn through the park ended far too quickly. Bowing and brushing a kiss across her hand as he left made her think of lingering kisses and roving hands claiming her body. If she had known how to swoon or have a fit of the vapors, she would have done so.

***

In the East End of London in one of the roughest ale houses, two men dressed in work clothes bent over a table talking. They looked like every other patron.

"Nothing but a costume ball to introduce the duke and his family. They're keeping everything under close wraps. We'll find out what costume the duke is wearing and duplicate it. The house will be heavily guarded. They'll think no one will dare try anything that night—too many ladies and men from the Home Office. Have our man get him alone and get it done. There can be no failure. A message will be sent to you in the usual manner."

A bag of coins passed hands, and the two staggered out of the tavern.

***

Caroline and Alexius called on Her Grace and her daughters every day that week. With their help, Anne started to understand the ins and outs of society. Ready or not, she and her family would soon have to venture forth into that back-stabbing gossip pool of humanity called the ton.

"Even if you are the mother of a duke, you're mixed blood and many feel you don't belong. Too many British believe the lines of the aristocracy are pure and everyone's antecedents must be traced back to the Norman invasion.

"As with Sar, life happens in many unsuspecting ways. People marry for love, marriages are arranged for alliances, those next in line to inherit die, and titles pass to those never expecting them."

Caroline never took for granted the influence one yields when you're the daughter of a powerful duke and are surrounded by friends of equal importance. Rallying round Sar and his family and inviting them to the most exclusive gatherings would push them into the highest echelons of society. Nevertheless, society was still going to be cruel.

Glancing at Anne, Caroline took note of her unique looks. Her rich skin tone set her apart from the other beauties of society. The daughters were exquisite, well mannered, and refreshingly forthright. They complemented Alexius perfectly. Each one was an intelligent young lady unafraid to be different. It was good they were becoming friends, because they might have to keep each other company for a long, long time. *Thank goodness Sebastian brought them into our lives.*

Regardless of Alexius's huge dowry and the incredible fortune left to her by her grandmother, Caroline doubted there was a man who'd appreciate and deserve her daughter. Perhaps they'd raised Alexius improperly. Perhaps wanting her strong and independent was wrong, but Caroline needed no reminder. Because of the laws of the country, some rakehell of a husband could leave her daughter penniless and totally at his mercy. Caroline winced at the thought.

CHAPTER 6

Dinner with the Duke

Madame Burgoff's gilded establishment shouted in a refined whisper, "Elite only." With mounds of soft cushions, golden chaises, and mirrors reflecting every movement, it was a fairy castle where dreams and fantasies became realities in the most exquisite way. Yards and yards of scrumptious silk, velvet, and transparent gauzy fabric were draped like spun sugar over Mer's body. Her reflection bounced at her from every direction. She should feel like a princess, but fittings and a new wardrobe were the least of her concerns. Forcing herself to smile, she vaguely felt the tugs of Madame Burgoff's gentle hands. Julien's touch, the ride through the park, and her desire to experience all of him had her absentmindedly nodding at what the seamstress was saying and turning when requested. She could end up in puce with tons of lace and roses for all she cared.

Julien, Julien, where are you?

She hadn't seen him since their ride in Hyde Park three days ago—no word, no note. She dreamed the same dream every night: she was in his embrace, his hands claimed her body, and when she woke the sheets were tangled around her. Once awake, going back to sleep was impossible. Each dawn reinforced her reality. It was up to her if she wanted Julien as her lover—her one chance, the opportunity to experience what most women assumed would be rightfully theirs one day. She'd find those books to teach her everything she needed to know about the art of seduction, and then all she'd need was time alone with him. From the first time she saw Julien, there was an attraction between the two of them. She felt it, and she knew he did too. Mer wondered what he'd say or do if he could read her thoughts. *He might back off because of Sar and his duty to the Crown,* the voice in her head reminded her. She shushed her inner voice and let her imagination take her to a bedchamber with only the two of them and magical kisses.

Alexius's conversation flitted through her mind. *Julien and Royce are London rakes of the highest order and among the most handsome. At the few balls they attend, they never dance with debutantes. Some matrons and widows vie for their attention by throwing themselves at them, dropping their handkerchiefs or slipping notes into their pockets. On several occasions, fights erupted in the ladies' withdrawing room over one lady taking him away from the other . . . Dresses were torn. After a particular vicious mêlée, one lady sported a black eye.*

Yet no woman has ever claimed either's heart. They avoid matchmaking mamas as though they were the plague. With the greatest degree of diplomacy, they evade marriage. They are two of the most eligible bachelors of the ton—wealthy, handsome, and titled. Knowledge of their mistresses and skills in the bedroom are legendary. Better than any Gothic novel. You'll find out if you listen to the whispers.

Alexius had blushed at the last.

"Please turn."

As though on automatic, Mer did as the seamstress requested. Whenever she thought of her dream, her heart fluttered. When she awoke, she had the feeling she'd been well kissed.

Forbidden thoughts danced in her head, and she tried to breathe, felt the heat rise, her skin flush, and turned once again at the request of the modiste.

It took over two hours at Madame Burgoff's. Mer hoped her impatience didn't show, but her tapping foot was a dead giveaway. She'd figure how to have Julien teach her about the intimacies shared between a man and a woman. Madame's establishment couldn't make her dreams a reality. It was up to her.

Dogs and ladies made a fine sight savoring ices at Gunter's. As they were about to leave, the Earl of Dumfrey approached their table. Thanking Lady Caroline for the invitation to the ball and assuring her of his attendance, he asked to be introduced to the lovely ladies. The dogs sniffed and licked.

"The ball will be a crush. Dumfrey will tell everyone he met you. They will tell everyone else and claim they have met you too. Each one will add something different to your description. This tidbit will be on everybody's lips. You'll be a two-headed human with spiked hair by the time all is said and done. Don't be surprised to find a mention in the society column."

"That quickly, Caroline?"

"That quickly, Anne—and don't forget, servants talk." Laughing like debutants, they discussed the ball.

It was late afternoon by the time all of the boxes were unloaded and Caroline and Alexius were on their way home. Oliver told Mer His Grace was in his study.

Well, if I want to know where Julien is, I can't be a coward. I might as well go and ask.

Without knocking, she opened the door, said "Sar," and looked into a pair of the greenest eyes she had been dreaming about for weeks. *Julien, he's here, in the house!* "Excuse me, Sar, I thought you were alone." She curtsied and then grinned. "My lords. I expect a full report, Sar, or should I stay?"

"Out, Mer!" They heard her laughing from the hallway.

"Don't say a word; her eavesdropping skills are almost as good as Perkins's." Sar sauntered towards the closed library door. "Do you hear that, Perkins? Your student may surpass you."

By the time he opened the door, she was gone. Perkins lurked in the shadow. "You can resume your position with your ear attached to the door. Is there anything you ever miss?" Sar laughed. Perkins saluted him.

"Now, as you were saying, Julien."

"The man murdered at the tavern near the dock used the general's name on the passenger list. The innkeeper said the dead man limped down the stairs, spoke to him, and went out into the night. The next day, he's found dead. No one saw him return to his room; no one remembered anything else about him."

"Jack, at the second house, was anything amiss?" Berkley wanted to make sure nothing had been overlooked.

"No, the lack of clues concerned me. Nothing, absolutely nothing was out of place."

The hard glint in the general's eyes was back. "It's quite curious the innkeeper sees the murdered man leave the tavern but not return. The man is later found dead in the locked room in which everything is in order. Let's analyze the facts again, shall we?"

Mer paced in her room. When she stopped to think, her tapping foot left an impression in the Aubusson carpet. All of her thoughts were focused on the man with the green eyes in Sar's study. Would she have to settle for kisses on her hand for a lifetime? That thought made her shudder. The bleakness of her future—long cold nights, no children, no love, no husband—caused a sharp pain in her stomach, and she doubled over.

How was she going to get him alone? Would he reject her? It didn't matter; the worst that would happen is he would laugh at her and politely redirect the conversation. She'd be humiliated to her toes. If anyone ever found out what she was planning, she'd be banned to Scotland forever. But it didn't matter. Society was nothing to her, and she was an outcast anyway.

Julien had spent three days in Southampton gathering information. Always dancing on the periphery of his mind was the sight of Mer as they rode through Hyde Park, her laughter, and her blush when she glanced at him. He walked around half-aroused most of the time. When his thoughts took flights of forbidden fancy, he couldn't think, couldn't focus, and he looked for a cold bath. His visit to Lady Walton's hadn't helped. He made his excuses and escaped quicker than he had arrived. This fantasy about Mer had to stop; she was out of reach. She couldn't be touched; she'd better not be touched. Then she had appeared, as if conjured up by his thoughts. Her laughter from the hallway still rang in his ears as he tried to focus on what the general was saying.

"Yes, I believe our conclusions are correct. There were two different people at the Anchor Inn. Both looked alike, but one was in disguise. The innkeeper didn't see the murdered man, but one who looked exactly like him. The man who attempted to take Sar's life was probably killed shortly after he shot the duke by the man the innkeeper saw limping down the stairs. The dead man is found in a room in which nothing is disturbed."

Berkley continued in his usual brisk clip. "The two men who looked identical knew each other. Only the Home Office and Foreign Office have my full name. Someone who works in or has access to either office gave the murderer my information."

Berkley had been using his alias and had been immersed in his invisible, secret life for the Crown for so long that most people in polite society had forgotten who he really was. The older members of the upper echelon of the aristocracy who remembered his parents were kept in line by the most senior revered dragon of the ton, Lady Horton. How she knew everything he could only guess. She would have been one of his best operatives.

They discussed this new turn of events. There were still more questions than answers.

"I'll send word where and when we meet tomorrow. Sebastian, I trust you and the others will be the dinner guests of His Grace tonight. Jack, come with me." The two of them eased themselves out the back.

"From this time forth, unless it's a social occasion, I suggest you also use the back entrance. Bring your families. Dinner is at seven. Not to worry, Perkins has already informed Her Grace and Cook." Sar's words were laced with concern. Someone's goal to kill him would include anyone around him.

"Cook has been used to this for years." Sebastian caught Sar's puzzled look and then a dawning of understanding.

By seven Mer was at odds with herself. Her maid had pulled out no less than a half dozen dresses. She couldn't decide what to wear until she slipped into a dark-peach-colored gown. Her skin glowed; she looked like a wanton. Wavy hair cascading down her back anchored only by diamond clips on either side of her head added to her allure. This was the picture she wanted to paint for him: enticing, seductive, and tottering on the edge of impropriety. God forbid if this wasn't enough to make him notice.

When she saw him this afternoon, her blood rushed to her ears and her mouth had gone dry. She'd all but drowned in the deep-green liquid pool of his eyes. Hell, she couldn't determine if he saw her as just someone under his protection, Sar's little sister, or maybe, hopefully, something more. His look had been friendly and amused. Her foot tapped in frustration.

There were fourteen for dinner. Tales of America, laughs about the gaffes they had made in "oh so proper" London, the ton, presentation to the king, and the ball helped everyone to relax. Anne added her impressions of London as the newest and only duchess with an American accent.

Mer's eyes sparkled. Beth's enchantment reminded Anne of a child in a candy store with unlimited choices. Sar sat at the head of the table sneaking food to the dogs, wondering how it all would end.

Julien watched Mer under hooded eyelids. If she ever wore her hair down like that again and a dress cut so low, it had better be in their bedchamber. The swell of the rich, creamy globes of her breasts begged to be touched. He imagined the feel of the softness of rich honey-colored curls wrapped around them, forming a cocoon of intimacy, and those luscious breasts pressed against him as they made love. He could smell her—that scent, a touch of almond and jasmine, deeply mysterious and seductive. His thoughts skidded to a stop. *In their bedchamber?* He shared his bedchamber with no woman.

After dinner, they gathered in the blue room to talk about the ball. The evening was unseasonably mild. Julien asked Beth, Alexius, and Mer to take a stroll in the garden. "Alexius and I have to make a few changes to our costumes. Take Mer," Beth replied.

"Mer, would you and America care for a walk in the garden?"

Mer threw her shawl over her shoulders and put her hand on his sleeve as he led them to the door. A jolt of lightning passed through her. Just touching him made every nerve ending come alive.

The terrace led to a large lawn and the gardens surrounding the house. The evening spring air was fresh and damp from the afternoon rain. He turned to speak. In the dim light all he sensed were huge brown eyes staring directly into his soul and an invisible force pulling him to her. She didn't move as his mouth inched closer to hers and took her demandingly. He slid his tongue against the seam of her lips. Timidly, she parted just enough for him to enter; he tasted. She was an innocent; he should stop. But the first tentative kiss had turned into a demanding assault and now a maelstrom of desire. Bloody hell, he hadn't meant for this to happen.

This is what she wanted, only more. Clinging to his shoulders, his hands cupped her breasts, found her nipples, and toyed with them. They felt as large as grapes straining against the barrier of her dress. She ached of a need and desire beyond her grasp. Heat pooled between her legs.

Mer tried to get closer and became aware of the evidence of his desire cradled against her stomach. She longed to feel him, touch him, and run her hands over the planes of his chest. Gulping for breath, she wondered if he heard the steady drumming of her heart.

He couldn't wait. When she was close to him, all he wanted to do was ravish. Holding his inner demons in check, he told himself it would go no further. When she pressed her entire body into him, his control vanished. Caressing her face in his large hands, he looked into the pools of chocolate flashing with gold. By its own accord, his mouth lowered to hers and her lips parted eagerly. She was leading the dance, and he followed. No words were spoken; the only sound was that of two souls in the beginning throes of passion.

Her breasts spilled free as he slipped the bodice of her dress down. The cool air assaulted her nipples; they peaked. His lips trailed kisses down her long neck and over her breasts. As he suckled, the nipples hardened. Nothing registered in his mind except the feel of her. Gently, he pushed the skirts of her dress up around her waist and his fingers explored the long legs encased in silk as his mouth continued to worship her breasts.

He couldn't stop, didn't want to stop, and wouldn't stop unless she told him to. God help him if she did. His fingers touched the curls between her thighs. He moaned, parted her, and found her sex. She was already wet and wanting. This was only the prelude as his demons screamed for him to take her right there. He tried to rein them in. He wanted her panting for him, gasping, writhing, and shouting his name. There were no rational thoughts. Everything had gone too far, but for this moment, ecstasy and desire. Her hand wrapped around her other breast and offered it to him. His lips pulled on the nipple as she tried to meld into him. The charged air changed.

She was in a daze when the cool night air hit her fevered body and she no longer had the comfort of his heat. He suddenly dropped her skirt and adjusted her bodice.

"Quickly, another way into the house where you won't be seen. Keep America close. Go now, run!" He straightened his clothes as he stealthy moved toward the sound he heard.

***

Jacob worked late and hadn't joined everyone for dinner. Something was wrong here, but he was no closer to finding out what it was than when he'd started this morning. Tonight, he'd talk to Sar.

His nose twitched, and he ran out of the building . . . Fire!

Flames were shooting out of the boat. Shouting the alarm, he raced to see what could be done. If the fire jumped, it would destroy everything in its path. Screaming orders to everyone who came to help, and battling against the wind, they fought the blaze.

***

Julien knew he'd find death around the hedge, and he did. One of Berkley's men stared sightlessly into the night with a hole between his eyes. The body was still warm. "Perkins, did you see anyone?"

"A dark coat turning the corner, about six feet, confident gait. Someone gave chase, but the man disappeared on horseback."

Julien continued his examination. "Why didn't we hear the shot?"

"A coach was conveniently passing by. I sent one of your men to Whitehall. Shall we inform the others?" Julien nodded. Rising, he noticed the piece of paper. *We'll finish this our way.*

Berkley eased into the duke's study from the garden. "We have additional clues. The murderer knew you were dining here. Except for the man at the Anchor Inn, all those murdered were in service to the Crown. And my man either knew the assassin, or the murderer acted in a nonthreatening manner. Julien, why were you the first to arrive?"

"I offered the ladies a stroll in the garden after dinner. Mer and I were talking. America growled and I heard a heavy thud. The sound was something out of the ordinary for London."

His mind flashed back to what they were doing when he had heard the thud. But for America's growl, he would have taken Mer right there and never heard the snarl. *Julien, man, get a grip. She's yours to protect, not ravish or think about taking every time you see her.*

"Perkins arrived seconds later."

All Julien could think about was Mer. She could've been killed. He hadn't heard anyone approach. Damn it to hell, he hadn't even heard the passing coach. When America started to menacingly move, he'd snapped back to his senses. But for America, he would have taken her in the garden. *The garden of all places, on the ground, her first time.* What the hell was wrong with him? *Dangerous, my boy. She is an innocent and her brother a duke. She scatters your wits. You'd best stay away.*

"The Pigeon Pie at dawn. Use the back stairs and arrive separately. Give the duke the directions." The general faded into the night.

Men in service to the Crown continued to plague Sar as he tumbled into bed. Within an hour, he was sneaking out of his own backyard and carefully making his way to Whitehall. It came to him just as he was about to slip into slumber—*men in service to the Crown.*

Berkley momentarily looked up from his nightly reading. "Sar?"

Sar knew it was crucial to add this piece to their puzzle. He wondered if it could also possibly be a link to begin to tie things together. "All of the murdered men except the one at the tavern were helping me in some manner. Find out what they did and find out who is still helping. Can you have that information by dawn? Also, get the names of those who helped in the past."

Clinging to the shadows as he left, Sar almost bumped into Perkins. "Home, Perkins."

"Don't think so. There has been a fire at the docks."

Sar made his way to the Pigeon Pie before dawn. His eyes were closed, his long, well-formed legs stretched out before him, and his feet were perched on the seat of another chair. He smelled of smoke; soot dusted his jacket. He sensed the arrival of the others as they quietly slipped into the room one by one.

Without opening his eyes Sar asked, "Do you have the information, Berkley?"

Berkley pulled up a chair. "Yes, the three agents were helping to get the official papers detailing the passage of title to London to be duly noted and placed in the official registries, along with notice to His Majesty and Parliament."

"Go on," Sar urged.

"The man murdered last night was the liaison officer between the Home Office and the courts in the discussions recognizing the legality of the marriage of your parents."

"Anything else, Berkley?"

"No. And your theory, Sar?"

Sar dropped his feet, stood, and started to pace. "My theory is simple. Anyone who helped me to legally assume the title of duke, or anyone assisting me now, is in danger of being killed.

"Someone's original plan went awry when I wasn't murdered at the docks. Everyone in this room is in danger.

"First, no one has the full name of the general except those in the Home Office and the Foreign Office. This information could only be passed by a minister or someone who has access to the records. Not completely understanding the web of connections, I'm assuming the person passed the information to an aristocrat.

"Second, the murder of the court liaison officer also suggests aristocrats are behind this. The murderer must have known the liaison officer and the role he played in ensuring the legalization of the marriage. Only a small circle of aristocrats, the court, some ministers, and a select few within the Home Office knew about the petition filed in court.

"This is an aristocrat who probably remained absolutely silent on the issue but had enough power to lobby against the decision through others. Only someone of considerable influence could do this and know about the envoys sent to escort us to England. It's important my family and I do not survive. The murder last night was just another message from them to us. They can get to us, and they are watching and waiting to pounce."

The general opened the folder. "Do you have the other names, sir?" Besides themselves, there were twelve others who needed protection.

"By the way, there was a fire on the docks in front of the shipping office," Sar continued. "It was deliberately set. I need the best from Scotland Yard—one you trust with your life. The murders and the destruction of the shipping business don't seem to fit together. It appears someone is trying to destroy records and disrupt the day-to-day business. If I die, I can leave the shipping business to anyone I choose, or it can be sold; business continues as usual. Destruction of files won't destroy the business, just the past. There must be something more to this.

"Are the notes connected to one crime or are these separate crimes? The man who shot me may or may not have killed my father. Whether he killed my father or not, we may never know. Why the fire?"

Berkley started shifting the pieces again and nodded, for he was reaching the same conclusion. "I think this deserves a closer look. Expect Daggs. He's one of us. If you should ever find you don't need Perkins, I have use for him."

Sar grunted. "Ask him yourself; he's right outside the door. He hears everything." And the door opened. "Did you need something, Your Grace?"

"Home, Perkins, home."

CHAPTER 7

———

Scotland Yard

Anthony Daggs rolled out of bed and looked at the clock—one in the morning. The missive stated, "Whitehall now." When he thought he'd finally get a good night's sleep, he's summoned by the general. He smiled. As part of the select group of wealthy nobles serving the government, he'd found his niche at the Yard. Except for those special assignments on behalf of the Crown when he worked alongside Sebastian, Julien, and Royce, he spent endless hours making London a safer place. To be summoned at this hour only meant a matter of great urgency and secrecy.

The elitist group of aristocrats working for the government always made him think of family. The war had forged a bond deeper than brotherhood. Assignments along with friendship blended into a seamless package of the whole. Now they were as close as ever as they continued to protect the country they loved. As during the war, they were commanded by the general.

Daggs wondered if Berkley was content sitting behind a desk instead of moving about in the field. Daggs's recent promotion was not to his liking at all. He found himself permanently glued to a desk, allocating responsibilities, and writing reports. *I hate it.* Years of thinking and acting on the go put him at sixes and sevens with being in an office. Sitting dulled his wits, made him feel out of sorts. Using the merest threads of evidence, along with a few facts, and mixing them together he solved cases, not wrote reports. Maybe there was something afoot to save him and get him back into the field.

Maybe I can talk my superior into giving me someone who'll write the reports for me or hire my own clerk. His laugh echoed through the silent night. Nobility couldn't pull rank at the Yard.

Daggs removed his coat, pulled up a chair, and immediately started to pace. He was given every detail about the eighth Duke of Westmoure and the murders littering his path.

"So, let me make sure I have the right of this," he began. "The new duke has been shot, his father murdered, an attempted assassin murdered, three men at the second house used by the Crown's operatives shot between the eyes, the liaison officer between the Home Office and the courts killed last night at the duke's house, and a fire started on a boat outside of the duke's shipping office. The duke is of mixed blood, and someone doesn't want him to live long enough to beget an heir. And there are potentially other victims. Someone's been very busy."

"To say the least," the general replied. "Now let's examine the obvious. Someone within the Home Office knows our every move. Secrecy is imperative. I hate to think how far up this goes. The duke will be murdered unless we stop this, and we must protect the other intended victims: Her Grace and her daughters. It's only logical to wipe out the entire family to prevent any mixed-blood offspring.

"Everyone who helped the duke assume his rightful place in society has been moved until this is over. Only two of us know their whereabouts. Anyone now assisting the duke is aware of the danger. Harold, the next in line to inherit the title, is being watched. Someone is trying to destroy the records and possibly the shipping business itself. The duke asked for the best from Scotland Yard."

Daggs's instincts were prickling. He could feel the hair on the nape of his neck rising. Murder and treason, crime at its worst. "Who knows about this?"

"The duke's family, Julien, Royce, Jack, Jacob, and Perkins. I'm looking into anyone who might have any knowledge about the duke through the Home Office, and I'm looking higher. You're expected at the shipping office now."

Daggs paced; his long strides ate up the space in the office as he continued putting the pieces of his theory together. "Treasonable acts have been committed with the death of the duke's father and attempted assassination of the duke. Trying to destroy the shipping office or trying to burn evidence may point to illegal activity within the shipping business. That places the shipping company and His Grace in a precarious predicament. Of course, the fire might have been an intimidating ploy, but I doubt it. We have to find the links tying all of this together, if there are any. If not, we are looking at unconnected crimes. But what is the why?"

Outside the general's door, a man slipped quietly down the hall and into his office. Scotland Yard's involvement meant everything needed to be tidied up by the night of the ball. Putting on his coat, he quickly exited the building and left the sign a meeting was needed immediately. No one would ever know he'd been in Whitehall that evening. The light in his office was out, as it was at the end of the workday. Later, no one saw him enter again.

Impeccably attired even at three o'clock in the morning,

Sar couldn't help but note that Daggs took command like the others. His demeanor silently stated he was in charge and to be obeyed without question. It was obvious; he was another member of the elite of society. The inspector's tall, lean, muscular frame bespoke of a man who was very active in the endeavor. Without a preamble, he started with questions and relentlessly kept pounding away. The interrogation left no stone unturned. Amber eyes locked with Sar's.

Jacob explained his suspicions. "Ships went out with the designated cargo. The Ships at Sea Report created by Westmoure's is an internal checking system. It's a second inventory of the cargo onboard, taken while at sea before gaining the first port to ensure the correct cargo is on the right ship and everything matches the original manifest on file in the office. The second-in-command completes the Ships at Sea Report. The crew doesn't know a second inventory is done. Upon the ship's return, the Ships at Sea Report is compared to the original manifest.

"During the last six years, some Ships at Sea Reports showed more cargo than what originally left the docks. Some manifests matched; others did not. The ships were different. At some port, the extra cargo disappeared."

Jacob let a few moments of silence emphasize his discovery. They all understood the consequences for carrying contraband.

"The records show nothing. There is no bill of lading for the cargo, and there is nothing else in our records."

Jacob continued to talk as Sar studied the reports before him. Sar laughed wryly to himself. *On top of everything else, we're in the smuggling business.*

"Is there a way to get your records out of this office without anyone knowing?" Daggs asked. "They need to be stored in a safe place. I have a private office. If you agree, it might do for now."

Like Berkley, Daggs was a man who took the initiative and was used to talking and making plans at the same time. "Shipping crates used for cargo would be perfect. This needs to be done in daylight, with the appearance it's just an ordinary shipment—and it needs to be done by this afternoon. Anything else you wish to save also needs to be crated. If my suspicions are correct, this building will be aflame before the week is out."

He confirmed what everyone was thinking. "It appears you have another business, shipping contraband. The lack of evidence in the files indicates someone has been using your ships for personal gain, and someone knows about the Ships at Sea Reports and their importance. Without the Ships at Sea Reports, nothing is amiss."

"Done," Sar replied. "Jacob, Perkins, my sisters, my mother, and I will have everything ready before three this afternoon. Julien and Royce will make sure there are no extra eyes about. No one will think anything of my family visiting the office."

Perfect foil, Daggs thought. "I'll put a couple of my men on the docks, just in case. You won't know they are there. Here are the directions, and this is how you enter without being detected. Three this afternoon."

"Three this afternoon," Sar confirmed. "Also, I think it best if we do not meet at Whitehall again. There's a spy who knows our every move, even if we meet at very odd hours."

"The general will be informed. Until this afternoon."

Daggs walked out of the shipping office knowing someone out there was becoming very rich at the expense of Westmoure Shipping. His curiosity about the American duke had his thoughts going in all directions. *What kind of man puts his mother and sisters in harm's way? Although his plan is ingenious, anything could go wrong. The mastermind behind this would think nothing of killing women.* That last thought seemed to take root in the far recesses of his brain.

At five that morning, Perkins entered the back entrance of the shipping office. Julien and Royce lurked about. Jacob was waiting. The work began.

Sar summoned his mother's and sisters' maids before seven. "Would you please ask Her Grace and my sisters if they would care to take an early ride in the park with me and then visit the shipping office?"

After curtsying, they went to inquire of their mistresses. Of course the maids didn't know the message conveyed was a coded one used by conductors of the Underground Railroad. His mother and sisters would be pleasantly surprised to find themselves involved in subterfuge in London and would come prepared for anything and everything.

Sar had never seen them look so beautiful, in their jaunty velvet riding habits in dark, rich colors trimmed with gold frogging and buttons, and hats with feathered plumes and veils. "Good morning, Mother, Mer, Beth. You look wonderful. If you're ready, let's take in the morning air."

To every passerby, he thought, it must be a beautiful sight to behold, a family out together for a morning ride.

Mer kept shifting in her saddle, looking for the green eyes that watched over her. She didn't sense him about. When the maid had come into her room, she had been gazing out of the window, reliving the night in the garden. She'd awakened shortly before dawn. The tangled sheets wrapped around her body reminded her of Julien's vice-like gentle arms that had held her against a solid wall of masculine strength. After the night in the garden, it was obvious; she would get her chance. He wanted her as much as she wanted him. Logistics, logistics, he was the expert. After her offer, she was quite sure he'd figure out the whens and wheres.

As they approached the park, Mer's mare stumbled. They stopped. Sar lifted them out of their saddles so they could take a look at the horse's limb. Quickly, he explained the purpose of the trip to the office. After making a great to-do about the horse, he helped them to remount. The horse had been taught the trick as a filly.

Except for Jacob and Perkins silently packing, the office was empty. Morgan and the office workers had been sent on various errands throughout the city. As the morning progressed, the office buzzed with the activity of crating as the ladies emptied file after file. Sar thought of his uncle's hard work and the memories the building held and offered up a silent apology. He knew Daggs was right, and the building would be ash very soon. Looking around the office at their handiwork, it looked as though it was business as usual.

The ladies left after their "tour" of the office. Jacob made his way to Browne's for a late luncheon with the office workers. A disguised Perkins drove the wagon to the docks and the boat that would take the cargo on the top of the wagon to Southampton.

Chief Inspector James of Scotland Yard had met with the directors before summoning Daggs. His furrowed brow and brusque manner were indications of high priority. The chief inspector hadn't been in this state since he'd ordered Daggs to work with Sebastian, Julien, and Royce to find the British spy and his French counterparts. Placing his hands on the back of the chair to keep from pacing, Daggs awaited his orders. The steely voice of the chief inspector didn't disappoint.

"The governors want this matter resolved with all urgency, without public knowledge. You're relieved of all other responsibilities. Let me know how many additional men you need, and I'll arrange it immediately. It's going to take the wits and talents of the best to see this through to the end. You're to report directly to me and no one else, except Berkley."

They discussed possible theories. Daggs requested three additional men with extraordinary skills. With a flourish and grin on his face, he personally handed the stack of paperwork for his unwritten reports to the chief inspector.

Following directions, John the dockworker, aka Perkins, drove the wagon to a secluded place within London. Looking for the signs, he came upon the entrance. The false bottom of the wagon was opened and quickly unloaded. Driver and wagon returned to the Westmoure Shipping Company and the driver disappeared.

Daggs caught up with Sar at the private office. "Sar, have Jacob meet me here tonight. We need to start examining the Ships at Sea Reports and look at the crews. Even though the ships were different, some of the ports and crew may have been the same. Perhaps there is a pattern of some sort."

CHAPTER 8

The Fire

Dinner that evening with the Marquess and Marchioness of Broadhurst was Sar's first venture into society. Sebastian's sons weren't down from Eton yet, so it was his wife, daughter, Julien, and Royce. Jack's demanding mistress required his presence. Tonight he would be the devoted paramour.

Sar wondered if he would ever get the way of society. For the last two weeks, Caroline and her family had cosseted his mother and sisters. With the season starting in a little more than a fortnight, they would become the specimens for society's fodder. He doubted if they'd ever be ready for the onslaught, and there was no way to protect them. *And what of you?* He couldn't afford to think about himself right now. His only hope was that he could be half the man his father had been.

Julien knew there was no way to get Mer alone. They'd be readily missed in this intimate group. Thoughts of her in his arms two nights ago were driving him utterly mad. His trousers were constantly uncomfortably tight. He could still sense her engorged nipples as they hardened at his touch, and the weight of her heavenly breasts in his hand. His mind's eye saw her wild, passionate look and parted, bruised, swollen lips. Julien felt her body melding into his, but it was the knife handle digging into the palm of his hand—a reminder that he was on the edge of a precipice he'd never walked before. He wanted to leap across the table and drag her to the nearest bedchamber, throw her on the bed, strip her bare, and make love to her until they were both sated. His craving was like the blood flowing in his veins, always there, unable to stop.

Mer tried to avoid looking at Julien, but all her thoughts centered on him. It was *Julien, Julien, Julien.* People had to repeat things to her two or three times. From the corner of her eye, she saw him glance at her, and her nipples pushed against the fabric of her chemise as they tried to get closer to be touched. The abrasion sent a shock to the center of her body, as though he had suckled her. Imagining his hands touching her had left her wanting and aching for the unknown. She felt her eyes closing in anticipation of the onslaught of her senses and blinked to fight the sensation.

"What do you think of London, Mer?" Julien's deep voice slid over her like a silken whisper fraught with undercurrents of possibilities. Heat pooled in her stomach; she struggled to think of something to say.

After dinner, the men decided to enjoy the remainder of the evening with cigars and port in the garden. Alexius took Mer and Beth to the ballroom for dancing instructions. Caroline swept Anne away to discuss menus and decorations.

"This won't do," Alexius announced. "I'm going to find Julien and Royce. We need them desperately. In addition to everything else, they're wonderful dancers; they're masters."

It didn't take much pleading before all of the men were in the ballroom dancing. Julien partnered with Mer for every waltz. Since this wasn't a ball, no one thought anything of it. He held her as close as possible. No one noticed his thighs brushing her skirts. He was branding her with his imprint, making sure she'd never forget their night in the garden.

His sleepless state of sweet torture since he first saw her was taking its toll. The memories were closing in as he led her into a turn of the dance. The arm around her waist was lower than acceptable. He could feel the indentation of her back and the beginning swell of her buttocks. The recollections of them, these memories, were holding him prisoner of erotic wonder.

Whenever he inhaled, his imagination conjured up her scent. Plumping his pillow reminded him of the feel of her breast in his hand. Cold baths would be the death of him.

Mer's breath was coming in short pants. He was literally taking her breath away. As he executed the turn of the waltz with precision, she felt like she was suspended in another dimension, supported only by the thinness of air. His closeness fed her need and the reality of the darkness of her lonely future. Being denied him was not an option. She'd find a way to take what she wanted.

His aroused state was apparent to both of them. He tried to increase the distance between them, but she kept edging closer. Looking up at him, she laughed, and his heart took a summersault to his knees.

"Anne, here are the dinner menus for the evening. I hope you approve of them and the decorations." Caroline handed everything to Anne. "Since two countries are coming together, I want the ball to represent unity and acceptance. I'd like to include dances, food, and other things done at American balls. What should we add?"

"The colors of the flags of both countries are red, white, and blue—"

Laughing, Caroline never let her finish. "I chose those colors for decorating. Red, white, and blue flowers will overflow from every conceivable space. The balcony and terrace will be draped with pale blue and shimmering white fabric with tiny flags of both countries. The garden will be lit with pure-white candles. I want to make sure the statement is clear: two countries coming together as one. Do you have any other ideas?"

"Caroline, this will be beautiful; it's perfect. It's kind of you to do this, but you realize the dangers as well as I." A knowing look passed between the two women. "We both understand my family and I may not be well received. We've been trying to prepare ourselves for cutting comments and being snubbed. Sar and Sebastian are concerned about protecting us. We may even be shot. I know we have to be introduced to society, but it might be an anxious and suspenseful evening for all of us."

In Anne's eyes, Caroline could see hurt, fear, and apprehension. "Well, that may be the way of it, but they'll only go so far. We'll find a way to guarantee even the highest sticklers will eventually beg to be introduced to you and your family." Caroline smiled. "What an interesting time this is going to be." And the little voice in her head said, *What a dangerous time this is going to be.*

"Yes, you're right, Anne. Some of society will be very cruel, and danger literally looms around every corner. Next week my father and some of our friends are returning from the country.

"Sebastian and I are giving a small dinner party to introduce you. Our friends are people you can turn to at the ball. Believe me, with their approval, others will fall in line. They are some of the most powerful in society, and you'll like them."

"Caroline, you may not have the right of it."

"Oh, Anne, but I do. Let's give the ton something to talk about." She laughed again. Anne didn't know whether to laugh or cry.

"But there is another reason I wanted to speak to you. You see . . ." Caroline paused.

Anne silently sighed and cringed. She knew Caroline was

going to ask her how it felt to be a Negro. Well, people were going to ask, so it might as well start now.

"You see, it is frowned upon by anyone in society . . . um . . . to be in trade and actually earn a living in that manner. My grandmother was the only child of a merchant who made the family fortune in fabrics, soaps, lotions, and perfumes. Her father taught her everything about the business. He died before she was eighteen. Upon his death, she ran the family business.

"Through business, she met my grandfather, the marquess. He encouraged her, and together they came up with innovative ideas that changed the scope of the business to include goods the upper classes wanted. My grandmother continued running the business after they married. Society hadn't known of her before the marriage, so it was quite easy for her to continue in trade.

"After my grandmother's death, my mother took over and expanded the business tenfold. Sometimes I believe that's why my father married her. He adored her and helped her in every way. His ideas are visionary.

"The business is passed from one generation to the next through the daughters. Unfortunately, I don't have the talent for it, but my mother saw Alexius did. She started going with my mother to the office before she was five. My mother died when Alexius was seventeen. For over four years Alexius has been managing the business.

"This is a secret the ton cannot find out. You can imagine if anyone ever discovered Alexius was in trade, she'd no longer be accepted in society. She is the daughter of a marquess and the granddaughter of a duke. To the silly ton, this is neither proper nor appropriate for a member of the aristocracy, let alone a lady of society.

"The business continues to grow and is much larger than Alexius can handle. Alexius and I discussed this. Do you think your daughters might like to work with Alexius? Of course, they need to spend time at the office and learn more. We may be presumptuous, but we don't think Mer and Beth want to spend their days making morning calls or acting like silly twits with nothing more than the weather or the looks of some young aristocrat to discuss."

Of all the things Anne anticipated, this wasn't one. They all had secrets and secret lives. One more secret didn't matter. There was much more beneath the surface of the woman sitting next to her than she ever expected. "And what of you, Caroline?"

"Well, I am one of the founders of Harson's, a school that trains young women to have a skill: accounting, business management, and other jobs of that nature. Some of the graduates are employed at Alexius's company. Perhaps when things settle down you might like to help at Harson's or with one of the other endeavors some of my friends are involved in.

"Alexius is a very clever businesswoman. Her personal fortune rivals her father's. She is in control of it, with the help of trusted advisors. It's our hope your daughters will be in charge of their own fortunes, so they too can be independent women of means."

Not knowing Anne's response, Caroline continued, emphasizing the importance of being an independent woman. "You may not realize it yet, but the aristocracy is fraught with men looking to marry a woman only for her fortune. The laws of this country give a woman's husband or guardian control over everything she owns, including her person. Once married, the husband is free to do what he wishes with his wife. In many marriages, this leads to abuse and cruelty.

"Sebastian and I have taken every legal step possible to prevent this from happening to Alexius. It's very important for a woman not to be at the mercy of one's husband or guardian."

Anne laughed. "I never thought you wanted to talk to me about something like this. I feared you were going to ask me how it felt to be a Negro and how we went about our lives in America without being detected. Thank you for not asking. Mer and Beth are fascinated with London, but they're becoming a bit restless without something meaningful to do. They were involved in the family business on a day-to-day basis. Here there's nothing but morning calls, shopping, and rides in the park. They feel a loss. There's a void."

Underlying all of this was danger, the rigid rules of the aristocracy, and the loss of Avery. Soon, the season would be here and rejection by society was probably going to be added to the list. Her daughters needed something to make them feel worthwhile and be meaningful for them. Doing something useful would take their attention off of the future.

"Knowing my daughters, they will bow down at your feet for saving them from utter boredom. They'll be ready to start the moment I tell them. So, that's why you and Alexius called on us so early the first day you came to visit." Smiling, Anne answered her own question. "You were on your way to work, weren't you?"

"Yes. We leave earlier than that on most days. Welcome to *our* real world of London. If possible, can we meet the day after tomorrow? It'll give you time to think about the offer and discuss it with Mer and Beth. Seven in the morning is the best time, if that isn't too early for you. We'll breakfast here."

"Seven is fine. Now, we must be leaving. It's late."

***

In the designated place in the East End, two men discussed the latest turn of events. Bringing in Scotland Yard to investigate the fire and help solve the murders complicated matters. Everything had to be brought to an end quickly and evidence destroyed. Loose ends needed to be sewn up tightly. Now he had to inform the others. He bade the messenger good night.

***

On the dock near the office of the Westmoure Shipping Company, a man slithered quietly within the shadows. Lighting the torch, he placed it where it would be most effective and then slipped quietly down the waterfront. He was nowhere in sight when the alarm was raised.

"Perkins, what is it?"

"The office is burning, Sar."

"Did anyone catch the culprit?"

"No, he got away without being seen."

"Wake me by six and make sure the others are here by seven." There was nothing he could do now. Their men were watching the building. In the morning they'd figure out how the person slipped in and out without being seen.

Everyone was there by seven, including Daggs. "I was at the fire, and I looked at what was left of the shipping office this morning. It was a job done by an expert. The torch was placed where it could do the most damage. Oil was thrown on the side of the building. The area is dark and shadowy. If you know what you're doing, you can skulk about undetected." His amber eyes, flashing like fire, burrowed into the general as he spoke.

Berkley knew the truth of it. The blueprint signature of the fire was undeniable. After all, he taught them. It was with a heavy heart when he discovered one of his men was involved in illegal activity, for there was but one consequence.

"This is how I see it." There was a pregnant pause. "An operative for the Crown set the fire last night." He knew Daggs had already reached that conclusion.

The study echoed in silence. Berkley was deep in thought,

searching for clues from men he worked with every day. Nothing came up—nothing but one. Why that one, he didn't know. His mind started focusing on that person. Nothing fit . . . yet.

"We need men out in the stews, in the East End, and in the dock area where gentlemen normally don't go. They're meeting somewhere. It's a gamble, but we might luck upon a clue, a missing piece. They think they've destroyed Westmoure's. For reasons we don't understand yet, the records had to be destroyed. Did the files contain evidence and clues about the extra cargo, or information which would lead us to those involved in the murders? Or did it cover up something else?

"If this is a separate crime, as Sar suggested, there may not be another move, since they think whatever was important for us not to find has been destroyed. That is, unless there is a connection between the fire, the different Ships at Sea Reports, some illegal activity—whatever it is—and it continues. I'm inclined to believe the fire and the Ships at Sea Reports are connected. Someone who knows the importance of the reports and our discussions passed this information along to the interested parties. If this is a separate crime, the answer may be in the company files. It would be that information, the link, someone doesn't want us to have. Daggs, how soon can we have the information about the Ships at Sea Reports?"

The general kept asking questions while juggling clues. "The duke is still alive, which means he is in danger. We have three different notes. These may or may not be a part of the same crime. What we can accurately conclude is that there must be another move by the criminals to implement their next step. That is, at least in case of the threat on Sar's life. After each step taken, they must meet, because the next move depends upon the success of the prior. This can only progress step by step like a game of chess.

"As for the fire, if they think the evidence of criminal

activity no longer exists, then we will need to rely on someone to reveal something, monitor the ships to see if the activity continues, or see if the Ships at Sea Reports can lead us to the culprits or their activity.

"It's clear someone within Whitehall is giving them information. We don't know where they're meeting. We only know one place where they can't meet—Whitehall." Berkley hoped that was true.

"Sar, why don't we just have Perkins come in? He's heard every word we've said." The general doubted if he'd ever had an operative as good as Perkins.

"I can't. It's a game. He needs to keep his skills sharp."

"Sar, besides Perkins, how many other men do you have?" Daggs could easily wear a hole in a carpet in a short time. He hadn't sat at all, and he pushed strands of thick, sable hair though his hands as he walked back and forth.

"Six. They are assigned to follow the ladies—seven, if you include me."

"My instincts tell me our time is running out. Sar, you stick close to your mother. Julien, Royce, see to Sar's sisters, and take those dogs with you wherever you go. Sebastian, you take care of your family."

Daggs continued his pacing and talking. "Three nights, operatives fanning out throughout the city to see if they can pick up any clues—talk of anything—someone with pockets to let who normally would not have so, someone who was in the area of the docks last night, anything. Everyone is in danger. We start immediately."

Berkley interrupted, "I think this might work. No one go near Whitehall—three men in the East End, three men at the docks, and three men in the stews. Daggs, can you coordinate?"

As usual, the general didn't wait for an answer. "Have all your men here by eleven. Julien and Royce, when you are out and about with Sar's sisters, make everything look normal.

Take it upon yourselves to introduce them to the city. We have to give the appearance nothing is out of the ordinary. Even if you have to go shopping and carry their packages, talk about the weather, or all of those other topics which are only appropriate for young ladies to discuss, do it.

"Sar, Sebastian, do you have any idea what the ladies were planning for the day?" Just looking at them, Berkley knew they had no idea whatsoever. "Never mind."

"They're together at Sebastian's house probably working on the plans for the ball," Sar said, but he knew the ball was the last thing on their minds. They were discussing business—how to increase profits, allocate responsibilities, and gain control of an expanding enterprise.

"For better protection, use closed coaches instead of open carriages. Sebastian, I'm sending your wife and daughter little presents."

Sebastian looked up and grinned. "Wolfhounds, I presume?"

"They'll be delivered before noon. Julien, Royce, meet at Sebastian's in an hour." There was no questioning Berkley's orders. Daggs left with a nod to everyone, and Julien and Royce followed. The general remained behind.

"Perkins, come in. There's something I need you to do."

For the next ten minutes, the general explained to Perkins who he needed to watch. Perkins left to become John the dockworker once again. Berkley learned from experience never to ignore his inklings. Something sent up red flags about this man, but he wasn't sure why. Somehow, George Mason was involved.

CHAPTER 9

Business and Pleasure

Ledgers and papers covered the tables. Five intelligent ladies sat around a table trying to figure out the best way to gain control of a growing company.

"With more rapid transportation available, it's important we capitalize on it," Alexius said. "It's probably expedient to move our manufacturing facilities closer to the expanding railways. The materials we need for manufacturing and the finished products can be moved more easily. There are so many things to consider."

As she methodically went through the distribution lines of the business and explained the day-to-day workings, Alexius tried to envision the company ten years from now.

"Since society strongly disapproves, how do you do this, Alexius? How do you go in and out of the office without someone seeing you or figuring out what you're really doing?"

"Oh, that's easy, Mer. My grandmother left me a house not too far from here. It's normal for me to check on my house and my staff. In a couple of years, I'll be so far on the shelf people will think nothing of it when I leave my parents' house and move in. As for you and Beth, I'll show you how to come and go without being seen.

"My employees take care of the contact with the public at the shop on Bond Street. On the rare occasions I need to meet with some of our larger suppliers or visit a manufacturing site, I go in disguise. I'm accompanied by one of my male advisors. Of course, they really think they're dealing with the advisor. It makes it easier, believe me—much easier."

Beth couldn't believe how right everything felt. "America is so different in that respect. It didn't matter who knew we worked in the shipping business. Spending my days going to balls, making afternoon calls, and longingly hoping for someone to pluck me from the marriage mart isn't my idea of fun. Thanks, we needed this."

Finally, something to do, she thought. London was becoming a bit of a bore. The only adventure so far was the escapade at the shipping office. She missed the excitement of being in the middle of the day-to-day business crises. It didn't matter what society thought. The two mixed-blood aristocrat sisters would be on the shelf for many years to come. Somehow, she'd learn to accept that.

They were discussing the shipments due in this week when the door opened and Sebastian, Sar, Julien, and Royce strolled in. Mer lost her thought the second she saw Julien. The day seemed bright, though it was cloudy and threatening rain. He smiled directly at her.

"Ladies." Sebastian looked around the room and saw papers spread out over various tables. "I see you're working on the upcoming ball."

He smiled at Caroline, raised his right eyebrow, and a knowing look passed between the two of them. "I hate to take you away from this, Caroline, but may Sar and I have a word with you and Your Grace in the library?" Alexius, Mer, and Beth were quickly gathering the ledgers.

"But of course, we were just chatting."

Sebastian caught himself before he almost rolled his eyes. His wife never chatted; if anything, she interrogated.

"And what do we owe the pleasure of your company to, Julien and Royce?" Despite all of the gossip, these two men were two of Alexius's favorite rakes—not that she knew more than a dozen or so rakes. They both seemed to be friends of other rakes.

To Julien and Royce, Alexius was like a pesky younger sister. When she started to crawl, she'd attached herself to the two of them. Julien remembered when she first reached out to him to pull herself up. Since then, she was always there, always underfoot, and always a pest. They rode together, taught her how to shoot and defend herself, and kept suitors they didn't deem suitable out of her path with not-so-subtle warnings. She had grown up to be a beautiful young lady—strong willed, stubborn, and independent.

Julien smiled. She was a bratty younger sister and best friend. "Brat, Mer and Beth haven't seen much of London. We thought a day's outing would be in order."

In the library, Sebastian and Sar were in the middle of explaining the latest events and the precautions to be taken.

"I don't know exactly, but Daggs thinks since their plan to murder the duke was muddled, they'll kill anyone in their way. Berkley and Daggs think Her Grace, Mer, and Beth are the other intended victims. It's best to make sure everyone is protected—everyone, Caroline. That includes Alexius and you."

"It's Anne, Sebastian. So, you think this is the best way?"

"Yes, Mother."

Sar was reading his mother's thoughts; he knew her well. She'd go to any extreme to protect her children and wouldn't hesitate to use the pistol in her reticule or the one in her garter.

They needed to talk. Try as he might, it was difficult to understand what it must have been like to be married to a white man and have children in America. How much time had been spent in fear? This madness surrounding the title had to be brought to an end. If anything happened to her, his very soul would be ripped out of him. She'd never know how much he loved her.

"Sebastian, I won't have maids or any of the staff put in danger. They can't be caught in the middle of this intrigue. There'll be talk if the girls are seen without the proper chaperones."

"Caroline, you never cared one whit about what society thought, so why now?" Sebastian was clearly confused. This wasn't like his wife.

"I want to be sure the duke and his family make the best impression on society. I don't want to give the ton anything untoward to talk about."

"I see, but I don't see," replied Sebastian. "Besides Dumfrey and the modiste, no one outside of our close circle has met them. Correct? This will only be for three days, and most of society won't return until later this week. I think we can do this for three days. We'll take the added precaution of having everyone ride in closed coaches."

"I'll not have you ruin my plans for making the duke's family the most sought-after family in the ton," his wife replied.

Ah-ha! That was it. She was going to ensure that, mixed blood or not, the duke's family could walk around with their heads held high, and she had the lineage and connections to do so. He chuckled and imagined those silly enough to give Sar and his family a direct cut. They'd find themselves excluded from the most exclusive gatherings—social suicide.

"Three days, Caroline. Three days only." Sebastian was grinning. This wonderful wife of his, he loved her even more than he did when they first wed. He thanked whatever gods were involved that theirs was a love match and not one of those arranged marriages for the sake of a proper union for family alliances or to beget a title. He made a mental note to tell her tonight how much he loved her.

"Three days, Sebastian, and three days only. We also have another little problem. Alexius has to go to her office the next three days. Julien and Royce have no idea about her little business."

Besides the two of them, only a select few knew about Alexius's business, which spanned Great Britain and the rest of the world.

"I don't know how she'd feel if they were to learn of this. Three days without going to her office is out of the question—and no, it can't be done here. Did you see the morning room? It was cluttered with papers, and that wasn't even the majority of it. And I don't think Julien and Royce would think we were going on about the ball. If we did, they'd think we were brain addled, and we would be if we spent that much time planning a mere ball."

He loved the spark of her fire when she was upset with him. "Let's have Alexius decide. I trust Julien and Royce with my life. How they'll feel about Alexius's little business, I don't know. By the way, my dear, the general is sending you and Alexius a little present."

"Um . . . the general never does anything little, husband. What is it?"

"You'll find out before noon. I'm not going to spoil the surprise. Now, let's join the others and make our plans for the day. I haven't had the pleasure of going about London with my wife in years, though I put a limit on how much shopping I'll do."

Alexius left the others discussing the day's outing. She found her parents in the hallway. "Mother, Father, may we speak for a moment?"

"Alexius, we wanted a word with you also." To trust someone with their secret could be a monumental mistake.

"Royce and Julien might never hurt me intentionally,"

Alexius said, "but their ideas about the role of women may be archaic. After all, they are renowned rakes."

Caroline smiled, frowned, and then arched an eyebrow. That fact is something her daughter shouldn't know, even though her father was once one of the most sought-after rakes in London. She caught herself sighing. Alexius shouldn't know so much. They'd discuss that tiny matter later, although she prayed her daughter would marry a reformed rake. After all, everyone knew they made the best husbands. She once thought Royce or Julien was the perfect match for her daughter, but there was never a romantic spark. They were friends, the best of friends. Rakes or not, they were honorable men. She smiled to herself again as memories of the fabulous years with her reformed-rake husband had her sighing wistfully.

Sebastian explained the seriousness of the situation and the plan to keep them safe.

"Dad, is there any way we can come up with another plan? I trust them both, and they are like brothers, but . . . I don't know. I could lose their friendship if I told them. They mean a lot to me."

"It's not easy being a woman of independent means. Just ask your mother. I know they'd never banter this about in society, but knowing about your business might change your relationship. You may never share your brother-sister regard for each other again. Alexius, I must do all I can to keep you and your mother safe."

"I know, Father. They've always been in my life, except during the war. However, I have a business to run. If they can't accept that I own a business, then are they truly my friends?" She'd soon find out. Julien and Royce had to be told.

"Excuse me, my lord. There is a man from Whitehall to see the ladies. I don't know if he has the right of it." Seymour was accustomed to the mysterious comings and goings of the household; someone from Whitehall usually meant it was for the Marquess.

"Seymour, this time he's here to see the ladies. Please show him to the morning room."

They were discussing the plans for the day when a man walked in trailed by two of the largest beasts Sebastian had ever seen. The wolfhounds were bigger than the three sitting on the floor. While the trainer was introducing the creatures to the ladies, Sebastian read the note from the general.

These were the smallest I could find. Let me introduce Felix and Oscar. They are well trained and love people, especially children. The handler will give you the commands. They've been taught to protect.

Caroline had the right of it; the general never did anything small.

"I suggest we finish discussing our plans over lunch. Cook is most patient, but I don't want her meal ruined. Sebastian, remind me to thank the general. Could he have found anything smaller?"

She grinned when, at that moment, Felix put his huge head on the lap of his new mistress. She hugged him, and he became hers.

"Before we eat, I need to explain something to Julien and Royce."

Julien and Royce looked at Alexius and realized she was serious about whatever she was going to say. It wasn't like the brat at all. When everything was said and done, Julien and Royce were actually smiling from ear to ear. The brat owned and ran Cummings. Everyone in all of Great Britain knew about Cummings. If their tailors needed something, they went to Cummings. Those special lotions and soaps their mistresses worshiped were from Cummings. How had she managed that? And how had she kept it from them? They were the operatives, not she. With Mer and Beth joining the company, it was up to them to protect everyone and everything.

"We've been here two weeks, and I've seen very little of London." All Mer could think about was finding ways to be with Julien. Most of her days and nights were spent imagining herself in Julien's arms and the feel of him. The craving, no, the need, the wanting. The thoughts of the moment in the garden and waltzing surfaced again and again and became the very breath she breathed.

Her nightly dream had changed. Now she dreamed of her legs spread wide, with Julien suckling her breasts and his fingers making her long for something that still eluded her. She always woke not knowing how it would end.

More than once, she'd started to touch herself as Julien had, only to stop and long for him. Hours spent in the library trying to find books explaining what happened in the marriage bed and the art of seduction proved futile. There was Bryon, Homer, and other such lofty tomes, along with those about flowers and agriculture. She was so frustrated in her search that on more than one occasion she considered burning the whole lot.

"Mer? Mer, where are you?" Beth looked at her sister and worried she wasn't adjusting well to England. "I've called you three times."

"Just woolgathering, Beth. I was thinking of . . . um . . . some of the things we discussed. I for one would like to see London."

Lunch was filled with talk about plans for the afternoon. Mer and Julien were going to the museum to see the Elgin Marbles and Piccadilly Circus. Caroline and Anne were off to Harson's to review applications. Sar and Sebastian would accompany them. Royce, Alexius, and Beth were spending the afternoon poring over ledgers.

Finally, they were alone in the carriage heading to the museum. He couldn't stop thinking about the two of them. Did she crave him as much as he yearned for her? If she did, it would be wonderful, but it spelled trouble—big trouble. She was looking at him with those gorgeous brown eyes that were saying *more, more, more, touch me.*

"Mer."

And she reached out for him. "I don't want to go to the museum. I want more of us. I want my breast in your mouth, and your hands claiming my body." The feel of him made her complete, and she wanted that. She needed him down to the inner core of her very being.

His forthright Mer. She was determined, especially when she was focused on something. When had he started thinking of her as his own? When had she started invading his every thought?

"Mer, we can't. As much as I want you, we can't let this happen. I want you in my bed so much I ache. Look at what you do to me." He put one long, sculptured leg up on the carriage seat, and the length of his arousal was visible. She leaned forward and touched the tip through the fabric. It jerked, and she stroked the length.

"Mer, stop!"

But she didn't. He was losing control. She offered him her breast, and he took it. Lost in desire, he did nothing but accept what she offered.

"This is what I want, Julien, only more. I'll never marry an appropriate man of society, because I'm mixed blood. I know that, and my family knows it. I'm twenty-three years old and on the shelf. I don't want to go through life without knowing what happens between a man and a woman. I want you to teach me. I'll be your mistress for as long as I can."

Julien couldn't get enough of her breast. The nipple was

large and peaked. She was starting to moan as he laved. He had to have her. Somehow her words penetrated the lusty haze of his mind.

"My *what*?"

"Your mistress."

He gently pushed her away from him. "Mer, you must listen. I see you and I'm aroused. I think of you. I dream of you. I long to teach you the pleasures a man and a woman can share. I want you wet, gasping, and shouting my name."

What he really wanted was to spill his seed in her womb and see her big and ripe with his child.

But he wasn't the marrying type, and he wouldn't litter the countryside with his bastards. He cared too much about her. Yes, that was it—he cared. He cared about her . . . and nothing more. And the armor around his heart struggled to close the ever-widening gap.

"You don't know what you're saying, and you can't be my mistress. You can't begin to understand the consequences. You'd never be accepted by polite society again, and your brother and mother would kill me." *Or I'd have to kill myself first.*

"I can't have an affair with you, Mer. You are an innocent, and I must leave you that way, whether you marry or not. What we are doing can go no further." He couldn't tell her she drove him to distraction with need and desire.

Straightening his clothes, he tried to look away from the swollen lips of the temptress before him. "We'll forget about this conversation and have a wonderful time at the museum." *Forget? How could he forget?* Inwardly, he groaned and pleaded with all that was holy that she'd stay on her side of the carriage.

She lifted her skirts, pointing to the patch of curls at the apex of her thighs. "You touched me here. I was wet. I am wet again; touch me." She was aching. She had to have him, and something else, but she didn't know what that something else was.

He could smell her sex and almost taste it on his tongue. He wanted to savor every bit of her—her texture, her taste, her smell. God help him, he wanted her. He adjusted his pants again and tried to think of something to say. His tongue was thick; struggling to put together a thought that didn't include her beneath him was impossible. His mind was blank, except for the roaring need raging within. He had to have her, but what of the consequences? *She is like none of the others.*

His honor didn't stand a chance with her body pressed to his in a most intimate way and her breast dangling before his mouth.

"Are you sure?"

"Yes, Julien. I need you to touch me and make me feel the way I did in the garden."

The coach stopped in front of the museum. Julien quickly adjusted her clothing. He helped her out, and he told the coachman to pick them up later. They went into the museum and out the back door. His thoughts centered on his driving need. He hailed a hackney. When it stopped, they were at the back entrance to his house. He let them in and led her upstairs to his bedchamber.

"Are you sure, Mer? If we start in this room, I probably won't be able to stop even if you ask."

"I'm sure."

When he looked up, she was struggling to remove her dress. "Here, let me; let me show you."

He eased her out of her clothes, piece by piece and layer by layer, revealing lush, soft, smooth skin. His breath caught, hands itched to claim and possess, and the thoughts of forever skipped along the fringes of his mind. Firm, large breasts graced a flat stomach, narrow waist, curvaceous hips, and long, firm, shapely legs.

"Why am I wet here?" Without any shyness or hesitation, she parted the curls of hair between her legs. Like everything else, she was forthright, unafraid, and facing their lovemaking head-on.

His imagination took flight, picturing her in various stages of passion. This woman was made for loving by him.

"Mer, there is much to learn about making love and giving and receiving pleasure. I need to show you how to pleasure yourself. If I'm not with you and you need me, you can do this and think of us. I can also give myself release, but it's not the same as with a woman."

As it would be for her; it wouldn't be the same without a man. But he couldn't make her his completely. Would this be enough to satisfy her curiosity? He would teach her, because he didn't want any other man to ever touch her like this, not even her husband, unless it was he. That errant thought slipped through his brain. His heavy arousal jutted out in front of him; he almost spilled his seed just looking at her luscious naked form and thinking about the infinite possibilities. Pulling a low, short bench in front of the looking glass, he asked her to sit.

"Show me, Julien. Teach me."

He kissed her and angled his tongue between her lips, and then slanted his mouth to plunder more deeply as he eased her onto the bench. She met him, eager for his kiss and whatever came next.

"Open your legs."

He stepped away; she was lost without his warmth. She did as he said and stared at herself in the looking glass.

"That's right; look. In order to be ready to receive a man and enjoy the pleasure, your passage must be wet. See? You're glistening. Open a little more." His fingers parted her and slid in between the folds. He pulled them out; they were wet. "Your sex is on my fingers," he said, and licked. She wanted to squirm; she wanted his fingers there and more.

He didn't know how much he could take. It wasn't his right to be here in his bedchamber with her, let alone take her virginity. That moment belonged to her future husband, but that thought didn't make him want her any less; he didn't want her being intimate with any other man, husband or not. Julien wanted her as he had never wanted any other woman. If he taught her to pleasure herself, he'd leave her virginity intact. She'd go to her husband as an almost virgin. She wouldn't be a total innocent when he was done, but at least she'd still be a virgin and know the pleasure to anticipate from the marriage bed.

You really like to fool yourself. There is no such person as an almost virgin. She'll never be the same. You could make her yours. What you are planning to do will make her feel incomplete; she'll want all of you, the small voice in his head echoed, and he ignored it.

He stood behind her with his stiff member falling on her shoulder, pointing directly at the mirror. She was looking at herself, gaping at the folds of her sex. Taking her right nipple between his thumb and first finger, he rolled it.

"Do the same with your other nipple."

She watched him and did. The nipples peaked and hardened. He leaned forward and tugged the nipple with his lips and nipped. Overcome with pleasure, she threw her head back.

"No, my sweet, I want you to watch. I want you to see you pleasuring yourself, and I want to see you pleasure yourself."

Sensations assaulted her, feelings never anticipated, nerves jangled from raw emotions; everything was focused on this moment and Julien.

"That's it, Mer. Look." He tugged on her nipple. "Before you were just glistening with moisture; now you can see the nectar of your sex."

Standing behind her, he watched her staring at herself with unbridled passion in her eyes. His arousal jerked madly at the sight. With his hand over hers, together they parted her folds and entered. He guided her finger and gently brushed over her mons once and then again. She jerked.

"Not yet, my sweet. There's much to learn. Open your legs a little wider and part yourself. What do you see, Mer?"

"I'm wet."

"Rub your fingertip over your mons. Let me show you."

Showing her how to pleasure herself was taking its toll on him. Beads of moisture covered the end of his stiff member. He was about to explode. He bowed in front of her, gently tying each of her legs to a leg of the bench with silk scarves.

"That's it. I can smell the essence of you. See how wet you are, and this is just the beginning. Keep pulling on your nipple. Pinch it slightly. Keep looking, my sweet. Pull on both nipples. Roll them in your fingers."

He leaned forward to taste. She didn't hesitate, opened her legs a little more, and arched her hips to force him to sample deeper. She dropped a hand and cradled his head to her. She could feel his tongue darting and swirling and bringing her pleasure she had never imagined. He licked, and she moved her nether lips closer to give him full access. Now she was beginning to understand how a woman could lose herself in a man.

He stepped away. "What I just did with my tongue, I want you to do with your finger over and over and over again. See how hard your sex can become." He placed her hand on her mons. "Now gently rub, and if it's not pressure enough, rub a little harder."

Looking at herself, she did as he said, but it wasn't enough. She rubbed harder and felt her wetness on the seat. He was standing to her side, watching. She rolled her nipple and instantly became caught up in the moment.

"Slow, Mer."

He knelt again and covered her with his mouth. His tongue swirled around between the swollen slick folds, and he went deeper. She was so wet, but he didn't want her to shatter yet. He sucked and nipped her mons. She lifted her hips to meet the thrust of his tongue.

"No, no. You must pleasure yourself." He stood, replaced her hand where his tongue and been, and kissed her hard.

Stepping behind the bench, her silky hair caught on his arousal as she moved her head from side to side. The feel of cool silk gliding over his hot member made him wonder if this was what her sheath would feel like, silky smooth. His body tensed, and he gritted his teeth.

Mer kept rubbing herself, looking for something just beyond her grasp. He took her other hand and guided her fingers to the swollen wet fold.

"If you can, I want you to put a finger into your passage and continue to stroke your sex. Is it hard, Mer? Can you feel how wet you are? Can you feel your passage begging for more? Keep looking at yourself."

She tried to spread her legs wider, her hips lifting, searching. He started playing with a nipple, and then he found the other and pulled on both.

"Keep your eyes open. Your release will come soon."

Her eyes were glazed with passion. She stroked herself again; he pulled on both nipples. She shattered and screamed his name. Wave after wave of pleasure hit her. Watching her explode, he could tell her contractions were powerful and deep. After witnessing the most erotic sight he'd ever seen, he had to get her dressed and out of there. Whatever control he had left was slipping by the second. Shaking his head only brought his eyes to feast on the erotic sight before him, and his manhood strained to reach her. His curious Mer could pleasure herself until she was married—or so he tried to convince himself. Muttering curses, he tried to rein himself in, but his tortuous body wasn't cooperating.

"Mer, you're still a virgin." Drops of sweat dotted his forehead. Barely able to breathe, he bent to untie her legs. "Let's get dressed. You can pleasure yourself when you are alone. You can go to your husband as a virgin. This should satisfy your curiosity until you're wed." He didn't know what else to say.

When he stood, his manhood was directly in front of her. She leaned forward to taste him as he had done to her, running her tongue over the tip and then up and down the hard, stiff length. He was definitely going to explode. Acting like an experienced courtesan, she took all of him in her mouth.

Warm, moist heat surrounded his length. How had she figured this out? He didn't want her to stop and would beg her not to do so if she would only keep doing what she was doing. He couldn't slake his inner demons. They had gone too far, over the line. His conscience didn't stand a chance. The little voice in his head was silent.

"Mer, if you keep going, I won't be able to stop." She sucked harder and pulled him in deeper. "Mer, do you . . . do you want me?"

With his length in her mouth, she nodded yes.

Freeing himself, he carried her to the bed and spread her thighs. He wanted her just as wet as she was a few minutes ago. He suckled her nipples, ravished her mouth, and his fingers parted her and plundered. Easing himself down the length of her and trailing kisses on her damp body, he greedily ran his tongue over her sex again and again and again. He tasted her nectar of honey, and she arched into him. She was wet and ready. He wanted her like this always. The more he drank, the more she demanded. She wriggled, and he feasted more. She would shatter soon, and he wanted to be inside of her when she did.

He worked his way back up her glistening body. Placing her legs over his shoulder, they locked eyes as he thrust into her very hot, slick, swollen passage past the barrier. She was his.

"I didn't mean to hurt you. Just wait a minute; the hurt will go away. It'll be fine. The first time may hurt a little, but it only happens the first time." He was bumbling like an idiot. Around her he frequently sounded and acted like one. Bloody hell, he'd never wanted someone so much.

She raised her hips, beckoning him to fill her. It was as though it was his first time too, and he was fourteen again. He thrust deeply into her and bent to kiss her. She was already pulling on her nipples, looking for more pleasure.

Reaching between them where they were joined, he found her sex and rubbed. As he stroked, she took him in deeper and began to pull on his stiff rod as her hips started that ancient dance as old as time. He rubbed more, and she tugged and rolled her nipples, unconscious of everything except the pleasure building within her. Hot, smooth velvet held him in a vice. She came on a surge of pleasure, and he threw back his head and joined her.

The arch of her hips, her flushed skin, swollen lips, and soft breasts pleaded for more. This was not an experienced lady, but one who had never given herself to a man before. He felt as though he had been given a prize, the brass ring. Now she was his to protect. Gazing down at her flat stomach, he envisioned a little girl with honey-colored hair and brown eyes growing within. He had emptied himself in her womb without a care about withdrawing. Yes, she was his—*his* . . . branded by him. He'd make sure no other man would ever touch her like this. He couldn't begin to imagine Sar's reaction, let alone Her Grace's, if they ever found out Mer was going to be his mistress. He rethought his theory about being killed twice, and the voice in his head echoed, *Mistress? This is the woman you are going to spend the rest of your life with—your wife. Keep on trying to fool yourself.*

"Let me get a towel and clean you."

She should have grabbed the towel from his hand as he tenderly stroked her swollen folds. Instead, she leaned backed and opened herself to him. His hypnotic caresses made her yearn for him. He rubbed her mons over and over again, showing her the liquid of her sex on the toweling. He couldn't stop; she didn't want him to. Julien knew once would never be enough for either of them. Mer licked her lips and pleaded with her eyes.

As though pulled by a force beyond him, he reverently slipped his arousal between her wet folds.

Rolling over, he pulled her on top of him so he could sink more deeply into heaven.

"Julien." He looked up to see Mer offering her breasts. "I want more. Make me feel again."

He reached up and covered each breast with his hands. She bowed, opened wider, and raised herself up and down slowly on his stiff arousal. Her nipples were hard twin peaks. As he tweaked and pulled, she started on a ride she couldn't control.

Her hands covered his, begging for silent guidance. He raised her off of him. "What do you want, Mer?"

"Everything," and she eased herself over his mouth.

She was dripping with pleasure and started to tense as his tongue plundered. He could tell she needed him inside of her. He licked her mons and she opened wider, begging. He guided her to mount him again. Slowly, he set the pace up and down on his rod until she found her own rhythm. He pulled on her nipple, and she leaned forward and dangled the other breast before his mouth. The nipples were large and sensitive to his attention. *Grapes,* he thought, *plump grapes.*

As he nipped, her hair fell forward, forming an intimate cocoon around them. Rolling one nipple, he took his other hand and found her mons. She arched, giving him better access as her body moved on its own accord. She couldn't hold back. He rubbed and tweaked and rubbed and pulled. She screamed, pulling him deeper and deeper into her slick sheath. He joined her scream, spilling all of him into her, because he belonged there.

Their breathing was almost normal again.

"We have to go, Mer, and later we must talk." She could be with babe, his babe, and he caught himself smiling.

As she finished dressing, she studied her reflection in the looking glass. Her lips were slightly swollen, and a subtle smile lit her face. Talking was out of the question. She wanted the memory of their moment to last.

"Mer, we still have time to visit the museum for a few minutes. Let's go. You'll be able to tell the others what you saw." She had no idea what she saw in the museum. All she thought about was what they had done. She hadn't known her body could feel that way, and all she wanted was more.

***

That evening, two men sat in the shadows of an opulent, dimly lit study in the other house in Mayfair.

"This is what the duke is wearing for the costume ball. It's simple and easily copied. With our note, the duke will come to the library at the requested time. Our man should be there very early, in case His Grace suspects a trap. Here is the design of the house and the best way in. There can be no mistakes."

CHAPTER 10

A Fortnight before the Ball

The London Daily

Society News

There seems to be more news and mystery surrounding the eighth Duke of Westmoure. Where you find the new Duke of Westmoure, the Negro duke, you are apt to find shots, murder, and fire. There have been five additional murders since the mixed blood stepped foot on English soil. All of the dead men, except for one, were in service to the Crown. The last murder occurred four nights ago at the duke's house.

Before dawn three days ago, the Westmoure Shipping office was set ablaze. It's very clear someone not only wants Westmoure dead, but that someone also wants to destroy his business and ruin him.

The Duchess of Westmoure and her daughters were seen at Gunter's along with the Marchioness of Broadhurst and her daughter Lady Alexius. If you missed being introduced, you will have the opportunity if you have been invited to the Marquess and Marchioness of Broadhurst's masquerade ball in two weeks. It's the ball to introduce the new duke and his family to the ton, and to open the Season.

But who will attend? Introducing a Negro to society, a duke no less, has never occurred before. Do Negroes belong in society?

As for the other news . . .

Caroline read the part about the Duke of Westmoure and his family again. This was nastier than the piece that appeared the other day. *How does that woman know so much? She must be a part of the ton or know someone in government in order to write in such precise detail about daily events. Someone . . . yes, someone in the government is talking . . . talking too much.* Her mind quickly rifled through the latest. Who in the ton was the mistress of a government official?

The ton was beginning to return to London in droves, and subterfuge was a game Caroline learned from her husband. *When I'm done, everyone of any importance will be groveling before the new duke and his family, and the Society News will sing their praises.*

The Duke of Grayson took one look at the mischievous sparkle in his daughter's eyes and knew she was in the middle of something that would set the ton on its ear if ever found out.

"Father, I'm so glad you're back."

At sixty-six, the duke was still a tall, imposing man with silver-streaked hair. They had been without her mother for four years, and every widow of a certain age in the ton chased him. After his wife's death, the daughter-father bond was even stronger.

"Caroline, so am I. How are you, my child?"

The last time Caroline's eyes had glistened like this was four years ago when they'd created Harson's. Harson's School for Social Deportment was to honor her mother, his beloved Violet. And what an adventure it had become. Under this unassuming name, women were taught business skills. Those who graduated could run every aspect of most businesses. It took two years to complete the coursework. In addition, an apprenticeship of one year was required—radical training for women. In the beginning he didn't think they'd ever find businesses to sponsor the apprenticeships, but they had. Now the program accepted new students every six months. He was eager to review the new batch of applications, but from the gleam in his daughter's eyes, that review would have to wait.

"Now, out with it. What are you about to do? Do you need my help?"

"Well, this is what has happened . . ."

For the next half hour, Grayson learned about the new Duke of Westmoure. Caroline left nothing out: her worries, her concerns, and her fears for the family.

"Now you want the duke and his family to assume their rightful place in society, with the help of your friends and me."

"Yes."

"You realize how dangerous this is. People have already been killed. This won't be easy. You're going against popular thought. It'll be difficult for some to ever accept a mixed blood among the peerage. Some will fall in line just to court the favor of the most powerful people in society and still hate Westmoure and his family. Among the aristocracy, there is much to be said if the lineage can't be traced back to an invasion.

"Your mother would have enjoyed this. Let's go over your plan and set everything in motion." Offering his advice, and suggesting the support of additional friends, the stage was set. By the time they finished, the *crème de la crème* of society would be involved, and the Duke of Westmoure and his entire family properly launched. Grayson couldn't wait for the first act.

"Now don't forget Wednesday—the small dinner party for the duke and his family. Father, thank you. This is the right thing to do, isn't it?"

"Caroline, your mother never followed popular thought if she knew it was unjust or unfair. Didn't we instill in you the same? This is something which must be done, even if it goes against what society thinks is proper and what society believes should be the sanctity of pure lines. All of that's rubbish. Intermarriages have occurred in England for centuries. It's wrong to deny this family their rightful place in society because of mixed blood. The duke legally and rightfully inherited the title. Society be damned.

"Caroline, you and your brothers are the sun of my life. When you do things like this—what is right—I'm exceptionally proud."

Caroline knew she was privileged to have such a father. A lump formed in her throat, and she tried to hold back the tears forming in her eyes.

"Yes, I'll do all in my power to help the duke, his family, and protect you. I know Sebastian has taken extra precautions." He reached down and patted Felix, who all but purred. "Now, tell me, how is that granddaughter of mine?"

"I think you ought to stop by the other house. The three of them are making plans to take over the empire. Do you think we raised her improperly?"

Marrying Alexius off had become one of Caroline's greatest concerns. At almost twenty-one, Alexius's love was business.

"Not to worry. The right man will come along, but he'll have to be strong and honorable. I think I'll do as you suggest. I'm off to see Alexius." What he really wanted to do was to check out Westmoure's sisters. He'd learn much about the new duke by meeting them.

At the headquarters of Cummings, Grayson carefully assessed the Westmoure sisters. The plans they were making astonished him. Yes, Caroline had the right of it. Cummings was going to be one of the largest companies in the world very shortly. He doubted if many men could match the three of them. Mixed blood or not, the duke's sisters were intelligent and knew the world of business.

He saw shades of his Violet in Alexius. *She's doing well, Violet. Remember, you taught her. The three of them make a powerful team. You'd approve. Watch over them.*

With misty eyes, he left knowing two things: the beginning of a new era for Cummings was about to commence, and the duke's family was kind and honest. No one could ask for more.

***

Perkins sensed a change in George Mason. Since trailing him, it had been the same routine day in and day out: home, work, and home again. After work today, George seemed overly cautious. Perkins as John the dockworker had changed appearances five times in the past five days. This evening George Mason was also in disguise.

Following him to a working-class area, Perkins slid into the shadows and watched and waited. A man also in disguise soon joined George. Perkins stumbled into the tavern found a table, ordered a tankard, and flirted with the tavern wench while observing George and the man he met.

Despite his stooped appearance, the man was tall. Smooth hands looked soft. Expertly trimmed hair artfully arranged to appear unkempt, and his air of confidence belied his shabby appearance. With heads close, the two men in disguise talked. A bag was passed to George. The man exited, leaving George alone to drink his ale. Some minutes later, a working-class man sat down with George. They leaned toward each other, talking softly. Shortly thereafter, he left.

Minutes later, George headed for home.

Perkins crept through the shadows of Whitehall and silently opened the door at the end of the hall. He handed the general a note and slipped back into the shadows. *His Grace's— one hour.* The general tossed the note into the fireplace and watched it turn to ash.

***

"Perkins, what happened?" Berkley trusted his instincts.

"George met a man in disguise at the Bull Tavern. George was also in disguise. They talked briefly. A bag of coins was passed to George. The bag could have held other things, but I only heard the jangle of coin. The man left. A few minutes later, another man joined George. He had also altered his appearance. After a brief conversation, the bag of coins changed hands once again. The second man left. George lingered for a while. I followed him home.

"The first man in disguise was hunched to shorten his height. Standing tall, I guess he would be a little over six feet. He walked with a confident gait, definitely not one of the working class. It reminded me of the walk of the assailant who killed your operative at the duke's house. The second man was tall—of similar height as the two of you—but he was of the working class, unkempt, rough demeanor, callused hands. One other thing . . . I haven't been able to figure out how the message was passed about the meeting."

"Someone will continue to watch Mason. Well done, Perkins," Berkley said. He thought messages were being passed within Whitehall itself, and the first man George met likely worked within the Home Office. *Dangerous, very dangerous.*

"The Pigeon Pie at dawn," he said, and the general became one with the shadows and air.

***

Daggs, Julien, Royce, Sebastian, and Sar found Berkley sitting at the table upon their arrival. Perkins lurked in the shadows. Jack watched George Mason.

"This is what we know. Based on the lack of information gathered by our men in the East End, on the docks, in the stews, and Perkins's personal observations, we are dealing with gentlemen and members of the aristocracy. Several people in the Home Office are involved."

The silence in the room became deafening. They were looking for one of their own. The game was now deadlier than ever and the stakes even higher.

"From this moment on, besides Jack and one other person, no one is to know our plans. Others who become involved will only be privy to sufficient information in order for them to do their parts. Sebastian, is everything in place for the ball?"

Without waiting for an answer, the general continued, "George Mason is our only link; we'll see where he leads us."

During lunch with the exchequer, Berkley realized what had changed about George. Normally, he worked all hours, including late at night. His pattern had been the same for the last five years or so. For the past several months, that had changed.

His office was dark at night. He appeared in the morning and left by early evening. Someone always saw him entering the building in the morning and leaving in the evening. Being seen was not a coincidence. There were never any coincidences in this game.

"Sar, have you completed setting up the new offices for the shipping company?" As usual, Daggs was talking and pacing.

Sar doubted if Berkley or Daggs ever stopped working. Their lives appeared to be service to the Crown, one inseparable from the other. And if he wasn't careful, he would fall into the same category—work, work, work.

"We set up two offices, as you suggested. One is run by the staff, which was in place in the shipping office at the time of the fire. They are given altered information. The other office has the correct information. We hired a complete staff from Harson's."

"Good, good," Daggs replied. "Jacob and I have studied manifests and the Ships at Sea Reports that didn't match up over the past six years. All of the extra cargo disappeared between Antwerp and Rotterdam. Both are thriving seaports riddled with smuggling and treasonous acts of espionage. Your ships have probably been used as a part of a smuggling ring—a hanging offense. No additional cargo ever came into England on your ships, only out.

"During the last six or seven years of the late duke's life, he spent less time in the office. Having trained his staff over the years, he knew they were capable of taking care of most of the day-to-day work. This would have made it possible for anyone he trusted to set up the operation.

"You have ships going to Antwerp and Rotterdam at least twice a week. My men will take command of your next ships leaving for those two cities. One of my men will be in charge of the Ships at Sea Report, and another a part of the crew. It's going to take some time to get to the bottom of this."

In all of his time at Scotland Yard, Daggs had never seen this much treason and crime by those within the Home Office and among the aristocracy. If he had the right of it, there were at least two people in the Home Office in this up to their necks, along with several members of the aristocracy. There was murder, attempted murder of the new duke, and a shipping business used for nefarious purposes. Everything had been carefully plotted and executed. Everything had gone according to plan until Sar wasn't killed. Ruining Westmoure's was probably a separate crime, and the why of it eluded him. Something wasn't fitting yet. There was more to this than the new duke's lineage, but the answers were still beyond the inspector's grasp.

"Done," Sar replied. "Have them come to the regular office tomorrow morning at six. Your men can become familiar with everything, as well as the crew. We'll meet at our other office on Sunday." Daggs simply nodded.

The general interrupted. "Our next step depends on what happens at the ball. If there is nothing else, I'll see you there, but I'll be in touch. If anything comes up, you know where to reach me," he said, and then he was gone.

***

Julien hadn't spoken to Mer for several days. His bed had become a shrine; a testament to all that was good between men and women. Everywhere he looked he saw her. When he inhaled deeply, her lightly lingering scent engulfed him. When he exhaled, he couldn't wait to take his next breath. He could taste her and see her climax. He wanted to watch her in erotic wonder as she tempted him and silently begged for his manhood. Had he spoiled her for anyone else? Or had she spoiled him for any other woman? He had to have her again . . . and again . . . and again. He wanted more of her—her smile, her direct approach, her intelligence, her tapping foot when she was irritated, moments in bed, and the feel of being connected, whole. She'd claimed a part of him; it was a strange feeling.

There had been many women in his life, but with her everything was different. Vivid pictures of their stolen moments made him fight his arousal, making the ride increasingly uncomfortable. *No one but I should ever be able to bring her passion to life. No one but I should make her cry out, and no one but I should ever touch her like that.* The mere thought of another man caressing her made him want to kill.

His horse snorted at the rough tug of the reins. "Sorry, Zeus." He patted the horse's neck. *This must stop. She's affecting everything in my life.*

Her offer to become his mistress was out of the question. Mixed blood or not, this just wasn't done. She deserved much better. She neither understood the ways of their society, nor the status associated with being a duke's sister. What a scandal *that* would be. There was little doubt in his mind Her Grace would kill him first and then Sar. None of them would ever be accepted by society again—not that society really mattered. Once again he reminded himself why he was feeling this way. He cared about her—cared, that's it, nothing more. He cared for her and kept repeating that fact to himself over and over again, as if that was the solution and absolution for his soul.

He'd find a mistress and forget about Mer. Yes, that's what he'd do. Better yet, he'd find her a husband and then banish her from his memory. Images kept dancing in his head. Every time he thought of finding another mistress, Mer's face appeared. He saw her pleasuring herself, he saw her bowed to take him all in, and on the verge of shattering. He had to have a new mistress fast, otherwise—yes, otherwise—he'd become her lust-starved sex slave.

At the office, he found Royce, Grayson, Mer, Beth, and Alexius poring over something on the table.

"Julien, look. What do you think?" Alexius thrust papers into his hand. "My grandfather believes most working women must make their own clothing and can't afford a seamstress. They spend hours after work sewing. If we made clothing at an affordable price, women would be properly dressed for work and have one less thing to do when their day ended—readymade dresses. We have the fabric and could supply it at a fraction of the cost while still making a profit."

Mer handed him more plans and smiled. "After having Beth and Royce cost everything out, if profitable, this might develop into another division of Cummings. There's a building near the market square which is available. Our idea is to make the garments in the back of the shop and have seamstresses available for minor alterations. Alexius's mother has a friend who runs a school for seamstresses. Possibly some of them are for hire."

"Give me a few minutes to look everything over," he said. He would buy her the building himself to always see that smile on her face. He found himself smiling also. Somehow she made his day better.

Like most of his class, he'd never thought about women in business. Women who worked had not been a part of his world until he learned of Alexius's "little" gigantic empire. Where did they work? Did they have proper clothing to wear? Was it difficult? Ready-to-wear women's clothing, working women, and a company that spanned most of the world run by women tumbled along with the thoughts of the woman who occupied his dreams and reality.

He had a lot to learn about women in business, starting with Mer. After today, she'd probably never speak to him again. That was the chance he took for their afternoons of . . . of pure carnal pleasure. The voice in his head whispered, *Is that all?* He couldn't come up with words to describe their afternoons. The plans before him blurred when his brain's eye froze on pictures of their last time together.

When he walked out of his tailor's, there she was shopping on Bond Street with her maid, two footmen, and America. He suggested another trip to the museum. Because it was Julien, she dismissed her maid and footmen, and climbed into his closed carriage. Once at the museum, he led her out the back door and hailed a hackney. Within minutes they were at his house.

By the time he locked the door and turned to her, she'd already pulled down her dress and chemise, offering him her breasts. Greedily, he took them. She wanted more, and he tried to guide her to his room, but she couldn't wait. Wiggling out of her clothes, she stood before him clad only in stockings, shoes, and her drawers. Untying the ribbon to her undergarment, he watched as it slipped slowly over her hips to the floor. He took in all of her, from the silk-clad legs, to the springy curls at the apex of her thighs, to the large breasts with nipples as large as plump grapes.

She looked him directly in the eye, parted herself, and began to rub her sex. He watched, unable to move. As she became wetter, she offered her slick fingers to him. He sucked and licked the very essence of her. Then she had backed away and leaned over the end of the sofa, with her legs wide and dangling so he could get a better look at the wet passage waiting for him. Fully exposed to him, she rubbed her mons and, with her other hand, toyed with her nipples.

He didn't remember how or when his breeches opened, but his hard rod was inching towards her. But she wouldn't let him touch her yet. She was wet, wanting, and hot. She continued to pleasure herself for him. Inserting a finger deep within her passage, she slid it in and out while brushing her sex. She was wild and uninhibited.

"Come to me and watch."

Moving closer, he could see she was about to shatter. Taking her finger out of her passage, she put it into his mouth.

He had stood spellbound. She thrust her fingers into her sex again, then rubbed the liquid on her nipples and offered the succulent orbs to him. Kneeling at her side, he took them and suckled like a babe. He was hot and heavy but would play her game. After all, he was a master in the art of seduction and loving—or so he thought.

Trailing kisses down her body, he went to the center of her heat. He nipped at her sex, and she shivered. Slowly gliding his tongue in and out while brushing her clitoris had her screaming for more, but he took his time, bringing her to the peak again and again, punishing her for making him wait. Didn't she understand what she did to him? Didn't she understand what her wet and wanting and desiring him made him want to do? His tongue rasped over her mons again and he gently bit. She tensed. Again his tongue found her center and plundered. Pulling abruptly away, he thrust into her forcefully. Finding her sex, he rubbed with one hand, and his mouth found a nipple. With each thrust, her muscles clamped more tightly around him, encasing him in her scorching sheath. He pulled out, because he wanted more.

He stepped back and looked at his wanton. Her swollen folds were wet. As he stared, she rubbed her sex; he watched as her muscles started to contract. Her scent alone almost pushed him over the edge. Julien had to taste again. He plundered and sensed she was trying to hold back for him.

His long, thick member was swollen from want, but she did it to him again; she made him wait. Mer wrapped her mouth around his manhood and slowly sucked him deeper and deeper into a cocoon of heat. He tried to push her away, but he lacked the desire and strength to do so, and the heavenly torment continued. Cradling her head to him, he watched as her mouth and tongue slid up and down his length and over the sensitive tip. As always with her, his control was gone; sweat trickled down his back.

She looked up at him and mumbled, "More."

He thrust into her. Finding her sex, he rubbed and felt her tense again. Offering a nipple, he took the hardened peak and bit softly. They climaxed instantly, with a force and intensity he'd never felt. It rocked his soul. His hot seed filled her womb, and he felt connected to eternity. He could still hear her screams of satisfaction mixed with his. The voice in his head said, *If she isn't increasing now, she soon will be.*

What she needed was a husband, and he'd find one for her—a suitable husband, one that met his standards. He glanced her way, hoping he hadn't missed anything important.

***

Julien spent the next hour tying to focus sufficiently to read the plans and make notes. "I suggest we go and look at the building. It needs to be large enough to handle the trade and accommodate a workspace. Also, the building must be in an area where people shop for other necessities.

"Readymade dresses are a new idea. To say the least, women will be skeptical at first. You'll have to win them over. Ladies who buy want to know they are purchasing clothes which will last. The name and the appearance of the shop will instantly set the tone. Have you thought of a name for the shop which implies quality and is still inviting?"

As he continued to talk and ask questions, Mer thought of their forbidden time together. This kind and generous man was a part of her. As his mistress, he would only be hers for a while. When he let her go for the proper wife, her heart would still belong to him. She loved him, and had known so when she begged him to make her complete. There was no denying it. He made her complete, whole. Even if there is a babe, everything would work out. She'd only be fuel for society's gossip for a few generations. They'd say, *See? We were right. Negroes are uncivilized and not worthy to be among people of society. Their blood is tainted, and they are from America. You cannot mix blood of the aristocracy with commoners, especially mixed blood. Americans are so uncivilized.*

She had found her one and only, and he was beyond her reach. Regardless of the social consequences, she prayed she was with child—Julien's child. Focusing, she willed herself to concentrate on business.

As they walked through the empty building and paced everything out, Mer vaguely heard everyone agree that both floors were needed: the first floor for the display of garments, fitting rooms, minor alterations, and an office, and the second floor for sewing the garments, creating the designs, and storage.

Grayson stood back and listened to his granddaughter and the others. As an aristocrat, he was going against every innate sense of what society deemed proper. And it felt right. It felt as though they were on the verge of something very big, something that would affect and help hundreds of people.

"I'll speak to Caroline, and we'll start looking for workers immediately," he said. "Mer, you know what you want and what will be best for the store. Can you be in charge of the hiring? Let me take the responsibility for setting up the shop. The store will be ready for your approval and additional renovations the Monday after the ball.

"Julien, I need to meet with you so we can set up everything as you suggested. Alexius, will you pick out the fabric? I recommend we use what we have in the warehouse at the onset, unless you know of something better. Beth and Royce, I need the costs of running this business."

Grayson smiled to himself. *Violet, I wish you were here. This group is bringing welcomed adventures to my life. I'll never grow old.*

"Now, a ride in the park is in order. Is everyone ready?"

Grayson's words floated over Julien's head as he tried to figure out a way to get Mer alone. Their liaison had to end immediately. As he covertly looked at her, he could feel his trousers becoming uncomfortably tight again. Bloody hell, she always did this to him. Did she know the power she held over him? Probably not; she was in love. That four-letter word resonated in his heart. How could she not be? He had taken the virginity of a woman who would never give herself unless she loved the man. She was taught to love and expected to be loved. He wanted to causally dismiss this by saying she would get over it, that he was just the wrong man, but the piercing pain in his heart caused his toes to ache, and he knew he was lying to himself. He'd been blindsided by the most beautiful woman he ever had the fortune to hold. How was he going to get out of this?

Glancing at Mer, he saw what the others didn't see: that certain tilt of her head, a tapping foot, and her big, expressive eyes, wider than normal, meant her keen brain was hatching an idea. He was so fixated on Mer, he wasn't sure he'd heard Grayson. A ride in the park?

"Not just yet." Mer hesitated. "I think the store should be named Paige's. It's simple, direct, and has a ring to it that suggests special, beyond the ordinary, but does not intimidate."

Everyone knew she'd hit upon it. She was invaluable for going straight to the heart of matters and getting it right. Julien thought Berkley would be lucky if he could have her as an operative. She was able to put pieces of puzzles together quicker than anyone he knew.

It wasn't the fashionable hour to be seen in the park, yet it was more crowded than it had been during the previous two weeks. The ton was quickly returning. By the time they reached the Serpentine, Julien, Mer, Beth, Alexius, and Royce were ready to walk. Grayson had been stopped by acquaintances and was busy laying the groundwork for Westmoure and his family's acceptance by society. It was easy to steer Mer apart from the others and still remain in sight of everyone and be within the bounds of the rules dictated by society. The dogs cavorted about.

"Mer, we have to talk, and there is no better time than now . . . in front of everyone."

Heat pooled in her stomach and her heart was beating the sturdy drum that always signaled he was close to her.

"You know I want you. I can't stop thinking about you, but we can't meet again. You are the sister of a duke; you are no longer a virgin. You'll marry, and your future husband will know you've been with another man."

He was making a complete mess of this. All he wanted to do was take her someplace and make love to her until she was totally sated. He wanted to spend hours and hours giving her pleasure and watching *his* passionate woman come alive. His head told him their forbidden moments of passion must stop. His heart told him something else, but he couldn't put his finger on what *something else* was. The little voice in his head said, *Not this lifetime. She is yours forever.* If she was carrying his babe, he'd marry her tomorrow. His? Yes, she was his. Marriage? Yes, marriage fit. The thought of marriage to her was more appealing than naught, and then his better judgment kicked in.

"Mer, you must listen to me. I care about you, but I can't cause your total ruin. If you're with babe, I must know immediately. We'll figure out something. Until we solve the murders surrounding your family and everyone is safe, Royce and I are assigned to protect you. I won't compromise your safety. We'll work together at Cummings and Paige's, but we can't and shall not meet again—and, no, you cannot become my mistress. That's out of the question. I have decided to take it upon myself to find you a suitable husband, one who will be understanding when you marry."

Haven't you found her husband already? his inner voice countered. And there was no way he could block his true voice, which said, *Tell her, tell her . . . tell her you love her.*

Her heart was breaking. So, she was just another one of his conquests. He wanted to auction her off to the highest bidder like a horse at Tattersall's and find her a suitable husband who understood she was not a virgin. Was he crazy? That wasn't going to happen. Her fury began to build. Unconsciously, she started tapping her foot.

Smiling for all to see, she looked directly at him. "Julien, you have spoken. Now listen to me. If I marry or not, I won't be a piece of horseflesh for you to auction off to soothe your conscience and arrogant manner. Listen to me very carefully. If I marry, I will not—I repeat, will not—need you to explain to my future husband I'm not a virgin. This wasn't, as you would say, an indiscretion. I'm very aware of what I wanted and what we did.

"You will not have me as your mistress, yet you will seek out someone else to be so. Rules of your society are a bit confusing. If I were a widow, you wouldn't think twice about making me your mistress, but I'm not. I'm mixed blood, which is common in England. However, I will probably never marry or find the proper aristocratic husband because of the aristocracy's idea that their lines are pure and must remain so."

Mer's heart was cracking inch by inch; she pasted a smile on her face. "Do you know how laughable that is? How many times has England been invaded? How many times throughout the centuries has royalty, including those from the Mediterranean and Africa, married those of the aristocracy in England? Nevertheless, I will be denied pleasure with the one I choose due to your society's crazy mixed-up code of propriety. If I am increasing, you'll never know. Unfortunately, I am stuck with you until this intrigue has been solved."

She turned and walked towards the others, hoping no one

would see the tears forming in her eyes and the pieces of her heart on the ground.

The ride back to the house was filled with talk of plans, schedules, and lists. Everyone had work that needed to be completed by the morrow. Alexius's grandfather would be at Cummings by early afternoon to review everything again. In the morning, he'd secure the lease. Mer smiled and said the right things as the cold ache of love loss settled deeper around her heart. She hadn't been prepared for everything to end so soon.

Upon returning to the duke's house, Julien excused himself immediately. He was off to see his solicitor and buy that damn building for *his* Mer and anything else needed to make Paige's a success and see her smile again. He was miserable. The light had gone from his day. The pain in his chest seared his soul. *Fool.* He had thrown away the only woman he'd ever cared about like a piece of foolscap. *Cared about?* Yes, he cared about her, but it was more than that. He knew it, had fought it, and had loss. Now she would never know. He'd be happy if she ever spoke a word to him again outside of business and what society demanded. He could give a damn about mixed blood. And the voice in his head said, *This is love.*

He cursed himself as he strolled into his solicitor's office and demanded in no uncertain terms what he wanted done by six o'clock that afternoon. The renovations were to be started immediately and finished in two days. His solicitor knew who to let the building to without them ever knowing the owner.

He returned to Sar's house to sit in the shadows and watch over Mer. *What a fool you are. You can live without her, but you'll be a shell of a man.* He'd figure out how to win her back.

Without her, his life was nothing, and that strange sensation filled his heart again.

Eleven Days before the Ball

Sar and Jacob sat in the second shipping office waiting for the Ships at Sea Report from the *Liberty*. At the inspector's suggestion, the plan was changed. The cargo listed on their manifest was loaded on Thursday, and each crate stamped with an identifying mark known only to them. Late Thursday night, the cargo was taken to Southampton. Using the inspector's crew, the ship sailed for Antwerp and Rotterdam early Friday morning.

Jacob glanced around the office as he spoke. "Daggs will be here shortly. He went to check with his men. By the time we loaded, someone had mixed in additional pallets with the cargo listed on the manifest. Fortunately, no one else knew of the change of sailing date. There was no way the contact in either Antwerp or Rotterdam was able to find out about the change. Our ship, commanded by Daggs's men, arrived in Antwerp and Rotterdam early. Apparently, sailing ships is one of their many talents.

"In the smuggling business, missing goods ensures some-one's death. There will be another dead body soon. With the smugglers' cargo missing, questions are going to start flying. All fingers will eventually point to the shipping office. We'll be more at risk."

Jacob wondered what Avery would have done.

"The *Liberty* was en route back to England on Monday. Six extra pallets left our docks, and the six extra pallets are being returned. They're being delivered along with the report."

Daggs walked into the office. "Jacob, Sar, we have the cargo that wasn't on the original manifest being unloaded in the back. You have a very angry crew. My man spread it about that the new captain read the schedule incorrectly and thought the crew standing about was his. Of course, the crew was eager to join him for the pay.

"According to the talk, he's to be reprimanded and will probably never command another vessel. I spoke with my men. No one heard talk of any extra cargo. My man sailed the *Liberty* to Liverpool. Someone will want to torch it, along with the cargo they think is on board. I thought it would be best to save your ship. Whoever is behind this may or may not catch on immediately that the switch was intentional. Eventually, someone will have to start snooping about. The cargo is here; let's get to it."

They stood in the loading area, watching as the crates were opened one by one. There was nothing but nondescript china statues, which might have been made at any one of a number of companies in England. These were pieces found in any working-class home. Several were broken. There was nothing inside.

Jacob examined the broken pieces—glass and dust. "We're overlooking something. Whatever it is, we're looking at it. Daggs, have your men stack the pallets in this area. I'll examine everything more closely this week. The office is about to open. Sar, all of the other ships are going out on schedule. Both offices have the same departure schedule. Let me know what you want to do. As for the crew which missed its run, I'm going to pay them as though they made the trip."

Mulling things over, Jacob realized this was just the beginning. They were dealing with a master. "No, it's better to take the cargo to Daggs's office where we have the other files. Do you have room, Daggs?" Daggs nodded. "I also want protection for the ladies. Leave seven or eight of those statues in the basket under my desk."

"Do you want a wolfhound too?" Sar asked.

"Yes, and get it here immediately. Sooner or later we'll be found out. When whoever figures out what has actually happened, we'll be the target. Whatever this is, those statues are invaluable."

"Someone won't take kindly to either their loss or the involvement of Scotland Yard." Sar was following Jacob's reasoning, knowing the ante had been raised once again.

Daggs replayed the opening of the crates over and over in his mind. Something was off, but he couldn't pinpoint what it was. "I'll get your request to Whitehall. Until tonight."

***

Grayson and Mer called on Caroline early that morning. "Readymade dresses? What a wonderful idea. I agree; start small. Between my friends and me, we should be able to find the workers to fill many of the positions. Sar just hired women to work in the shipping office. Maybe we can use them as models for the patterns."

Mer was half-listening. When she'd finally fallen asleep, it was just before dawn. This morning she dragged herself out of bed knowing her future was one endless tortured night. *Damn you. Julien, damn you. I never knew love could feel so bad.*

Love? Yes, love. I love him. Hopefully she heard Lady Caroline's question correctly.

"We want to finish the renovations to the building and begin working on the patterns as soon as we find someone competent to make them."

"If you want to accomplish all of this within the next forty-five days, and limit your workday to ten hours a day and a half day on Saturday, it's best to add two more seamstresses." Caroline studied the lists again. "You'll need to have one or two seamstresses available for alterations in the store. One designer will work. Your mother and I are going to Harson's today. We'll pull the files of students who are about to finish their apprenticeship. There might be someone right for you.

"You'll meet Miriam tonight. She runs a sewing school. Diana has an eye for decorating. I'm sure she'll be happy to help put final touches on the store to give it a special twist." Caroline smiled. "Two other things . . . There will need to be a private entrance and office for those who need to come and go unnoticed. I also suggest a Saturday afternoon for your opening. Serve tea and put an announcement in the news sheet. We'll send an invitation to all of the graduates and post notices at the schools."

Being with Caroline reminded Mer of being aboard a ship in rough rolling seas, assaulted by one huge wave after another. The ideas kept coming and coming on swift currents as they rushed forth to collide with other forces. She felt bruised and battered. *Will the world always keep spinning as I stand on the sidelines watching it pass me by?* All she wanted was to be by herself and figure out a way to go on without Julien in her life. In time, maybe business would be enough to fill the gaping hole in her heart.

"I'll leave the rest to the two of you. I have a building to see about leasing." Grayson felt as though he were a child filled with the excitement of getting one's first pony.

"I must leave too. I'll meet you and my mother at Madame Burgoff's this afternoon." Mer and America followed Grayson to the waiting coach.

Anne was impressed by the extent of training required to graduate from Harson's. This was avant-garde education for women. "Caroline, some of the recent graduates look promising for Paige's."

She put the list of names, along with their qualifications, in her reticule for Mer. Ah, her daughter. Lately, she seemed listless and uninterested, out of sorts. As Anne played the events of the last few days in her mind, she smiled the knowing smile of a mother who knew her children very well.

The fittings at Madame Burgoff's went smoothly. After being assured everything would be ready before the ball, the girls returned to Cummings. Anne eased back into the comfortable squabs of Caroline's coach. For the first time, she felt a promise of hope. Her children were finding their way. Once this mystery surrounding Sar cleared up, they'd be able to better handle the challenges of society and their new life. Sar could always find a bride and have the requisite heir, but she wanted him to find love. A loveless marriage was worse than the hottest pits of hell.

Thoughts of all that had occurred brought tears to her eyes.

She regretted that her daughters might never marry and have a love like the one she shared with their father, for there was a stigma attached to being mixed blood in the aristocracy. If lines weren't pure, it would taint someone's lineage. *Ha, unlikely.* And she smiled again. If things were as she thought, maybe that might change. If so, the family was about to turn the stodgy ton upside down again. Just a little talk with Perkins and she'd have all she needed to know. She sighed and patted Duchess and Felix as they slept curled together at her feet.

Caroline sat on the other side of the coach with her eyes

closed. Today was another busy day, and this would be the only time she would have to herself. Her life had become fuller and more exciting with the duke and his family. She reviewed her carefully laid plans and reminded herself to privately introduce Anne to Lady Hortense Horton. She was the senior dragon and most revered woman of the ton. The dowager duchess was in a class by herself. No, she was a class by herself; even the patroness of Almack's kowtowed to her.

Caroline's eyes flew open when a shot rang out and the ball hit the coach's door.

Anne pulled *Bessie* out of her reticule. "Down, Caroline, and keep Duchess and Felix down too! I'll shoot anything approaching the coach. I *will* shoot to kill."

With eyes bigger than saucers, Caroline crouched between the dogs, sneaking sideway glances at the pistol in Anne's hand. The coachman was trying to bring the horses under control and stop the coach. One footman was trying to track the assailant, and another was on his way to find Sebastian and Sar.

"Caroline, tell your coachman to keep moving. No one is injured; it's best to go to the house. Trust me, both Sar and Sebastian will already be there, if not far behind us."

Caroline did as she was told. Then, for the first time in her life, she considered swooning.

"Look at me, Caroline. No, don't you dare faint. Stay down. I'll teach you how to shoot after the ball. I never go anyplace without *Bessie*." For the remainder of the ride through fashionable London, Her Grace rode shotgun.

The coach thundered into the drive. Sar and Sebastian were both there.

"Where are the girls? I need them here now, Sar." Anne had to see for herself no one was harmed.

"They're with Julien and Royce. I sent Perkins to bring everyone here."

"Examine the coach; get that damn ball out of the door. Find out what the coachman and footmen saw and meet us in the morning room."

Sar hated to think of how many near misses his mother had as a conductor of the Underground Railroad. She'd helped hundreds of slaves to freedom and had gone to the southern states on several occasions to lead runaway slaves to safe points. Without concern for her own safety, she put her life on the line for others. His mother, an underdog, championed the rights of those less fortunate and had become a target in England, all because she married his father.

Anne handed Caroline a snifter of brandy. "Drink it now."

A dazed Caroline gulped the amber liquid. Anne poured more. Within the hour, Sar and Sebastian joined them. The girls arrived with Julien and Royce. Berkley silently entered. Daggs was the last to appear. Caroline's color was restored, although she was a bit unsteady on her feet. Perkins didn't even attempt to eavesdrop. He stood inside the door. This time it was Seymour who stood outside with his ear glued to the door.

Berkley spoke first. "Considering what everyone saw and how this happened, it appears as though the shooter saw you and decided to take aim." Outside of the obvious, he wondered if there was something else. "Our men at the second house were murdered because they just happened to be in the right place at the wrong time. This may be the case with you."

Berkley hoped this was the situation, and he trusted he sounded convincing enough to those in the room, but his mind kept asking if there was more to this than being a mixed blood.

Daggs paced as usual. "Your Grace, who knew you were going to Bond Street?"

That thought lodged deep in the recesses of his mind popped to life: *He will think nothing of killing women.* Berkley might have soothed Caroline, but his gut instinct was telling him that the killer wanted Her Grace dead. By the looks of the other men and Anne, no one had believed the general.

"Inspector Daggs, here is a chair if you would care to sit." Anne looked directly at him and patted the seat next to her. He looked as though he hadn't slept in a week. Deep lines of worry and concern etched his face, though his neck cloth was as neat as ever, and he was faultlessly attired.

"No, no, I think faster when I am moving about. Did anyone know you were going shopping?"

"It wasn't exactly a secret. I'm not sure if Sar or Sebastian knew exactly where we we'd be today."

"Do you always carry a gun?"

"Always, Daggs, always." Anne handed Caroline more brandy.

***

Jacob kept looking at the statues in the basket, lifting them, and turning them over and over when his office door opened. In loped a magnificent curly beast. "She is a beauty, isn't she? Her name is Bella—ah, just what I came to see." The general pulled one of the statues out of the basket.

"Empty, from what Daggs tells me. Do you think we'll need to break them all?"

"If need be." Jacob was letting Bella sniff him. "Hello, beautiful girl. I need you to keep everyone here safe." As he petted her, he continued to whisper in her ear. "I'll introduce you to everyone in the office and have Rose make up a schedule so everyone has a turn walking you, so that you have the opportunity to get to know them. One day their lives might depend on it."

Bella plopped down at his feet, clearly understanding who her master was.

"I want to examine them closely," Jacob finished. "As the last resort, we'll break each one."

"Let's clear this up by Monday. She has the same commands as Sar's dogs. They were trained together. Until this evening." Without a sound, Berkley left.

Jacob put the statues back under his desk. Bella sniffed the basket and whined. "Oh, you want to go for a walk? Good girl. I'll take you myself."

***

After the events of the day, the dinner party turned into a very relaxed, informal gathering of the best of friends. The hostess was foxed, and by three-quarters of the way through the meal, so were most of those present. New friendships and bonds were formed. Besides the Duke of Grayson, there were the Duke and Duchess of Northampton, Marcus and Diana Ryerton; the Duke and Duchess of Carrington, Evan and Georgina Marston; and the Duke and Duchess of Edgerton, David and Aurelia Rothingham. The ladies had known each other since they were in leading strings and were now referred to as the "dragons-in-training" by those of society. The mantle of responsibility of the upper echelon was passing to them.

"Caroline, remember the time we caught the butler and cook kissing by the lake? We were ten years old and told everyone we saw. By the time we returned to the house, half of the county knew. How were we to know they married the week before?"

"Miriam, I don't know how you remember these things. My mother warned me to mind my own business, and she didn't let me ride my pony for two days. Cook didn't make me my favorite treat for a week. I went to the kitchen and offered to help her if she'd forgive me."

Caroline was glad her friends were with her this evening; she needed reassurance of good in life.

The Duke of Grayson chuckled out loud. Thoughts of his daughter brought a smile to his face and peace to his heart. Caroline never minded her own business, and it had always been that way. If she did, they wouldn't be sitting here right now, and she wouldn't have the massive head she was going to have in the morning. His family—nothing could be better than to have his Violet near.

Mer and Miriam spent the better part of dinner discussing the particulars for the sewing area. Miriam couldn't keep the excitement from her voice as she revealed her thoughts. "It must be designed to meet the needs of the sewers: adequate light, proper ventilation, and space. The hours cannot be taxing. If the workplace is comfortable and clean, the work will go more smoothly. Pay must be adequate.

"Creating sizes and patterns will revolutionize making clothes. Grayson's idea is ingenious. Next week let's meet at the store and go through the list of requirements for the workplace. I'll speak with the instructors at the school. Their experience has given them ideas for work areas which meet the needs of the sewers."

Miriam's mind was spinning—innovative ideas and revolutionary approaches, better working conditions, adequate pay. *We're blazing the way for change.*

When Mer looked up, she was staring directly into Julien's dark-green eyes. Her heart tripped. He smiled. She loved him. Would her heart ever stop breaking? The thought of him with another woman turned her stomach and her food dropped like an iron rock.

With a smile that didn't quite reach her eyes, she tried to continue as though nothing was out of the ordinary. "Julien created the physical workspace. Next week, let's go through the building. Julien, will you be available Tuesday morning?"

"I'm available anytime you need me. Why don't I pick you and America up at eight thirty? We can be at Paige's by nine."

His voice rippled across her skin like fine silk. Flashes of their afternoons in his bed, his mouth worshiping her breasts, and his tongue in a place no one had ever been before raced through her mind. She felt her skin flush. Need, craving, and hunger sprang to life. As if he knew what she was thinking, he arched an eyebrow and, with a wicked glimmer in his deep-emerald eyes, smiled.

She belonged to him, and no other man would ever touch her as he had. *Belonged to him? Yes, belongs to you. I'm glad you're facing it, old boy. You can't live without her. Your days as a rake are over.* He pushed that thought out of his head.

***

Dinner was over, and the men took their cigars and port to the terrace. The ladies sat in the garden.

"I want to help create Paige's. The time for ready-to-wear dresses is now. Women work, and they may not have a position which provides livery. I'll stop by Paige's on Monday." Diana Ryerton, the Duchess of Northampton, was mentally clicking off the things to do to make the shop special. The fiery redhead was already creating a look that said comfortable quality but not high society.

Aurelia and Georgina sat talking with their heads close together. "This is what we are going to do. Georgina will give the first ball or soiree after Caroline's. I'll give the next affair, Miriam after that, and Diana and Marcus will give their annual end-of-the-season ball. We'll confer and make each event spectacular. My mother will make sure Anne and her family receive vouchers for Almack's. Anne, will you teach me how to shoot?"

Aurelia, the Duchess of Edgerton, was also the daughter of

a duke. She'd run the family businesses and taken care of the estates when her husband was away during the war. Together, Caroline and she created Harson's. To this day, she still took care of the family businesses and the estates. Her husband David was partially blind and had lost his peripheral vision from injuries sustained in the war. He was like the rest of the men, honorable men in service to the Crown.

In less than a heartbeat, the Duke of Westmoure and his family were swept up in the protective bosom of the elite of society.

Anne laughed. "Are you sure you want to learn? I told Caroline I would teach her the Monday after the ball. Don't you think your husband will be concerned if you associate with someone who has shots fired at her? This is serious, ladies. Someone is trying to kill my son and me. Our entire family is a target; whoever it is won't stop until we've been eliminated. I won't put anyone else in danger. It's kind enough for you to do all that you are, but your safety is paramount."

"Anne, we own several of the largest companies in all of England. It'll be good to learn how to protect myself. You and your family are here because of a quirk of fate. I think all of us can be friends. Many people may not accept you because you are part Negro. The ton is a very strange animal. Society doesn't accept anything that's not like itself.

"The purity of their bloodlines has been pounded into their heads for generations, yet many of the men have illegitimate children throughout all of Great Britain—and to them it didn't matter who they slept with. Purity of lines, or the minor fact they were probably married when they begot these children, never entered their heads. They wanted. They took, because they knew most women didn't have any recourse or protection—no rhyme, no reason, just pure animal lust. I wish all of the children were recognized as legitimate. The children didn't cause the problem. Stay close to us. We'll all sail through this eventually. Now, about those shooting lessons . . ." Aurelia smiled.

Cigar smoke hung in the garden air, along with the sounds of hushed male voices.

"Berkley, I've decided to take the family to the country tomorrow, and we'll stay until next Thursday," Sar said. "We haven't been yet, and now is a good time. After what happened today, I want to give you and Daggs time to investigate with everyone out of the way.

"Julien, your family's home is next to mine. Will you be able to join us and bring Royce along to act as my additional eyes? In the country, I'll be able to control things better."

Having just made the decision to leave, no one else would know about the sudden trip but those present, and Sar wanted it that way.

"I'll send a couple of my men along. I hope this won't inconvenience your staff." Daggs moved his cigar through the air as though it was pacing. "This afternoon was probably not a preplanned act, but one of opportunity presenting itself. Her Grace is one of their next victims."

"So my speech of reassurance earlier wasn't as convincing as I hoped it would be?" Berkley sat in the shadows with only the embers from the tip of his cigar visible. Daggs was right. If nothing else, today's incident confirmed that Her Grace was one of their targets.

✳✳✳

In the dimly lit library of the house on Grosvenor Square, two men talked. "Where is the cargo?"

"No one knows."

"What do you mean no one knows?"

"No one knew of the change in the schedule. It's going about that the new captain read the schedule incorrectly. No one had any information. Everyone was working out of the office as normal, expecting the ship to sail on Monday."

"Where is the ship?"

"Not at Southampton."

"Find that ship. Someone knows something. There's always talk or someone willing to talk for coin. We must have that cargo. Bring me that rogue captain. Remember, in this game there are no coincidences."

Now alone in the silence, he reviewed everything. One of the others should know what happened. If not, this meant all but the inner circle was privy to what was being planned. He replayed the events in his mind: wrong shipping schedule, new captain, different crew, ship disappearing. No, not a coincidence at all, but a carefully executed Berkley or Daggs plan. They have the cargo, but would they know what they were looking at? He'd send a note immediately, and tomorrow he'd personally call on the Duke of Westmoure.

***

Perkins had everything ready for their departure by eight o'clock. According to Oliver, Cook had already left for the country to make sure all was in order for His Grace's arrival. The lavish morning meal she prepared was laid out on the sideboard.

"Good, we'll be able to leave shortly. Thank you, Oliver."

Of course, he knew Cook's plans. Part of his job was to know everything. As for Oliver, Perkins sensed he very much liked the duke and his family. He was doing everything possible to make life for them comfortable and show them what to expect from the house staff of a duke. Oliver even asked to be taught the fine art of eavesdropping. It was always good to have an extra set of ears.

A knock on Sar's study quickly brought his head up from the last-minute instructions he was writing. "Enter."

"Your Grace, may I have a moment, please?"

"Of course, Morgan." *This must be very difficult for him,* Sar thought, *so much upheaval since our arrival.*

"Last night I received a message; my only relative is very ill. I know it's customary to give notice, but it's necessary I go at once. I don't know when I'll be able to return. For everything to continue to run smoothly, I must resign my position."

"I understand." The death of his father was still raw in his heart, as were the memories of their hasty departure and journey to England.

"Would it be possible to ask for a reference? I apologize for any inconvenience, Your Grace."

"You served my uncle for twelve years. I'll have the letter written before we leave within the hour."

Sar finished the last-minute household instructions and reference letter for Morgan, including wages for six months. Giving an order to leave the knocker on the door, the duke and his family departed for the country.

Making sure he was leaving nothing behind, Morgan quickly loaded his belongings into the waiting coach.

❄❄❄

Alexius toyed with her toast. "Mother, I know the ball is only a few days away, and you need my help, but there is so much to do for Paige's. In order to meet our schedule, I ought to be in the country working with Mer and Beth. We're losing valuable time."

"A few days in the country would be ideal for all of us. Yesterday, to say the least, isn't an experience I wish to repeat. I'll complete the last-minute preparations for the ball and we can leave tomorrow. We'll see if your father can come with us."

Caroline thought about her sleepless night. Around dawn, determination had replaced fear. No one was ever going to catch her at a disadvantage again. *I will learn to shoot my own Bessie. And I will never ever drink that much again.* Before Seymour slipped her that vile concoction, there were little elves—no, big elves—stomping inside her head in precise rhythm, and her stomach rolled.

That afternoon, the Earl of Thornton called on the Duke of Westmoure, just to be told the duke was not in. He left his calling card and made his way to Westmoure's shipping office, only to receive the same response. He'd call upon the duke again tomorrow.

***

Sebastian, Daggs, and Berkley huddled around Jacob's desk looking at the statues. Bella was by his side.

"We should break the contents of a crate. Daggs, can you and your men do it today?" Jacob wanted to get to the bottom of this. So far, the ordinary statues were just that—ordinary. He hadn't been able to figure out why they were so valuable. Maybe only a few held something of value. "Before you break the statues, look at each one. There may be a mark we're missing."

Daggs was not pacing but carefully examining the statues. His mind's eye told him something was off. Mentally he played and replayed the opening of the crates over and over again. "We'll take care of it immediately. No one has started asking questions yet, but I wager this will change within the next twenty-four hours. We should close this office and move it to His Grace's house. When the questions start coming, someone will figure it out and start looking for another office. Whoever *he* is will look for Jacob first."

"My thoughts exactly," Berkley said, petting Bella. "Jacob, spend a little more time at the other office. Let's get this office moved and the ladies out of here today. I suggest the morning room at the back of the house. You'll know who enters and leaves."

Jacob placed the basket of statues back underneath his desk. Bella whined, and he patted her velvet coat. "Time to go for a walk, girl? Let me have Rose take you."

Daggs began pacing. "How long will it take you to get the office ready to move, Jacob?"

"With additional help, we can be packed by this afternoon."

"Done. My men will be here within the hour." Daggs was about to slip out the door.

"No, wait, I have a better idea." This time Sebastian paced as he spoke. "All of you know about Alexius's business. Let's move this office to Cummings. We can provide better protection if everyone is in the same place. Cummings uses three front rooms. Westmoure's can use the rooms on the other side of hallway. No one will think anything unusual of the ladies coming and going. I'll show all of you how to enter without being detected."

"Since everyone associated with the duke and this office is in danger, that might work," Berkley said. As events unfolded, more and more people were in danger. If one of the women were killed, it would haunt him the rest of his life. "Will this interfere with Alexius's business?"

"No, the house is set up to conduct business. The workers will enjoy the luxurious surroundings and being catered to by a very attentive staff. With Daggs's men there also, no one will be the wiser, only safer."

✻✻✻

Jack was at the shipping office, looking for the general. He had missed him. There was nothing unusual here, although the duke, Morgan, and Jacob were elsewhere.

Sebastian found Caroline and Alexius at home. "We're moving the real shipping office into your building, Alexius. If my instincts are correct, it's best for everyone's safety. I didn't ask you first, but I want you to know what I have done. Westmoure's will set up in the rooms opposite yours."

"Is everyone in danger?"

"Yes, Alexius, unfortunately. I don't know how long this will last, but it's necessary. Originally the idea had been to move the office to the duke's house. That wouldn't do; it would be an intrusion into the personal life of the duke's family. Secrecy is still important. The staff is being told they are working in a building which is an extension of Westmoure's. If you're uncomfortable with this arrangement, we can move your work here. It will minimize your presence at the office and the off chance of contact with the other workers."

"Everything should work as it is," she replied. "If I find it doesn't, we can always move things later. Mer, Beth, and I will use the back entrance; we can come and go without anyone knowing."

"Thank you, Alexius. Daggs is adding some of his staff for additional protection. You won't even know they're present, except when you see new footmen who look like pugilists."

When Sebastian had helped Alexius design the office, he'd insisted upon a back entrance that went directly into Cummings. The garden at the back of the house was cleverly divided in half by a wall covered in greenery, with a row of tall evergreen trees on both sides, and lush gardens. Even in winter, the private entrance looked like an enchanted forest of another residence. Unless you knew what to look for, the interior hallway looked like a solid wall of rich mahogany wood. This eliminated the need to go through any other areas of the house or someone unexpectedly walking into Cummings.

"Sebastian, I think we should join Anne and her family in the country tomorrow. Alexius can work; I can learn how to shoot. I'm buying a *Bessie* like Anne's."

Sebastian chuckled. "First, *Bessie* is the name Anne gave her pistol." Caroline's mouth formed an *oh*. "I think going to the country is an excellent idea. Alexius should also learn how to shoot. Are all of the preparations for the ball ready?"

"If we return by Thursday evening, everything will be ready by Saturday. Alexius already knows how to shoot. Julien and Royce taught her when she was fourteen."

This time it was Alexius's mouth that made a surprise *oh*.

"I promise both of you a *Bessie*. Can you be ready to leave by seven in the morning? I assume you have sent Anne a note telling her of our arrival."

Caroline nodded. Sebastian saw the wariness in her eyes. Yesterday was a shock and had brought her a little too close to the dark, ugly reality of being an operative. He sighed; she'd never be the same. It would take time, but he could ease her through it. *Leaning to shoot and some training will help.*

Miriam stopped by to see how Caroline was doing after her ordeal of yesterday.

"We're going to Anne's in the morning, and we'll stay until Thursday," Caroline said. "I'm going to learn how to shoot. I won't be helpless again."

"Do you think Anne would mind two more?" Caroline shook her head no. "Ash and I can be ready by morning. I'm going to learn how to shoot too. Ash thinks it's a good idea. The girls and I can also work on Paige's. I'll send Anne a note immediately. Caroline, I cannot stay a second longer if we're leaving in the morning. We'll be here by six forty-five."

The shipping office moved into the building housing the offices of Cummings. At Daggs's private office, statues were examined and broken. Nothing was found but glass and dust. Bella loved her new luxurious surroundings but continued to whine whenever she was near the statues. It was clear that she didn't like them. The why of it plagued Jacob.

One day later, a hunched man with a limp going under the name of Baron Elias Phineas Perkins boarded the *Liberty* in Liverpool bound for America.

CHAPTER 12

Ivy Hall

County Hampshire
Eight Days before the Ball

"It's from the *History of the Westmoures*." Beth snorted as she continued to read. "Honorable renegades. Ha, they were all rakes! This is what I was looking for. Listen! 'Ivy Hall, the ancestral seat of the Dukes of Westmoure, is made of pale-gray local stone, with ivy covering half of the manor house. The original square building has been added on to by every successive duke. Each brought his own personality to the family home which has produced a building with a mixed hodgepodge of additions, including turrets jutting out in different directions, connecting passages, and glassed enclosed conservatories.'"

As the carriage rolled down the lane that evening, the trees looked like tall soldiers standing sentinel, giving the impression there was a small town nestled at the end. The lane opened onto a meadow, and Ivy Hall sat in the middle. The circular drive leading to the front door was flanked by fountains and lush gardens. Taken as a whole, the mansion looked like a little village with the odd spire here or there.

Of the one hundred and fifty rooms, there were forty-six bedrooms, several receiving rooms, a dining room large enough to accommodate one hundred, an art gallery in addition to the gallery of ancestors, several libraries and studies, a morning room, a music room, two ballrooms, and numerous other rooms. The two-story entrance, topped with a dome of pale blue trimmed in gold, gave the illusion of being outside on a sunny, cloudless day. A massive double-sided staircase led to the family apartments and guest rooms. The duke's apartment, housed in the east wing of the mansion, overlooked the sea. Oriental and Aubusson rugs sat atop marble and hardwood floors.

Her Grace and the housekeeper, Mrs. Spencer, were discussing menus when two messages arrived. Caroline and her family were joining them, as were Miriam and Ash. Both notes said, *Coming to learn to shoot.*

"Mrs. Spencer, we're having company, the Marquess of Broadhurst and his family, and the Earl of Danford and his wife."

"Your Grace, the families have been friends for generations. If they're coming, the Duke and Duchess of Edgerton won't be far behind. You should also expect the Duke and Duchess of Northampton, and the Duke and Duchess of Carrington. If I may suggest, you might want to send an invitation asking them to join you."

"Thank you, Mrs. Spencer. We need to get those notes dispatched immediately. Do we know their favorite dishes and which rooms they prefer?"

"I'll check our menu cards and files. It will be good to have the house filled with guests again. I must let Cook and the rest of the staff know of their arrival. I'll send Oliver to you, so he can make sure the notes are dispatched at once."

The footman assisted Caroline into the carriage and inquired if she needed anything else to make her trip more comfortable. Seymour handed her the news sheet, opened to the Society News.

"Thank you, Seymour." As the well-sprung traveling coach headed out of London, Caroline read the latest gossip.

The London Daily

Society News

Once again, the Duke of Westmoure, the mixed blood duke, and his family are in the news. And yes, more shots, or should I say another shot rang out. From our reliable sources, the coach carrying the Duchess of Westmoure and the Marchioness of Broadhurst was shot at on Bond Street. Not only does someone want the duke dead, but it appears someone wants his mother dead also. Is it safe for anyone to be in their company, let alone actually befriend them?

At the afternoon soirée of the Countess of . . .

Sar worked in his study with the estate manager. It was a beautiful day in the country; fresh air, blue sky, and colorful blooms dotting the landscape. This felt more like home in America. It also felt safe. They'd left the dangers of the city behind. After visiting the tenants, he'd spend the afternoon with the family and meet his cousin Joycellyn and her mother. He wondered if they'd welcome the Americans, or anyone in the family.

Matthews, the estate manager, was a wealth of information about everyone and everything in the community. Frances ran a shop in the village. "Joycellyn usually helps; she's an artist. Everyone in the area knows they're relatives and accepts them. They lead a very quiet life. Very fine ladies indeed." Sar said nothing and continued the task at hand.

***

Mer threw off the bedcovers. Exhaustion and fatigue still claimed her, even though for the first time in days she'd slept through the night. *Maybe the country will be good for me. I won't have to run into Julien every time I turn around. This will be the place to learn to forget him and go on with my life.* With that thought, she turned her head into the pillow to muffle her sobs. Their time together was forever burned into her essence, the loss unbearable.

Beth had been to the stables, explored the gardens, and found the manmade lake before she sat down to breakfast. Several days ago, she'd thought London tedious. Now she sighed and grinned. Cummings and Paige's gave her something exciting to do, and they'd stepped deep into intrigue. She still worried about Mer, who lacked her usual sparkle. They hadn't talked about being mixed blood, Poppa's death, and all of the upheaval since then. It was unnerving, and she found herself somewhat off-center. She didn't know if Mer felt the same, but she was confused. *Who was she?* Pulling herself out of her blue mood with the thought of the challenges of work, Beth headed to the library.

***

Julien had another sleepless night. He'd come up with a plan, and bloody hell hoped it worked. If not, he'd be the walking dead for a long, long time.

Royce took one look at him and laughed. "Julien, old man, who is she? It has to be a woman. No one but a female ever affects you like that. When was the last time you slept? What opera singer can't you have? I'll put in a good word for you."

"Don't say a word, Royce; don't say a damn word."

Royce's smile became even bigger and wider. His friend was in love. He wondered about the mystery woman. Was she someone acceptable to the ton? Well, he'd have to carry on by himself. If this was any indication, Julien's days of being a rake were over. At twenty-nine, his best friend was succumbing to the parson's trap. *Better him than me.*

"Beth and I are working on the store this morning. Are you coming with me to Sar's?"

"Might as well." Julien stabbed the kippers on his plate.

To see her and to be with her in the same room was better than nothing. At the first available moment, he'd put his plan into motion. If the duke ever found out, he was a dead man for sure. And once again, he imagined what it would be like to be killed twice. When the duke was through with him, he was quite sure Her Grace would shoot his brains out.

❦❦❦

Beth had taken over one of the libraries as an office. Already, papers were stacked in neat piles on the desk.

"Good morning, Beth."

Royce stood at the door. For the first time, she realized how handsome he was. His six-foot-plus frame dwarfed the door. Rich, deep-ebony hair, worn a little longer than the current fashion dictated, broad shoulders, narrow waist, and muscular thighs and calves made her look twice and sigh. *A hero of a gothic novel.* When he married, some woman was going to be very lucky, very lucky indeed.

She blushed. "Good morning, Royce. Can we begin to determine the actual cost of making a dress? This will form the basis for the selling price. We think we know what price will attract buyers, but we'll have to see if we can make the dresses, meet that price, and still make a profit."

"The country is beautiful this time of year. Very different than London, isn't it?" he replied.

"Yes, it is. It reminds me of the gardens and woods around the house in New York. It's as though my father brought a little of this house with him to America." Beth wondered if she would ever come to think of England as home. Sometimes she missed America so much she cried, but going back was impossible. Her life and future were here in England.

"We'll have to factor in the cost involved in setup and designing the dresses also. I have the list of most of our costs up to now. Do you have the lease fee? We'll also make a list of the anticipated costs, and fill those in as we receive them. At least we can set up the ledgers."

Before Royce could answer, Julien's deep voice echoed through the room. "Where's Mer?" She hadn't noticed him standing next to Royce. "In the west garden."

"I'll get her."

Julien found Mer staring off into the distance, absentmindedly petting America. "Mer." She turned and looked directly at him. "Julien."

I will not give him the satisfaction of seeing me cry. She bent down again to pet the dog for her own comfort and to mask the tears forming in her eyes. Thank goodness America's woolly coat covered her tapping foot. Would her heart always break when she saw him?

"Mer, we need to talk." He was bumbling again. She looked tired and hurt. He knew the cause of her pain. "I apologize for what I said in the park." *Tell her you love her,* his inner voice chimed. "I've thought about what you said and . . . um . . . your offer to be my mistress." *This sounds so formal, less than passionate for the woman you want to hold forever.*

"You know one day I must take a wife, and I'll be faithful to her forever. I'll not keep a mistress." *That might forewarn her you are going to get rid of her at some point. Are you an idiot?*

"Until I marry, if you still want to be my mistress, I know we can work out a suitable arrangement." *You haven't told her that she's the one you are going to marry. You just told her she isn't suitable. Are you crazy? That's right; make it sound like a business arrangement. You'll be happy if she doesn't slap your face and call her brother out here now and have him kill you.*

Mer wanted to fly into his arms and stay there forever. However, forever was impossible. He just made that perfectly clear. One day he'd marry a proper woman of the ton. Now he was offering her what she wanted, but did she want to take it? Her heart was pounding.

"Mer, I want to see you smile again. I want to give you pleasure and see you pleasuring yourself. I desire you wild and passionate in bed. I need to hear you scream my name when you shatter. I'll teach you all I know about the pleasures between a man and a woman—and I will do everything possible to keep you from getting with babe. I'll be with you as long as possible." *You forgot to mention as long as possible would be forever.* "Please, Mer, I need you."

Julien was begging. He couldn't go on without this woman. If it took begging to get her back, then that's what he would do. *Good, keep it up. She may pay attention.*

His plan was to make her addicted to him. He had to become the drug she couldn't live without and the very air she breathed. No man would or could ever touch her as he. Mer belonged to him. *Mine. She is mine. Branded by me.* He'd make sure of that, even if he had to get her with babe to do so.

So, I lied to her about that part. If that's what it takes, that's what it takes.

For the first time, she felt hope—a sliver of hope. He needed her. Heat pooled in her stomach, taking the place of anxiety. She had what she asked for, but when he left, would it be too much to bear? He was already a part of her and would become more so if they continued. But what would she do without him? Was not a short time better than no time at all? *Won't I have these moments to hold fast to until the day I die? Or am I being foolish?*

As if she needed confirmation of Julien's effect on females of all species, America stood on her hind legs, put her paws on his shoulders, and licked his face—another one of his victims.

"Hello, America. How's my beautiful girl?" America let out a woof of pure delight. Mer swore the dog was grinning.

"I need time to think, Julien. How do I know you'll keep your word? In a blink, you might decide I am either not good enough for you or you want another mistress. I couldn't stand it if you left me for another woman before you married. That would just make me another one of your many conquests."

Tell her you love her. "Mer." It was on the tip of his tongue to say those three words, but they froze. Most marriages of the ton did not include love. They were arrangements. Could they have love?

"There will be no other mistress or woman until I wed. This I vow on my life. You will be my only one until then. I'm committed to you and only you. Once I'm married, there will never be another." And that strange sensation filled his chest again.

"I still need time to think about your offer."

This wasn't going as Julien planned. *Did you really think she would jump into your arms after what you said in the park? Why can't you just tell her you love her? Your days of being a single man about town are over, done. Your marriage doesn't have to be like the others of the ton.*

You've seen too much hate and deceit in the world, but it doesn't have to be you. Look at your parents. They love each other.

There was only one way to convince her. His senses told him no one was about. Pulling her into his arms, he started showing her what they have. His lips claimed her mouth; his hands laid siege to her body. He pulled up her dress and found the silk covering the curls between her legs. The fabric became wet. Pushing it aside, he parted her, found that magic spot, and rubbed lightly.

Mer swayed.

He whispered, "Tonight, meet me at the lake at midnight," and dropped her dress. "Shall we join the others? There's a lot to be done."

***

Anne was flitting about, waiting for Frances and Joycellyn. It was a terrible thing to be labeled illegitimate. People blamed the child who was not responsible for being born, and seldom thought ill of the man who sired the child. It was always the woman's fault for enticing, for being a wanton. She wondered what emotional scars Frances carried from the cruelty inflicted by Charles. Eleven years old and speechless for six years—the nightmare, the torture of being locked within the chamber of one's self, the horror. If Charles were alive, she would take great pleasure in shooting him herself. No man had any right.

According to Mrs. Spencer, Frances and Joycellyn lived in one of the houses on the estate. They were frequent guests of the late duke. The late duke's daughters would have nothing to do with them "because, you know . . ."

Sar had returned from visiting the tenants. Mer and Beth worked in one of the libraries. Their guests from London were arriving shortly. People were being murdered, and shots were being fired at her and those she loved. Now she was about to meet the woman who was violently misused by her husband's family. *Yes, I am nervous.* Anne wanted to laugh from the tension. Where was her duchess's magic wand when she needed it?

A huge wolfhound greeted Frances and Joycellyn with slobbering kisses; they instantly fell in love with the enchanting beast. Calling Duchess to her, Anne studied the women. Both were absolutely beautiful. At forty-two, Frances's blonde hair, curvaceous figure, and stunning smile would still turn many a head. Joycellyn inherited the best of her mother and parts of the aristocratic, Westmoure bearing—the famous Westmoure broad forehead.

Both curtsied. "Your Grace."

Anne rose and hugged them both. "Welcome, welcome. I am so glad to meet you. My name is Anne. Sar will be here soon. Oliver, will you ask the girls to join us?"

Perkins stood rock still as his heart plummeted into love. She was shorter than the average woman. Freckles dotted her face, and clear, blue eyes with a hint of melancholy gazed at him, along with a smile that didn't reach her eyes. He smelled the scent of rosewater as she passed. She was the most beautiful woman he had ever seen.

"Let me introduce you to Perkins. He is in charge of everything and knows everything before we do. Perkins, I would like to introduce you to our cousins, Frances and Joycellyn."

For the first time in his life, Perkins couldn't think of anything to say. His mouth wouldn't work, and his tongue stuck to the roof of his mouth. He barely managed a smile and was saved by Sar walking into the room.

"Cousins." He embraced them both.

Mer and Beth rushed in. "We're so glad to meet you." Mer hugged them both, until Beth pushed her aside.

"Excuse our informality. As Americans, we are much laxer than the British. We have a lot to learn about your society. Sar is my son who inherited the title when his father, my husband, died several months ago. You don't know us yet, but we would very much like you to be a part of our family. But you must know, to many in the aristocracy we are outcasts. We are Negroes, mixed blood. If you choose not to associate with us, we'd be disappointed but would try to understand. We can't force you to be a part of our family."

Anne was babbling and trying to find the right words to make them feel comfortable. She sensed they were as cautious and inquisitive of the family as the family was of them.

"Thank you for welcoming us to your family."

Joycellyn was curious about these people. They were warm and eager for them to become a part of the family. Did they mean it? Didn't they know what she was? Of course they did. They didn't seem to care. As a child of an unwed woman, she was the outcast and was labeled all that was unholy. *I'll carry the shame and disgrace of being a bastard all of my life.* As the illegitimate daughter of a brother of a duke, acceptance by polite company was never a consideration. *Will the new duke and his family also be ashamed of me and shun me when others are about?*

But the duke and his family were Negroes. The old duke had told her how Negroes were treated in America. Were the indignities Negroes endured like that of being a bastard? The question hung in the back of her mind.

"Mrs. Spencer told me you manage a shop in the village called Winters." Anne saw the fear and shame still lurking in Frances's eyes. *We'll work on making your eyes sparkle with joy,* she silently pledged. *Oh, Avery, what are we to do to make this right? Damn your brother.*

Old fears, anxiety, and hatred welled up from deep within. The scars festered. Trying to smile, Frances answered like an obedient servant, revealing little of herself. "The late duke asked me what I wanted, and I told him a shop. He trained me. When I was ready, he let me create Winters. On one side of the shop there are bolts of fabric and trimmings. On the other side are soaps, perfumes, and lotions. Joycellyn helps in the store, but she would rather be designing clothes and painting." Frances almost curtsied but stopped herself at the last second.

"Can we see Winters tomorrow?" Mer asked.

What a find—a mother and daughter team, manager and designer, and relatives! Unable to contain herself, Mer asked, "Have you ever thought about moving to London?"

Frances was taken aback with Mer's excitement and questions. "Of course you are welcome in the shop." An air of fear, shame, and something else was evident in her hesitation. "We are happy in the country. Except for my business trips to London, this is our life."

Without waiting to be announced, and in a most unladylike fashion and inappropriate manner, Alexius flew into the room.

"Alexius!" Beth rushed to hug her. "Mer and I didn't know you were coming. Come meet our cousins."

Anne, Frances, Miriam, and Caroline talked while the girls peppered Joycellyn with questions. As usual, Mer went directly to the point. "Show us your designs. We need to see them."

"Why the interest in my designs?" Joycellyn looked at each of them. Her heart was singing. *They want me to be a part of their family.* The late duke told her the American brother was kind and honest, and he'd been right.

"Let's talk about it after we see your designs." Alexius looked at Joycellyn. *Yes, she could possibly be our designer, but would they ever leave the country permanently?*

Dinner was a lively affair, with everyone swapping stories. Anne looked at Sar at the end of the table and saw Avery was standing next to him, smiling. She raised her glass in silent salute as a tear slowly trickled down her cheek. Perkins sat next to Frances, and Sar saw a side of him he had never seen before—Perkins trying to court a woman.

***

In London, the Earl of Thornton called upon the Duke of Westmoure, only to find once again he had missed the duke and Morgan.

Jacob was as confused as ever. The open crates revealed nothing. Whenever Bella was next to the statues, she whined.

"All right, Bella, let's see what we really have here."

He took the statues out of the basket and gave her the basket. She sniffed and plopped down. Then, one by one, he gave her the statues. She whined at each one she sniffed.

"I understand you don't like the statues, but why, girl? Tell me why."

Bella was his friend, one of his confidantes. Frequently, he held one-sided conversations with her, and she occasionally answered with a *woof,* a whine, or a lick. This time she looked at him, lolled her head to one side, and rolled over, requesting the requisite tummy rub, as though she was making him work for the answer.

"That's it, girl. I need to rub the statues!"

He found glaze remover and rubbed off the finish. Everything looked normal. He gave Bella the statue again. She sniffed, whined, and tried to knock the statute out of his hand.

"What do you want me to do, girl? What are you trying to tell me? We found nothing but shards and dust when we destroyed those other statues, shards and dust."

Seconds later, he went looking for tools. He settled back

behind his desk and sawed off the head of one of the figurines. Turning the headless figure upside down, he found his answer.

"Bella, let's go."

Daggs was in his office.

"Daggs, good to see you," Jacob said, slipping him the note.

The two kept up mindless patter for a few minutes and Jacob left. Daggs cautiously made his way to Whitehall. Within the hour, Daggs and the general were at the second shipping office.

"What have you found, Jacob?" They were at loose ends. The general hoped it was something that would begin to tie everything together.

"Watch!" Jacob removed the head of another statue and turned it upside down. White powder floated to the paper. He did the same again.

"My guess is that someone is bringing opium in from India. Whoever it is, is using the Westmoure ships to transport the opium out of England. As you know, this circumvents paying taxes to the Crown. If you can get opium into China, or any other country, in this manner, it's a very lucrative and illegal business venture. English ships carry kilos and kilos to China every year, despite the prohibition, protests, and opposition of the Chinese government. Westmoure ships are being used for smuggling."

Daggs and Berkley examined the power. Jacob was right: kilos and kilos of opium.

Daggs replayed the opening of the crates in his mind again. "There may be more to this than meets the eye."

At the mention of smuggling and circumventing the Crown, the hair on the nape of his neck started standing on edge. There was only one thing left—the crates.

"Let's go; we need to examine those crates again carefully." In Daggs's private office, the men studied the pallets.

"Irregular sizes are not unusual for crates, but something

isn't quite right about them. Let's take this crate apart," Daggs said.

For the next twenty minutes, they worked at tugging off the strapping. Daggs examined the sides and started pulling the various layers apart. "Here, this is what someone doesn't want us to discover. The sides are partially hollow. Inside there's enough room to slip papers or other flat objects. There's nothing in this one. On to the next."

They were on the fifth crate when Berkley found two dispatches: one from the Home Office and one from Quinn's, the Foreign Office—both highly sensitive documents, treasonable offenses. There was nothing in the last crate.

"Daggs, get the last of the statues emptied," Berkley said. "After the statues have been emptied, clean one and give it to Bella to see if she still whines. We don't want to miss anything. Have your men put the crates back together exactly as they were. Next week, take the crates to the original shipping office. Have the workers set them ablaze. In the next few days, let's see who comes to us. Whoever is behind this must have this cargo and will kill to get it. The hunt will intensify.

"Burning the crates at the shipping office will confirm we have them. This will also buy us time. Our traitors will think we burned all of the evidence. We're using their trick—*B* and *D*—burn and destroy. Be ready to leave for Ivy Hall at first light. I must speak to Quinn.

"Daggs, have your men make sure no one enters the second shipping office unless they're supposed to be there. Jacob, leave Bella with Rose. Tell her to keep Bella close. I assume everyone in the office knows her commands." As usual, there were no wasted words as the general made clear their next plan of action.

Berkley slipped out and headed for Quinn's office. He'd served with Ethan Quinn during the war, and both of them were still dedicated to the Crown. Quinn was his counterpart, the director of the Foreign Office. What he handled within England and most of Great Britain, Quinn handled with foreign countries. Frequently, their responsibilities and operations overlapped, as it would be with this. Only now they were looking for their own. The Home Office and the Foreign Office were deeply involved in espionage and treason.

His meeting with Quinn was brief and to the point. Their only goal: find them as soon as possible.

***

That evening in the opulent house on Grosvenor Square, two men sat. Neither was pleased. "What does Morgan have to say?"

"Morgan has disappeared. I went to the duke's house and the shipping office. He wasn't at either place. I went to his lodgings. According to the agent, Morgan received a note informing him his only living relative was very ill. He went to his relative's and didn't know when he'd return. He left on Thursday, two days ago."

"Do you think he's still in England?"

"Honestly, no. Should we try to find him?"

"Yes, and if you find him, kill him."

"Have you talked to the crew who works for us?"

"I'm meeting with them tomorrow."

"Find someone who'll talk for coin. Get the information, and then kill the person. They've moved the crates to another location. The captain of that ship?"

"He disappeared. The ship sailed for America from Liverpool today."

"So the ship was moved to Liverpool. Berkley and Daggs know about the cargo. The question is, do they know what they are looking at? We must find the crates immediately. They'll smash the statues and be none the wiser of the contents. Have you been able to locate Westmoure?"

"He hasn't been seen."

"And Whitehall?"

"There's no information we can get. Meetings are held elsewhere. Only Berkley, Daggs, Broadhurst, and Westmoure know what is going on."

"Have someone watch Jacob. He's in charge of the shipping office and will know where the crates are. Are you going to the ball on Saturday?"

"Yes."

"Report to me immediately after. I declined my invitation. Who would want to attend a ball introducing a Negro into society? Whoever heard of such foolishness as a Negro in society? What absurdity. Westmoure and his family will always be outcasts, just as they should. Such a ridiculous notion, tainting the aristocracy."

***

In the East End tavern, two men discussed Saturday night. "Is everything ready for Saturday?"

"Yes."

"There can be no mistakes or near misses. Make sure the duke receives the note during the ball ten minutes before the meeting."

"Meet me here afterwards."

***

Mer left by the backdoor shortly before midnight. The bright moon in a cloudless sky provided the backdrop for thousands of twinkling stars. America and she walked quietly to the lake.

She'd debated over and over again whether to meet Julien, but her double-crossing body betrayed her. He was as essential to her as a heartbeat, and she yearned for his caress and touch. Without him she wasn't whole. She pushed aside her thoughts of forever and cold lonely nights after he wed his proper wife of the ton; she wanted all she could take before that time.

Julien didn't know whether she would come. In the garden she wanted him, but was it enough to make her remember what they shared and risk meeting him? He had to become the drug she craved, the addiction she couldn't live without having flow through her veins. No other man would ever be able to satisfy her as he had. When he heard them before he saw them, he expelled the breath he didn't realize he was holding.

As she walked from the copse of trees through the garden surrounding the clearing by the lake, her breath caught. He stood like an Adonis bathed in moonlight. The moonbeams highlighted the broad expanse of his finely chiseled torso. Her body thrummed with anticipation as she approached him, taking in his magnificence, the body that belonged to her for a short time.

"Mer." His voice was like the touch of the gentle wind. "Undress for me."

Standing on the blanket before him, she couldn't refuse. He observed under hooded eyelids as she reached for the buttons on her bodice. Barely containing himself, he watched the ancient dance of seduction, a woman pleasing her man by slowly stripping layer after layer of clothing. He gasped as the last piece of clothing slipped to the ground. She was more beautiful than before. Mer stood like an elusive goddess offering herself to him in the shadows of light from the moon and stars. He saw her shudder from the cool air and what he prayed was anticipation. She skimmed her hands over her naked body in an open invitation for him to touch her. Tonight, he had to pleasure her over and over again.

"Don't touch yourself." He gazed at every part of her body, taking ownership. She was a bewitching goddess waiting for her lover, legs parted, begging to be filled, loved, and fulfilled. "You are so beautiful. Tell me what you want, Mer."

"Julien, I can't breathe when you are near me like this. I wanted to pleasure myself as you taught me, but I waited for you, for us . . . together. My nipples are hard and longing for your mouth."

She rolled a nipple in her fingers. My God, where or how did she learn how to tempt a man so? The fierce need in him kicked in. He sucked and licked her fingers as she stroked his arousal with her other hand.

"You are so beautiful. Spread your legs a little more. Let me worship your body. Let me do this, Mer. Don't touch yourself."

"Julien, I need you." Her hands ran over her body again, and she rubbed her sex.

He touched the parted folds and she jerked. "What is it that you want, Mer? Tell me. I need to bring you pleasure. Do you want me? Tell me."

She was heady with desire. The wind brushed her like flickers of fine kisses, caressing every part of her body, heightening her nerve endings. She shivered. "Julien, I need all of you." She ran her hands over his body.

"I can see you won't let me pleasure you. Your hands are busy. I need to take care of all of you tonight," he said. "Let me; let me teach you more." He gently tied her hands behind her back with his neck square. "Let me give you everything you crave."

She stood there looking directly at him. She was helpless. With her legs parted and her hands tied behind, her breasts thrust forward, and puckered nipples strained toward him for attention.

"Oh, my beautiful Mer." He got down on his knees in front of her; her scent was driving him mad with something more than longing. He parted her and found her sex with his fingers. "You are already wet and ready for me."

Parting her more deeply, he found that special spot with his tongue. She felt his hot breath, the cool wind, and moved closer to him. He swirled, nipped, and tasted. "Listen to the sound of your nectar, Mer. You are wet and wanting." He tasted.

She threw her head back in unbridled ecstasy. "More."

He eagerly and willingly obliged. He found her nipple huge and ripe. It pebbled at his touch. She spread her legs wider as her hips began a rhythmic rise and fall—the mating call. He brought her to the brink and pulled away. Kissing her stomach, swirling his tongue in her navel, he worked his way up her fevered body, caressed a nipple, and suckled.

"The other too."

He chuckled. "I will take care of all of you."

He pulled on one nipple with his lips and covered the other with his hand and rolled it to a hard peak. His other hand roamed her body and found her dripping folds. Lips laved her nipple. What he was doing with his tongue, he did with his fingers. He brought her to the brink again and pulled back. His hard, stiff rod was throbbing from need.

"Look what you do to me, Mer. If you were able to touch me now, I'd spill my seed."

She looked. His manhood jerked; she loved knowing she had this effect on his body. He kissed her inner thighs and found the curls between her legs again. He parted her with his tongue. She swayed. Her hips arched. He feasted anew.

"Julien, I can't hold back much longer."

"Let me untie your hands, my sweet, but you must promise not to touch yourself."

"Julien, I need more now." She was so lost in the throes of passion that she was unaware his fingers had replaced his tongue.

"I need you to kneel."

He helped position her while caressing her breasts. Then he entered her from behind, his thighs outside of hers. One hand found her mons. His other arm braced her and brushed her nipples as he rode her. The abrasion set her aflame. She couldn't think and was reaching the point where the world stopped. He knew she was about to shatter; she tensed and tightened as her contraction started pulling him into oblivion. He withdrew, entered again, and rubbed her where they joined.

"Come, my sweet, pull me into you. That's it, Mer, give me more."

She pulled him in deeper and deeper. Her muffled scream of satisfaction enveloped them. He held her as she drained the last of his seed. Totally sated, they let the cool air wash over them.

"There's much more, Mer. Let me take the time to show you. Think about us during the day and before you go to bed. If I cannot be with you and you desire me, you can bring yourself to that point and climax. Just think of us."

Bloody hell, he was giving her the tools to become a total wanton for him. Thinking about him, knowing how to satisfy herself, and remembering their passion was bound to set off an avalanche of want, craving, and desire. Her nerve endings would be taut, and she'd be on the verge of shattering whenever he was near.

"It's getting late. Get dressed. I'll walk you part of the way and watch until you and America are in the house."

What he wanted to do was make love to her again. His stiff arousal pushed into her. She felt him, found his hand, and led it to the apex of her thighs. His fingers opened her.

"It's late. The house staff will be up soon," he said, but she rolled on top of him and took him in. He couldn't resist. She arched, and he found the spot and rubbed. She leaned forward and put a nipple in his mouth. He was lost. Up and down she rode, setting the pace. Frenzied with desire, Mer was unaware of anything except their joining. He let her pull him in deeper still. She tensed and squeezed. He lost all thought, and captured her mouth as he spilled his hot liquid into her womb and caught her moans.

The thought of withdrawing never entered his mind. He wanted her big with his child, and the sooner the better. If she was increasing, she'd have to marry him. *Knowing Mer, she'd think I married her out of obligation and didn't love her. Something has to be done soon to prove my love . . . yes, prove my love.* He craved and wanted pleasure like this forever. When had the tables turned? She was his addiction; she was a drug flowing through his veins. He'd die without her. The armor around his heart shattered and a strange feeling filled his inner being.

Mer couldn't deny him herself. She belonged to this man and refused to think about the ending: his marriage and the other woman. *No one could ever love him as much as I.* She hoped the memories warmed her on cold, loveless nights amidst her longing and tears.

CHAPTER 13

Ivy Hall's Unexpected, Distinguished Guests

"Just think of the last time your husband made you angry, and then aim for his favorite part of his anatomy."

In their first shooting lessons, Anne was using the easiest possible way to teach Caroline and Miriam to focus. Soon, fingers, limbs, and various other parts were missing from the targets.

"Shooting someone is serious business. It's very difficult to shoot another human. Always remember in situations in which guns are used, someone is going to get shot. Don't play the victim, and don't think twice if the situation calls for it. Never threaten to shoot anyone unless you intend to do it. You have the advantage. Most men don't expect a woman to be able to shoot at all. It is not ladylike." Anne laughed. "Remember, death isn't ladylike either."

The girls joined them, and they squared off in teams to compete. "We'll challenge the men before we leave."

Lunch was interrupted three times with the arrivals of Aurelia, Georgina, and Diana. For the first time in eight years, the house was brimming with sounds. Cook had outdone herself. Oliver was pleased. The house was as it should be, filled with people. The staff could shine.

"I shall escort the ladies to the village," Perkins said. "We'll return in time for tea."

The thought of seeing Frances again made his heart turn upside down. He might as well keep the ladies safe and see his heart's desire at the same time. There was little else to do in the country.

No messages had arrived from London yet. Besides, this would give him time to think and sort things through. Different surroundings always brought new ideas and theories.

Three coaches filled with ladies and dogs descended on the village of Winchester that sunny Saturday afternoon. Villagers stopped to gape at the new duke's family as the line of coaches wound its way through the streets.

Entering Winters was like walking into any one of a number of fine shops in London. The warm, creamy yellow of the interior was offset by vases of fresh flowers and displays of perfume, soap, and lotion decorated with trimmings and flowing curling ribbons. Fabrics were artfully arranged along walls displaying the richness of their colors and textures.

"These are our cousins, Joycellyn and her mother, Frances." Anne introduced them to Georgina, Aurelia, and Diana.

Diana, Caroline, Georgina, Anne, and Frances moved about the store, discussing the layout and rearranging things for better effect. Perkins hovered near, in order to lend a helping hand and stay as close as possible to Frances. The others cornered Joycellyn, demanding to see her designs.

Joycellyn's studio behind the store was lined with exquisite watercolors. "Wait until Diana sees these; she'll buy them all." And then Miriam came to an abrupt halt. She was standing in front of one of the most elegant dresses she'd ever seen.

The ivory satin-silk sleeveless dress fell straight to the floor. Instead of ribbon, the bodice had a band of deep blue and green gemstones. Gemstones were sprinkled throughout the dress. The vee-neckline bodice was held up by one-inch shoulder straps secured with blue and green gemstone brooches, which matched the band of the bodice. The back plunged to a deeper vee, and the gemstones in the band of the bodice continued down the center of the back of the dress to the end of the foot-long train.

The matching long-sleeve jacket had a stand-up ruffle collar and ruffled sleeves. Blue and green gemstones lightly covered the jacket. On the back was a three-inch band of gemstones which extended from the middle of the shoulder to the bottom edge of the jacket and matched the band of stones trailing down the back of the dress in width and position.

"Exquisite, Joycellyn. Simply exquisite." Miriam examined the stitches closely. "May we please see your other designs?"

Joycellyn's work was too couture for Paige's, but not for the ton. Society ladies would beat down her door, stand in line, and scratch each other's eyes out to be seen in one of her elegant creations.

The others joined them in the back. Diana's breath caught when she saw the watercolors.

"Winters is incredibly beautiful. Frances, I'm speaking for all of us. We need you and Joycellyn in London. I suggest we close Winters for the afternoon and discuss this over tea. What we are going to tell you may come as a pleasant surprise."

Perkins's thoughts were so clouded with Frances that he didn't know whether he was thinking clearly. Every time he shifted the pieces of the puzzle, Frances appeared in the center. The clatter of a carriage rolling quickly by the store caught his eye. He glimpsed Jacob, Berkley, and Daggs barreling towards Ivy Hall. Raising his hand slightly, he got Beth's attention; she nodded. Giving the footman orders and putting America and Duchess *en garde*, he headed for Ivy Hall. A few minutes later he pulled alongside the coach, gave them a salute, and raced ahead.

Conversation rose to a fever pitch of pure excitement as the plans for ready-to-wear dresses and Paige's were revealed. Miriam thanked the heavens above for her knowledge about sewing.

Pausing for a second, Miriam collected her thoughts before she spoke.

"Joycellyn, your individual designs for commissioned dresses are too elegant for Paige's. You're more than capable of creating and designing dresses for ladies of the ton. We need help in creating the ready-to-wear dresses, the patterns, and sizes. Once we get the basic concept of sizing developed and the reusable patterns made, the ready-to-wear dresses can be easily duplicated. Then you can turn your attention to making the ladies of the ton envious of those who are fortunate to wear your dresses. Your work rivals the finest I've seen in Paris. Your talent can best be used making the ladies of the ton jealous of each other.

"There's a lot to figure out. No one has ever created ready-to-wear dresses. We're the first. We'll be setting the standard for others to follow, including good working conditions, decent hours, and adequate pay."

Somehow Mer had to say the right thing to persuade them to move to London. Mer examined the dress as she talked. The dress was beyond beautiful; it was the perfect wedding dress. A dress she'd never wear. Mer tried to focus on business, but she could feel the tears forming in her eyes. She was nothing but a mistress—never a bride, never a wife.

At some point in time she'd be abandoned by the man she loved, a man who would be faithful to the woman he married. Trying to distance herself from the pain of her future, she kept talking.

"Word will spread if we treat our workers fairly. Sewers will inquire about work; customers will know they are supporting their own . . . working women." She inhaled deeply. "Where's Perkins? We need to start back."

"He left some time ago to return to Ivy Hall," Beth said. "By now he has told everyone we won't return for tea." The signal Perkins gave Beth was one used by conductors of the Underground Railroad: *must go immediately, something urgent has come up.*

Mer kept talking. It pushed the inevitable to the far recesses of her mind—her bleak lonely future. "We need to create soaps, lotions, and perfumes for Paige's also. The simple pleasure of a fragrant bar of soap or rich luxurious lotion makes one feel special. How long does it take to get this done?"

"I love the idea," Diana said. "I think everything should be out of the ordinary for the ladies who shop at Paige's. With each sale, gift a small bottle of lotion or a small soap square, and serve tea while women are waiting for alterations. The customers will become familiar with the scents, luxurious lotions, and accustomed to the friendly service. When they can, they'll buy or ask for lotion and soap as presents. This will be an added plus to keep them coming back to see what's new. This is just the beginning."

She continued to take in the feel of Winters. "The soaps, perfumes, and lotions make the shop smell heavenly. Joycellyn, are your paintings in the back for sale?"

"Yes."

"Would you take one hundred pounds for all of them?"

"One hundred pounds?"

"That's not enough? All right, two hundred pounds."

Joycellyn was stunned. "Diana, one hundred pounds is more than enough. Don't you think it is a bit much?"

Miriam laughed; no, she caught herself actually giggling. "Diana, give her the two hundred pounds. I knew this was going to happen the moment you saw those paintings."

"Work will start on Paige's the Monday after the ball," Caroline said. "Joycellyn, you and your mother are expected to attend. We'll talk about your move to London next week." Joycellyn's sobs caught Caroline off guard.

Between tears, Joycellyn tried to talk. "You . . . you don't understand. I am the . . . um . . . um . . . illegitimate child of Sar's dead Uncle Charles—a bastard." Tears flowed from pain and shame.

"May Charles forever rot in the hottest part of hell. You're expected at the ball." Caroline wondered why a grown man would force himself upon an unwilling woman, let alone a child.

With a slight movement of her body, Frances seemed to back away from the group. Anne glanced at her and could have sworn for a split second the look on her face was pure malevolent hate. Whatever was there had been quickly masked with a smile. Shifting her way, Anne picked up on an unspoken thread of apprehension—scars from Charles's abuse. Frances still carried them.

While working on the Underground Railroad, Anne had come in contact with women who had been abused by men. There was a hollow look in their eyes—vacant, no light, just fear. It was as though they were disconnected from their feelings. Anne cried silent tears for the humiliation suffered when white men forced themselves on Negro women. The woman had no one to defend her honor and integrity. To the men, she didn't have any honor; she was nothing. Anne would be dammed if she was going to allow her daughters to be abused.

Would her thoughts always drift back to America and the constant state of danger they lived in? *Avery, we did what we had to do to protect our family. Didn't we?*

Beth's voice snapped her back to the present. "Frances and Joycellyn are family. No sense in hiding this fact. I suggest we give the ton more to talk about, and the ball is the perfect place to start the gossip wheel spinning. It's apparent we're the talk of the ton anyway."

The resilience of her daughters amazed her once again.

***

In the library at Ivy Hall, Sebastian, Julien, Royce, and Sar awaited the arrival of the carriage racing to Ivy Hall. Perkins lurked about somewhere. The door to the library opened. Oliver was about to announce them when four gentlemen swept in, smiled at him, and closed the door.

"Nice job, Perkins."

Berkley thought he heard in *sotto voce*, "Thank you, my lord."

"Sebastian, Royce, Julien." Quinn was shaking their hands. "In the thick of it again I see. Good to see you. Your Grace, I'm Quinn." Quinn was taking measure of Sar. Berkley had filled him in on the American duke, but like all good operatives it was necessary to make his own assessment.

"I am Sar." Without hesitating, he turned to Jacob. "I assume you've found something." Quinn chuckled to himself. *The man is pure duke. He dismissed me as though I was an underling.* Quinn reminded himself to stay on the duke's good side. "Yes, Sar. I think it best if we sit. This will take some time."

The door opened, and food was brought in. Decanters were placed within easy reach. In the kitchen, Cook was singing. Mrs. Spencer told her there would be twenty-six for dinner. Oh, how she loved the new duke!

"Is there anything else, Your Grace?"

"Oliver, we aren't to be disturbed." Oliver quickly left the room to allow Perkins to become one with the door. "Let's hear it, Jacob."

"Remember how Bella whined whenever the basket of statues was near her? It was clear she didn't like them. But why? They were just ordinary statues. After taking the glaze off one and letting her sniff the statue, she still whined. We smashed an entire crate, and all we had were fragments and dust. I sawed off a head and turned the statue upside down—opium. Someone is shipping opium to other countries using our ships to transport the contraband out of England.

"I contacted Daggs and Berkley. Daggs thought there was something more. Something wasn't right about the crates. I kept visualizing the six of them. Something appeared off."

Daggs's pacing had already taken him around the room twice. "We took a crate apart and found a hollow opening in each of the sides, an opening large enough to hold a document or flat item."

Berkley continued without missing a beat, "In the fifth crate, we found two documents, both highly sensitive items— one from my office and the other from Quinn's, the Foreign Office. Sar, your ships have been used for smuggling contraband and espionage. It's fortuitous we discovered this."

The hard glint was back in the general's eyes. "We have spies in the Home Office and Foreign Office. They're working together. And, there's little doubt that at least several members of the aristocracy are involved. God only knows who else. I thought it best if Quinn joined us." Berkley refilled his glass.

Quinn stood and walked to the fireplace. "Gentlemen, the first thing we must do is find the lynch pin between the two offices. When we find that person, we'll be able to get to the others. In my opinion, someone very close to the late duke who was privy to all of the shipping information is also involved. That person passed the information to the contact.

"We know George Mason gave information to someone. Working in the Home Office, Mason would have been able to gather information, spy, and act as messenger to someone higher up in the scheme."

Berkley gazed out the window onto the flowing fountains and lush gardens. The last time he'd stood here was a decade ago. Then they had discussed the use of Westmoure's ships for the war effort, and here he was again dealing with another Westmoure duke, the American who had been ensnared in a web of espionage, smuggling, and murder for reasons unclear to him, except one: his lineage. Every instinct in his body told him there was more. But what, and why?

Daggs took another sip of brandy, then said, "There's also a go-between, someone who can come and go without question in either office. One other thing . . . I, like Sar, believe we are dealing with separate crimes. The first is the murder of the duke's father, the attempted murder of the duke, and the eventual murder of the entire family. The second is espionage and the smuggling of contraband. And maybe a third: the attempted murder of Her Grace."

Their discussion was tense and urgent. As they comprised the list of names of people close to the former duke and those who could walk in and out of both offices without question, they also realized without a doubt there was one person close to the late duke who could get information to those involved in smuggling and espionage: Morgan. The other list was quite long. Upon Berkley's return to London, he'd have George Mason detained for questioning, and his men would bring Morgan back from his relative's. Sar's cousin Harold appeared not to be involved.

That left nothing but more questions and few leads.

"Gentlemen, I haven't been here for years. Sar, do you mind if I walk in the gardens?" Quinn needed time to think; time to shift the pieces again, mix them up and see what fell into place. There was no better way to think than while walking in a gorgeous bit of nature with a profusion of colorful early blooms and fresh air.

"No, not at all. Dinner is at seven." Quinn left through the terrace door. "Tell me, Berkley, was my uncle an operative too?"

"We all do what we can for our country. I for one am going to ring for a bath. Until dinner." "There's no need to ring for a bath. You said it, and Perkins is already seeing to it."

"Sar, if you ever find you don't need him, send him to me."

The general neither saw nor heard Perkins, but his bath was indeed waiting for him.

Daggs paced as he sipped on the amber liquor. "It seems you hit upon it at the time of the fire, Sar—separate crimes— and I'll go one step further. These crimes originally started out unconnected, but somewhere along the way the lines will cross, if they haven't already. Someone is very well connected."

***

In London, Jack attempted to stand up. Blood trickled from his head. He staggered and fell forward again. He had to stay awake and get up. How long had he been here? He crawled to the front of what appeared to be an alley. Someone would find him. Where was George Mason?

Blackness pulled him back into its depths.

In a nondescript black coach, George Mason thought of his new life in America and what he was leaving behind. He would be second to none again. Each turn of the wheels brought him closer to Southampton and the ship to take him away from the aristocracy and England.

***

Around the dining room table at Ivy Hall, conversation was light and lively. No one would guess there was anything more important than the weather and its effects on the *al fresco* luncheon planned for after church. As soon as possible, Anne would have a private conversation with Sar. Something had happened; the air crackled with tension. Having Daggs, Berkley, and Quinn as house guests until Monday was in itself sufficient to call out the cavalry and the navy. They didn't leave their offices unexpectedly to journey to the country unless it concerned a matter of grave national importance. Before the ladies left, she'd make sure they'd be able to seriously harm anyone who threatened them. Anne felt the urgency down to her toes and smiled at her son.

Mer sat next to Julien, and his hands roamed the lower part of her body while she ate. Going to the lake tonight would be impossible. There were too many people about, but he'd make her think only of him and their stolen passion-filled moments. She burned wherever he touched her and didn't know how to continue the conversation with Julien's father. *What had he just said?*

Frances and Joycellyn were swept up within the group, as though they had known everyone all of their lives.

The men left the women for their port and cigars. Along with five wolfhounds, the women strolled in the gardens. The men never rejoined the women; no one asked why.

Early Monday, Jacob, Daggs, Berkley, and Quinn returned to London. After their shooting lesson, the ladies set up offices in two adjacent rooms: one for Cummings and the other for Paige's. Everyone ran back and forth between the two, making plans for the new store and taking care of the day-to-day business of Cummings.

Sketch after sketch littered the floor where Joycellyn

worked. "We want simple and stylish, yet practical. What do you think, Alexius?"

Joycellyn and Frances were moving to London immediately. Joycellyn's responsibilities included designing the ready-to-wear dresses and creating patterns. Frances would be in charge of Paige's.

Another store and dresses to design. Well, what do you think of that, Sir Duke? The sudden abundance in her life kept her mind spinning with thoughts of what was and what was to be. Sir Duke, the name Joycellyn called the late duke, told her the American family would accept them. She hadn't believed him. *I know you know what's happening. I really have a family. Thank you.*

Memories of the past assaulted her. For the first six years of her life, a wild-eyed woman called Mother grunted at her. Joycellyn had spent most of her time with Cook and Mrs. Spencer. When her mother started talking again, the late duke put her in the school room, and Joycellyn joined her. Under the same strict tutor, they were educated as though they were sons of a duke.

Once her mother's formal education was completed, Sir Duke taught her about running his business empire and his estates. During the last years of the duke's life, she learned everything about Westmoure Shipping and ran the company. Together, they created Winters. He gave it to Frances "for the shame of my brother that I can never undo, and so you will never be at the mercy of another." Joycellyn was holding his hand when he died.

***

In London, Jack was in his bed being attended by a physician.

"It's a concussion, and I'm afraid he has amnesia. There's no doubt his pain is severe. I'm not dosing him with laudanum;

he needs to stay awake as much as possible. He needs rest—total rest. Have someone take him to the baths by the sea in Brighton. That may help. These cases are tricky. You never know when or if the memory will return." Dr. Stanley Altman could only hope for Jack's eventual recovery.

Berkley nodded as he sensed another piece of information slipping from his grasp.

***

At Ivy Hall, it was late Monday afternoon before Anne, Mer, and Beth found Sar by himself. "Sar, you do not have two of the government's highest officials suddenly show up for dinner at your house in the country and stay two nights," Anne said. "Something has happened, and it's serious. Your sisters and I need an explanation."

There was no way around it; they had to know. "It appears there are two or three separate crimes. Of which, we are either indirectly involved or the targets."

As he told them what he'd learned, he fought the urge to take everyone to Scotland until the danger had passed. "We have to carry on as though we know nothing of the shipping crimes and proceed with extra caution. We walked head-on into danger."

***

In the north of England, a young aristocrat snarled. At the age of thirty-three, the evidence of extreme excesses was beginning to show. The veins of his bulbous nose made his sagging jowls more prominent and accented his expanding stomach.

"She must die. He is old, and damn it to hell, he can't leave his fortune to a stranger. Next time don't miss. We'll keep him alive until she's dead. From now on, no one is to enter the old man's room without my permission. He'll never know." His stomach churned just thinking about the unentailed fortune slipping through his fingers.

In another part of the mansion, the cook, butler, and physician were helping an old man escape through a secret passage. They had a long journey, but if this was the last thing he did, it had to be done. They were saying good-bye to their home forever. Regardless of the outcome, there could be no return. He prayed he'd live long enough to reach London. He'd forever be in debt to the late duke.

CHAPTER 14

The Ball

Daggs was already pacing by the time Berkley arrived at the duke's house. "I sent an escort to bring Morgan back. I'm beginning to think he played a pivotal role in supplying information to the traitor in Whitehall and the person responsible for the murder of Sar's father. Morgan may be able to connect us to a go-between in Whitehall and the Foreign Office."

But why had Morgan turned on his employer? Another question without an answer and nonexistent clues.

Every way they turned, Berkley felt they were running into brick walls. The web of deceit became more entangled and was spreading like an epidemic. And there was the other obvious conclusion—a carefully laid plan in effect for some time.

"As you know, Jack was watching George Mason. Someone got the better of him. He is at the baths in Brighton under the care of a physician. He has amnesia and doesn't remember a thing. George Mason can't be found. As soon as Morgan is returned, we'll begin to put the pieces together. Someone is trying to find the cargo. Jacob is being followed. He is aware of this and not going to Cummings. We'll see if their man leads us to someone in the next few days."

"Someone had to start looking for the cargo. It's far too valuable to dismiss as an incident of the pitfalls of business." Daggs paused in his pacing to look at the drizzling rain. "If each incident is a separate crime, is there a common thread? What are we looking for here?"

They discussed final plans for the ball and joined the ladies for tea. Berkley occupied most of Anne's time, regaling her with stories of his misspent youth and watching her smile. Mer slipped Julien a note: *Ten tomorrow night in the library.*

***

That evening in the other opulent Mayfair house, two people discussed the ball on Saturday night.

"Are you sure everything is ready?"

"Yes."

"Our man knows what he is to do?"

"He knows what is to be done."

"Make sure he never sees Sunday."

"I'll do it myself."

"This mixed blood shall not survive and be a part of our world, the disgrace and the shame."

"Thank you for standing up for what is right. I love you."

***

On Saturday, Sar, Anne, Sebastian, and Caroline made their way to the royal residence. They were the talk of everyone present.

"Your Majesty." All watched as Anne bowed flawlessly before the king.

"Your Grace, a mixed blood from America. That should make things very interesting around here. From what I hear, people are a little upset." His Majesty laughed. "Knew the late duke very well. It's a time-honored name. Let's hope you don't disgrace the family." Anne was dismissed.

Anne sighed with relief. "Well, that's over."

"Your conversation will be repeated over and over again and embellished along the way," Caroline said. "We won't recognize the *tête-à-tête* when we hear it again. You were perfect, Anne. He didn't have to receive you at all. Now, *that* would have spread through the ton quicker than the blink of an eye. There have been times His Majesty snubbed people presented to him. He simply turned away."

Caroline cleared a path to make their way to the side of the room, so they'd be able to easily leave as soon as possible. She'd anticipated the possibility of His Majesty giving Anne a direct cut, and had a rather dramatic backup plan, which included a faint worthy of the stage. *Thank God that didn't happen.* Recognition, even with the cloaked warning, gave Anne royal approval and paved the way for acceptance by the ton.

Every eye in court followed them around the room. Whispers behind fans and discreet glances let Anne know Caroline was correct. The mixed-blood American duchess was definitely the only talk of those present.

"Lady Caroline, Lady Anne."

Both turned to see Diana, Georgina, Aurelia, and Miriam coming in their direction from the opposite side of the room. Making sure they had the entire room's attention and with all the grace and hauteur of their aristocratic bearing, the four ladies of the elite of the ton slowly glided across the room.

"We just wanted to give everyone something else to gossip about. As soon as one and all accept you have our support, we can leave." Diana laughed as she talked. "We couldn't let you face this den of vipers alone and miss all the fun, now could we?"

Fans fluttered more rapidly as the entire room shifted and inched closer step by step to the group to hang on every word overheard.

That evening, Sar and his family dined with the Marquess and Marchioness of Broadhurst and thirty others before the ball. He didn't know what the others were thinking, but the undercurrent of tension running through the dinner conversation suggested everyone was worried. Someone's life could end within the next few hours. All of them were targets.

The receiving line stretched down the stairs of the Marquess's house. Everyone who was anyone was there to meet the new Duke of Westmoure. Two ladies with elaborate masks greeted each guest. Caroline laughed at the comments she overheard and the deceit the men had put into play. To their disappointment, Westmoure wouldn't be introduced until midnight. To make it harder to figure out who was Westmoure, six men were dressed identically alike in dark-brown trousers, threadbare shirts, dominos, and a dark-brown hat pulled low over their eyes. Being similar in height and build, there was nothing to distinguish one from the other.

Lady Hortense Horton was the last to arrive and make her way through the receiving line. All attention turned to her. Everyone in the far corners of the ballroom heard hard-of-hearing Lady Horton's conversation with Anne and Caroline.

"So, this is the mixed blood. I was expecting a dark savage. Don't know much about you people, although you are a pretty thing. The ton doesn't like to think of itself as anything but pure—pure bloodlines. Well, we all know that is impossible." She laughed.

Openly assessing Anne, she inched closer. In a stage whisper for the world at large to hear, and worthy of Covent Garden, she declared, "I think you'll do. You'll stir things up a bit. Call on me tomorrow." Fans fluttered around this latest bit of gossip. Before dawn, all of London would know.

"Lady Horton is the queen of the ton. She is above the lady patronesses of Almack's. There wasn't time to introduce you to her before tonight. Don't mind her hearing; it's an act. She believes people should pay deference to her because of her age. It works." Caroline continued in a whisper, "She's been around for ages, but mind her cane; she's wicked with it. I believe she likes you."

"If that's an example of someone liking me, I'd hate to think of those who don't. They're probably planning my demise as we stand here. So far, I've received sixty direct cuts, barbed comments, and an invitation from an old harridan. That's enough for one evening, Caroline. There're over three hundred people in attendance."

"Yes, and they are all trying to figure out which one is the new duke. Shall we join them?"

Mer went to the library early to check to see if it was arranged to her liking. A fire was burning. *Tonight is for enticement.* She was setting the scene just as the book said: *raise his ardor with a little preview of what is to come . . . the fine art of seduction,* a tool in the bag of tricks written about in the books she'd finally found.

Approaching footsteps snapped her out of her reverie. It was too early for Julien. She'd be totally ruined if she was discovered in the library with a man, one she didn't know or want. Just as she slipped into the office off the side of the library, a man entered, helped himself to brandy, and sat down. She hadn't noticed him in the ballroom. He needed to leave before Julien arrived. As if hearing her, the man rose, but he ambled over to the drapes and hid in the shadows of the alcove.

Six men walked cautiously into the library. Two positioned themselves on either side of the door, one at each end of the terrace windows, one near the fireplace, and the other in the middle of the room. The sound of a cocking pistol reverberated through the silence.

"All six of you by the fireplace." Slowly and reluctantly, all the men came to the center of the room. "By the fireplace, now!"

Coming out of the shadows, he walked to a table that held the candelabra and pointed his pistol directly at the heart of one of them. "There are six of you, and I was looking for one. I guess six will have to do."

Demonic laughter echoed throughout the room. Without taking his eyes off of them, he threw a candle on the rug. The rug caught. A second candle burned at their feet. The third candle landed on the couch. Draperies were set ablaze. Through the slight opening of the door, Mer saw his left arm and shoulder. *Crack.*

"I'm sorry, but you cannot harm anyone I love."

Over her words, a scream rent the air and a pistol fell to the carpet.

"Perkins, get Simmons and Quinn." The demand fell on empty air. He was already gone.

The others were putting out the fires while Sar held the assailant. The back of Sar's neck tingled.

Of course he knew. He'd taught them. He sensed the presence of one of two people who could have pulled off this feat.

"Mer or Beth, come out of that office, now!"

Mer stepped boldly out of the office and stood with pistol loaded again in the ready. The library door opened. Simmons threw off his jacket.

"Get the ball out of him. Try to keep him awake. We must talk to him," Sebastian barked in his usual manner.

"Hand me the brandy."

Sebastian passed the decanter to Simmons and watched while he poured it on the wound and gave a little laudanum to the assailant. Simmons extracted the ball, and the assailant's eyes rolled back into his head.

"Simmons, can you wake him? How long will he be out?" Sebastian's instincts told him morning would be too late.

"I administered some laudanum to dull the pain sufficiently to extract the ball. He should come around shortly, but he'll be going in and out of consciousness. He'll need more laudanum to get through the night, otherwise he will be screaming in pain. Let's see if he can stay awake long enough for you to talk to him. Unless you protect him, someone probably won't let him survive the night."

The assailant stirred. Quinn entered, windows opened, and all attention turned to Mer.

"Mer, I know you didn't follow us. What are you doing here?" Sar's scalding look almost burned her.

"Alexius talked about the library, and I came to see it." She trusted Sar believed her Banbury tale. "I heard footsteps and hid in the office. That man entered, sat on the couch, drank several glasses of brandy, and then rose and stood in the shadows. I watched all of you enter and saw him aim his pistol. It wasn't until he started throwing candles that I had a clear shot. I fired."

He could see the impact of the shooting was beginning to dawn on her. Would she be able to get through the remainder of the evening without crumbling? He passed her a glass of brandy.

"I had a clear shot," she said. "I couldn't let him hurt you." *Or Julien or any of the others.* She unconsciously tapped one foot.

"Don't scare me like that again, Mer. You're one of two of my favorite sisters." Her color was returning. "He'd have killed you. Thank you for saving us. When you're ready, Perkins will accompany you back to the ball. Try to put on a good face and act as though nothing happened. Tell Mother and Sebastian's wife we'll join them as soon as possible. Ask Jacob to stay by your side."

Sar leaned forward and brushed a tendril of hair back into place. "Go now, Mer. We'll finish up here. Thank you." With that assurance, she hugged him and left.

"Sar, does every member of your family carry a pistol?"

"Always, Daggs, always." And if he knew what else, he would enlist them for help. "Let's get him awake and see what he can tell us."

Daggs sat him up. The assailant stirred again, and eyes dulled with pain opened. Slurred, listless words wracked with hisses were uttered.

"Pa . . . ain. Hell, it hurts. I've been shot." Blood flowed from the wound. "What is your name?"

His eyes fell shut and a muttered "John Smith" escaped on a shallow breath.

Daggs didn't believe him. His name was John Smith; the John Smith who hired him was a nob. The nob was tall, hunched, walked with a limp, and dressed exactly as they did. They met at the Bull Tavern in the East end. His eyes rolled to the back of his head, and John Smith the assailant passed out again.

"Newgate, master's side," Quinn ordered. "No one is allowed to see him unless directed by me. Make sure my order is clear."

Julien couldn't erase the image out of his mind: Mer in an elegant blue ball gown and a smoking pistol in her hand. It was laughable, and he'd have done so if she hadn't placed herself in danger. When he saw her emerge from the library office, his heart stopped. With all of the planning to be done before the ball, he'd forgotten to tell her not to leave the ballroom. Now all he wanted to do was keep her safe, lock her in her room for a week, preferably with her beneath him.

*I'll have to guard her more closely. She could've been killed. She saved our lives. What did she think—*He stopped. Mer knew what she was doing; she had the shot. He hoped she wouldn't give him cause to have heart palpitations over the next fifty years. *The next fifty years. I truly love this woman and can't imagine life without her. I must tell her.*

At midnight, masks came off and Sar was officially introduced to the ton by Grayson and Sebastian. More than one woman nodded her appreciation of his tall, fit, masculine form, and quietly commented about the possibilities and pleasure of bedding forbidden fruit—mixed blood. More than one gentleman thought it shameful a Negro legally held the title of duke. All smiled, ate, drank, and played merry. The tidbit about a shooting in the library spread like wildfire. By the time Sar heard the ballroom gossip, three people had been killed and the library destroyed.

CHAPTER 15

Death and Deception

In the East End tavern in the early morning hours, two men talked. "The duke is still alive. Our man was shot."

"What?"

"There was someone in a side room who saw what was happening, took aim, and shot."

"Is our man still alive?"

"Yes."

"Where is he?"

"Newgate, master's side."

"I'll send a message to the others. They'll best handle it."

In the other fashionable house in Mayfair, a note was handed to the gentleman: *The duke is still alive. Our man shot; he's at Newgate, master's side.*

"Our man failed to kill the duke. He's at Newgate and was the only one shot."

"I'll take care of it myself."

In an opulent study on Grosvenor Square, two men sipped brandy.

"And?"

"Someone attempted to kill Westmoure but was shot himself."

"Any word of our cargo?"

"Nothing, which only means they still have it. Do you think they know what they have?"

"I doubt it, but we can't take chances. Too bad the guy didn't get off a shot. As for Jacob?"

"He goes from the house to the office. If he goes anywhere else, it's with the duke and his family. Our man is being tailed. I suggest we change men twice a day."

"I'll call upon Westmoure myself."

***

Just as the ton climbed into bed, a woman at Newgate Prison begged to see John Smith.

"No one can see him. Direct orders from Quinn." The jailer looked at the tasty wench, with long black hair, full ruby lips, and the largest, ripest breasts he'd ever seen.

"But I can give you this."

She pulled down her bodice. The partially exposed breasts tumbled out and dangled within the jailer's touch. The keeper's dirty hands reached for the lush orbs. She looked him directly in the eye and pulled the trigger.

Opening cell after cell, she finally found him half awake and half dazed.

"I've come to take you away from all of this—no mistakes, no link, no trace." She pulled the trigger, closed and locked his cell, and rushed to the waiting hackney.

Quinn, Berkley, and Daggs found a dead jailer and prisoner,

both shot between the eyes. All of the cells leading up to John Smith's were empty.

"Daggs, get your men in here to see if any of the other prisoners saw or heard anything," Berkley said. "We'll meet at His Grace's at three. If you haven't finished, send word. Quinn and I must meet with our superiors."

Berkley and Quinn slipped out into the morning.

***

Sar, Sebastian, Royce, and Julien were explaining what happened in the library to the ladies when Perkins interrupted.

"Perkins?"

He gave Sar the note: *Assailant dead, meet at Newgate.*

Without missing a beat, Sar snapped out orders. "No one—I repeat, no one—is to go out unarmed and without Julien, Royce, Sebastian, or myself. If we can't be with you, you'll have two footmen escort you, and let everyone know where you are going. No exceptions, and that includes you, Mer."

Thoughts of her exiting from the side office of Sebastian's library and the danger she'd put herself in made him want to send her to Scotland for her own safety. It reminded him of the particular night in America when three slaves almost didn't make it because the hunting party set the woods ablaze. By the time he'd reached her, she was unconscious.

"I am moving part of Cummings and the shipping office here. Until this is over, we need to keep everyone as safe as possible. Jacob will work on Westmoure's here. He's being followed. No one is to go near Cummings. Is the private entrance in place for Paige's?"

"Yes," Julien responded.

"Use that entrance only. I suggest you have a late noon

meal. John Smith, the assailant, is dead. No one is to leave until we return."

A somber group met in Sar's study late in the afternoon.

Berkley sat behind the desk with an unlit cigar in hand. "As I see it, the only objective last night was to kill you, Sar. We have three facts confirmed by various prisoners: a soft female voice, very light footsteps, and no struggle. We only have one name—John Smith. After last night's incident, I'm convinced we have separate crimes."

"I am trying to think of anything else the assailant said or didn't say to connect us to the person who hired him." Quinn looked out over the garden as the beating rain fell like large crystal drops on the blooms. "We know the aristocracy is involved. Only those present at Sebastian's knew of the shooting in the library, and only someone in attendance could set in motion the shooting at Newgate so quickly. I'll need a list of all those invited."

The general lit his cigar. As smoke curled up and dissipated, he wondered if their clues would continue to lead them to dead ends and fritter away like the smoke.

A rider jumped off his horse, raced up the stairs of His Grace's house, and asked to speak with Lord Berkley. Perkins quietly knocked on the door and entered the study.

"Lord Berkley, one of your men needs to see you immediately."

"Perkins, show him in."

"Sir, am I at liberty to speak?" Samuels queried. Berkley nodded.

"Morgan never went to Ipswich. William Morgan is hale and hearty and has only met Morgan once. They're not related."

"Sit, Samuels. Sar, can you ring for refreshments?"

Berkley mulled over the information. For anyone to know about the envoys sent to America, his name, the fire at the shipping office, and the attempted murder of Sar only confirmed that everything was orchestrated by those very well connected and who had inside information about the duke's affairs.

"Samuels, start from the beginning, and repeat your conversation with William Morgan word for word."

There was another knock on the door. Cook and Oliver brought in carts of food and drink. After repeating the conservation with William Morgan several times and answering their questions, Samuels left.

The general sat with paper and pen. "Now that we have two people identified, which crimes did they assist with? Let's analyze this through."

"Wait," Sar interrupted. "Perkins, have someone bring me the slate board and chalk from the nursery. Someone must have brought children to visit."

Sar didn't bother to open the door to speak directly to Perkins. Within a few minutes, courtesy of Cook, a slate board and chalk were in hand.

"Shall we?" Sar handed everything to the general.

"We have three separate crimes, even though the victims are the same. Assuming the first three notes are connected to the same crime, the first crime is to kill Sar, his father, and others. The second crime is to kill Her Grace. The third crime involves espionage and smuggling. Morgan was privy to all of the late duke's business, including the shipping business and the information regarding Sar's father inheriting the title."

Drawing lines with the chalk, Berkley connected Morgan's name to the possible crimes. "This involves Morgan in at least two out of three of the crimes. George Mason passed information he gathered within Whitehall to someone. The question is, what information could he have gathered? It's obvious he spied on our meetings in Whitehall and heard everything we discussed. Like Morgan, Mason directly or indirectly gave information to those involved in at least two of the different crimes. As for the other crime, we have a ball from a pistol, no names, and no note. Curious, very curious.

"We must find Morgan and George Mason. Royce, Julien, check with ticket agents for ships leaving Liverpool and Southampton. See if their names are on any of the passenger lists. Look for John Smiths and other names which look suspicious. Daggs, see what your men can uncover. These two hold the key to solving these crimes." Berkley knew this implicated the higher echelons of the Foreign Office.

Quinn lit a cigar. "We've interviewed half of the people on our list that can come and go between the Home Office and my office. We still have a half dozen more to interview. Then we'll discreetly start with the ministers."

Berkley poured another brandy. "Daggs and I will travel to Brighton tomorrow to see if Jack remembers anything. Sar, Sebastian, you're welcome to come with us."

"Thanks, but I prefer to stay here. I'll feel better if I'm close to my mother and sisters. How long will you be away?"

"Three days. We'll return on Wednesday," Berkley replied.

"I'll stay here too. Sar and I will help track down Morgan and Mason," Sebastian added.

"Royce, Julien, if you find out anything, report here. When we return, we'll come directly here and send word to all of you. Regardless of the hour, come immediately. Until then." Berkley walked to the terrace door to move quietly out, but stopped when he heard Daggs's comment.

"My curiosity is peaked by the reports of the prisoners—the sound of possibly a female's voice and light footsteps. I am sending a couple of my men back to the prison. You never know." Daggs's instincts told him there was something to it.

"Gentlemen, until Wednesday." The general left, trailed by Quinn. "Until Wednesday," Daggs said and slipped out the side entrance.

CHAPTER 16

The Week after the Ball

"I don't think we'll have the darlings of the ton sending posies and dropping by to proclaim their undying love in poems. Do you, Mer?" Beth grinned.

The morning room was empty of bouquets and callers. No one had danced with them besides Jacob, Julien, Sar, Grayson, and Royce. After the shooting, Jacob never left their side.

"Not unless he fell in love with your face from across the room. Are you reading those gothic novels again where the man rushes in and declares his undying love from a mere glance?" Both sisters laughed. Mer didn't care that no one else asked her to dance. She had danced with Julien.

"I'm going to accept the fact we'll be on the shelf for a long time." Mer didn't know how to respond to her sister. Beth struggled to take a breath. "Does it bother me? Ask me in about ten years."

Mer was dumbfounded by Beth's confession. They would

be on the shelf together. She'd be without Julien. Teardrops leaked from the corners of her eyes.

***

After two days of rest in Northern England, the old man, cook, butler, and physician started their journey to the coast. Even if the search turned north, they were too far ahead of his captors, and there were too many different northern routes.

"We're three hours away from the coast; we'll reach the yacht by nightfall and sail in the morning." The old duke felt the mistakes of a lifetime had caught up with him, and there was only one way to correct the future. In London there was hope.

The physician studied his patient. Yes, indeed the old duke looked better. "You're getting stronger by the minute, Your Grace."

In the mansion in Northern England, the young aristocrat thought about his strategy. He sent his men south to comb the area looking for the old man. After a week of searching, they'd neither found the old man nor had anyone seen him. Even for coin there was talk, but all leads led nowhere. Tomorrow his men would search to the north and he would go southeast to London.

The old man had to be found before he reached the city.

***

The ladies met at Paige's. The gloom of the gray day was chased away by the newly invented gas lights on the walls.

"Can you believe this?" Alexius went from room to room, touching the cabinets and tables. "It looks as though the owner knew our thoughts when he completed the renovations."

The extra-large, airy rooms with wide windows shouted, "come see what we offer!"

"And the garden in the back is a magical touch, like an enchanted forest. The workers will have a place to relax."

Next to Paige's was a busy candle shop. Both buildings were owned by the same company. The courtyard wall and canopy covering the street side of the stores made it look as though the two buildings were connected. One could only access the private entrance from the back through another courtyard—if one knew what to look for. From the back it also looked like the two buildings were one. The obvious back entrance went directly into the candle shop.

Lady Aurelia brought out the scale models of the store they'd painted in the country. Upstairs, Joycellyn mapped out placement of tables for the design area. Mer and Miriam walked through the workspace.

Mer looked around, envisioning the room filled with workers. "Do you have any sewers available to work for a few days? Before the painters come, we need to see if the work area is adequate. If not, the carpenters can make the necessary adjustments. By the look of what Joycellyn is doing, we'll be able to start work by the time the paint dries."

"When do the painters come?" Although the space looked sufficient, Miriam understood the necessity to make sure. Insufficient space meant unhappy workers and compromise of the quality of the goods.

"Wednesday, but we can change it if necessary," Mer answered.

"I can arrange to have three seamstresses here tomorrow morning. What are they to sew?" Miriam inspected the stacked fabric in the warehouse area.

"Window coverings, displays, and the other embellishments Lady Diana wanted."

The words tumbled from Mer's mouth, but her mind was

elsewhere. She hadn't seen Julien since before the ball. She *saw* him, but it was always in the company of others as the ever-vigilant protector. Their moments of passion always hovered on the fringes of her mind. Alone in her bed at night, she was filled with longing.

She had to refocus. Their time would end when he found his proper wife. Long, lonely nights awaited her. Her days would be just as dismal—no warmth, no laughter, no love. For her, there would never be another. Besides being the unaccepted mixed-blood lady of the aristocracy, she'd be the unaccepted mixed-blood spinster of the aristocracy. There was no going back in her life.

At least here she was free.

"Mer, I'm going to bring seven seamstresses in the morning. The workspace doesn't feel quite right." Mer nodded at whatever Miriam said.

"Joycellyn, come to the school with me," Miriam continued. "Bring the dimensions for the window hangings and sketches; we'll take the fabric with us. You can explain to the students exactly how you want the window hangings constructed. Everything will be made to your specifications. This is an excellent project for the students, and a gauge of the quality of our teaching skills. We've never had a project of this caliber before; they'll be excited to have *real* work to do."

Miriam made a note to find more projects like this. "You can also take measurements of those students who are willing. The more measurements you have, the easier to create the patterns."

"Take a footman with you to the school. Need I ask, do you have your pistol?" Mer laughed.

"Yes, Mer. Like you, I always carry my *Bessie*."

The Earl of Thornton called upon the duke and found His Grace and Broadhurst in the study. "Wanted to call on you personally, Westmoure, to welcome you to London. Incredible crush on Saturday, Broadhurst." They were soon joined by three other men.

"What about our visitors, Sebastian?" Sar questioned when the two of them were alone again.

"The curious. Since you haven't presented yourself at White's yet, they couldn't find out the details of the shooting. I'll wager there are bets in the books as to the day you'll be killed. We can look; never know what we'll pick up. I'll have Grayson meet us there tomorrow."

Julien and Royce went from one shipping agent to the next, collecting an interesting list of names and taking what information they cajoled from the agents. Julien wondered if the duke would allow him to pay his addresses to Mer. He had to see her, to be close to her, and to breathe her into him. It was really simple, if he wanted to admit it. Love had found him in the form of a gun-toting, intelligent, foot-tapping, honey-haired American beauty. Marriage to a woman acceptable by the ton's rigid standards made him shudder from distaste.

Thinking of Mer as his wife sent an exhilarating jolt to his soul. He wanted to laugh, think of a future with honey-haired children, and keep her close forever. Clearing his head of images of their evening at the lake, Julien tried to concentrate on what the ticket agent was saying.

***

That evening in the other fashionable house in Mayfair, the two talked. "Unfortunately, the duke is still alive."

"No one else is alive to talk—no mistakes, no link, and no trace. Everything was taken care of."

"You amaze me, my dear."

"It is unfortunate the sniveling idiot Harold will inherit the title."

"It's better than a Negro."

"What is the mixed blood like?"

"Definitely not one of us, the pure. Besides Westmoure, Broadhurst, and myself, there were three other gentlemen present."

"We need to get rid of the duke as soon as possible."

"Come here and please me."

"What do we do next?"

"Patience, my dear. John Smith is dead. Let everyone think the death of the assailant put an end to everything. When things quiet down, I promise I'll kill him. Come to me."

He caressed her white globes as she rode him.

***

In the opulent study on Grosvenor Square, two men sipped brandy. "And our cargo?"

"Nothing, no word. Besides Westmoure, Broadhurst, and myself, three others were present."

"Maybe it was good others were present. They weren't able to figure out what you wanted. When is our next cargo due to be shipped?"

"Next week."

"Let's change things around a bit. Ship our cargo to Le Havre. Notify our contact. The documents will be delivered on Saturday. I want Jacob watched at night too."

Talk turned to the new opera singer who was looking for a patron.

***

Julien and Royce stopped by Paige's to speak with Sebastian and Sar. Maneuvering Mer into one of the fitting rooms, Julien kissed her like a man finding water after crossing the desert.

"Think of us at night." Then, unexpectedly, he released

her and rejoined the others. She was at odds for the rest of the day.

On the eastern coast of England, a lone yacht made its way towards London. By coach, an angry young aristocrat traveled to the city. Westmoure's continued as usual, with three exceptions. An identifying mark was put on all cargo going to Antwerp and Rotterdam. Three of Daggs's men were on every ship going to those ports, and one of his men was in charge of the Ships at Sea Report.

Frustration mounted as Daggs and Berkley tried to jog Jack's memory. Jack didn't know George Mason. He alleged he was John Smith. They tried names and places, but Jack had no recollection of a past.

Dr. Altman shook his head . . . his concern mounting with the lack of progress of his patient. "Nothing has changed, my lord. Visits from those he knew in the past are good. One never knows when something will spark a memory change. Will you come next week?"

"No, we'll return in two weeks. If there are any changes, send a message immediately." Berkley looked at Jack, wondering how to unlock his recall.

"As you wish." Dr. Altman nodded.

"What do you think, Daggs?" the general asked.

"John Smith must have been the last name he heard before he lost consciousness. Is that a true name, or is it an alias?"

"Good question, Daggs, good question. Let's hope Royce and Julien discovered something about George Mason and Morgan. Maybe someone at the prison remembered more."

They both rode in silence, mulling things over.

In the book at White's, there were indeed bets as to the day and time Sar would be killed, as well as the method in which the deed was done. Most members were cordial. All were angling to find out the details of the shooting. Grayson learned the way the wind blew from a few of his friends. More than one member thought Sar's death before he begot an heir would solve the problem of a mixed blood among the peers.

Over dinner, with the Society News spread out before them, the women dissected the most recent article.

The season started with a crush at the Marquess and Marchioness of Broadhurst's ball. Most of the elite of the ton were present to take a look at the mixed blood duke and his family.

Someone wants the duke dead. The shot which brought down the assailant who tried to kill the duke was fired by an unknown person who still remains a secret. Rumor has it a lady fired the shot. Of course, this can't be true. Ladies do not carry pistols or shoot humans. Whoever saved the duke will surely ingratiate Westmoure to this person for life. The assailant was killed in Newgate by an unknown assassin.

At her presentation, His Majesty actually received Her Grace and prayed Westmoure and his family would not disgrace the family name. The Duchess of Edgerton, the Duchess of Northampton, the Duchess of Carrington, and the Countess of Danford were seen speaking with the Marchioness of Broadhurst and the Duchess of Westmoure at the palace.

For the ball, the Duchess of Westmoure was elegantly gowned in a deep-blue, jeweled-and-beaded dress lined in the most shocking peacock green. More than one comment was heard regarding the duke's masculine form and mixed blood amidst the peerage. Like His Majesty, we hope the family does not disgrace a time-honored name.

> *At least the Duke of Westmoure does not have an heir, and there is no line of matchmaking mothers pushing their daughters in his path, even though he is one of the richest men of the ton.*
>
> *What will happen next?*

"Vicious," Anne commented. "At least no one knows who shot the assailant."

"There will be more, much more," Caroline added. "This is just the beginning. All eyes are on you and your family. Georgina's ball is next. Joycellyn, is there a dress you're working on which would be exceptional for Her Grace? If what she is wearing is being mentioned, this is as good a time as any to have tongues wagging about who is designing her elegant clothes."

"Yes, I've designed gowns for everyone."

After dinner, Sar and Jacob worked on the shipping business. Everyone else worked on ready-to-wear dresses. Mer tried to join in, but all of her thoughts were on Julien, the lake, his touch, the caresses, their precious few moments together. She wondered how long they had before he'd dance the proper tune of society and leave her for the fitting wife of the ton.

Before now, she'd never realized how abnormal life was for those who were mixed blood. For those in America, it meant you didn't have choices to do what white Americans did. You didn't count. Here in England, no one cared what you were, unless you were an aristocrat. Bloodlines, purity of lineage, antecedents, that's what counted. She sighed knowing what she wanted was forever out of her grasp. Julien was twenty-nine. She'd be lucky if they had a year together—lucky and then lonely.

"Will I be able to interview seamstresses to work exclusively on my designs tomorrow? Production needs to start immediately." Joycellyn chattered on about patterns, fittings, and creating her shop.

"We own the building next to Cummings. It's the perfect place for your shop. For now, it's best to create the first of your fashionable garments here." Alexius talked as she looked through Joycellyn's designs, trying to envision which gown to choose. "What do you think, Mer? You're the expert on scheduling and timelines. Can we do this?"

Alexius's question had Mer scrambling to remember what was being discussed. "We'll have to see."

Knowing she would be drawn into a conversation she couldn't and didn't want to follow, Mer excused herself. Her bedchamber had become a prison of torture, imagining her future without him. Images of Julien in bed with her turned the room into a pleasure palace. She replayed the feel of his exquisite touches, heated kisses, and searing moments of rampant bliss. His murmured words *think of us at night* were her only thought.

The bed linen brushed across her nipple and sensations shot through her. Heat pooled in her stomach. Her hips arched in desperation to be filled. He had taught her how to pleasure herself for moments like this. Seeking relief, she touched the curls at the apex of her thighs, slid her fingers into her wet folds, found her nub, and stopped. She wanted him. Love was about sharing, about two, and it wouldn't be the same unless he was in her arms.

The following day, after listening to the comments of the sewers, Sebastian, Julien, and Sar completed the sketch of the changes for the sewing room and redesigned Joycellyn's sewing area. Julien found a way to get Mer by herself. She could barely stand when he finished kissing her.

After several days of rain, the sunny day was a touch of

heaven. At the duke's house, Cook laid out an extraordinary noon meal on the terrace. As if conjured up, Berkley and Daggs stepped into the garden.

"Ah, just in time." The general found a place next to Anne.

Perkins summoned Quinn and Jacob. Lunch became a prelude to work. Anne sensed the men wanted to discuss Jack, and she knew there was no way any of them would be pleasant company until the business had been thrashed out. Smiling at Sar, she announced the ladies were going for a ride in the park. With the dogs, eight footmen, and two carriages, they were off to enjoy the warmth of the day, over the protest of the men. Of the eight women, five carried pistols.

"Let's adjourn to the study, shall we?" Sar summoned Oliver. "We're not to be disturbed." Perkins leaned into the closed door.

"Jack can tell us nothing. He thinks he's John Smith. Daggs believes that was the last name he heard before losing consciousness. Dr. Altman will send word if there are any changes. Julien, Royce, did you have any luck?" Berkley sat while categorically going through every event in his mind as he spoke.

Julien replied, "There were thirty-four John Smiths who sailed to America within the past two weeks, of which twenty were accompanied by their families. However, on Friday, eight days before the ball, a Baron Elias Phineas Perkins sailed on the *Liberty*, destination the port of New York. Sar, what is Perkins's name?"

"Elias Phineas Perkins. Clever, very clever indeed. That had to be Morgan. He was the only one who would have access to Perkins's full name. He even had the gall to sail on one of our ships."

The depths of treachery puzzled Sar. Had his late uncle's man of affairs been deceiving him from the beginning? If so, why?

Berkley's intense gaze swept the room and settled on Sar. "Get him back. We must have a little chat with him."

"There might be a way."

"Find a way."

The direct order reflected the tension in the room. If looks could kill, Sar mused, they'd all be dead.

"Were there any leads as to the whereabouts of George Mason?" Daggs paced as usual.

"Yes." Royce's ambled over to the fireplace and leaned against the mantle. His words weren't going to help them move closer to solving the mystery. If anything, they had just lost another key suspect. "Mason George booked passage on a Westmoure ship and sailed to Boston on Monday."

"There must be something we are overlooking," Quinn interjected. "Sar, if you can get those men back to England, the Crown would be most appreciative."

The general's resigned sigh was that of a man plagued with deceit and treachery. "We're returning to Brighton in two weeks. Jack may or may not be able to tell us anything. I agree with Quinn; we're overlooking something."

All hell was breaking loose. The master plan had been thought out and implemented with precision, the precision of trained men.

The burden weighed heavily on Berkley's mind; several of his men were traitors. "We need to examine everything from another angle. Let's look at those in attendance at the ball. Only those present knew of the shooting. Someone was able to inform the person behind this conspiracy and immediately set in motion the murder of the assassin. Or the mastermind was at the ball. Who would be able to do this so quickly? Who was spying on the scene unfolding in the library? Sar, how did you receive the note about the meeting in the library?"

"Julien. A footman gave the note to him."

"Would you remember him?"

"Yes. We questioned him, but there is no reason why we can't interview him again. The person who slipped him the note was in costume. The footman went to Julien first, thinking he was Sebastian."

"Sebastian, speak with your servant again today. Now, where do we look next?" Berkley pushed the lock of fallen hair from his forehead, leaned back in his chair, and waited for answers.

"I think we should send Grayson back to White's. When we were there, some of his friends told him of the talk going around. Many think Sar's death would solve the problem. We'll keep checking the books. Maybe someone will make a heavy wager on a particular day."

"Good, Sebastian. Can anyone think of another way to find those involved?"

"Morgan worked for my uncle for twelve years. Jacob, I want you and one of Daggs's men to begin to go through all of the files from fifteen years ago to the present. Morgan's deceit runs deep. We need to find out when things started to change, a shift in the usual pattern, or has it been consistent from the beginning. Look at the correspondence. Look at everything. Our *why*, or at least a clue, may be in the past and closely associated with Morgan's actions. If you need additional help, let me know." Jacob nodded at Sar's request.

Daggs paced as usual. "I'll check with my men to see if any of the prisoners remembered anything else. Maybe someone who fled has been returned to Newgate. We can always offer a prisoner the chance to leave the country permanently in exchange for information."

"The interviews of those who have access to both offices are completed. We'll be able to narrow the list. I haven't started interviewing the ministers. Someone has inadvertently told us something. I'll be in touch." Quinn left through the terrace door.

"I want them back—the sooner the better," Berkley said.

"It might take six months or longer."

"Sar, bring them back."

"I will do my best, General."

***

In Brighton, Dr. Altman was completing the transformation. As an actor, his skill with stage makeup was quite adept.

"Sorry I hit you so hard, Jack. Always wanted to go to America. Thanks for the chance." He finished altering Jack's face. "Take a look. You won't recognize yourself."

Jack looked. There was no resemblance of his true self. "Amazing, Brian. Amazing. Do you think they guessed?"

"No. There wasn't the least bit of suspicion, but let's not push our luck. I prefer not to hang."

"Neither do I. We sail on Friday. When they return in two weeks, we'll be far from these shores. Make sure you leave nothing behind."

***

Joycellyn fitted Her Grace with one of her latest designs.

"I can't wait to wear it. If the other dress gave them reason to comment, this will make them green with envy."

Anne stared at herself in the mirror. Never had she seen a dress so beautiful. The rich amber color made her skin glow and turned her eyes to shades of brown with flecks of honey. A contrasting bronze underskirt created the effect of a glistening waterfall.

"Anne, you look elegant. I'll finish this by tomorrow."

Joycellyn had never seen her cousin look so exquisite. The material floated, giving her an ethereal, regal look.

"Joycellyn, do you sometimes think life just grabs you and carries you along? I never thought our lives would be like this."

"Things have changed. Thank you for making me a part of the family. Besides my mother, the late duke was all the family I had."

She didn't know how to explain her mother. Frances had never healed from Charles's abuse. It affected everything. At times, the depth of her melancholy made her uncontrollable. She was angry, vengeful, hateful, and existed in another world. Joycellyn bit her inner cheek to hold back the tears.

In the empty building that was soon to be Paige's, Sar explained to the painters what was to be done. Julien did a walk through with the carpenters and showed them the changes to be made. Thinking now was the time to ask Sar if he could pay his addresses to Mer, he tried to put a coherent sentence together.

This is serious, old chap. She's the one you'll spend the rest of your life with. There will be no crying off. If the duke finds out what has been going on, you're dead. You can't talk about your lineage. He knows you're wealthy. Why don't you just say you love her? But that isn't the way of the ton, is it? Not only do you love her, you can't live without her. You're addicted to her. She's stronger than any drug. You'd better put the ring on her finger soon. She may be increasing.

"Julien, is there anything else for us to do here? The painters assured me they'll finish by tomorrow. We'll return later to check on the progress of the carpenters."

"I'd like your permission to pay my addresses to Mer." He'd gotten it out. *What had Sar just asked me? I'm making a hash out of this.*

"Julien, did I hear you correctly?"

"Yes."

"We'll talk about it at the house. When will the carpenters finish?"

"This afternoon. We'll return later to check on the progress of the carpenters."

Sar shook his head. He'd just said that. Julien was a man in love. He'd seen the symptoms before with his friends.

In Sar's study, Julien felt like a child before the schoolmaster. He wanted to squirm. He hadn't done anything wrong, not really. Like a bouncing ball, the devil and angel in his head talked back and forth.

If your illicit moments and taking Mer's virginity hadn't been wrong, then what was?

I was always planning on making her a part of my life. And you think that justifies your actions?

When he was with her, there was an invisible force pulling him to her. Everything was right with her beside him. Without her, there was no sun in his life. The thought of her in his arms brought an instant reaction to the lower half of his body, which he was trying to control in front of Sar.

He prayed Mer's brother wasn't a mind reader.

"My parents married for love," Sar began. "It was a wonderful marriage, and one that beat all of the odds. They had an astounding capacity to love, and they loved each other and us under extraordinary circumstances. I want my sisters to share that type of love with a very special man of their choosing. I expect their husbands to be faithful and loving and always honor them. I don't expect them to have marriages like those of many of the ton. If you ever do anything to hurt her, Her Grace will kill you, and I'll have to take care of a very unhappy sister forever. Am I making myself clear? You know all about us. I don't have to explain.

"In America, unlike here, we normally don't arrange marriages. Mer will have to decide if she's interested. If she says yes, you have my permission. Perkins, have you gone to ask

Mer to come to my study, or are you still lurking about? I have no need for the bell pull with Perkins. Do you love her?"

Julien looked directly at Sar and felt relief, and something much bigger to finally be able to say he loved Mer out loud.

"Yes. I love her, and I will take care of her for the rest of my life. Have no fear. Your sister will lack nothing and will always come first in my life. In England, there is usually a dowry settlement accompanying the marriage arrangement. I don't know if the custom is the same in America. I don't want her dowry; I don't need it. I want arrangements made for her to keep it and always be in control of her own money. It's important for her to know she is an independent part of me."

Sar nodded. Now he understood the depth of Julien's love for his sister. It would be a marriage filled with all life brings—the joys, hopes, disappointments, and the sad times. If Julien's declaration was a true indication of his intentions, it would be a good marriage. He wondered how Mer felt. If she felt half of the same for Julien as Julien did for her, the two of them were indeed lucky.

The door to the study opened. "Sar, I'm busy. What? Julien."

Looking at Julien, her stomach did a flip-flop. *Oh my God, has Sar found out? Possible, but improbable. Definitely safe on that account, the room is not in shambles, and Julien is still alive.*

"Come in, Mer."

Mer crossed to the front of Sar's desk. On its own accord, her foot started to tap.

"This may come as a surprise, but Julien asked me if he could pay his addresses to you. In England, that's the beginning of the engagement which will probably lead to marriage. I want you to have a marriage full of love like our parents. Marriage and life are full of surprises. Is this the man you want by your side for the rest of your life? It's a lifelong commitment. This is your decision to make, and I want you to think about the seriousness of this step. Just because we're in England, I'll neither arrange nor force you to marry. I told Julien it was up to you. You don't have to give him an answer now."

He wants to marry me. Her heart beat a staccato. *Marry me. Marry me.* Her mouth was wide open in shock as her foot kept moving.

"Close your mouth, Mer." Sar grinned. *I've been so busy; I didn't notice. She glows when she's around him. She is in love.*

The door opened again, and Her Grace entered. "Sar, Perkins told me you needed to speak with me."

"You see how it works, Julien. Perkins is in control."

"Mother, Julien has asked to pay his addresses to Mer. She hasn't said anything. She's standing here with her mouth wide open."

"I think I'll sit." Mer walked to the table, poured herself a full glass of sherry, and sat. She drank the sherry in one gulp.

"Mer!" Sar laughed. His rich robust laugh was the same as his father's.

When Anne looked up, she saw Avery with his head tilted at the same angle, laughing. She blinked and he was gone.

"Pour me a glass like yours, Mer, and pour yourself another."

Her Grace grinned from ear to ear, and whispered, "Thank you, Avery, for giving them your blessing."

"Would one of you say something of consequence? Julien doesn't know what to think. Julien, care for a brandy? I'll wager you never knew affairs of the heart could be so risky, did you?"

"Sar, leave your sister alone; she's thinking. As a matter of fact, the two of you take your brandy—no, take the decanter— and go for a walk in the garden."

Sar smiled and opened the door for Julien. "After you."

"Do you love him?" Anne sat with that all-knowing look of every mother.

"Yes."

"Well, his honorary title is Earl. He will be a marquess one day, and he's very wealthy in his own right. We know he's honest and kind."

"Mother, how do you know all of this?" Mer poured herself a third glass of sherry.

"When he started looking at you with lovesick puppy eyes and your moods went from happy one day to distracted the next, then to gloomy, and then back to happy, I started making inquiries.

"You *are* my daughter. I want you to have a love match with a wonderful man. Does he love you?"

"I don't know. He has never said. I don't want him to marry me because he feels he must protect me, or out of obligation to Sar. I don't want him if he thinks I'll never find anyone else."

"Perkins, please come in."

"Yes, Your Grace."

"Did Sar ask Julien if he loves Mer?"

"Mother, you can't ask Perkins that!"

"Yes, I can, and I just did. Well, did he, Perkins?"

"Yes, Your Grace."

"What did Julien say?"

"Yes."

"Thank you, Perkins. As usual, you are of invaluable service."

"Thank you, Your Grace."

"Come, Mer. Let's take a walk."

Mother and daughter linked arms and leisurely strolled through the garden, away from the overly sensitive ears of Perkins and the prying eyes of Sar and Julien.

"Don't hesitate, Mer. If this is love, take it. Your father and I chanced everything for love, and I'd do it again. If you're lucky, you find the love of your life. On Saturday, we are the guests of the Marquess of Briarcliff and his wife at the theater. You can learn a great deal about a man by observing his father.

You don't have to say yes to Julien now, but if it's love, give it your heart."

"What do you think they are saying, Sar?" Julien asked. "Do you think she'll have me?"

Sar threw back his head and laughed. "Love is grand. Not to worry. Women are wonderful, complex creatures. Don't ever forget that. I suggest we talk Cook into fixing us an early lunch. Then we'll go back and check on the progress of the work at Paige's."

Sar couldn't help but laugh again. "I think when we return, you'll have your answer."

CHAPTER 17

Mothers of the Ton

It was late afternoon when Daggs walked into the duke's study.

"My men interviewed everyone close to John Smith's cell. A prisoner was recaptured and talked in exchange for a one-way passage to America. According to the prisoner, John Smith and the jailer were killed by a woman or a man dressed as a black-haired tavern wench. She said, 'I can give you this.' There was a rustle of what sounded like clothes, and then a shot. She ran down the stairs, opening cells. The other prisoners below John Smith's cell confirmed light footsteps and a female voice. Since it appears she offered her body as a diversionary tactic, I believe we're dealing with a female."

Berkley fired one question after another. "Several questions come to mind. What woman wants to see the duke dead? Was the lady in question in disguise? Is there a female member of the aristocracy so bold, or was she hired to do the job? Was this woman someone's mistress? Did she act on her own?"

"We know the late duke's daughters won't receive the

family. Does this make them suspects? Do they know how to shoot?" Quinn's questions hung in the air.

A discreet knock on the door interrupted them. "Yes, Perkins."

"Your Grace, this just arrived. I retained the messenger."

Sar opened the note: *You will be dead within the month.* He passed it to Berkley.

The messenger, a skinny, dirty, lanky lad about ten, looked around him in awe. He couldn't tell them anything and cried, "'e give me two shillins. Don't take 'em from me." The *he* was an older boy.

"Where are your parents?"

He cautiously looked around and attempted to bolt, but Sar reached out, grabbed, and held. Flailing arms and legs connected with Sar's shins. "We ain't goin' to no orp'nage!"

Perkins walked in holding a little girl dressed as a boy. "Good job, Perkins. Why don't you take these two to Cook."

"No, you ain't gonna eat us." Legs kicked out again. Arms were swinging. "Calm down. Cook may have a treat for you in the kitchen."

The lad looked at Sar unbelievingly.

"Perkins, they need to be fed and bathed. See if Cook can use two more helpers. Make sure he has a safe place for his shillings."

"You ain't takin' me shillins?"

"No, you earned them. They're yours to keep. After Cook feeds you and you take a bath, we'll talk. I think we may have a job for you here."

"'Ere?"

"Yes, now you and your sister go with Perkins; we'll talk later."

The lad almost smiled and then followed Perkins cautiously.

"Another clever move, having an older lad hire the younger one to deliver the message. They are just two of the many orphans on the streets of London. There's no way to trace the person who wanted the message delivered. Daggs, what do you think of all of this?"

"The note is written on a piece of ordinary scrape. Anyone, male or female, could have written it." Daggs paced as he shifted the pieces in his mind once again.

"We have a month or less; we must make the assailant come to us. With Morgan gone and our meetings held outside of Whitehall, they have no way of knowing where you'll be. We'll let them know. Do you know what parties you're attending?"

Berkley looked at Sar and knew without a doubt he didn't know. "Never mind. Anne and Caroline will. We need to put it about you're looking for a wife. It doesn't matter who believes it; the people who want you dead will know where to find you. A little note in the Society News will do the trick. Can you take care of it for tomorrow's edition, Quinn?"

"Yes, if I can get it to my contact within the next hour. I'll send a note now telling him to expect it. He'll get it to the person who writes the column. No one knows the author of the Society News. Everything is done by secret messengers. Sar, would you ask Perkins to send for my man?" Quinn was writing as he spoke.

Sar chuckled and didn't bother to answer him. "On Saturday we are the guest of Julien's parents at the theater. Oh, by the way, Julien, it is yes. Carrington's ball is the next Saturday. As for the other engagements, you'll have to speak to the ladies."

Sar was interrupted by a knock on the door. "Enter."

Quinn's man entered. "Please deliver this immediately. Sar, I'll take Perkins if you find you don't need him." Sar smiled.

Julien was also smiling. His world had righted itself. She was his—or would be soon if he had his way of it—diamonds and emeralds for her ring, perfect against her beautiful skin tone.

Daggs began writing. "I suggest we make the entry for the column short. I'm going to have my men watch the late duke's daughters and follow up on our theories. It's time this ends before someone else is murdered, the sooner the better."

Julien was the last to leave. "Please tell Mer I'll pick her up at seven thirty for the theater. Beth will come with us. You and Your Grace should follow. Sebastian and Royce will meet us there."

***

In the other opulent house in Mayfair, she removed the men's clothing, wig, and makeup. Job accomplished. Venom flowed through her veins. That mixed blood must die. Her lover will never know she sent the note.

***

At the duke's house, Joycellyn along with her three seamstresses worked on the dresses for Lady Georgina's ball. Everyone else worked on Paige's and Cummings. Another ready-to-wear dress was delivered.

Mer slipped it on. "My, my, this is unbelievable."

Anne asked the ladies to join her in the conservatory. "I believe we're going to have a wedding. Julien asked to pay his addresses to Mer. She loves him, and he loves her." Anne's brown eyes sparkled with flashes of gold.

"Wonderful. We've known Julien since he was a child. It's time someone snatched him off the marriage mart. He needs an exceptional wife, one he loves. He'll make an excellent husband." Caroline looked at Anne and then Aurelia and extended her hand. "My one-pound note please." Both laughed.

Anne glanced at them, confused.

"Caroline and I made a wager. She suspected Julien had a tendre for Mer. Knowing Julien as I do, I said no. I've been carrying a one-pound note in my reticule since we made the wager. Not to worry, Anne, we'll help. The wedding must be at St. George's on Hanover Square. The banns need to be read. Do you know how soon before they're officially betrothed?"

"My guess is by the time of Georgina's ball. We may only have weeks to plan the wedding. Are you sure he'll make a good husband?"

The ladies nodded yes. They knew firsthand. They'd all married reformed rakes.

Julien spoke to his father and retrieved the family jewels he wanted from the safe. After telling the jeweler what to do, he stopped by the florist and was assured his order would be delivered immediately.

The Marquess of Briarcliff found his wife with the housekeeper. Leading her to his study, he poured her a glass of brandy and pulled out the gift in his desk drawer. "Years ago, I had this made for you. I decided to give it to you when our son announced his intention to marry. Evelyn, you will soon have another daughter—one of Westmoure's sisters, the older one, Mer." He handed her the diamond necklace and his linen square. He knew his wife. Evelyn didn't disappoint him upon hearing the news they'd waited on for so long.

When she opened the box, more tears fell. The diamond-encrusted necklace had a magnificent center stone flanked by a black pearl on either side of it.

"Don't you worry about mixed blood?"

"No, this is a love match. I'm glad he found her; she's intelligent, kind, and has a head for business. We both know within our class most marriages are for anything but love, and many relationships turn out to be miserable arrangements. Fools worry about mixed blood. I gave him our blessings."

The marquess had been fortunate to have his marriage grow more wonderful with the passage of time. Thanking God he'd set a good example for his son, he prayed Julien's marriage would also hold incredible joys and be blessed with amazing children.

"Good." She sniffed and wiped away more tears of joy. "Our son is like you, a good, kind, honorable man. Thank you for being who you are and loving us. I must call upon Her Grace at once."

***

After carefully observing Perkins's every move for over a month, Oliver was beginning to get the hang of the way the duke's household operated. If he was ever to be like Perkins, he'd have to learn to anticipate every move and always be at the ready. He patted the pistol in his pocket for assurance. His lessons with Perkins were making him an expert marksman and eavesdropper extraordinaire.

Oliver heard the carriage halt. If his instincts were spot-on and the conversations he'd overheard correct, the carriage signaled the arrival of the Marchioness of Briarcliff. As he opened the door, he smiled. He was right, and again sent up a silent thanks to Perkins. Before she could hand him her card, he stated in his most butlerish tone, "The Marchioness of Briarcliff," and bowed. "My lady, good afternoon, Her Grace is waiting. This way, please."

"Anne."

"Evelyn. How soon can we expect a wedding? This is such a wonderful surprise. I'm glad you came immediately."

Evelyn took in the countenance of Her Grace and knew without a doubt she wanted to get to know her better. Their initial meeting at Ivy Hall had left the impression of a very warm American unused to the stodginess of aristocratic

British ways. Her Grace was like a spring breeze, welcoming and refreshing.

"I guess eight weeks at the most."

"We have our work cut out for us."

Anne rang for Perkins, ordered champagne, and asked the housekeeper to tell Cook to prepare dinner for eighteen, with a request to be able to accommodate more if need be. Perkins told Cook to expect a wedding within six to eight weeks. Cook started singing. Oh, how she loved this family. They were kind and generous. She looked at her new helpers, little Elizabeth and Edward, and quickly dabbed the tears forming in her eyes. Her heart was overwhelmed with joy. Who else would have taken in two orphans?

Stems of orchids arrived for Mer. The card read: *Think of us.*

Beth screeched when she saw the huge bouquet. "Mer, those are gorgeous. Who are they from?" Bouncing up and down, she tried to read the card over Mer's shoulder.

"Julien."

Alexius laughed. "Julien? That's impossible. He's a rake. Rakes don't send flowers to ladies like us."

"He asked Sar if he could pay his addresses to me," she said and sighed.

Alexius grinned. "Reformed rakes make the best husbands. Joycellyn, there's a wedding dress and trousseau to make." Alexius rolled her eyes and *harrumphed.* "Our mothers left to discuss this without giving us a hint. The wedding will be at St. George's. Did he ask you to marry him yet?"

Without stopping to take a breath, Alexius laughed again. "The mamas of the ton will like you a lot less once they find out a prize catch has been removed from their grasp, snatched away by the American. I love it. I love it. I love it!"

For the rest of the day and through dinner, there was only wedding talk.

***

Friday morning, John Smith and John Smith boarded a ship for New York. They were so unsteady and fragile that the two old men needed help from the crew to board.

Miriam stopped by the duke's house to deliver the remaining ready-to-wear sample dresses. Beth and Alexius modeled. They decided which three styles to make to sell.

"Lady Miriam, do you think the other two seamstresses I interviewed will be willing to come to work for me now? With the wedding, there's much more work." Joycellyn sketched as she talked.

"I'll send a footman to bring them here immediately." Miriam completed the note and handed it to Oliver.

Alexius glanced at the news sheet handed to her and screamed, "You won't believe this. Listen!"

The London Daily

Society News

The Duke of Westmoure is actively in the marriage mart. With shots being fired at him, he needs an heir. Even as one of the wealthiest men of the ton, this will take some doing. He is attending Saturday night's performance at the theatre as the guest of the Marquess and Marchioness of Briarcliff and the ball given by the Duke and Duchess of Carrington the following Saturday for those interested.

Everyone gasped in surprise.

"There will be more visitors at the marquess's box

tomorrow night than you'll care to meet. Some matchmaking mamas who can't get their daughters married off in any other way will throw their daughters in Sar's path. Tell Sar not to be caught in a compromising position. The mothers purposefully plan that. With your brother's wealth and looks, nothing will be beyond them."

This time Beth *harrumphed.*

***

Watching Mer descend the stairs in a deep-green gown that set off the richness of her skin tone made him wonder why he hadn't recognized she was the love of his life when he first laid eyes on her. She was beautiful. Mer's eyes focused on Julien. Her husband-to-be looked exceptionally handsome in his dark-blue jacket with silver waistcoat. Forbidden thoughts filled her mind. As though reading her inner thoughts, he brushed his hand down the bare skin above her glove. She shivered at the touch of his skin kissing hers and blushed. A knowing smile lit his eyes. He bowed; she curtsied and took his arm.

Alexius was right. The marquess's box was the center of everyone's attention. Before the play and during intermission, the family was hounded by those wanting introductions, and debutants and their mothers giving Sar the once-over. While the marchioness engaged the ladies in conversation, Alexius was busy pointing out the who's who of those there. Looking around the theater, they counted at least a dozen pair of opera glasses trained on them, a wall of eyes scrutinizing their every move.

"Your Grace, Lady Evelyn." The Countess Fatson curtsied as she elbowed Lady Margaret out of the way. Lady Margaret fell onto the lap of His Grace and poked him in the eye with the flowers in her hair. Somehow this caused the Countess Fatson to lose her balance and end up on top of the duke and Lady Margaret. Extending her hand, Evelyn tried to help the countess up, and almost tipped over herself. Lady Fatson was as her name implied and weighed at least twenty stones.

"Charlotte, allow me to introduce you to His Grace and the Duchess of Westmoure, his mother." Countess Fatson had the nerve to actually blush.

Evelyn didn't know if she could endure another boorish intrusion. Lady Margaret made the sixth person who'd been rudely pushed out of the way to garner an introduction to the duke. There were going to be some very visible bruises in the morning.

Besides the current debacle in their box, three women had dropped handkerchiefs in front of His Grace and one fainted. Manners dictating, he had been forced to meet at least ten simpering debutants. The duke was being molested. She looked at him, and he arched an eyebrow and grinned.

"Worse than being in battle, Your Grace."

"But this is a battle, and this is just one of the many battlegrounds." His eyes twinkled, and a mischievous grin lit his face.

He was a handsome scoundrel, and this was only the beginning. The mothers of the ton weren't going to let him rest until he married. She'd have to warn his mother.

"And just how many battles do you think you will survive?" He looked at Evelyn and let out a robust laugh.

"Beth, look at the woman on your left staring at your brother."

"I can't believe this. If they aren't forcing themselves on him, they're trying to get his attention. This is worse than it was in America. Don't ask, Alexius. We had more temporary friends than you can imagine. When he lost interest in them, they tried to befriend us to get to him. He's handsome, rich, and available. He looks like our father."

A tear rolled down Beth's cheek. *I miss you, Poppa. Mer is getting married, and Mom is still sad.*

On the other side of the theater, a woman seethed behind her smile. Her husband was speaking to his latest mistress, while she tried to deflect any comments or conversation about the Duke of Westmoure. Unfortunately for her, that was the only gossip.

CHAPTER 18

The Week of the Duchess of Carrington's Ball

On Monday, Daggs, Quinn, and Berkley stopped by His Grace's for a luncheon and were regaled with stories about the evening at the theater. Mer's only regret was that Brian O'Keefe didn't perform. According to the critics, he was brilliant in the role of Dr. Stanley Altman. The forks of the men stopped, suspended in midair as they listened more closely. Their food congealed. Then they readily excused themselves.

Daggs prowled around Sar's study as he spoke. "An actor playing the role of a doctor! Damn it! He duped us all. Berkley, can you be ready to leave in the morning? We must return to Brighton. Is Jack a part of this, or will we find him dead upon our arrival?"

Berkley responded, "If Jack is a traitor, then he's one of the lynch pins. If he is, both of them will have already left Brighton.

Julien, Royce, check with the ticket agents. See if you can pick up any information. We leave at first light."

What was there about Jack he missed? Had he given any clues? Berkley inwardly sighed. When had he come to work for him? *Ten years ago when we were at war.* He started retracing every year they worked together.

***

An angry young aristocrat presented himself at the London townhouse of the Duke of Brockton. The house hadn't seen visitors in years, let alone the owner. Well, it would all be his soon, and he might as well start enjoying it now. After a bath and a short rest, he'd visit *Les Dames de Bois d'Ebène de la Soirée.* He needed a dark prostitute—one who liked it rough— to wipe away days of traveling.

***

At the house of the Marquess of Broadhurst, Seymour bowed. "Your Grace, the marquess isn't in, but you're expected. It's good to see you again. Would you care for refreshments or to be shown to your room?"

"Seymour, I'm glad to be back. My cook, butler, and physician are with me."

"Your Grace, welcome back."

Feeling better than he had in months, the Duke of Brockton took refreshments in the morning room. Carefully thinking about his plans, he methodically ticked off every step of his strategy. Everyone should have joy in life. He smiled, wondering about his talents as a matchmaker.

Maybe Seymour is looking to wed. Cook and he would rub along well together. For the first time in years, he felt like living forever.

The physician silently made a visual examination of the duke. He wasn't as lethargic, and his color had returned. It was probably as he thought. The nephew, Basil, had been slowly poisoning the old man. *Thank goodness we escaped when we did. Eventually I would have been forbidden to see my patient.*

***

In his now empty study, Sar paced. *Hell, I'm picking up Daggs's habit.* He continued to think about what he was considering and paced as though it was the solution. The outcome and ramifications had him questioning his sanity, and rightfully so. Lifelong commitments, but was there any other choice. *For God's sake, I am a bachelor.* But in his heart, he knew it was what his father would have done.

He stopped abruptly, glanced at the door, and stated, "Perkins, will you ask my mother, Frances, and Cook to join me for tea in the library? I need you also."

"My oh my, Perkins. What is his lordship up to now? Cooks don't have tea with the lord of the manor," she said when the duke's man summoned her, knowing it was a privilege. The American duke kept surprising her in all manner of things. Cook prepared the tea cart, quickly changed aprons, and hurried to the library.

"Cook, good you're here. Please sit. How are little Elizabeth and Edward doing?" Sar smiled at Cook and she beamed.

Just like the rest of the female staff, this handsome man with the blue eyes rimmed in green and reddish-brown hair made her heart patter. That he asked about the little ones made her heart sing. Most employers would care less. She was taken aback when Her Grace handed her a cup of tea.

"Cute as buttons they are, and they catch on quickly, Your Grace. It appears they've been on their own for a while, abandoned by their parents when the little one was still in nappies."

I've never been treated so well in my life, Cook mused, *like quality.* She sipped her tea.

"I thought as much."

"Mother, I've been thinking about this for a while. Little Elizabeth and Edward need to be educated. They're now under our care and protection. I don't want Edward growing up without having a chance to be what he wants to be. Little Elizabeth may have talents like my sisters."

Sar laughed to himself. *Another independent woman in the making.* He couldn't allow her to grow up unable to fend for herself and be at the mercy of some man.

"This huge house is too quiet. It needs noisy children. What if we made them a part of our family? I know it'll be different having two children about, but I'm sure we'll manage."

"This is your house, Sar, to do as you please, but you're right. My answer is yes. It'll be wonderful having little ones underfoot." When Anne spoke to Sar, she saw Avery standing next to their son smiling, and she knew he had given his approval. *Continue to guide him, Avery.*

"Please ask Miss Engles to find the appropriate teacher. Perkins, I am holding you personally responsible for their education. Do not teach them to eavesdrop . . . yet."

Turning his most charming smile on Cook, he asked if she'd act as their grandmother. "They'll need a lot of cuddling, hugging, and treats, but they still have to obey and do chores."

"Your Grace, I'm honored." Cook excused herself to return to her kitchen.

These Americans are odd. It wasn't at all the thing to do to give those of her class a chance. There was so much poverty in England; children were abandoned to fend for themselves every day. People were starving, yet there was so much wealth. The aristocracy didn't often reach back to help those below them. And here His Grace was giving those little ones a chance. Her heart overflowed with joy.

Imagine that; I'm a grandmother. Finally, a family of my own—two grandchildren and a wedding to plan. My oh my, the late duke would be so proud. She dabbed away the tears. The soft lilt of Cook's voice was heard throughout the kitchen.

"Sar, there's more to this than educating Elizabeth and Edward. What's going on?" Anne sensed he was struggling with something.

"Our lives have been turned upside down and taken directions we never anticipated," he said. "In America we freed slaves, and there are free Negroes, but they don't have rights and aren't considered equal. There is no freedom without rights. One day I had rights, and the next day I had none. To be free, we had to come to England.

"I've been thinking about Frances too. As a servant, there was no one to protect her. To be a victim of capricious whims and degradation and be at the mercy of another is equivalent to slavery. Without the kindness of my late uncle, where would she be? And I think about Father. What would he do in a situation like this?

"In America we were taught to believe everyone is free, but we know that is only true for people who are white. However, we can take the American principle of freedom for all and allow our servants to change their lives. Here there're no repercussions, except the gossip of the ton, which means nothing to me. I don't want anyone working in my employ to be helpless. I know this is radical thinking, but I want all of the servants to learn to read and write if they choose."

As the duke spoke, Frances was taken back to that ill-fated day thirty-one years ago. Lord Charles had been drinking, and a meaner man couldn't be found when he was drunk. She still felt his sweaty hands grabbing her and stuffing the gag in her mouth. She struggled. At age eleven, she was no match for a man. His laughter echoing in her brain woke her many nights.

Ripping her clothes off, he threw her on the bed and tied

her to the posts. Undressing himself, he leered at her. *I am going to give you what you have been teasing me with and asking for during the last year. You want this, and I am going to give it to you rough, just as you like. You've been serving all of the others. Serve me.*

Threatening to kill her if she ever told anyone, he fell upon her, spread her legs, entered, and ripped her apart. Pain seared through her. She screamed, but not a sound was heard besides his rutting grunts. Breathing became difficult. His hands mauled her body. Tears ran down her face. Seeing her tears, he punched her until her swollen eyes shut closed. Over and over again he thrust in and out. Once was not enough. She lost consciousness when he started again for the third time.

She awoke alone with the gag still in her mouth, her body bruised and bloodied. They found her later that morning acting like a crazed, wild animal caught in a trap trying to eat its leg to escape. For the next six years, she stared at her world locked within the cavern of her memory of that night. That memory was her only tortured company until she saw Charles again.

Perkins handed Frances his linen square. From her anguish and tears, he could feel her reliving the memory of that horrid, fateful night. No woman should ever have to experience rape, the birth of an illegitimate child, nor years of tortured silence as a result of shock from the abuse and the inhumanity of another. Perkins offered the only thing he could, a shoulder to lean on.

Avery, even though people are trying to kill us, I'm glad we're in England. Our son is turning out to be as thoughtful, honest, and as kind as you.

"Sar, yes, this is the right thing to do. I'll check with Georgina. Her school trains governesses. She can recommend someone for Little Elizabeth and Edward. Tomorrow, let's have tea with the children. If we talk about what we plan for them, they'll be less frightened. There has been much sadness in their young lives. They had to fight to survive. Slowly, we have to earn their trust.

"As for the staff, I think if we speak with everyone at the same time and explain our intentions, we'll be able to work out a schedule for those who want to learn. They too will be cautious of our intentions and the change. Remember, we're going against class and tradition."

Well, well, one more thing for the ton to talk about. Ah, the mixed-blood American family changing the order of things again. Anne felt like singing. Happier than she'd felt in months, she started making plans for changes within the entire house.

***

The Duke of Brockton rose as Sebastian entered the room. "Your Grace, I am very glad to see you. Now what is this business you've come to London to see about?"

Sebastian shook the old man's hand. For someone approaching seventy, he looked quite healthy. "Sit. We have experienced too much together to stand on formality."

"Broadhurst, thank you for putting up with an old man. I need to take care of some business, which must initially be done in the utmost secrecy. This may take a few weeks, and then I'll be out of your way."

"You always had the most intriguing network for getting things done." Sebastian smiled. The Duke of Brockton's service to the Crown during the war had been invaluable. His holdings in the north and connections to the ports allowed major operations to be launched.

"Now tell me what's new in London. I've been away for ten years."

The old Duke listened as Sebastian filled him in. When he mentioned the new Duke of Westmoure, Brockton became all ears.

***

On a ship destined for America, the night sky sparkled with stars. At the railing, Brian O'Keefe gazed upward at the wonder. This was his favorite time. All was calm and still; he felt he owned the world. Alone, he planned his future and his new beginning.

With no one about, Jack slipped behind Brian, hit him, and pushed him overboard. Morning came and Jack complained. He couldn't find his friend John Smith.

In Brighton, Daggs and Berkley found no trace of Dr. Altman or Jack. No one had seen them for several days.

"Interesting, there are no bodies and no trace of either one of them. Do you think Jack has been killed?"

"I don't know, Daggs, I don't know. He was injured, and there is a possibility he was murdered, but he's a trained operative. We'll check his lodgings in the city."

***

By midmorning on Wednesday, Paige's was a beehive of activity. The ladies, with the help of Perkins, Sebastian, Sar, Julien, and Royce, put the window hangings in place and arranged the furniture. Joycellyn's five seamstresses completed the ball gowns and started the wedding trousseau and commissioned gowns. Joycellyn secretly worked on the wedding dress.

***

Jack's things were still at his lodgings and the rent paid for the next three months.

"We were worried the injury might have killed him." The talkative agent was more than willing to tell Berkley and

Daggs everything he knew. "We look forward to his return and hope he'll be back to normal soon. Please give him our regards."

"Well, Jack wasn't planning on moving, or he was planning on moving and taking nothing with him. Maybe Julien and Royce discovered something," Berkley commented as he and Daggs headed to His Grace's house.

In Sar's study, the men tried to fit more pieces of the growing puzzle together. "This is what we know. Jack is gone. Whether he is alive or not or an integral part of the scheme is what we must try to figure out immediately. Julien, Royce, did you have any success?" Berkley's clipped tones resonated throughout the study.

"No names, but there is something of interest," Royce said, his instincts on full alert. "One ticket agent said two old men, each going by the name of John Smith, booked passage to America on a ship which left Friday. They looked old but acted years younger. He thought their voices, walk, and mannerisms odd considering their age. I would wager that was Jack and Brian O'Keefe."

Julien knew he wasn't wrong. "The ticket agent was very emphatic about what he saw. He watched them closely, envious of their youthful movements even though they were quite old. That's why he took special note of them. My instincts tell me those were our two, and Jack is in this up to his neck."

The general was always pleased when men he trained turned out so well. "If the two of you feel that way, then I believe you're correct. Instincts are rarely wrong. Sar, I want Jack back alive. Whatever it takes, bring him back. With Jack involved, there's no telling who is behind this, and the why eludes me."

"Brian O'Keefe will be easy to find. He'll use his name and credits from the theater here to find work in America. I don't know if finding him will lead us to Jack." Sar knew only one man for the job.

Quinn sipped his brandy. "Damn the actor. Bring me Jack. I want Mason and Morgan also. Daggs, do we know anything else?"

"There has been no additional cargo on the ships going to Antwerp and Rotterdam. I'm watching this closely. My gut feeling is they assume we know something. If so, they'll move the extra cargo onto ships going to other ports. None of the crew is talking. Eventually someone will.

"Smuggling and espionage don't stop suddenly, unless you're caught. There's still activity. But where?" Daggs was pacing while talking. "Quinn, Berkley, check your offices to see if you are missing any documents."

"This implicates some very high officials. We'll have to inform the prime minister. We're overlooking something. Why did it start? When did it start?"

The prime minister would want answers, and all Quinn had was theories.

***

The invitation to dine with the Marquess of Briarcliff's family on Thursday hinted to expect a declaration of a formal engagement. Anne told Perkins, who told Cook. When one neared the kitchen, one heard singing.

It was Thursday afternoon when Jacob entered the shipping office used by the original staff and crew. This was the best time of the day. All was quiet. He looked about. Noting everything in order, he settled into his office. The knock startled him.

"Enter."

"Sir, I am sorry to bother you so late in the day, but we have a matter of some urgency."

"Captain Coomes, come. Please sit. Now, what is this matter?" Jacob looked at the sea-worn leathery face of the captain of the *Britain*. Years of weathering the sea were evident, but today he saw worry too.

"We were three days out when we picked up a man floundering in the ocean. How he managed to stay alive is a miracle. Once we fished him out, he was able to tell us he'd been pushed overboard the night before. We got his name and tried to treat him. He died before we docked. Since this may be murder and he told us he was an actor from London, I brought the body here. His name is Brian O'Keefe."

Jacob stopped what he was doing and gave the captain his full attention. "Who knows of this?"

"The entire ship, but only the physician and I know his name."

"I'll have Scotland Yard investigate immediately. His name is to remain known only to you and the physician. Inform the doctor. No one else is to know."

There was another knock, and Sar entered. "Guard the boat with your life until the body is released to Scotland Yard. This is the Duke of Westmoure; I will inform him of the incident. Thank you, Captain. Well done. Well done indeed."

The captain quickly left.

"Perkins, get Daggs here at once!" Jacob was writing as he spoke. "Give him this message. So you both know, Brian O'Keefe was pushed overboard. One of our other ships picked him up. He died onboard. The captain brought the body here. Daggs and his men will handle the investigation. We need everyone else at His Grace's."

Within the next two hours, Daggs viewed the body and made his way to His Grace's. Jacob retold the Captain's story.

"I assume you also spoke with the captain."

"Yes, and I viewed the body." Daggs's pacing was just short of a run. "His story is exactly as you stated. As Julien and Royce suspected, O'Keefe was in disguise. Bits of theatrical makeup were still on his face. Surviving the night in the water was beyond a miracle. He received a blow to the head and back of the body. No other injuries were apparent. The finger is pointed directly at Jack as the murderer."

The general, using his cigar like a baton, punched the air to emphasize his words. "Unless other facts come to light, it appears Jack is a key person in this scheme. Sar, he must be returned."

"Yesterday, Jacob and I sent a dispatch to Chief Red Cloud. Along with their descriptions, the boats they sailed on, and their particular habits, we also sent pictures. Joycellyn made sketches of all of the men. Red Cloud is in charge of our business in America, Avery Jacob Shipping, and he is the best tracker we know. We trust him with our life. If they're to be found, he'll find them. We told him you want them back alive. This will take time."

"I don't care, Sar; just bring them back."

By the time Sar and his family arrived at the Briarcliffs', the gathering had taken on a festive air. Julien's mother was giddy with anticipation.

Evelyn hugged Anne and whispered, "Tonight is the night. His father and I have waited twenty-nine years for this moment."

Julien couldn't take his eyes off of Mer. He wanted her now. Since he had asked Sar if he could officially see Mer, everyone conspired to keep them apart. One of the mothers or Sar chaperoned them. Tonight he'd take steps to put an end to their forced separation. Thoughts of her being so close and unable to touch her had left him off center and at odds with everything. Zeus was still complaining about his sudden bursts of rough handling.

"Mer, shall we take a walk in the garden before dinner?"

"That would be lovely."

Mer didn't know what he planned, but she hoped there was a secluded spot where they'd have a moment alone. Unfortunately, the wall of windows overlooking the garden gave everyone a ringside seat, and the prying eyes weren't moving. She smiled and placed her hand on his sleeve. Together they went out into the warm evening.

He found a bench partially concealed in the shadows. "You know they're intentionally keeping us apart." His chuckle sounded ragged to his ears.

"I know. I overheard them. They want to make sure society knows this is a love match, not one for family alliances. Julien, I need you. I dream of us making love. When I awake, I am wet and wanting."

He'd have to remember he would never be able to keep anything from her. Her eavesdropping skills were as good as Perkins's. "I need you too. When I get you in my bed again, expect to stay there for a week." And he meant it; forever wouldn't be long enough to fill his need for her.

Boldly, she looked him in the eye. "I've been reading the *Kama Sutra*. There are a few things I want to try." Mer didn't blush or bat an eye. All she craved was him and the feel of them together.

He wasn't shocked. He knew *his* Mer would find ways to enhance their love and strengthen their bonds. Thoughts of their future daughters acting like this with some rake made him put in a request for sons only.

"Why don't we just go through the *Kama Sutra* together? There may have been things you overlooked."

"Mer." With one graceful move, he was on his knee. "I didn't know anything about feelings until you entered my life. I never thought I'd ever utter, let alone declare, my love for another. You are my world. I love you and I need you. I love your intelligence, your wit, your straightforwardness, and your passion. I'll be faithful to you always. I can't live without you. You are an extension of me, and I am but a shadow of a man without you. Meredith Anne Roxbury, will you do me the honor of becoming my wife and the mother of our children?"

The silence was almost his undoing. His nerves took over and he started questioning his sanity.

What if she said no? *She might turn me down.* The bottom dropped out of his stomach. Endless battles and covert missions had never put him on the edge like this. Why did Sar leave the decision to her?

"Please say yes. If not, we'll end up sneaking around trying to find moments to be alone. I don't want that. No, I don't want a mistress. I want all of you and all of what married life brings."

From the terrace windows, a sea of eyes was staring at them. "I sense we have an audience."

Hearing the words she thought would never come, Mer tried to brush the onslaught of tears from her face and still her tapping foot. "Julien, you are my life."

"I assume that is a yes."

All Mer could do was nod her head. He slipped the ring on her finger. One look at the ring and her tears flowed like a flood. He wondered if she would always cry this way when she was happy. If she did, he'd cherish every single teardrop.

"One other thing, my sweet." He pulled out a box and handed it to her. She opened it. "My father gave this to my mother the night their betrothal was announced. Please do me the honor of wearing it Saturday?"

The diamond collar sparkled in the evening light.

"Oh, Julien." Her tears stopped her from saying anything else.

"Here, let me wipe your eyes. I think we should give our audience something to talk about." He embraced her and ravished her mouth. Reluctantly, he pulled away. "We have to face them soon or our mothers will join us out here. Will you marry me in a month?"

"Can it be any sooner?"

He wiped more tears from her face. "Are you ready for them?" She nodded.

There was little to be said when they entered the house, because everyone had unashamedly witnessed their very private moment from the windows. The gentlemen produced their linen squares for the waterworks that followed.

"Congratulations, Julien. Much happiness." Royce handed Julien a glass of champagne, and for the first time envied someone about to be married. He felt their joy and love and wished he'd find a love like Julien's. Where did that thought come from? *Oh, face it; one day you'll have to set up a nursery. You are a future duke. And if happiness came with it, wouldn't that be different.* He *harrumphed.*

"Mer, I'm so happy for you. Your ring is beautiful," Beth said.

A huge emerald winked from a chunk of gold. On either side of the center stone were very large diamonds. The fire from the ice was enough to blind a person.

"Can you believe this? A wedding? You're about to be married!" Beth barely contained her excitement. She doubted if Mer heard her; she only had eyes for Julien.

"I can't believe this, Beth. The ton is going to go crazy. Mer did it." Alexius looked at Mer and Julien. *My God, they're in love.* She wondered if love would ever come her way.

"Mother, Julien and I would like to be married four weeks from Wednesday. Is a month sufficient time to have the banns read and everything prepared? If not, we can elope."

Anne noticed Joycellyn's slight nod. "Don't think about eloping. Yes, Mer, we'll have time. We need the wedding fuss and bother." So far, the year had brought one upheaval after another. Finally, something joyous in their lives to celebrate—the beginning of new beginnings.

"I'd like to make the formal announcement at the ball on

Saturday." Georgina couldn't wait, gleefully envisioning the shocked look on all the faces.

This will put those matrons and busy-body matchmaking mamas in a real snit, one of the most eligible bachelors snatched off the wedding mart by the mixed-blood American. Wonderful! She could almost hear the gossip. *They'll wonder if Sar bought him for her. When people realize it is a love match, it'll set the ton topsy-turvy.*

Perkins slipped away for a moment and then returned to his place as one with the door.

At His Grace's house, Cook received a note: *Lady Meredith to marry Lord Julien four weeks from Wednesday.* Cook cried. Oliver handed her his linen square.

On Friday, work started in earnest on the wedding. Beth, Alexius, and Joycellyn would attend the bride. Announcements were sent to the news sheets to appear on Monday. St. George's was available, and the banns would be posted on Sunday. The ladies conferred on the wedding feast menu and decorations. Her Grace met with the housekeeper and Oliver.

"Mer, I would like to create your dress in a pale shade of peach, with touches of buttercream and hints of very light lavender. What do you think?" Joycellyn handed her sketches of the wedding gown. "I know you like the wedding dress at Winters. We can send for it if you wish, but I thought you might like this better."

Mer studied the design. "Beautiful, Joycellyn, beautiful. Will you have time to get this made?"

"Yes. The attendants will wear rich butter-cream-colored dresses with similar sleeve designs. You'll look gorgeous, Mer. Do you have any idea what color ribbons you want for your groom and groomsmen?"

"I want ribbons of all three colors in the dress woven together in some fashion. Will that work?"

"That will be stunning and unique. Thank goodness Paige's is set to open the week after the wedding. We'll be fine."

"We're postponing our wedding trip until after the opening." She looked down at her ring. *He loves me; he loves me.* Her smile brought tears to Joycellyn's eyes. She didn't dare hope for such happiness.

***

The general slipped into Sar's study. "Gentlemen. Congratulations, Julien. Have we learned anything else?"

Daggs paced. "Brian O'Keefe's body was claimed by the actors from the theater. We went to his lodgings. According to the agent, he took everything with him when he left. He'd planned to move to America."

"I had three missing documents," Quinn said. "Two were discovered in a place where I would never leave a document. The other is gone. Four men are being watched."

In setting his trap, Quinn moved all of his sensitive documents to another office. Those missing were fake documents listing in code old tide charts of countries on the Continent.

"I have two documents missing and haven't found them yet." Berkley knew they were gone.

Like Quinn, he had moved his classified documents to another locale. Those taken were useless.

Daggs sat and just as abruptly stood again. "So, we have continued espionage and probably smuggling. Sar, I'm putting my men on all your ships going into ports we think they might use. Here's a list of the most obvious ports. Jacob, you'll have other ideas. This starts immediately. We have cargo to mark and men to train by Monday.

"I need your shipping schedules. They'll want to deliver the documents as soon as possible. Shipping opium is probably done more frequently than secreting sensitive information out of the country. There're crew members who know something. We have to find them. Jacob, are the shipping schedules posted?" The pieces were coming together slowly, but there wasn't a why of it just yet.

"I've posted the shipping schedules in the office for a month out. Is that sufficient notice for them to arrange their nefarious operations?" Jacob took note of the men present. The seriousness and urgency of the matter hung over the room like a threatening storm.

"Daggs, we need another entry for the *Daily*," Berkley said. "Caroline and Anne gave me the list of engagements for the next two weeks. If the note forewarning Sar of his death within the month is to be taken seriously, my hunch is they'll try to kill him at Edgerton's affair at Richmond.

"They wouldn't dare try at Almack's. The lady patronesses know all who enter and would themselves take the assassins to task if they tried anything untoward in the hallowed halls of the matrimony mart. Their families would forever lose their vouchers, which to most in the aristocracy is worse than hanging."

Berkley studied the list of ports ripe for espionage and smuggling. "Take a look, Quinn. See if you agree."

"On Saturday night, everyone must stay within the ballroom, card room, and dining room," Daggs said. "I don't want to take any chances. This isn't a masquerade ball. Things haven't quieted down since John Smith was murdered. I don't think our killer will strike again so soon, but you never know. Sar, don't let your family out of your sight. After the announcement of the engagement, everyone's focus will be on that startling bit of news."

Writing while talking, Daggs started the next entry for the Society News editor.

From what we have learned, the mixed blood duke has met the approval of many of the ton's mothers. Is it his fortune, looks, or title? Of course, it is his title and wealth. His future duchess will want for nothing. Anyone interested will find him at Almack's the Wednesday after the Duke and Duchess of Carrington's ball. We understand Lady Sarah Jersey personally gave the Duke of Westmoure's family the voucher. The following week he will attend the Duke and Duchess of Edgerton's al fresco luncheon at Richmond. Who will be the lucky bride?

***

In a bedchamber in the other fashionable Mayfair house, he marveled at her beautiful form. Huge breasts arched up to him as he trailed kisses over her body. The late afternoon sun bathed her in a rich glow as she opened herself to him.

"My contact gave me Westmoure's upcoming schedule. Saturday's ball won't be the right time to kill him. There'll be other perfect opportunities. I also found out the oldest Westmoure sister will soon be engaged to Briarcliff's son."

"Just kill him and the rest of the family. The sister cannot beget an heir. Just think of what it will do to our society. Future generations will be mixed and contaminated forever."

"Patience, my dear. I'm putting my child in you. I'll never withdraw again. Your husband be damned."

"Now," she purred. "Please me." He let her fly as he spilled his hot seed into her womb.

***

To say the Duke and Duchess of Carrington's ball was a crush would be an understatement. As they stood in the long line waiting to be received, Anne looked around at the elite of society dressed in every imaginable color. Lights from hundreds of candles reflected against the jewels artfully decorating hair, draped around necks, arms, and on fingers. Prisms and tiny rainbows danced about.

Georgina sparkled like a child savoring her favorite treat. "Anne, you look beautiful. Joycellyn, you outdid yourself designing our dresses. Thank you. At midnight, we'll make the announcement."

Mer took in the ambiance of the room. This was her night, the night she'd remember always, their declaration of love to the world. White orchids and roses edged in gold overflowed from arrangements in the ballroom and on the terrace. The gold and white candles cast the ballroom in a soft light. Flowing white fabric tied with gold flounces and ribbons turned the terrace and balcony into a translucent gazebo. Behind gold and white screens and bouquets of flowers, the orchestra played—a magic land created just for the two of them. Glancing around the room, Mer was trying to remember everything. She'd have these memories forever and stories to tell her future daughters.

Matchmaking mamas were angling for an introduction to Sar, and in turn the chance to introduce their daughters. Acting as though the duke was an old family friend, Countess Fatson cornered him. None too politely, Sar was forced to dance with her oldest daughter, who also weighed at least twenty stones and was adorned in layers and layers of lace and roses. If she weighed less, the dress didn't help. Regardless of the countess's poor taste in clothes for her daughter, she was beautiful.

Absentmindedly, Mer tapped her reticule and felt her pistol. The older matrons and dowagers were in their usual place and participating in their favorite sport: gossiping and *tsk-tsking* at the tomfoolery. Widows and some wives were giving Sar, Grayson, Royce, and Julien come-hither looks. Soon, those same women would learn Julien was out of their reach. *That* made her smile.

Before the final waltz preceding supper, the Duke and Duchess of Carrington managed to silence the ballroom. Standing next to them were the Marquess and Marchioness of Briarcliff and the Duke of Westmoure and Her Grace.

"It is always a pleasure when we have something special to enhance a celebration." Carrington paused, making sure he had everyone's attention. The silence was deafening. Questioning looks passed from one guest to the other. "The Marquess and Marchioness of Briarcliff are pleased to announce the betrothal of their son, Lord Julien, to Lady Meredith, the sister of the Duke of Westmoure."

His words seemed to reverberate through the silent room, and then the buzz started.

Alexius first heard a whisper of noise, then an uproar, and caught snippets of what was being said. "No, this can't be true." "Did he buy him for her?" "My daughter wants him." "They aren't married yet; she still has a chance." "They are Americans, mixed-blood Negroes." "Well at least it is not a love match. He'll be available tomorrow."

The newly affianced couple led the waltz. As they glided about the room, the world blurred around them and a diamond collar sparkled around her neck. More than one distraught mother required smelling salts.

Above the din of noise, one voice clearly carried. "Snatched him right out from underneath all of those matchmaking mamas' noses. They've been after him for years, and he got away. This is good. New blood for the aristocracy."

Lady Hortense Horton cleared a path with her swinging, tapping cane and headed directly for Anne. "That's it, my girl.

I knew you'd stir things up a bit. Call on me tomorrow. We'll discuss the wedding. Three o'clock." Cackling with glee, she left a stunned Anne to join her old cronies.

"You have the unqualified blessing of Lady Hortense Horton, Anne. You'll be surprised what her approval will do. We'll both call on her tomorrow." Caroline knew the major topics of gossip for the next few weeks: the match of the mixed-blood American to one of London's richest titled rakes, Lady Horton's approval, and those fortunate to receive an invitation.

Alexius and Beth made their way to the ladies withdrawing room and opened the door, only to be stopped cold by the scene unfolding before them.

"He's mine. No upstart American, let alone a mixed blood, will take him from me." The countess lunged at the widow and yanked her hair.

"Oh, but I had him, and you never will." The widow, primed and ready, ripped the dress of the countess. Alexius and Beth quickly closed the door and heard a crash.

Supper was a mix of congratulations and comments of disbelief and envy. Mer and Julien glowed. One of his past lovers caught a tear rolling down her cheek. In a corner, a smiling earl knew he had to kill all of them soon.

CHAPTER 19

Almack's

In church on Sunday, the banns were read. Alexius thought she heard a collective sigh from some of the ladies in the congregation. At exactly three o'clock that afternoon, Anne, Caroline, and Mer were shown into the receiving room of Lady Hortense Horton. The dowager duchess was the granddaughter of a duke, the daughter of a duke, and the wife of the late Duke of Horton.

"I like people who are prompt. Come here, my child." Lady Horton beckoned to Mer. Mer curtsied. "So, Briarcliff's son chose you. Let me see the betrothal ring."

Mer felt like a prime piece of horseflesh being inspected at Tattersall's. The thin, old, veined hand clasped hers. Laughter filled the room. "Oh, I do love this. The ton is going to have a royal fit. This is a love match."

She saw it in Mer's eyes. Asking to see the ring was a good way to get a closer look at the child. The ring meant nothing without love. It was a stunner, and only someone in love would have a jeweler create such a masterpiece. She patted the seat next to her. Mer sat.

"I knew you'd do. Stir things up a bit you did, Your Grace. This twaddle about pure lines is nothing but poppycock—not possible if their lives depended upon it." Lady Horton continued, "My husband's title passed to him from a distant cousin whose wife's ancestors were from Northern Africa. Your Grace, your daughter looks exactly like you. She and Julien will have beautiful children."

Anne thought she saw the gloss of sheen from tears in the old lady's eyes.

"Please call me Anne."

"Knew I liked you when I first met you. You keep excellent company." She nodded in Caroline's direction.

"By the way, Lady Caroline, how is that school of yours? I believe it's called Harson's. Wonderful thing you did. I assume you did it in memory of Violet. Don't be surprised I know. I keep up with those changing the old order of things. Needs to be done."

"Thank you, Your Grace. We are busier than ever." Caroline wondered how the old lady knew, but it didn't matter. She knew and there were no recriminations.

"Now, let's talk about this wedding. It's at St. George's, I assume. This needs to be another event of the season. Who's creating the dress?"

"Joycellyn."

"Who is Joycellyn? I've never heard of this modiste."

"She's the one who has been designing our gowns," Anne replied, hoping the dowager duchess was satisfied with her answer.

"I know that, but *who* is she?" Lady Horton pinned Anne with a stare.

"She's our cousin."

"On whose side of the family?"

"The late duke's side."

"Who is her mother?"

"Frances." *She's like a dog with its bone and won't let go.*

Just tell her the story, Your Grace. You don't know the half of it. She heard Avery laugh.

"Frances who? Who is she connected to?"

"She was a servant of the late duke. Charles took advantage of her when she was eleven." Anne felt the shame and burden of the family for what had been done to a child; it didn't matter what Lady Hortense thought. "Frances and Joycellyn are family. The wedding dress won't be designed by anyone else."

Ah ha! She's willing to tell the truth and recognize Frances and Joycellyn. Anne has a backbone of steel. She'll think for herself and do well in the ton. She also has integrity and a soul of compassion, and she doesn't give a damn about what the ton thinks . . . good, good.

"Charles was always a worthless, devious worm, even as a child. Knowing the kindness and honor of the late duke, he'd take care of the mother and child. Charles has more than one child born on the other side of the blanket. Don't know what the late duke knew about."

Lady Horton didn't think she could keep the pretense up much longer, but she pressed on. "Good you're making Joycellyn a part of the family. Make sure the ton finds out about her. No need to be ashamed of Joycellyn. The fault lies with Charles, even though people are too stupid to realize it."

At that moment, Anne knew beneath Lady Horton's gruff exterior beat the heart of a kindred spirit and adventurous woman. *She must have been incredible in her day.*

Avery laughed again. *Her day isn't over yet. Wait till you learn the rest of it.*

"I want the church to be decorated in a spectacular fashion—flowers at the end of the pews and at the altar. I'll send my gardener to discuss things with your head gardener.

Your cook is excellent, some French training as I recall. If she wishes, my cook has recipes to share and will be at your disposal. Both cooks are friends. Who is attending you, my girl?"

There was a discreet knock and tea was brought in.

"Cook, glad you came. I'd like to introduce you to Her Grace, the Duchess of Westmoure, and her daughter Lady Meredith, and the Marchioness of Broadhurst. Her Grace's daughter is to wed Lord Briarcliff's son in four weeks. Please help Her Grace's cook in any way possible. I expect you to visit her tomorrow."

"It would be my privilege, Your Graces." Cook curtsied and left with an additional spring in her step.

"Remember, servants talk. Those two have probably already started on the wedding feast. Now where were we? Ah, yes . . . Who is attending you?"

"My sister Beth; Lady Caroline's daughter, Alexius; and my cousin Joycellyn," Mer responded. She was beginning to like the crackly old lady who smiled with her eyes.

"Good, good. I want everything to be correct and precise and the ton jealous with envy."

For the next hour the detailed list became longer and longer. "I will see you tomorrow at four. If possible, I wish Joycellyn to design my gown. When the season is over, Lady Caroline, I will help in any way I can with Harson's. I may be old, but my mind is sharp. Continuous balls and gossip can be such a bore. They dull the mind."

"Thank you. It will be wonderful to have your help."

"Your Grace, I don't have grandparents who are alive. Our only relatives are the late duke's daughters and a distant cousin, Harold. The late duke's daughters won't receive us. Will you please act as my grandmother and be a part of our family for the wedding?" Mer peeked up at the old lady and smiled.

"Well, no, no, that is not quite—" The dowager duchess

stopped. Looking at Mer, she realized the request came from the child's heart. "It'll be my pleasure."

Mer leaned forward and kissed her cheek. "Thank you."

Sadness and happiness pulled at her heart as tears gathered in the old eyes that had seen much.

Thank you, my dear, for this wonderful American family of your brother's.

On the way home, Caroline and Anne were dumbfounded as to the why and what of everything that just happened at Lady Horton's.

"I'd have never guessed. I'm amazed," Caroline said. "She's making herself a part of your family. There's more to her than I ever imagined. You had her blessing at the ball, but to offer to help and become a part of the family makes you her family. This only means she thinks you are above reproach. Welcome to the highest echelon of society. Anne, tomorrow go over your wedding list with her. There may be a few people she knows you need to invite."

"I'll need to speak to Joycellyn," Anne said. "There's another dress to be made. The gardener is very particular about his blooms. Short of ordering them, maybe the two gardeners can work well together. On the other hand, Cook will welcome her friend."

Anne thought about the wedding to orchestrate, the ton securitizing their every move, and people trying to kill them. *Avery, can you believe this? What is it that you know about Lady Horton?*

You'll find out soon enough, Your Grace, Avery replied, and he laughed again.

Dowager Duchess Horton stumbled as she was being helped up the stairs by her housekeeper and good friend, Mrs. Kiggins. "I'm fine, Kiggins. I just need to rest for a moment."

Once in her bedchamber she pulled out one of the

well-worn letters, and tears fell as she read the memorized words.

My Dearest Hortense,

I have loved you from the first moment I saw you. You were standing by your husband at your annual ball. At the time, we were both married. Having taken my vows, I promised to always remain faithful to my wife, as you to your husband. I watched you from afar, and I was envious of the man who had the privilege to hold you at night.

It was at your husband's funeral I decided to see if we could one day become friends. Although we had both lived through marriages made in the usual manner for those of our class, you never gave any indication that your marriage was anything less than a love match, but we both had endured marriages that were miserable and only severed by death.

It was two years later when we met again. The sparkle in your eyes told me you were the one. I love you, my dear, and you know this. As the years are quickly passing, I want you to remember the things we have talked about and my requests if I should happen to die first. Remember, you are the love of my life, and I will be with you through eternity.

My brother Charles was a dishonorable man. Frances and her child, Joycellyn, who I think of as my own, are under my protection. If there is any way possible, please watch over Joycellyn and be there to protect her if necessary. I will do all in my power to ensure she is cared for.

After visiting my brother in America, I can only tell you again that he is a fine and honorable man. If you should ever need anything, go to him. He will help. I have written to him about you, the love of my life.

His wife Anne is the granddaughter of a freed slave. He has three children. The son Sterling, Sar, is named after me. The two daughters are Meredith and Elizabeth. He and his wife have done a fine job with them.

One day they will be in London. This will mean I am no longer with you. Help them navigate the waters of our society. I know you will grow to love them as I love you.

Tears clouded her vision. *Sterling, I love you. I miss you so much. I have met them, and they are as kind as you said. I wish you were here instead of hovering about watching.*

Exhausted, she closed her eyes, and images of their time together floated through her mind.

Well done, old girl. You never knew you'd be a grandmother. They'll grow to love you. I miss you too, but it's not your time yet. I need you to be there for the other weddings and the birth of some of the grandchildren. I'll be watching and waiting for you. I'll love you always and beyond eternity.

She woke the following morning to the smell of his cigar smoke. *Thank you, my love. I have a wedding to help plan, and I'm the grandmother of the bride.* She quickly wrote her note and rang for her maid.

***

Anne met with the staff in Mrs. Spencer's office.

"Dowager Duchess Horton has offered her assistance with the wedding and the availability of her staff. This may be highly unusual, and I don't want any of you to feel as though you're being replaced. It's important to be comfortable with this arrangement and for all of us work together. The cooks have already started the menu."

"Your Grace, Lady Horton's gardener is one of the best around. With all the blooms we need and fancy designs, his help will be appreciated." The gardener asked for a clearer picture of what Her Grace wanted for the designs and the types of flowers to be used. Orchids needed to be found, hot houses raided, blooms forced.

"With your permission, Your Grace, may I call on the gardeners of the other ladies involved with planning the wedding?"

"Yes, if they don't mind. Talk with each other and Lady Horton's staff as the need arises. Things will be easier to co-ordinate if we're moving forward together. Lady Horton's staff will stop by today. Mrs. Spencer, please let me know what additional help we need. Approximately five hundred invitations are being delivered.

"I also received a note from Lady Horton, advising me that with the announcement of the betrothal there'll be a long line of afternoon callers. We'll only receive between two and three until after the wedding. For things to be easier for Cook, let's have sweetmeats and pastries we can leave on the carts for the entire hour."

"Your Grace, that should work very well. If Cook could assign someone to watch the carts, we'll be assured there is always plenty. Might I suggest we receive in a larger room."

"Thank you, Mrs. Spencer. We'll use the other morning room; it's twice as large. Cook, arrange for someone to watch the carts. Oliver, will this work for you?"

"Yes, Your Grace."

"Julien is sending bouquets to Mer. Let's place them throughout the house. This will help the gardeners concentrate on the wedding and the grounds."

"Thank you, Your Grace." *How thoughtful and considerate,* the gardener mused.

"Cook, we'll have twenty-four for dinner tonight. Count on that number for dinner most evenings before the wedding, but be prepared to accommodate more."

Mrs. Spencer, knowing her best friend well, informed everyone as to what to expect. "Mrs. Kiggins has been with the Dowager Duchess for the past eighteen years. She'll do anything to help Lady Horton. If Lady Horton wants this wedding to be spectacular, Mrs. Kiggins will make sure of it."

As soon as the meeting was over, Mrs. Spencer made a beeline to Lady Horton's house to compare notes with Kiggins.

***

In the luxurious bedroom in the other house in Mayfair, she reclined on the deep-blue-velvet counterpane in only her silk stockings and garters. "Do you think this will work? They will be on the lookout for something to happen at Richmond."

"Yes, and we'll give it to them. When they discover him, I'll be far away. I want you increasing by then. Your child will be mine, and your husband will raise him as his own. My blood will inherit his title."

By five minutes after two, just as Lady Horton had predicted, the receiving room was packed. Anne underestimated the number of curiosity seekers. Even a few of those who had given her the direct cut were among the callers. At promptly three, Oliver informed additional callers that Her Grace was no longer receiving but would receive between two and three tomorrow. She wasn't able to shoo the last stragglers out until three thirty.

Avery, I have never seen such a group of silly young ladies and their mothers. Sar is going to have a difficult time finding the right bride. If they weren't interested in marrying off the daughter, they wanted to know about the wedding or give their advice. Our Mer is getting married to a wonderful young man. You would like him. I miss you.

"Pardon me. Did you say something, Your Grace?"

"Oliver, please make sure this room is straightened. We'll be using the room next to the conservatory for planning the wedding. Have this desk moved there."

Oliver wondered if Her Grace always talked to herself. He'd have to ask Perkins. Once again, he patted his pocket. She was his to protect.

As the combined staffs of the great houses joined forces, the wedding planning took on the epic proportions of a major battle. The room next to the conservatory became the command center, and Lady Horton the commander. Papers and lists were spread everywhere. Invitations were designed, flowers ordered, and menus transformed from wonderful to extraordinary. The Dowager Duchess approved the design of her gown and added seventy-five names to the guest list. Rejecting design after design of flowers for the church, she forged on.

"No, no . . . above the door of the church. I want the bower to represent the fruitfulness of their home to come. Those who enter are welcome. For the end of the pews, two different floral arrangements, and complementary designs for the front of the church."

Joycellyn sketched and sketched, trying to find the look Lady Horton wanted. "Yes, that's what I want for the front of the church, only fuller and richer."

Cook sang as she and Lady Horton's cook made dinner. Once released from their lessons, little Elizabeth and Edward started their chores and ran through the kitchen grabbing treats.

That evening in the hallowed halls of Almack's, the patronesses were doing their weekly review, determining if anyone should be granted vouchers or if anyone should lose theirs due to *déclassé* behavior. But the real topic of discussion was the surprise announcement of the engagement of Briarcliff's son to the Duke of Westmoure's sister.

"With this marriage, Westmoure's family will solidify their position within *le bon ton*. Her Grace was perfect when presented to His Majesty, and he even received her. Their behavior has been impeccable. Now it's up to us whether to give the younger sister the ultimate status." Lady Sarah Jersey had given the voucher to His Grace herself. It was impossible to deny the request of her godmother.

"But they're mixed blood, and *that* has some of us in society concerned about the sanctity of the purity of lines of future generations. We pride ourselves on the breeding of those we allow vouchers. It sets us apart from the rest. What would happen if one of our granddaughters or grandsons married one of the sisters' children? Just think about one of our daughters marrying the duke." Lady Emily Cowper wasn't quite sure what to think of this mixed-blood family.

Connections and wealth put aside, they were Negroes; mixed blood didn't belong with the elite.

Lady Anne Stewart, Marchioness of Londonderry and the Viscountess of Castlereagh, wondered why the most revered woman of the ton had befriended the Roxburys. The Viscountess of Castlereagh voiced her concerns. "The younger sister hasn't had her come-out. Regardless of their breeding, by the company they keep, it's evident the family is already accepted by some of the powerful of the elite of society. Granted, we have always prided ourselves on the breeding of our members, but we are going to have to make a choice. If we ignore them, where will that leave us?

"We can either sanction the family or sit back and watch.

With or without us, the duke's family is connected to the highest echelon of society. We, the patronesses of Almack's, would be remiss and lose our status as the arbiter of the elite if we don't accept them. Goodness, they have the backing of Grayson, Broadhurst, Lady Horton, Briarcliff, Edgerton, Carrington, Northampton, Aston, and Danford."

Countess de Lieven couldn't imagine falling out of grace with those members of society. They would be slitting their own throats, instant death. "Since they're new to this country and the ways of society, it's only proper for us to give the younger sister her come-out. We can guide her. The wedding is a month from Wednesday. We'll have her come-out a month later. Ladies, with or without us, the family will be a part of the elite of society. We'll call on them tomorrow. Her Grace only receives between two and three."

Lady Sarah Jersey and the other six patronesses of Almack's continued their weekly business.

***

On Tuesday, Lady Horton arrived for lunch, along with Caroline, Diana, Aurelia, Georgina, Miriam, and Evelyn. They were calling it the mothers' lunch. At one-thirty Oliver interrupted to ask if Her Grace was receiving.

"The Countess of Jersey, the Marchioness of Londonderry, Lady Emily Cowper, Lady Sefton, Countess de Lieven, Baroness Willoughby de Eresby, and Countess Esterhazy are requesting to be received."

Lady Horton's eyes sparkled, and she hooted with glee. "The patronesses of the Assembly Rooms of Almack's, the committee of the exclusive, have come to call. Have Oliver show them to the front room and let them wait a bit. You don't want to seem too anxious. It'll be interesting to see what they want."

"Lady Horton is right. Have Oliver tell them you're receiving." Caroline's eyes gleamed with amusement. She couldn't wait to hear why they were calling.

"Have Cook send in refreshments. I'll receive them, Oliver."

In all of his years of service, Oliver had never heard of all of the lady patronesses of Almack's calling at one time. He'd check with the butlers of other fine houses to see if anything like this had occurred before.

When Anne and the other ladies entered the morning room, she thought she saw a look of approval on Lady Jersey's face. When she looked again, Lady Jersey had slipped into her stern role of grand arbiter of *le bon ton*.

"Your Grace, thank you for receiving us. Your younger daughter, Beth, has not had her come-out yet. We'll allow her to make her come-out at Almack's two months from Wednesday. It's necessary and required of a young lady of rank and privilege to be presented to society. It's a slight if she isn't."

Lady Jersey quickly glanced around the room. The elite of the elite were having lunch with Her Grace. And the grand dame of all was present—Lady Horton. Yes, they made the right decision. She saw herself falling from her elite perch if they'd snubbed Westmoure's family. She shuddered. "Could we discuss the details here at lunch on Friday?"

Anne surreptitiously glanced at Caroline and Lady Horton. The imperceptive nod of their heads was all the answer Anne needed. "Lady Jersey, we're honored."

This appeared to be the answer the patronesses wanted, for they all gave their smile of approval.

"We must be going. Callers will be arriving soon; we know you receive between two and three. We'll see you Friday at noon." As the ladies were leaving, those arriving noticed the patronesses of Almack's.

There were more callers today than yesterday, and the receiving dragged on and on. Finally, the tedious hour was over.

"Well, what do you think? What if Beth doesn't want a come-out? Only her brother, Jacob, Grayson, Julien, and Royce have asked her to dance at the balls. Should Beth do this?" Anne was at a loss. Her children had been through enough in the past few months. She didn't want them subjected to the humiliation of the *ton*. Beth, at her own come-out and no one asks her to dance; the gossipmongers would have a field day.

"Ah-ha, now they're courting you. You've been enclosed in the sacred bosom of the elite. This will get those high sticklers in an uproar. I can't wait until the rumors get back to us." Lady Horton patted Anne's hand. "You'll be fine, my girl. You're doing more than stirring things up a bit. The pot is about to boil."

Sterling, I wish you were here. What a kick you'd get out of this.

"Don't worry about Beth's dancing partners. The patronesses will pick them. And no gentleman dare refuses them. At Almack's, the come-out balls are usually very boring, but I'm sure we'll be able to change things." Aurelia stopped speaking when Perkins slipped into the room.

"You needed me, Your Grace?"

"What is being said about the patronesses of Almack's call?"

"Most assume your voucher has been revoked. The comments were quite cutting; you've been tried and found wanting. After all, you're mixed blood; your lineage isn't impeccable."

"Thank you, Perkins. You're of invaluable service as usual."

"Thank you, Your Grace."

"He's worth his weight in gold. I'll take Perkins anytime you don't need him." Lady Horton imagined the juicy bits Perkins could uncover for her.

Beth was the first to see the gossip column on Wednesday. "Oh my goodness, oh my goodness, I don't believe this!" She handed the paper to her mother.

The London Daily

Society News

I should state, but for the Duke and Duchess of Carrington's ball, this entire column is about the Duke of Westmoure and his family. The ball was a veritable crush. The Duchess of Carrington looked spectacular in her gold-tone dress. The Duchess of Westmoure, the Marchioness of Broadhurst, the Duchess of Edgerton, the Countess of Danford, and the Duchess of Northampton were also stunning in dresses of various shades of gold. No one knows who is designing these fabulous gowns. It remains a secret, and the ladies of the ton need to know.

The talk of the ton is the Duke of Westmoure and his family. All tongues are wagging about the surprise announcement at the ball of the betrothal of the Marquess of Briarcliff's son, Lord Julien, to the Duke of Westmoure's sister, Lady Meredith. Since doubtful this is a love match, the question is: how much did Westmoure have to pay the perspective groom, one of the renowned rakes of London, to accept the bride? At least no gunshots were fired. The wedding is in a month. Who will be among those invited?

We understand at the ball in the ladies withdrawing room a confrontation erupted over the news of the announcement of the betrothal. Hair was flying and a dress ripped to shreds. Shards of porcelain littered the floor.

It is also rumored one of the duke's sisters was there as a bystander.

The seven patronesses of Almack's called upon the Duchess of Westmoure. Why? No one seems to know. There is the speculation of the obvious: their voucher has been revoked because of their less than perfect breeding. Tonight, all eyes will be on those attending Almack's.

There is a long line of mothers and debutants wanting an introduction to the Duke of Westmoure. As of this writing, he has not singled out a young lady as his perspective bride.

Will the Duke of Westmoure and his family be all we talk about?

To Caroline, the hallowed halls of the matrimony mart appeared more crowded than usual that Wednesday. Mer only had eyes for Julien, who to her stood out in the crowd in his formal attire and knee breeches. Unfortunately, there was no way for Mer to avoid the necessary meeting of the patronesses of Almack's. It was worse than her interview with Lady Horton. Lady Jersey and Lady Castlereagh scrutinized her closely. When asked, she showed them her ring. She didn't understand why everyone wanted to see it.

Once through the receiving line, she and Julien then faced the elite of the ton. Much to the chagrin of some of the ladies in attendance, he stayed close to her. They danced once and spent most of the evening answering questions about the wedding and watching women gasp at her ring.

In a corner, the Duke of Brockton's heir apparent smiled, for everything would be his soon. The old man was still missing. In another three weeks, he'd send out a search party to bring back the body, if one could be found.

Lady Jersey and Lady Castlereagh introduced the Duke of Westmoure to eligible young ladies and suggested he dance with a select few. The other part of the evening was spent watching over their charges and discussing Julien and Mer.

"Did you see that ring?" Lady Jersey asked.

"It is not as we thought." Lady Castlereagh smiled at one of this year's debutantes.

"No, not at all. This is a love match. No one but someone in love gives a ring like that to one's intended." Lady Jersey thought of her mother-in-law, one of the notorious mistresses of the Prince of Wales. She'd never received jewelry half as spectacular as the ring on Westmoure's sister's hand.

"It would have been a *faux pas* of disastrous social consequences to deny them a voucher. The sister's come-out is important." The Viscountess of Castlereagh looked around. It was five minutes before the doors closed at eleven, and the assembly rooms were packed.

Anne was laughing and dancing her way through the evening, when Berkley and Quinn slipped through the door at one minute to eleven. All heads turned to watch their progress, and whispers started. The patronesses expected nothing less than the two men to pay the correct homage to them, and they did.

Berkley took Anne's hand and escorted her to supper. Unlike private balls, supper was the usual Almack's matter: day-old, thinly sliced bread with fresh butter, and fresh cake without frosting. The dry cake, as it was called, was scrumptious, and Berkley smiled at Anne's surprise with the first bite of the treat.

The band struck up a waltz, and he led her to the dance floor. People didn't know who to watch, the Duke of Westmoure, the Duchess of Westmoure, or Julien and Mer.

After the dance, Julien turned Mer over to her mother and

joined Berkley and Quinn. The group, which included Sar and Sebastian, seemed to form an exclusive circle. Everyone else steered clear of them and watched. Sar passed the note he had received earlier to Quinn: *Enjoy yourself. This may be your last dance.*

Later in Sar's study, they added the note to their mounting stack of clues. "There were over two hundred people in attendance at Almack's. Can you recall anything that suggests when and where the note was slipped into your pocket?" Quinn asked.

"With so many people about, getting in and out of the coach, the attendants, the receiving line, and the assembly rooms themselves, I don't know. People bumped into me. People wanted my attention for introductions, and there were the curious." Sar hated the idea that the assassin was within reach and he'd probably met him—or her.

Daggs paced as plans were made. "Another attempt on your life will be made soon. How do we keep everyone safe and catch the murderer?"

*****

On Thursday, like every other day that week, there was a long line of callers. Sar avoided the morning room. He had never seen so many mothers trying to marry their daughters off to a total stranger. What if he was a lecher? The mothers didn't seem to care. All they wanted for their daughters was a title and wealth.

Anne sat through endless inquiries about her son, Julien and Mer, and the wedding. Her Grace unclenched her jaw at the end of the hour and poured herself a brandy.

By Friday morning, all of the wedding invitations had been delivered. Lady Horton went through her list. The gardeners met with the ladies, reviewed the sketches of the plans, made suggestions, and left. The candle maker arrived, and departed with designs that were pieces of art.

Promptly at noon, the seven patronesses of Almack's arrived for lunch. "This is my daughter." Anne introduced Beth and noted their approval.

The patronesses set about discussing the come-out. "Sarah, this will have to be a come-out unlike any other at Almack's." Aurelia knew Lady Jersey's and Lady Castlereagh's weakness. They had to be above *le bon ton*, the first to bring things of note to society, and the first to bring society up to their supreme level.

"You're right; the child's come-out can be like no other. We have the privilege of having the sister of one of the richest men in all of England make her debut at Almack's, even though her breeding is unusual, and she is an American not used to the ways of our society. We must guide her and show our society that she is the elite of the elite, in the class of the esteemed few. Yes, we must make this different. Look at her. The child has impeccable manners."

Beth smiled. The other patronesses stared at Beth and agreed with Lady Jersey. Beth felt like the animal in a scientific experiment. Everyone was prodding and poking. She wondered if she had to show her teeth next.

When Lady Jersey started extolling about the exclusivity of the come-out, Aurelia knew all the standard rules set for other come-outs were going to be tossed out the window.

"With your permission, we can only have those of Beth's elite rank plan the affair," Aurelia said. "I suggest my cook, along with the Duchess of Carrington's cook, create the menu. The Duchess of Northampton and the Countess of Danford can take over the responsibility of decorating the assembly rooms. The Marchioness of Broadhurst and the Marchioness of Briarcliff will handle the invitations and other details. Lady Horton can oversee and coordinate everything. Her Grace will learn from all of us. We want her prepared when her son marries. She is part of our society now and must be the epitome of decorum and grace."

Aurelia smiled her best smile, and watched as Sarah, like a fish out of water, grappled with the change in the old order of things.

They discussed the come-out and approved Aurelia's plan. The usual tea and lemonade only served at Almack's wouldn't do. They added champagne, brandy, wine, and port. Setting the bar for exclusivity, the invitation and a special voucher would have to be presented to gain admittance. To all others, Almack's was closed. As for Beth's dress, the design and designer were a secret.

"We will see you next Friday, Your Grace. Do not hesitate to contact me if need be." Lady Sarah Jersey, the dragon guardian of Almack's, left, with the other patron saints trailing behind.

As the patronesses were leaving, the first in a long line of afternoon callers began. Cook and her staff refilled the carts four times during the hour. Before Aurelia left, Anne had to find out how she managed to get the patronesses to agree to a come-out that was totally different for Almack's.

"Anne, I just played on their vanity. They set themselves up as arbitrators of society and perfection by making their own rules. Sarah Jersey is my mother's godchild; I have known her all my life. She tries to ignore the fact her mother-in-law was one of Prinny's mistresses and involved in the prince regent's scandalous private life, which was really a public life of notorious orgies, gambling, other debauchery, and mindless spending. Parliament passed a special bill to increase his allowance just to pay off his debts.

"The politics of being Prinny's number-one mistress for many years involved backstabbing, cat fighting, and maneuvering to eliminate any competition. Their affair started in

1782. I believe around 1803 or 1804, others caught Prinny's eye. For twenty years, she was his lady love. She kept his interest longer than most marriages.

"One other thing—Sarah's mother-in-law's father died before she was born. Her mother-in-law's father, the Reverend Philip Twysden, Bishop of Raphoe, was shot and killed attempting to rob a stagecoach in London, a very disreputable man of the cloth. No one knows how she managed to marry as well as she did. It's rumored it's the king's influence. With all of the scandalous behavior of society, nonacceptance of your family is unacceptable."

Avery, this is pure madness here. Most people are not what they seem. We need you.

As if summoned, Perkins appeared. "You needed something, Your Grace?"

"Perkins, callers saw the seven patronesses of Almack's leave. What are the rumors today?"

"Some believe the patronesses are giving you lessons in deportment. Others think they are warning you your voucher may be revoked, since you are uncivilized Americans." She and Aurelia shook their heads with laughter as Perkins told them more.

The *crack* shattered the glass. Her Grace ducked and pulled the gun from her garter. Aurelia rolled to the floor. Perkins flew out of the house. The note stated: *You didn't think anyone could get this close.*

With pistol in hand, Oliver found His Grace, Royce, Julien, and Sebastian in the study. They joined Perkins outside.

After dinner, the men took their port in the garden. "No one saw anything today?" the general questioned.

"Perkins was with Her Grace when the rock was thrown through the window. He was out of the house immediately. Oliver informed us. We joined Perkins outside and thoroughly combed the area. There was nothing. Perkins didn't even see someone turning the corner." Sar had difficulty believing the square was empty. There wasn't even a carriage about.

"Too close . . . too close. Whoever it is, they are getting too close. Who was the message intended for, Sar, Her Grace, or both? I don't think this is a new crime, but a continuation of one of the original crimes." A pacing Daggs sipped his port.

"All of the notes were written by different people. Does this support our theory of co-conspirators, or are these different crimes? Perkins, follow His Grace wherever he goes. Stay particularly close to him at Richmond." Quinn was talking to Perkins through a closed door.

"Perkins, you might as well come in."

"He can't. It's a game. He has to keep his skills sharp. Trust me. He heard every word you said," Sar said with a smile.

"Gentlemen, I believe we are about to solve something." But what? Quinn hoped he could keep the Graces alive.

Mer stood silently in the shadow hearing every word spoken. Perkins hadn't even detected her presence. She was getting very good at this, or he was so in tune with her that he sensed everything was safe. The first fitting of her wedding gown was Saturday, and she intended for everyone to be alive to see her wear it. She wasn't waiting another year to marry Julien, and she didn't think she looked particularly stunning in black.

CHAPTER 20

The Hunting Accident

Without a doubt, Alexius heard a collective sigh when the banns were read in church for the second time. She gently nudged Beth and raised her eyebrows. Only the two of them seemed to notice. The Marchioness of Briarcliff smiled to herself. She remembered when the banns for her wedding to Julien's father were read; she'd heard the same collective sigh. Thoughts of little ones running through the house brought tears to her eyes.

With the wedding a little more than two weeks away, the house was brimming with activity. Mrs. Spencer's additional help was cleaning and polishing every room from top to bottom. The house took on an extra sparkle along with the excitement of a celebration. The feeling was contagious. Cook kept little Elizabeth and Edward busy running errands for the bustling kitchen. Oliver held meetings with the footmen, and the gardeners worked from sunup to late in the evenings. Her Grace and the Dowager Duchess Horton stood for the first

fitting of their gowns. Lady Horton took the stack of accep-
tances from the salver and continued working on the seating
arrangements.

Oliver interrupted. "Your Grace, a royal messenger just delivered this." He handed the envelope to Her Grace.

The ladies gathered for the mothers' lunch to discuss the
plans for the wedding. "Excuse me, Your Grace."

"Yes, Cook." Cook and Lady Horton's cook stood before
them.

"For lunch, you're sampling some of the dishes we plan to
create for the wedding feast. We've taken the liberty of making sheets so you can check which ones are your favorites. The
gentlemen will do the same. A miniature replica of the wedding cake will be ready next Monday."

"Thank you both. This is an excellent idea. Will you also
have Mrs. Spencer, Mrs. Kiggins, and Oliver taste everything?"

Anne smiled. She was becoming a little nervous about the
wedding and the proper this and that's when a familiar voice
invaded her thoughts. *You'll do just fine, Your Grace.*

Avery, she thought, but as usual he was gone.

"We'll need to make additional arrangements for the wedding. His Majesty has accepted and will attend the ceremony
and wedding feast. I need your help more than ever."

"Not to worry. Just follow our lead. Everything from the
ceremony to the food will be exceptional. The tasting is a brilliant idea of the cooks." Diana thought of the endless meals
she'd eaten with His Majesty and spooned up another bit of
delicate melon soup. "Never become concerned about serving His Majesty. He loves food. If what we are eating today is
an indication of the feast, the cooks have outdone the Royal
Kitchen."

"If His Majesty didn't indicate how many people will be
attending him, plan on thirty," Aurelia said. "Also advise the

cooks, Oliver, and Mrs. Spencer. The patronesses of Almack's are going to be thrilled."

Aurelia thought of Sarah Jersey and wondered how she handled functions with His Majesty present. The scandal surrounding her mother-in-law as the king's mistress was a juicy bit of gossip passed from one generation to the next; it would never die.

"The receiving hour will start soon. Probably half the ton already knows His Majesty will be attending the wedding. I'll receive the callers alone today. You can continue working on the preparations. Do people do this all the time?" Anne looked at the other women and caught herself rolling her eyes and snorted. "One more comment about the weather or someone's dress and I'll weep."

"Yes, some people do this all of the time and think it is the only proper thing to do. I'll receive with you. It will probably continue until after Sar is married. Maybe the men should do the receiving. Calls wouldn't last more than ten minutes. They'd put an end to the endless babble." Caroline laughed. "Sebastian receiving callers, after a few minutes he would excuse himself and never return."

***

The Duke of Brockton saw his solicitors and gave them the information sent to him by his friend, the late Duke of Westmoure. He'd have answers soon. While he waited, there was no reason why he shouldn't do a little matchmaking. As much as possible, he put his cook in Seymour's path.

He wanted everyone happy.

***

On Tuesday, lunch tasted better than the day before. "Excellent! Your cook's French training is apparent. You may not know, but she was taught by the great chef Marie-Antoine Carême. He was in England when His Majesty was Prince of Wales, and served as his *chef de cuisine*. Monsieur Carême prepared the great feast. Your cook worked beside him every day. I can't wait to see the *pièces montées* for the wedding. He was known for the elaborate centerpieces and your cook will try to live up to his reputation."

It seemed to Anne that Lady Horton knew more about the late duke and Cook than any of the other ladies. Avery's familiar laugh echoed in her mind, and he whispered, *If you only knew.*

Her mind shouted, *Tell me everything!* Silence was her only answer. *Avery, we need to talk.*

Laughter was his response.

There were more fittings, and the number of callers increased. Of the 575 wedding invitations sent, 287 had already responded *yes*. Another stack of envelopes was given to Lady Horton. If she was correct, they'd have over a thousand people witnessing the marriage—more for the ton to chew on. She laughed to herself and silently thanked Sterling.

On Wednesday morning, Oliver handed the news sheet directly to Her Grace and secretly smiled. He'd opened it to the Society News. His star among the butlers of great houses was rising.

The London Daily

Society News

Is there anything newsworthy other than the Duke of Westmoure's family? No. It is a love match! The ring is a stunning emerald-and-diamond masterpiece. Only someone in love would give a ring like that. Another notorious London rake is no longer available. As we all know, reformed rakes make the best husbands. Sorry, ladies.

The wedding will be an event of the season. Of course, it is being held at St. George's on Hanover Square. It is a most coveted invitation. Will you be among the invited?

Almack's last week was a crush. Wherever the duke and his family go, others follow. He was seen dancing with a select few young ladies, but he still hasn't picked a lucky one for his bride. His duchess will want for nothing, except love. We trust she can be kept alive. If she presents the duke with an heir, the contamination of society continues.

Lord Berkley and Lord Quinn were in attendance and spent their time with the duke's family. In all the times Lord Berkley has attended Almack's, he has never danced. On Wednesday, he waltzed with the duke's mother.

The younger sister of the Duke of Westmoure, Lady Beth will make her come-out at Almack's this season. The patronesses of Almack's have embraced the family. The patronesses meet with Her Grace once a week to plan the debut. Special invitations and a special voucher will be issued for the ball. Without these, you cannot attend. The ladies of several great houses are planning the event, including a supper unlike any other at Almack's.

Who is Joycellyn? She is the modiste who

creates the gowns worn by Her Grace and several other ladies of the ton. Rumor has it she is so exclusive that she will design only for a very select few. Joycellyn's by-invitation-only establishment will open shortly on Bond Street, next to Cummings. But who is Joycellyn? That remains a mystery.

His Majesty will attend the wedding ceremony and wedding feast.

Will there ever be anything else to discuss other than the Duke of Westmoure and his family, the Roxburys?

That evening, Mer went to find Julien to persuade him to take a walk in the garden. She discovered the men in Sar's study and stood in silence.

***

A dark, gloomy Thursday morning greeted them. Gray clouds hid the sun. Sar hoped the weather wasn't an omen for the day. Over breakfast, Beth babbled on about the glories of Richmond.

"It will be a day in the country. Parts of Richmond will remind us of America. The two hundred and seventy-five acres were originally designed as a royal park for hunting by Charles the First in 1637. Some of the trees he planted are still standing."

"Beth, what did you do, read every book about Richmond?" Mer said with a laugh.

By the time the family set out, the dark clouds had blown through and the blue sky was dotted with an occasional fluffy puff. The scene at Richmond was just as Beth described: bits of

America and manicured lawns like a sea of green glass. Guests strolled about, sat in garden chairs, or on blankets. Tables covered in pristine white linen were laden with an abundance of succulent morsels and sweets in silver and crystal. Servants scurried here and there, ensuring all the guests were well catered to and their every wish fulfilled. Even the fussiest of diners seemed to be pleased.

The fresh air reminded Anne of the crispness found in the woods surrounding the house in America. She inhaled deeply for the first time in weeks and scanned the area, checking on everyone.

Julien was speaking with his parents. Alexius, Beth, and Royce were walking towards Pen Ponds. Berkley ate with her, keeping up a dialog of funny stories and pointing out people she may not have met yet. Daggs and Quinn were somewhere about. Sar was exploring the park. Perkins followed closely behind. She couldn't account for Mer. Before she panicked, she'd have Berkley look for her.

Sar felt a sense of freedom in the open space. This is what he missed, and decided they'd spend more time in the country. It was difficult trying to get the right of everything in England.

Dad, I miss you so much. How can I do this? Images and thoughts raced through his mind: his father's death, finding out he was mixed blood, being stripped of all rights in America because of that, a title, being shot, smuggling, espionage, and society. Finding a wife among the available debutantes or acceptable women of the ton was not a priority on his to-do list.

Having Joycellyn become a part of the family was one of the pluses of being in England. The two little imps running through the house made the family more complete. Discreet inquiries had been made as to the whereabouts of their parents, but little Elizabeth and Edward were just two among the hordes of abandoned homeless children in London.

With the help of Daggs, Quinn, and Berkley, they'd solve the murders and problems within the shipping company. He wanted to introduce bills in Parliament to eliminate abuse of children in orphanages and workhouses. Looking to the future, there was much to be done.

Thinking about Mer's upcoming marriage shifted his thoughts to his mother. They needed to talk about everything. Occasionally he still saw grief in her eyes and knew she missed her father deeply. She made an excellent duchess. One might think, with her aristocratic demeanor and grace, she'd been born into the role. Being in the elite of society came as naturally to her as breathing.

He could feel himself relax as the calmness of the woods and grass engulfed him; he wanted to keep walking until he'd covered every inch of the park. It was hard to believe this bit of paradise was only twelve miles from London.

The form on the ground a few feet in front of him looked like a man. Preparing himself in case it was a ploy, he checked his pistol and slowly approached the body. He turned the man over.

Blood flowed from the gash in his head. "Perkins, get help now!" Perkins ran for help, passing Mer in the bushes. She moved toward Sar.

When he looked down again, a pistol was aimed directly at this heart. "Now, Your Grace, don't utter a sound. Slowly remove the pistol you just returned to your pocket, the knife in your sleeve, and take your boots off. That's it."

The gentleman tossed the boots far out of Sar's reach without taking his eyes off of him.

"Good, now I will tie your hands. Kneel! If you so much as attempt to make a move, I will kill you before we talk. It makes no difference to me."

Sar's hands and feet were tied behind him. The man faced

Sar and backed out of reach. He knew his only chance to live was to keep the man talking.

"The blood was a clever bit, wasn't it? Learned that from the actor, Brian O'Keefe." The man laughed. "I want you to understand why I'm going to kill you. Your father was killed, and you'll soon join him because he married a mixed blood, a Negro, and begot an heir—you. My love and I, and many of us in society, understand the importance of the sanctity of pure lines and know the superiority of our lineage. To have our lines tainted by blood of inferiors is not acceptable. The aristocracy would no longer exist in its purest form. It's fine if commoners choose to taint their blood by mixing it, but it isn't acceptable for those of the aristocracy. We are a class above the ordinary human being.

"Having you and your heir become a part of our society is totally unacceptable. We can't allow anyone in your family to live. You don't understand the importance of keeping everything pure. How could you?" He laughed. "You're mixed blood. We must do this for future generations and to uphold the sanctity of the purity of lineage."

Perkins's instincts were screaming at him, telling him something was wrong. It was too far to go all the way, but he was close enough. He let loose two sharp whistles, kept running, and whistled again.

Her Grace was about to ask Berkley to look around for Mer, when she heard the distress signal used to indicate trouble on the Underground Railroad. "There's trouble. Follow that whistle. Go quickly!"

The general rose and signaled Daggs, Quinn, and Sebastian. They slipped away from the crowd without being noticed.

Beth, Alexius, and Royce were strolling towards the picnic area when Beth heard the faint shrill. "There's trouble. Get Julien and follow that whistle. Hurry! Alexius, do you have your pistol? Where is Mer?" She saw her mother, but Mer was missing. Once out of sight, she ran as fast as she could, following the direction of the sound of the whistle.

The second set of whistles came and Her Grace slipped out of sight. Caroline and Aurelia followed.

Once Julien and Royce were clear of the picnic area, they ran. Reaching Perkins first, he pointed them in the direction. "Go quickly. Something is wrong. Go!"

Mer stood several feet away from Sar and his captor. Neither saw her. Sar heard the whistle and knew help was on the way.

"Who are you? At least let me know who is going to kill me. You look familiar." Sar thought he recognized him as one of those who came to call on him after Sebastian's ball.

"Of course, of course. You don't know me, don't associate with inferiors. We met once at your house after Broadhurst's ball. Didn't attend. Who ever heard of introducing a Negro to society? You're outcasts, as you should be. I am the earl—"

But he never got any further.

Crack! The ball hit the captor's leg. He turned and saw Mer. "Bitch!" He aimed his pistol directly at her heart.

Sar was too far away to fall forward on the earl.

Julien saw the pistol aimed at Mer; his heart stopped. The moment froze. He couldn't reach her and was going to watch the love of his life die.

"No!" he screamed and reached for his pistol, but the man didn't waver. Guests heard the shot and rushed toward the sound.

The words of her mother echoed in her head. *Do you want to be the shooter or the one lying on the ground? Don't play the victim, and don't think twice if the situation calls for it. Most men don't expect a woman to be able to shoot at all. It's not ladylike. Remember, death isn't ladylike either.*

Crack! A second shot rent the air.

The surprised man looked down and saw a bright red stain saturate his shirt. His pistol dropped as he crumpled to the ground. Mer stood braced with a pistol in both hands.

"Get her out of here, Julien, before the others arrive!" Sar shouted.

He scooped up Mer and carried her away in the opposite direction. His life without her had flashed before him in that split second. His heartbeat still wasn't normal. When this was over, they'd talk. He couldn't live without her.

With the second retort, guests started running towards the sound.

Royce quickly untied Sar and threw a jacket over the man. Quinn, Berkley, Sebastian, and Daggs surveyed the area. Simmons arrived, as did several of Daggs's men. Her Grace, Caroline, and Aurelia had their pistols drawn. Beth skidded to a stop. Perkins slipped in beside Sar.

"Mother, Caroline, Aurelia, put your pistols away. It's over. Others are right behind you. We'll talk at home."

Other guests came upon the scene.

"Just an unfortunate hunting accident. We'll take care of it from here," Quinn told the first group to arrive.

Somewhat mollified, they in turn told everyone else who arrived. After a while, the excitement died down and the group slowly returned to the picnic area. Then the gossip started.

Beth couldn't find Mer or Julien. Somehow, she knew Mer was in the middle of this. Beth released the breath she didn't realize she was holding. Mer was safe.

When he'd carried Mer far enough away from the scene, Julien sat down with her in his lap and started kissing her senseless.

"Everything is fine, my sweet," he whispered between kisses. "It's all right."

He knew the internal turmoil that followed after you killed another. Why did it come down to that? You killed the person or got killed. You take another's life and you witness the person's last breath. When the shock wears off, the memory lives with you forever. Her eyes were still unfocused and glazed. She clung to him like a barnacle on the underside of a boat, not even aware she was doing so.

"It's fine, Mer. I'm here. I'll always be here for you." His love, his life, through eternity. "Julien, make love to me now."

He also knew this emotion too, the reaffirmation of life, the need to feel alive.

"Just let me hold you. Let me tell you about the wedding night I'm planning. It'll be a night you'll never forget, the beginning of many nights we'll share. I love you. I love you so much. You're my life. I'm nothing without you." He continued to whisper as she came back to reality and the impact of what just happened started to dawn on her.

Daggs and Simmons examined the body. "Cause of death: a direct shot through the heart, dead center. Julien is a fine marksman." Simmons looked at Sar. "That's what will be in my official report."

"Thanks, Simmons."

They had to protect Mer. A pistol-carrying lady of the ton who shot to kill wasn't acceptable in society, not done among the elite.

"Who is he?"

"That is the Earl of Landingham. Daggs, have your men clean up the area. We'll meet at His Grace's." Berkley walked back to the picnic area, not seeing the beauty of the park surrounding him, his mind spinning, plotting their strategy.

News of the hunting accident would spread like wildfire and have the gossip wheel whirling out of control within hours. Hopefully, this would force the other conspirators to show their hand. The death of the earl was only the beginning of the twisted path surrounding this intrigue. He wondered where the dead earl fit into the scheme of things, top or bottom, and which crime?

Who did he work with?

So absorbed was he in his thoughts he bumped into something and automatically reached for his weapon. When he looked up, he was facing something deadlier than a pistol—Anne's complete trust. The haunting look in her eyes scared him. She was holding him personally responsible for her family's safety. Damn. At that moment, he knew he would die before he disappointed her, or kill anyone who threatened the Roxburys.

Taking another path, Julien guided Mer back to the others. Only her family, Sebastian's family, Berkley, Quinn, Royce, and the Edgertons remained.

"We'll meet at His Grace's," Berkley said. "Julien, we'll need to speak to Mer." Berkley noted she had that glazed, frenetic, after-battle look, but she was coming around.

***

In the opulent bedroom in the other house in Mayfair, she paced back and forth. He should have been there two hours ago. Something was wrong. Double-checking to make sure everything was neat and tidy and there was nothing of hers in the bedroom, she removed all of the jewelry, money, documents, and stocks from the safe and quickly left through the back.

***

Finally, the Roxburys reached town. Anne poured Mer a brandy and informed Cook there would be twenty-one for dinner. Daggs was the last to arrive.

Quinn poured himself a brandy. "Sar, why don't you tell us what happened?"

"After our busy days in the city, the park was a refreshing bit of the country. I decided to walk and came upon a man on the path bleeding from a gash in the head. This was a trick. It seems he learned something from Brian O'Keefe too. I sent Perkins for help. When I turned around again to assist him, there was a pistol pointed at my chest. He took my weapons, made me take off my boots, and threw them out of reach. I was told to kneel. He tied my hands behind my back and backed away.

"Before killing me, he wanted me to know why. A mixed blood is not acceptable in the aristocracy. The lines must be pure, he said. He and others found me unacceptable. No other names were mentioned. Mer shot him in the leg. He turned and aimed the pistol at her and was about to fire. She fired again—this time at his chest."

Sar had never felt such a feeling of helplessness and despair as when the late earl turned the pistol on Mer. Before his eyes, his sister would die. Just the thought of what almost happened caused the bile in his throat to back up and pain to sear his heart. She could have died. *But she didn't. You trained her well, and like you she is a protector of all she holds dear.* Sar smiled and shook his head. *Julien, I believe you've met your match. Your daughters are going to be hellions.*

"Two other things . . . His plan included killing my father. He also called on me after Sebastian's ball."

"Mer, can you tell me what you saw and heard?" Berkley knew her mind had not quite assimilated everything.

"Of course." Her foot tapped to the beat of her words. "Perkins followed Sar, and I followed Perkins. After going some distance, Perkins ran past me, heading back towards the picnic area, and I ran towards Sar. I hid behind the bushes and saw Sar on his knees. The earl was talking. They didn't notice me.

"He said, 'My love and I and many others in society know the superiority of our lineage. To have our lines tainted by blood of inferiors is not acceptable.' He continued to talk as I looked for the shot. I didn't concentrate on what he was saying. When I got the shot, I aimed for his leg and fired. He turned to me and shouted, *'Bitch.'* My mother's words echoed in my head. 'Don't play the victim, and don't think twice if the situation calls for it. Death isn't ladylike.' I aimed for his heart and pulled the trigger. He fell to the ground. I heard Sar shout to Julien, 'Get her out of here!' Julien picked me up and carried me away. Royce was there too." Mer's foot was rapidly tapping its own beat.

"Very good, Mer." Berkley wondered who trained her besides her mother. *Probably her father, Sar, and Perkins. They did a damn fine job. Pistol-packing women of the ton.* Berkley smiled to himself. *Always something new.*

Her Grace handed Mer another glass of brandy. "We shouldn't keep Cook's dinner waiting any longer. It'll be easier to think if everyone is relaxed. Other things will come to mind, and we can fill in any missing gaps. Berkley, who was he?" Anne also sipped on a brandy.

"The Earl of Landingham—and I agree. Let's dine. We can talk after dinner." After dinner, the women relaxed on the terrace and the men adjourned to the study.

"Who is the Earl of Landingham?" Sar couldn't shake the image of Mer with a pistol pointed at her heart.

"The Earl of Landingham lives very close to you here in Mayfair," Berkley replied. "As I recall, he spent time on the Continent and has close friends in the Home Office and the Foreign Office. He isn't married. We don't know if he had a mistress, a lover, or an intended. We'll do some digging to find out his habits. He hasn't been vocal about the title passing to you."

Berkley understood the plot to kill the Roxburys was held in the utmost secrecy by all of those involved. Without a doubt, finding the others would take stealth and cunning.

Daggs added his thoughts. "I'm curious about the woman. When Mer heard Landingham explaining the reason for killing Sar, he said 'my love and I.' Could she have been the one at Newgate, or is his lover a man? Have Grayson check the book at White's. Also, who knows the most gossip of the ton? If we want to find out about the Earl of Landingham's life, we need to find those who know the secrets. Our clues will be there. Sar, how many pistols do the women in your family carry?" He was curious as to the answer.

"Two."

"Even Her Grace?"

"Even Her Grace."

"Mer saved your life. Killing someone is difficult. Eventually she'll recall all of the details of the shooting, including the look on the earl's face and the copious amount of blood. She reacted like a threatened, seasoned solider." Quinn realized her reaction was one of a trained veteran: the enemy must be defeated. "She has been trained to kill, hasn't she?"

"Yes."

"Amazing. Well, gentlemen, this wasn't what I anticipated. I think the death of the earl will force the others to come to us." Quinn glanced at Mer again and his instincts murmured, *Pistol-packing women.*

"The woman who killed John Smith at Newgate may be Landingham's mistress," Daggs said.

"One of the clues we have from Landingham is 'my love and I and many others.' If we can believe his statement, they're working with others. My men are searching the late earl's house. I was there before coming here. Nothing seemed to be out of order, but it didn't feel right. It was as though the house had just been cleaned. There were no clues."

Daggs wrote as he talked. "Here, this should work. Quinn, can you get this to your contact at the *London Daily*? Nothing else is to appear in the paper."

> *The Earl of Landingham was killed in a hunting accident on Thursday. He was discovered by a passerby. Based on the investigation conducted by Scotland Yard, the earl tripped on a tree root and his rifle discharged.*

"One other question, Sar. Mer had two pistols in the ready. Do you know why?" The general waited for the answer.

Sar paused, wondering how to break the news to him. Within his house, he had a spy system that would probably outperform anything the general had. "Well, she overheard every word we said in my study. She's a Perkins student. He demands excellence."

"She'd make an excellent operative."

"*That*, you'll have to discuss with Julien. But if you ever need her, I would ask her first. She won't take kindly to Julien running her life or making decisions for her." Sar laughed. "Julien, did I ever tell you about Mer's pistol collection? You'd be impressed and amazed."

Two things became instantly clear to Julien. He had to have that little talk with Mer. She'd almost given him a heart seizure. And dictating to Mer would never work; she was her own woman with her own opinions and would do what she thought was right. *Maybe that's why you love her. You'll never have a dull moment.*

"Find the person who Landingham's title passes to and watch him," Berkley said, disappearing into the evening. Quinn followed.

***

Two days later, the woman read the article in the *London Daily. A hunting accident. Ha!* The gossip had reached her before the news sheet. Everyone there heard two shots. When people arrived at the scene, they found an inspector from Scotland Yard, the heads of the Home Office and the Foreign Office, the Duke of Westmoure, Broadhurst, Aston, and Briarcliff. Men from Scotland Yard were searching the area. Someone else shot her lover twice. Who killed him?

Why the cover-up? She would find them all. *Consider yourselves dead.* The plan couldn't be stopped.

***

At church on Sunday, the banns were read for the last time. The sigh was slightly louder. Mer grinned. Alexius raised her eyebrow. Beth nudged Alexius. Caroline and Evelyn sat with a knowing look in their eyes.

On Wednesday, Oliver handed the open news sheet to Her Grace.

The London Daily

Society News

Where there are shots you will find the Duke of Westmoure. The Edgerton's affair at Richmond was the event to attend. It ended in a blast, two blasts.

The Earl of Landingham was found dead on a hunting path. According to the official report, his rifle accidentally discharged when he allegedly tripped on a tree root. It was a clean shot through the heart. But those attending heard two shots.

When guests arrived at the scene, they found the Duke of Westmoure, along with Lords Berkley and Quinn and Lord Inspector Daggs of Scotland Yard. It is curious that all of these gentlemen arrived at the scene before any others. Did it have something to do with shrill whistles?

Rumor has it that the man who saved the Duke of Westmoure at the Broadhurst ball fired the shots in the park and saved Westmoure once again from imminent demise. It could not have been a lady. Ladies do not carry pistols in general, and they do not carry pistols to al fresco affairs.

Or do they?

Two shots were heard. Does this intrigue go deeper? Was there a cover-up? Will we ever uncover the truth? If I could enter a bet in the book at White's, I would bet on the lady.

Is there any other news which does not involve the Duke of Westmoure and his family? No! What will be next?

A Few Days Later

Unmindful of the garlands wrapped around the Corinthian columns, she hurried up the steps of St. George's Church on Hanover Square. She neither saw nor smelled the peach, pale lavender, and rich buttercream orchids, roses, and hydrangeas that formed a lush double arch over the doorway. Sliding into the back pew without looking about, she bumped into the young aristocrat already seated, who collided with the man sitting on his right. They smiled at each other as though they were old friends and uninvited guests with a secret shared only by the three of them.

From above, he looked over the crowded sanctuary and fixed his gaze on the three in the back row. *So, they have finally met.* He felt like a puppeteer pulling the strings of their destiny.

Glancing around, she didn't see the flower arrangements draping the ends of the pews, or the candles covered in crystals and pearls softening the severity of this most holy place. Staring at the wrought-iron railings of the pulpit stairs decorated with buttercream flowers made her think about what should have been hers but for the son-of-a bitch who was her sire. And that brought her back to the present moment: the desecration of the aristocracy and the root of her problems. Music from the organ housed in the five-towered case that had been played by George Handel floated through the air. So pre-occupied in thought, she didn't hear a sound.

His Majesty was seated and requested the Duchess of Westmoure and the Dowager Duchess of Horton to join him. Julien stood with Royce and the archbishop.

"You look beautiful, Mer." Sar had never seen his sister look more radiant. "Thanks, Sar. I wish Dad was here."

"He would approve." He put a stem of pale-peach orchids in her hand and the two of them proceeded down the aisle.

Anne couldn't take her eyes off the center aisle. Walking beside Sar, smiling broadly, was Avery. He winked at her. *I approve, darling,* he whispered. Then he was gone. A tear slipped down her cheek.

Mer's eyes were fixed on Julien. Sar placed her hand in Julien's and she felt connected, whole. She was more nervous when they signed the church registry than she had been during the ceremony. When they re-entered the sanctuary, she was wearing the Briarcliff coronet. The archbishop officially pronounced them husband and wife. Julien gave her a kiss, which curled her toes. They bowed to His Majesty, and church bells pealed as they stepped into the sun.

The back pew was empty.

Sar stood on the steps of St. George's and gazed at the tableau in front of him. Rose petals were everywhere. His family was happy. Mer laughed as Julien tossed coins. An old man who looked somewhat familiar was talking to his mother. Lady Horton was quite the stately, elegant matron in the pale-rose creation by Joycellyn. She could catch the eye of any older gentleman.

As if hearing his thoughts, the Duke of Grayson stepped forward and offered her his arm. "Seeing as though we are the grandparents, we should act as such." Grayson smiled down at a beaming Lady Horton.

Perkins stood near Anne. His big hand held little Edward's small one, and he carried Elizabeth in his other arm. Berkley, Quinn, and Daggs talked as they surveyed the crowd. Did they ever stop working?

Royce, Alexius, Beth, the Countess of Fatson's daughters, and Joycellyn stood together. *My God, she's beautiful,* Sar thought. Her hair, shades of blonde mixed with light brown, sparkled in the sun. Those large blue-gray eyes smiled at him. Sar reached for her hand and just as quickly thrust his wayward appendage behind his back.

The wedding feast filled the house with joy and laughter. His Majesty insisted on sitting with Westmoure and Her Grace. Food to tempt the most jaded palate was served: *soufflés de homard une La Montglas, saumon à la Rothschild, galantine de volaille, glace de jambon.* The *pièces montées* were ships, family crests, and a replica of the home in America with a rose garden.

She was married, and the joy and excitement of being Julien's wife outshone the sun. Unable to eat, Julien took her hand and guided her around the room, speaking to everyone in attendance. First, he introduced her to His Majesty, who looked forward to visiting them after the honeymoon. She met the Duke of Brockton, a delightful old man who reminded her of a doting grandfather. They laughed with Lady Hortense. After dancing with Julien and Sar, she took a turn around the room with the Duke of Brockton.

The evening was a magical moment. Every time Anne looked up, she saw Avery smiling. Beth and Alexius never left the dance floor. Sar was having a difficult time escaping widows, and certain matrons, debutantes, and their mothers, especially the Countess of Fatson.

Royce was having the same problem. By the looks and actions of the matchmaking mamas of the ton, he would be the next one to be leg-shackled.

His Majesty laughed with everyone. The lady patronesses of Almack's actually smiled after giving Beth permission to dance the waltz at this very special occasion only.

"Time to go, my sweet." The silk timbre of his voice spoke of promises and a lifetime of togetherness. They said good-bye to His Majesty, their parents, and Sar, and departed amidst best wishes and another shower of rose petals.

***

In the Duke of Brockton's mansion, the young aristocrat and the Earl of Severson dined with the lady they met in the back pew of the church, Sylvia Meacham, the Viscountess of Truvo.

Clearly, she was married and in the market for a lover. Her inviting breasts were barely contained by her gown. Severson could sense them hardening under his leering scrutiny, and from the look on her face, she would take him right now if she could.

Basil, the future Duke of Brockton, was curious as to the best house for his particular lascivious tastes. Severson was more than pleased to recommend one of his favorite establishments, but Basil's inner thoughts focused on the wedding and his goal: the Duchess of Westmoure's death. Who was this damn stranger, and why did his uncle leave his unentailed estate to her?

Sylvia's question brought him back to the present. They discussed the wedding they'd witness and the disgrace of mixed blood in the aristocracy and marrying into one of most prominent families of the aristocracy.

While participating in the conversation, Severson thought about his shipping business and his various sidelines. He had to ensure nothing interfered with his thriving enterprises. The elimination of Westmoure meant his wealth and stability would continue as it had for the last six years. The lean years flashed through his mind and he inwardly shuddered.

Sylvia's smile was an invitation to plunder. Licking her lips, she leaned towards Severson, giving him a better view of her lush orbs. She was thinking about Jack, Sam, and Boss, and what needed to be done in order for their plan to succeed. Next week when she met with Basil and Severson, she could better gauge if they might be worthy allies. She wondered about the unspoken: all of their hidden agendas.

Helping her into a hired hackney, Severson gave her his card, leaned forward, and laved her nipple.

***

The London Daily

Society News

The event of the season was the wedding of the Duke of Westmoure's sister, Lady Meredith, to the son of the Marquess and Marchioness Briarcliff, Lord Julien. The bride wore a gown of pale peach covered in a pale-peach tissue fabric. A band of gemstones encircled the bodice. The train was attached by a brooch at the V of the back. Gemstones and pearls were sprinkled on the tissue overskirt. Sheer sleeves ended in points over the back of her hands. Embroidered throughout the train and on the sheer sleeves were the intertwined crests of both families.

After bowing to His Majesty and hugging her brother, who escorted her down the aisle, the bride embraced her mother, the Duchess of Westmoure. Lord Julien took her hand, and together they approached the archbishop.

After signing the church registry, the bride reappeared with the Briarcliff coronet adorning her hair. This replaced the pale-peach veil worn down the aisle.

Upon entering St. George's, one walked through an enchanted garden. Bowers of cream, pale lavender, and peach flowers formed the arches above the door. The pews, altar, and canopy over the pulpit were similarly adorned.

Candles sparkled with crystals and pearls.

His Majesty immensely enjoyed the wedding feast.

The wedding cake of six round layers sat on top of a square base covered in the whitest of white frosting imprinted with the intertwined crests of the families. Spun sugar flowers and butterflies adorned the cake.

Well, there is no need to guess who designed the dress. It was Joycellyn. Joycellyn was also one of the bride's attendants. Rumor has it Joycellyn is a cousin of the bride. Rumor also has it that Joycellyn is the daughter of the duke's late uncle, Lord Charles Roxbury, and was born on the other side of the blanket. If there is any truth to this, it makes things very interesting, very interesting indeed.

Her Grace was exquisitely gowned in pale blue studded with pearls. Sitting with the family and acting in the capacity of grandmother of the bride was Lady Hortense Horton. (The question everyone is asking is why?) Yes, they too wore Joycellyn's designs, as did the Marchioness of Briarcliff, the Marchioness of Broadhurst, the Duchess of Edgerton, the Countess of Danford, the Duchess of Northampton, and the Duchess of Carrington.

Joycellyn has been accepted by the Duke of Westmoure and his family. Is the old order of things changing? Is a welcome to the ton in order for Joycellyn and her mother, Frances? They will never be embraced by the ton.

One other thing, a store by the name of Paige's is opening soon. It will sell readymade dresses (what are those?), soaps, lotions, and trimmings for working women. Is there finally something afoot in which the Duke of Westmoure's family is not involved? Who has ever heard of readymade dresses? If I could make an entry in the book at White's, I would wager you'd find an uncivilized American Roxbury involved.

The sanctity of the aristocracy has been compromised. What will be next?

After reading hundreds of romance novels, I felt there were other dimensions and avenues to explore in this genre. This was written for fun, but little did I know there were missing pieces of my family history that would come to light. I had always been told my great-great-great-grandmother was from Ireland. We had never been able to trace her entry into the United States. My great-great-great-grandmother was probably among the last groups of women from Ireland sold to America as slaves.

Bringing the Roxburys, the Broadhursts, Julien, Perkins, Royce, Berkley, Quinn, and Daggs to life reminds me of the quirks of fate that take all of us to places we had never previously imagined. The correct historical basis to the book is one that is very different from the incorrect version of history and slavery many of us were taught.

The Regency Period and the reign of King George IV was an incredible time in England. There was vast wealth and power, extreme poverty, and an old order of things, which started to shift. In my creative imagination, my characters are among the shift, as were the real people of this era who enacted change: Anand, Thomas Clarkson, William Wilberforce, and Olaudah Equiano.

Enjoy the life of the Roxburys and the aristocracy as it has not been portrayed before.

—August Jade Sterling

HISTORICAL NOTES

1. Slavery was abolished in England in 1602. Slavery was abolished in all of the British Empire by the Slavery Abolition Act of 1833.

2. On March 25, 1807, An Act for the Abolition of Slave Trade was passed in Parliament and became effective May 1st of that year. This act abolished slave trading. Anand, Thomas Clarkson, William Wilberforce, and Olaudah Equiano were real forces behind the twenty-year campaign to end slave trade.

3. Slave ships were an abomination and more deplorable than mentioned. Slaves were sold to America from several countries, including Africa and Ireland. Irish women were bought to breed with African men; Irish slaves were cheaper to purchase than African slaves. "Satan's Highway to Hell" took years to end, despite the laws and patrols of British and American ships.

4. Many history books overlook the fact that thousands upon thousands of Irish women were sold to Americans as slaves. After the 1798 Irish Rebellion, records show the number of women sold to America as slaves increased. Many Americans classified as black will find their ancestry

deeply intertwined with Ireland and other countries. The same is true for many Irish Americans and others from various countries who will discover their ancestry interwoven with, and relatives include, African or Black Americans.

5. Britain has a long history of interethnic marriages. These marriages have been common since the seventeenth century. Mixed marriages were generally accepted by 1817. There have never been any laws prohibiting interethnic marriages in Britain.

6. Captains of ships are able to perform legally binding marriages. Under the principles of international law, a marriage on the high seas in international waters is legal and binding if the country of which the ship is registered and sails under its flag recognizes the marriage as lawful.

7. The Prince Regent, King George IV, began an affair in 1782 with the mother-in-law of the patroness of Almack's Sarah Jersey. The mother-in-law lured the Prince of Wales away from his secret wife, Maria Fitzherbert, in 1794. The decline of the affair started in approximately 1803.

8. Almack's assembly rooms were the place where the elite went to see and be seen. It was the marriage mart for those of its class, and it existed to exclude the *nouveau riche*. Breeding, along with wealth, behavior, and address, were key factors for being granted a voucher by the lady patronesses of Almack's. The cost of the voucher was ten guineas (a guinea is a little more than a pound). During the height of Almack's supremacy, it was ruled by the six or seven patronesses. The number of patronesses changed depending on who was involved with Almack's at the moment. The Lady Patronesses were the Countess of Jersey, the Marchioness of Londonderry, Lady Emily Cowper, Lady Sefton, Countess de Lieven, Baroness Willoughby de Eresby, and Countess Esterhazy. Their reign lasted until

approximately 1824, when the exclusivity and strictness of the rules were no longer in effect. Today, a high-rise building stands where the elite once danced and were matched. A plaque commemorates the existence of Almack's.

9. Richmond Park was created by Charles I in 1637 as a hunting park. To this day, it is one of the beautiful attractions of the London area. Trees planted by Charles I are still standing.

10. Marie-Antoine Carême was abandoned by his destitute parents when a child. In 1798, he was formally apprenticed to Sylvain Bailly, a famous *pâtissier*. He gained fame in Paris for his *pièces montées*. After the fall of Napoleon, he went to London and served as *chef de cuisine* to the prince regent who became George IV. Today he would be considered a celebrity chef. He raised culinary standards and revised the tastes of the upper class. Besides creating the standard chef's hat, the toque, he is credited with writing at least five cookbooks.

11. The British Empire was the world's leading drug trafficker in the nineteenth century. Although the Chinese used opium as a medicine, there was no widespread addiction before the British arrived. In 1799, an imperial decree was issued prohibiting smoking and importation of opium. Opium addicts and corrupt officials collected bribes to allow smuggling; they effectively became allies with the British in subverting the efforts made by the Chinese government to stop opium smuggling. In 1821, the British responded to the Chinese government's attempt to stop opium importation by moving the base of its opium-smuggling operations out of Canton to the small island of Lintin inside Canton Bay, where the Chinese navy could not threaten it. By 1831, the opium trade into China was two-and-a-half times greater than the tea trade. It was probably the largest traded single commodity in the world.

12. St. George's in Hanover Square in London, England, was built by John James between 1721 and 1725. The organ in the west gallery is housed in a five-towered case. George Frederick Handel was a parishioner from 1724-1759. It is a favorite venue for society weddings.

DON'T MISS THE NEXT BOOK IN
THE AMERICAN DUKE SERIES

TWICE A DUCHESS

COMING SEPTEMBER 2023

CHAPTER 1

———

Breakfast with the King

Her Grace, Anne Roxbury, the Duchess of Westmoure, skipped softly down the stairs of the Duke of Westmoure's town-house in London. She stopped midway and turned her head to listen to the snores of the men. His Majesty had decided to spend the night. Besides her son, Sar, the current Duke of Westmoure, there was Sebastian Standerson, the Marquess of Broadhurst; Grayson, the Duke of Grayson; Richard Quinton, the Marquess of Briarcliff; Royce Thortonshire, the honorable Marquess of Shone; Ashby (Ash) Wyndham, Earl of Danford; Marcus Ryerton, Duke of Northampton; David Rothingham,

Duke of Edgerton; Evan Marston, Duke of Carrington; and Thomas Berkley, the Duke of Hampton, a royal duke, moniker: "the general."

Simmons, the Earl of Carlyle, was also abovestairs, as was Lady Hortense Horton, queen of the ton. Yesterday, they had all witnessed the marriage of Anne's older daughter, Meredith (or Mer, as they usually called her), to Julien Quinton, the son of the Marquess of Briarcliff.

The last guest left at three thirty this morning, but Anne was as wide awake as though she had slept for eight hours. She had dismissed and ordered none of the house staff to appear until two this afternoon. Her Grace was even able to give the footmen a rest. With the king in residence, all the king's men were literally guarding the house.

Anne had promised everyone her American-style celebration breakfast. Anne hummed her way to the kitchen, checked the clock, and donned an apron. For a moment, it felt like being in America preparing Christmas breakfast. Everyone would still be upstairs as she scurried to make the best meal ever. Then she thought of Avery, and tears formed in her eyes.

With all the hustle and bustle of the wedding, the quiet seemed odd. Breakfast for forty. Laughing to herself, she got to work as she replayed the events of yesterday in her mind. Mer's walk down the aisle with her father on one side and Sar on the other was one of the highlights of Anne's day. *Thank you, Avery, for giving your blessing. We wish you were here instead of hovering about with angel wings.*

I wish I were there too. She heard him and felt a soft touch to her cheek. Then he was gone, receding from the niches of her mind. Her Grace understood people would think she was crazy if they knew she communicated with her dead husband. *But that's our secret, isn't it, Avery?*

Every day brought new challenges, heightened awareness, sorrow, and incomparable joys. She didn't want to think about murder always lurking around the next corner, or the smuggling and espionage.

"Your Grace. Please let me help. I couldn't sleep. Too used to being up at this hour." Cook was tying her apron.

"Cook, are you sure?" Anne knew Cook had worked long hours to create the perfect wedding reception and an incredible cake. Anne also realized Cook would feel shamed if she didn't help. "All right then, can you wash and split the blueberries in half?"

"Of course, Your Grace."

"You and the rest of the staff did an outstanding job yesterday. You made Mer's day perfect."

"We appreciate that, Your Grace. I'll make sure the rest of the kitchen staff know how pleased you are. Now, how many for breakfast?"

"Just forty." They both laughed.

Ignoring the stirrings from abovestairs, Her Grace went about her business. The batter for the cinnamon blueberry pancakes was done. Bacon had been started. The perfectly seasoned small steaks and eggs would be last. Glancing at the clock gave her assurance that the first meal of the day would be on time. Cook was slowly adding batter to a hot pan. Anne looked up and then suddenly ran from the kitchen. She got as far as the hallway and deposited anything in her stomach into the umbrella stand and hung on for dear life, shaking worse than a *crème à la vanille*.

Sar saw his mother pitched over the umbrella stand, shaking and crying. "Perkins, get Berkley and the rest of the men." Gently, he picked her up and headed toward the beckoning couch.

Anne had become their human barometer. When this happened, someone was about to die. Guessing who would die next had become an art form. Every time Her Grace sensed death, her reaction was always the same. When the rest of the men arrived, one look at Anne confirmed they were being stalked by murder once again.

A cool, damp cloth was draped over her forehead. "And before you ask, there was no warning. I found myself hurrying out of the kitchen. My only thought was to make it to a dustbin. As you can see, I didn't make it." Anne shifted to a more comfortable position.

"Let's get her upstairs. I want all the men to meet me in the kitchen." Sar watched as Berkley gingerly lifted Anne from the couch and carried her to her bedchamber. The Duke of Westmoure headed to the kitchen and donned an apron.

"Cook, I'll need an apron for all the men here, even His Majesty. Her Grace taught me how to make celebratory meals. May not be as good as hers, but we will survive."

By the time the women descended the stairs, the scent of burning pancakes and the stench of overcooked bacon wafted through the air. Knowing something was wrong, they headed directly to the kitchen. There, standing at the stove, were the king, trying to flip pancakes, and Sebastian, turning the charred bacon. Cook, Mrs. Spencer, and Mrs. Kiggins were leaning against the wall, laughing.

"Ladies, I think we will wait in the blue room and let the men have at it." Caroline wondered if Cook would ever get her kitchen clean. With the rest of the ladies in tow, Caroline turned and found the safety of the blue room before laughter took over.

"Did you see them?" Aurelia's bouncy red curls were doing a happy dance of their own. "It appears most of them have never been in a kitchen to cook before. His Majesty looked a little out of his league. That pancake almost hit the ceiling before it hit the floor. Can you imagine a pancake on the ceiling dripping batter?"

"Thank goodness Cook won't let this get too out of hand or the kitchen staff would be cleaning for days. We'll have our morning meal shortly." Miriam had no idea how they were going to fake enjoying the meal, but what a story this was going to make for future generations. "Should we ask Sar to bring Her Grace down? This might just be the thing to cheer her up."

Just as the women predicted, the meal was a disaster. The only thing that could be said was that the men had cooked the meal. The women listened as the men each told of their part.

"Never done anything like that before. Cousin, remind me to give the royal cooks a raise. I can only imagine what it takes to prepare a feast." The king sat back and marveled at what their morning endeavors had produced. The ladies politely looked at the mess the men had created and served. It took a lot of stamina to pretend to eat and enjoy the meal.

As the men finished their breakfast, Sar brought his mother down. Her Grace looked as though she hadn't slept for a week. Shaking hands demonstrated how deeply she was affected by these bouts that took place before someone died. When she was settled in the most comfortable seat, Cook brought her weak tea and toast.

After they had sufficiently praised themselves for their endeavors, the men headed to Sar's study. As soon as they were out of sight, the women stampeded to the kitchen to see what Cook had prepared for them.

"Anne, is there anything we can do? Do you want to talk about it?" Miriam was gingerly applying another cool cloth to her forehead.

With a shaking hand, Anne clung to Miriam and stared into space. Tears escaped from her eyes, and she sobbed softly. Simmons quietly took Miriam's place.

"I'm here, Anne." The doctor made a visual examination of his patient. Her color was returning.

Cook brought breakfast to the blue room and more weak tea and toast for Her Grace.

In the study, the men were more than puzzled. During this spell, and for the first time, Her Grace had seen still people in smoky, shady shadows. "She didn't see anything but shadows and still people. Were they dead? Were they men or men and women? Anne is becoming more and more ill each time she has one of these spells. Let's keep her more closely guarded. She'll have a fit and accuse us of all sorts of things, but that is the best thing to do for now. Simmons is with her."

Julien strolled in and stopped. He could feel the tension like an oppressing ton of bricks on one's chest. By the looks on their faces, he could tell something had happened.

"Gentlemen, I take my leave. Keep me posted, my cousin. Let me know what you need from me."

As His Majesty rose to leave, Berkley said one word: "gossip."

"What say, cousin?" The king leaned in closer to hear what Berkley was saying.

"We need to know as much gossip as possible. Who has a lover or lovers in the highest realms of the government? Anything that seems to be a little off, we need to hear it. Regardless of how insignificant it seems to you, it may be a link to us. My men and I might be able to connect it."

"Done." The king took his leave.

"Now, is there anything else?" Berkley looked at the men around him. "Okay then, let's go and talk to the women. We will find out all about the wedding and what people were really thinking. Also, we can check on Anne; she may have remembered something else."

They knew where to find the women by following the trail of their noise and laughter. There was no way you could put a group of women together and not have gossip.

"Perkins, make sure there is plenty of brandy in the blue room. It appears the women have decided to roost there." Sar and the other men headed straight to the front of the house.

The women were doing exactly as they thought, dissecting the wedding from top to bottom, left to right, laughing, and throwing out bits here and there. When the talk turned to local gossip, the men listened more intently. Tomorrow they would focus on Paige's and preparation for its opening.

Even though there was laughter all around them, Berkley took one look at Anne and knew they needed to talk, alone. The haunted look in her eyes scared him. The slight trembling of her hands indicated how badly she was distressed by the last episode of seeing people who were still. He would meet her tonight in the kitchen if the staff could get it clean.

On the ride to Whitehall, Berkley couldn't help but chuckle remembering one of the first times he had met Anne in the kitchen. He had ordered everyone to dinner at His Grace's house and didn't show up himself. He thought back and smiled. His men had been in Sar's study discussing the latest murder. When Berkley left the meeting, he had come around to the front of the house to be let in.

Perkins had answered the door with a raised eyebrow and said, *"Did you come for dinner?"*

Berkley was in no mood to banter with Perkins. He had simply stated, *"I would like to speak to Her Grace. Can we cut to the chase? Perkins, I need to speak to Anne."*

Without so much as a twitch, Perkins asked, *"Why didn't you just come through the back of the house? You were already here."* He raised his eyebrows. *"I will see if Her Grace is receiving."* Perkins had closed the door in his face.

The general chuckled. He had just received his set down. Perkins was all what you saw and more. He was there to protect the family in every way at all costs.

Minutes later, Her Grace opened the door and took one look at him. She didn't offer the normal salutations but immediately started to put him in his place. She said things he would never forget. *"You haven't eaten, have you? We can have our little chat while you eat. And you know what little chat I am talking about. The kitchen, now."* Berkley responded like a child in leading strings. He laughed at this memory, wondering how many more memories they would create.

That night, she gave him an earful. Laughing again, which was completely out of character for him, he had failed to notice he was close to Whitehall. Berkley replayed everything in his mind's eye. He had literally been stuffing his mouth when Anne's deadly whisper reached his ears: *"Don't ever use your high-handed methods with me again. I am not one of your elite operatives."* He wanted to grin, but he knew she would shoot him with her little pistol.

Ah, the beginning—or close to the beginning—of his love for Anne. She made him whole. There was never a day he could go without her. Until she came into his life, he was nothing. He was without a heart. This is something he could fix. Now, it was business of the Crown. The rest he would take care of later.

***

The night of the breakfast fiasco with the king, shadows danced along the corners of the tavern in the East End. Two laborers were in their usual spot, heads hunched, solving their worldly problems. Jerkily, they stood. Staggering, they gave the impression of drunken men drowning their sorrows. They dropped the act as soon as they were safely enclosed in the warehouse.

Pallets of containers filled with opium stood in the middle of the otherwise empty room. The Earl of Severson was leaning forward, examining the pallets, thinking about profits and sampling the delights of Sylvia Meacham, the Viscountess of Truvo, later tonight. For a second or two, he only felt the sting of the deep cut and a neat zip across his throat.

"You will never threaten me or anyone else again. Can you

still hear me, Severson? I want you to go to the devil remembering that." Blood dripped onto the floor; a thud was the only answer. His frantic eyes darted around and his long talon-like fingers clawed at his throat as he struggled to grapple with the reality of the moment.

How many minutes had passed? The earl realized he was on his stomach. How? He didn't have the strength to figure it out. He thought he heard a rustle of fabric and something being stuffed around his throat. Severson felt he was being lifted, or was he floating? *So this is what death and hell are like.* Then nothing.

August Jade Sterling is allowed to live with her cat, Sir Prince Charming, in Minnesota. Like all good cats, he runs the house. While she is busy working away, he takes his daily naps in between thoughts of food. August Jade holds a graduate degree from the Maxwell School of Citizenship and Public Affairs at Syracuse University. When not writing or singing jazz, she creates programs for television.